MORE THAN COURAGE

MORE THAN COURAGE

HAROLD COYLE

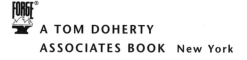

FORGE®

A TOM DOHERTY
ASSOCIATES BOOK   New York

This is a work of fiction. All the characters and events portrayed in this novel are either fictitious or used fictitiously.

MORE THAN COURAGE

This book is printed on acid-free paper.

A Forge Book
Published by Tom Doherty Associates, LLC
175 Fifth Avenue
New York, NY 10010

www.tor.com

Forge® is a registered trademark of Tom Doherty Associates, LLC.

Library of Congress Cataloging-in-Publication Data

Coyle, Harold, 1952–
    More than courage / Harold Coyle.
      p. cm.
    "A Tom Doherty Associates book."
    ISBN 0-765-30188-1
    1. Special forces (Military science)—Fiction. 2. Soldiers—Fiction.
I. Title.
    PS3553.O948M67 2003
    813'.54—dc21

                        2002154963

First Edition: April 2003

Printed in the United States of America

0 9 8 7 6 5 4 3 2 1

MORE THAN COURAGE

PROLOGUE

Isolated within the tight confines of his aircraft, Lieutenant Commander Kevin Shiflet found it difficult to maintain his focus. The muffled roar of jet engines and the sound of his own breathing accentuated by the mask he wore were the only sounds that broke the eerie stillness. Like his aircraft, his mind seemed to be suspended in a void. Mechanically, Shiflet turned his head this way and that, peering into the pitch black that his aircraft wore like a cloak. The night sky and featureless terrain below offered his unaided eye no clues as to where he was or what lay below. Only the faint light of his instruments, dimly reflected off the interior surface of his canopy, was visible.

The chatter of other Coalition aircraft operating throughout the region offered little in the way of distraction. While the data and mission reports the Coalition pilots rattled off at infrequent intervals were vital, they were not mentally stimulating. The monotone exchange of information between other strike aircraft and an aerial tanker came across to Shiflet as being no different than the canned audio clutter that instructors piped into every simulator scenario he was required to go through back on the carrier. At times like this, he had to remind himself that the arming switch before him was not a dummy but was, in fact, connected to very real bombs that would, if circumstances permitted, soon be dispatched against very real targets.

When he had opted for naval aviation after graduating from the Naval Academy, Shiflet had envisioned his career as being more akin to the zoom and boom dogfights that Hollywood was so fond of. Though far from being a Tom Cruise, Shiflet always thought of himself as an adventurous sort who had the "Right Stuff." Unfortunately for the naval aviator, the right stuff these days required a pilot to be more of a delivery boy than a swash-buckling brigand. This mission was a case in point.

The run-in to the initiation point had been uploaded into the navigational system hours before Shiflet set eyes on his aircraft. Likewise, data concerning the target, the ordnance to be used against that target, and the sequence of its release were fed into the F-18's fire control system. If all went well the entire mission would be about as routine and unspectacular as a high-speed ride at an amusement park.

From somewhere out of the darkness Shiflet heard his wing-man call out. Equally bored, Lieutenant James Jefferson was pick-ing up a conversation that the pair had started back on the USS *Truman*. "So, you haven't told your wife yet. I know if my Sally found out that our deployment was being extended from some-one other than me, she'd be fit to tied."

When their rotation had begun eight months before, engag-ing in such nonessential chitchat in the midst of a mission would have been unthinkable. But like everything else, as their time on station stretched into months and one redeployment date after another came and went without any relief in sight, things had become looser. When senior officers on the *Truman* described the current state of their mission, they referred to unraveling of discipline or inattention to detail. The truth was, pilots and sea-men alike were finding it harder and harder to care about what they were doing. Infractions of standard operating procedures and regulations had become so prevalent that even the most stri-dent disciplinarian in the *Truman*'s air group was now turning a blind eye to deficiencies that would have previously resulted in a written reprimand. If the truth were known, commanding officers considered the ebbing of morale justified because they too were just as angered by the breach of faith that had become routine, as the deployments kept getting extended.

"It's not going to make any difference to Peg who tells her or how she hears about it." Shiflet grunted. "She'll just saddle up that high horse of hers and go on a tear that will make a pornographer blush."

Jefferson chuckled. "I've got to hand it to your wife. She *does* have a gift for expressing herself."

"So, Jimmy, what do you think it's going to take to get shore leave in Athens?"

"Hey, you're going to have to find another dupe this time around. Do you know how much money I blew the last time we were there?"

The navy lieutenant commander chuckled. "As I recall, you managed to lay waste to a fair amount of my own disposable income."

"Well, you know what they say, Kevin. A fool and his money are soon parted."

As the attack aircraft continued to cut through the darkness that offered little real protection, the pair of aviators exchanged their views on how, exactly, they had managed to waste as much money as they had during their last shore leave. Back on the *Truman*, the personnel manning the ops center charged with monitoring the activities of their air group, heard the banter but didn't pay attention to what was being said. Like the pilots flying the mission they struggled to maintain the high state of vigilance that active air operations demanded, but the mind-numbing routine and long months on station made that difficult.

The first warning of imminent danger to the flight of F-18s being led by Lieutenant Commander Kevin Shiflet came from an officer aboard an E-3A Sentinel slowly orbiting Saudi airspace. "SAMs, SAMs, SAMs. All aircraft in Echo Seven, SAMs have been fired. I say again, all aircraft in Echo Seven, SAMs have been fired."

Startled, Shiflet blinked twice as he scanned his radar warning receivers. As if on cue, they lit up. Not knowing just how close the enemy missiles were and having no desire to waste any time finding out, Shiflet snapped, "Jimmy, we're it. Pop countermeasures, and break right on my count."

Without waiting for acknowledgment, the lieutenant commander triggered his chaff and flares and began counting. "On three—two—one—break."

With a violent jerk Shiflet threw his aircraft into a hard bank as he increased his airspeed and began to dive. He didn't bother to look back to see if his wingman was following, or search the night sky for the surface-to-air missiles that were in pursuit. He didn't pay attention to the excited chatter as the E-3 AWACs issued vectors to a flight of air force aircraft assigned to SAM suppression. The naval aviator was focused on fighting the effects of the G force that was pushing him back into his seat, while doing his best to put as much distance as possible between himself and the countermeasures that he hoped would spoof the Syrian missiles. Time, which moments before had seemed to be plentiful, was now as much a foe as the SAMs dispatched to kill him.

CHAPTER ONE

By the time the sun began its final swift descent in the west it had been drained of all its harsh cruelty. The great solar orb that had the power to suck the life out of any creature foolish enough to show itself during the day was now little more than a harmless orange ball receding in the distance. Within minutes it would be gone from sight completely, giving the parched desert it ruled over by day a few hours' respite. Sensing the coming darkness, creatures of the night began to emerge from their holes and coveys. Even before the last long shadows of daylight were absorbed by the gathering gray twilight they would be out and about, pursuing those chores that were so necessary for survival in this harsh and most unforgiving land.

Those creatures that were native to Syrian desert could only rely upon natural skills to track prey. When they managed to corner their quarry, they had to employ their own teeth, claws, venom, and sheer brute strength to bring it down and kill it. When times were hard and victims scarce, these same predators had no qualms about turning on each other in order to survive. Under the right circumstances, any animal will turn on its own for self-preservation.

Not all the predators that populated Syria's barren landscape were indigenous. Few of the fourteen members of the U.S. Army Special Forces unit known as Recon Team Kilo thought of themselves as predators. None would have considered themselves to be the most dangerous ones in the area. But by any measure, they were. Unlike the creatures that crawled and slithered in the sands about the laager where RT Kilo's vehicles lay hidden, the Americans conducted themselves in a well-disciplined, methodical manner that thousands of years of civilized warfare had distilled into something of a science. Aided by instructional memory and state-of-the-art weapons that enhanced their own ability to seek, strike, and destroy, RT Kilo was the tip of the mightiest killing machine ever assembled.

Still, it was a fragile tip, one that was in danger of becoming dull due to overuse and prolonged exposure to a harsh and unforgiving environment. Its very existence depended upon adhering to the same laws of survival that all predators live by. The first law is avoiding positions and actions that threaten that survival. First Lieutenant Ken Aveno understood this principle very well, which is why he followed a strict routine when moving about within the confines of the team's laager while it was still light. He began by pulling himself up from the reclining position he had settled into hours before. Using the same cautious, almost hesitant motions that a prairie dog does when emerging from its burrow, the Special Forces officer paused to scan the trackless horizon through the broken pattern of the camouflage net that protected him from observation and the brutal daytime sun. Only when he was satisfied that it was safe to do so did he rise out of the shallow pit he had dug just prior to dawn that morning. He parted a seam in the tan net, stuck his head up through the opening like a swimmer breaking the surface, and continued to look around now that his view of the flat, barren landscape was unobstructed. Satisfied that all was as it should be, he ducked back under the net and started preparing himself for another long night.

Slowly he slipped into the flak vest he had shed during the heat of the day, took up his weapon, and did his best to muster up some enthusiasm. With each passing day he was becoming acutely aware that the amount of effort he needed to motivate himself was increasing. It was as if he had only a finite reservoir of élan, a supply that this mission and his duties were depleting at an alarming rate.

Pausing, he shook his head. "Gotta keep it together," he mumbled as he adjusted his gear and glanced to his left and right, catching quick glimpses of other members of the team as they prepared for their nocturnal labors. To a man they moved in a deliberate manner that was purposeful while at the same time reflecting the same lack of enthusiasm he himself was struggling to overcome.

This concerned Aveno. He knew they were tired. But it was more than simple physical exhaustion that worried the young officer. They had been deployed for six weeks plus with no downtime, no opportunity to kick back and simply rest and relax. Their area of operation and the nature of their mission required that they maintain an around-the-clock vigilance in a harsh environment that was taxing for even the hardiest of them, physically and emotionally. The same fine grains of sand and grit that worked their way into the gears of their vehicles and the actions of their weapons also found their way into every mouthful of food they consumed, breath they took, and bodily opening left exposed. The sand was a constant irritant. It could be tolerated. It could be joked about. But it was always there, like the unseen dangers that added mental stress to the physical duress that the desert inflicts upon any and all who reside there.

The result was an attrition that could not be stopped. Efforts to lessen the stress and gradual but steady erosion of each man's health could only do so much. Each member of the team had sufficient opportunities to rest, plenty to eat, and medical attention as soon as it was required. But nothing short of removing them from this milieu would restore both their full mental and physical well-being. That this would not be happening anytime soon only served to accelerate the ebbing morale and growing strain that was becoming more and more evident with each passing day.

When originally conceived, the plan allowed each Special Forces recon team three days to infiltrate along a predetermined route to its designated sector in Syria. Once it was in place the unit would spend two weeks gathering intelligence, observing known terrorist training camps and, if necessary, employing their laser designators when someone thousands of miles away decided that a target required immediate attack. At the end of this two-week phase, when a new team was en route the deployed team would extract itself. All of the preceding ten recon teams dispatched as part of Operation Razorback had started out following a schedule that placed them in harm's way for just under three weeks. But like RT Kilo none of them, Alpha through Juliet, had been able to stay within this schedule. Each team had its deployment extended time and time again by unforeseen operational requirements as the war on international terrorism siphoned off already scarce special operations resources to deal with other, more pressing needs. The days when a recon team's deployment in Syria was extended by a mere two additional weeks was now nothing more than a memory. Six weeks in place had become the norm, with eight not being unheard-of.

It was not knowing when they would receive the word to disengage and head back to The World that Ken Aveno suspected was most wearing on them. As he finished tending to his personal chores and prepared to turn to his assigned duties as the team's executive officer, he wondered just how much the other members of the team were being affected. Though part of being on a Special Forces A team meant that rank was often ignored, Aveno was still an officer. There were conventions within the United States Army that even the camaraderie and professionalism of an elite unit could not overcome. As with any other officer, he depended upon two things when it came to judging the combat effectiveness of those entrusted to him: his personal observation of the men and his own physical and mental state. While not quite at the end of his rope, he could feel himself slipping and he suspected that the motivation and endurance of the others was ebbing as quickly as his own. Still, he remained confident that in terms of materiel, they were more than capable of executing their assigned duties as when they had begun their tour of duty.

Kilo was basically a reinforced Special Forces A team, armed to the teeth with the best weaponry the lowest bidder could provide them. Most carried the venerable M-4 carbine, which was nothing more than a modified M-16A2. Those who had connections sported an MP-5, the weapon of choice for special ops types around the world. With a cyclic rate of eight hundred rounds per minute and a muzzle velocity of four hundred meters per second, the German-designed Heckler & Koch MP-5 fired 9-mm parabellum, full-metal-jacketed rounds, with a surprisingly high degree of accuracy due to its action, which fired the first round from a closed-bolt position. In the hands of a highly trained professional it was a most effective instrument. Rounding out the category of individual small arms were 9-mm pistols as well as one good old-fashioned Remington 870 pump-action shotgun.

To augment these personal weapons, RT Kilo's arsenal included a number of heavier weapons. Among the more impressive was the Beretta M-82A1 .50-caliber sniper rifle, capable of firing standard 12.7-mm cartridges. With a ten-power telescopic sight this rifle had a range in excess of 1,000 meters, or a tad over .6 of a mile, allowing a good marksman to reach out and touch his foe long before that unfortunate soul became aware that he was in danger. The sheer size of the slug, .5 inch in diameter, ensured that even a glancing blow was more than sufficient to ruin someone's entire day.

The crew-served weapons mounted on the unit's vehicles were the real heavy weapons. The Hummer that gave them the mobility to range far and wide also provided them with platforms for weapons that their Vietnam forebears could never have imagined humping on their backs.

Kilo Six, the Hummer used by the team commander, sported an M-2 .50-caliber heavy-barrel machine gun. Based upon a German World War I 12.7-mm antitank rifle and classified in 1921, it was fast reaching the century mark with no end to its useful military career in sight. Like the Beretta, it fired 12.7-mm balls or armoring-piercing rounds. Unlike the sniper rifle, the M-2, known affectionately by its operators as the Ma Two, had a rate of fire that was 450 to 500 rounds per minute. Newer by a full half century was the M-19 40-mm grenade launcher that graced the ring mount on Kilo Three, which was Aveno's Hummer. Capable of chunking out sixty baseball-sized grenades per minute up to a range of 1,600 meters, its only major drawback was the limited number of rounds that could be held in its ready box.

Range was not a factor for the crew-served weapon affixed to SFC Allen Kannen's Hummer Kilo Two, which was the only all-enlisted humvee. Kannen, the team's senior NCO, fully appreciated what was probably the most unusual weapon for a Special Forces team—the tube-launched, optically tracked, wired-guided missile, or TOW. The decision as to whether or not to include this long-range antitank weapon had been an issue hotly debated at every level of command that had a say in the organization, deployment, and operational control of the recon teams. In the end the choice had been left to the individual team commanders. Captain Erik Burman, Kilo's commanding officer, explained his decision to use the TOW by telling his people that when one goes wandering about in bear country, it's not a bad idea to take along a bear rifle even if it's not bear you're looking for.

The only RT Kilo Hummer that did not have an oversized weapon protruding from it was Kilo One, which belonged to the two-man air force team headed by First Lieutenant Joseph Ciszak. Instead of a ring mount and crew-served weapon, Kilo One's hard shell was adorned with an array of antennas and a small satellite dish. Ironically, it was this innocent-looking vehicle that was responsible for all the devastation that RT Kilo had managed to rain down upon their foes during the past six weeks. The members of RT Kilo were hunters in every sense of the word but they did not do any of the actual killing. None of them had fired a single round since they had crossed the Turkish-Syrian border. Rather, it had been Lieutenant Ciszak and his collection of high-tech radios connecting him to his fellow aviators that did all of Kilo's killing. Using all the wonders of modern electronics and his trusty handheld laser designator, Joe Ciszak was able to employ

the full spectrum of conventional munitions available to the
United States Air Force. Were it not for the need to provide security and locate hard-to-find targets, the Special Forces A team
would have been totally superfluous.

In and of itself this impressive array of weaponry and comms
equipment had no real value. The most accurate firearm in the
world is worthless unless it is used by someone who possesses
both the training and the motivation to use it. Military history is
replete with accounts of lavishly equipped armies being humbled
by ragtag forces that won through a triumph of will and courage.
The United States Army itself has seen both sides of this coin,
once at its birth when it faced the best-trained army in the world,
and later in Vietnam when opposed by a foe who refused to yield
to logic and the cruel mathematics of attrition. It is the willingness to soldier on and do one's duty in the face of daunting odds
and seemingly insurmountable difficulties that often determined
who is victorious and who is vanquished.

So the question of a unit's morale, even when made up of elite
warriors, is always of the greatest importance. Lacking a definitive
means of measuring this critical element and suspecting that the
other members of RT Kilo were suffering from their protracted
deployment in much the same way as he was, Ken Aveno found
himself worrying how his state of mind was impacting those
around him. Perhaps one day, he told himself, he would find a
surefire away of steeling himself against the slow, subtle corrosive
effects of sagging morale. Perhaps when the twin silver bars of
captain were pinned to his collar they would shield him from that
demon and give him the strength to be the sort of soldier that
everyone expected him to be. Until then he would have to mud-
dle along, executing those duties that were assigned to him as
best he could and keep morale from robbing him or his unit of its
ability to carry on.

Climbing from the shallow hole that he had spent much of
the day in, sleeping when the heat permitted, the executive officer
of the small A team stretched his five-foot-ten frame for the first

time in hours as he continued to look around. There was not much to see. Each of the team's humvees was hidden under tan-and-brown nets. It never failed to amaze Aveno how the squiggly strips of material laced through the squares of the knotted nylon nets managed to hide something as large as a Hummer and those who operated it. Yet he knew that from a surprisingly short distance, a net that was properly set up blended in nicely with the surrounding nothingness of the desert. From even farther out, the nets and Hummers tucked underneath them simply disappeared, just like Team Kilo.

Shaking off his lethargy and anxious to get started before the faint light of early night was gone, Aveno chugged forward. As the XO he was charged with the maintenance and logistical affairs of Team Kilo. This required that he check each of the team's specially modified Hummers on a daily basis to ensure that they were being maintained in accordance with established standards and ready for that night's operations. Unlike unit morale, this task had established standards and procedures that could be measured and relied upon. In the process of overseeing maintenance, he was also expected to keep track of current levels of ammo, food, fuel, and water. After six weeks this drill had become second nature, as routine as the setting sun. In fact it had become so routine that the young first lieutenant found he had to guard against complacency.

Each member of Recon Team Kilo was a professional in every sense of the word, men who had been in the army long enough to appreciate the reasons behind Aveno's precombat inspections. Yet it still irked some of the enlisted men to have someone poking and prodding every nook and cranny of their vehicle and equipment day in and day out. They were after all the crème de la crème, the best of the best, professional soldiers who expected to be treated as professionals, not rank recruits. Only through quiet diplomacy and an occasional threat was Sergeant First Class Allen Kannen, Kilo's senior NCO, able to keep their tongues in check.

Still, not even he could stop their every effort to let Aveno know just how much his daily inspections irritated them.

On approaching each Hummer, Aveno would call out to its driver, who was usually tearing down a camouflage net or checking out his humvee. The men assigned to the Hummer would greet him with whatever subtle sign of resentment they thought they could get away with. For his part, Aveno ignored this as he set about following a script that had been burned into his memory from repeated use. The routine never varied.

First, he unscrewed the cap of all water cans hanging on the side of every vehicle in order to check their contents. Then he'd crawl inside each door, pulling out any opened cases of MREs tossed in the rear and counting the number of meal packs remaining inside. After inspecting fuel gauges, and drawing dipsticks during his examination of the engine compartment of each Hummer, Aveno would drop to the ground and crawl under the vehicle checking the suspension. Everything had to be touched by him to confirm that every Hummer was functional and in order. Only the crew-served weapons, inspected by the commanding officer himself were ignored during this obsessive daily ritual that caused Kannen to secretly nickname Aveno Captain Queeg.

If Aveno reminded the enlisted members of the naval officer who commanded the USS *Caine*, then their commanding officer was without question the team's Captain Ahab. It had been the only other officer assigned to RT Kilo, Lieutenant Ciszak of the U.S. Air Force, who had graduated from Notre Dame with a B.A. in English, who first made this comparison. One night, while he was waiting to direct an air strike, Ciszak turned to his driver, Airman Jay Jones, and commented that Captain Burman's single-minded dedication to duty, aloofness, and drive to accomplish every mission regardless of difficulty or danger reminded him of Melville's fictional captain, a processed man who prowled the seven seas on an endless quest. Amused, Jones shared this observation with his fellows, who immediately started using nautical terms whenever possible, including calling out "Thar she blows!" whenever they located a target they had been dispatched to find.

Ignorant of its origin, Captain Burman joined in on what he took to be a harmless attempt to liven up their harsh and monotonous existence. It was three weeks before Aveno discovered, through a slip of his driver's tongue, the true story behind the adaptation of seafaring clichés. Unsure of how Burman would take this piece of information, Aveno decided to keep that knowledge to himself. With the irritating sand and stress already eating away at Burman's nerves, Aveno knew that it wouldn't help to tell his commander that he was the butt of a collective joke.

Adding to the strain of their protracted deployment and the stress that living in the desert placed upon them was a gnawing doubt Aveno had concerning the value of their efforts. Like the cold war that his parent's generation had endured, the current war on terror seemed to have no end. To many of his fellow countrymen, people to whom 9/11 was just another news story that was little more than a bad memory, the war on terror had become a distraction, a drain on national resources that some felt would be better spent on social welfare programs, education, or new roads. To them the idea of chasing terrorists and eradicating the threat they posed was a quixotic notion, a foolish dream that could never be achieved. Even Ken Aveno found himself wondering from time to time if it made sense to dispatch a group of highly trained professional soldiers like those belonging to RT Kilo to chase small cells of terrorists and call in bombers to drop high-tech precision-guided bombs on their tents when they were found.

This point was driven home every time a nation that was supposed to be an ally took a step to undo those small successes that RT Kilo did manage to achieve. In truth, Aveno could find little fault in what the French and others were doing. He believed that if his own national leaders were not prisoners of their own rhetoric, they would be seeking some way of getting out of an open-ended policy that was only costing American lives. Of course, such considerations were well above Aveno's pay grade. His personal mission was to follow orders and finish his current tour of duty with some degree of pride and sanity.

These dark troubling thoughts were in Ken Aveno's mind as he approached Kilo Six, Captain Burman's Hummer. Through the camo nets were still draped over the vehicle, he caught sight of Burman perched on the hood. This was a bad sign, for it had become something of a ritual for his commander to assume this particular posture when translating orders he had received during the day into detailed instructions. It was his way of announcing that the team had been tasked to go out into the gathering darkness once more and find something that a cabal of staff officers, ten thousand miles away, had suddenly taken an interest in. While most of these forays resulted in the discovery of targets that were subsequently bombed into oblivion, more times than Aveno cared to count, the forays had turned into a snipe hunt, but one in which the snipe had sharp teeth and long, deadly claws.

Stopping a few meters away, he watched as Captain Burman pored over maps and scribbled notes on a pad lying next to him. It didn't seem right to the young officer that in this age of computers and high-tech wizardry success and failure in combat still depended upon illegible scribbling on a page made by a human being. It was as if they were insulators placed within an increasingly high-speed system to keep it from overheating or spinning out of control. That there were fellow officers sitting in the Pentagon and at Fort Leavenworth trying to figure out how to eliminate those insulators was no great secret. Rubbing his irritated eyes, Aveno thought that the sooner those guys finished their work and made him obsolete, the sooner he would be free to pull pitch and turn his back on Syria, its people, and its fucking desert.

It was several minutes before Burman noticed that his executive officer was standing off to one side watching him. Determined to finish what he was doing before he lost the last bit of useful daylight, Burman ignored Aveno.

The task his team had been given that night was another routine mission. A Syrian ADA missile battery had become active some sixty kilometers southwest of where they were. As far as anyone knew there was very little in the region where the battery was located, and nothing of military value. The small villages scattered throughout the area relied on camels and goats. Half of the population was still nomadic, real Lawrence of Arabia stuff, as SFC Kannen put it. Hence the reason for curiosity and concern by various intelligence agencies.

Though the operations order he had received made no mention of it, Burman knew that someone back in Washington, D.C., was hoping that the barrenness of the area was an indication there was something worth defending hidden among the sun-dried brick huts and seemingly innocent expanses of nothingness. So Team Kilo was being dispatched to find out if it was just another cluster of terrorist training camps, or something more significant, especially installations involved in the development, testing, and manufacture of special weapons, the modern catchall phrase used to describe nuclear, biological, and chemical weapons. Everyone knew that facilities dedicated to this purpose existed somewhere in Syria and that the Syrians were doing their best to hide and protect them. But not everyone agreed on where they would most likely be found and how best to go about finding them. So even the relatively simple mission of locating and designating the Syrian ADA battery for aerial attack carried with it the implied task of uncovering any evidence of unusual or suspect activity that other intelligence resources had, to date, failed to detect.

Even so, the evening's mission was pretty much routine. As such Burman saw no reason to make a big fuss over the way it would be executed. When all precombat checks and briefings had been completed they would move out in a dispersed column. He would lead out with Kilo Six, followed by the team's senior NCO in Kilo Two and the air force liaison officer, or LNO, in Kilo One. Aveno, who was still patiently waiting, would bring up the rear in Kilo Three. Once they were within striking distance of their objective the team would find a concealed spot from which Burman and Aveno would sally forth, either mounted or on foot, to sniff out the exact location of their target while Kannen stayed back with Ciszak. How they would proceed depended on what they discovered during this preliminary recon. So other than mapping out their route of march, Burman saw little need for any additional detailed planning.

Having finished jotting a few notes just as the last modicum of light waned, Burman laid his map and pad aside and looked around. When his eyes finally turned toward the dark shadow of his executive officer, he acted surprised. "I didn't see you standing there, Lieutenant Aveno."

Burman slowly eased his way off the Hummer's hood. "I imagine you're waiting for me to vacate this spot," he quipped, "so you can finish your appointed rounds."

"No rush, sir. I knew you were in the midst of putting together an order." When Burman turned to walk away without saying a word Aveno called out, "Anything exciting, sir?"

"Nothing to be concerned about, Lieutenant."

Aveno remained where he was, struggling to suppress the anger he felt welling up in him. The bastard was fucking with him. He was always fucking with him. It was as if they were still back at the Point, and Burman was still a first classman and Aveno was still a plebe. Since they were in different units and first classmen seldom took the time to bother with plebes who were not in their own company neither man had known the other then. Still, after all these years the psychological gulf remained.

There wasn't a man in the team who hadn't taken note of the "Me Tarzan, you Jane," attitude that Burman showed in all of his dealings with his number two. Aveno knew it wasn't personal. As best he could tell, he had never said or done anything that could even remotely be considered improper or offensive to his commanding officer. Yet from day one the two had never really clicked. In Aveno's opinion Burman's policy of keeping him at a distance and his insistence on using proper military titles instead of establishing a more amiable relationship did not prevent the two from working together professionally. But it did create unnecessary friction. Like the fine grains of sand that he could taste with each bit of food and feel every time he blinked his eyes, Burman's manner was irritating and wearing. All Aveno could do was to endure, just as he endured the harsh and uncompromising desert. The same could be true for the rest of Team Kilo. For better or worse the fourteen men had to keep functioning and surviving until such time as the Fates smiled upon them and their circumstances changed.

Arlington, Virginia
11:45 LOCAL (15:45 ZULU)

Pushing away from his desk, Lieutenant Colonel Robert Delmont studied the document he had been working on for the majority of the morning. It wasn't a particularly long piece of correspondence. In fact it was less than a page in length. Nor was it of any great importance. If it had been, it would have been long gone rather than undergoing revision after revision after revision. The particular version Delmont was currently working on was by his count number eleven. While excessive even by Pentagon standards, it was far from being a record. Within the army's Directorate of Special Operations that dubious honor belonged to another single-page response concerning training ammunition for an exercise being conducted with navy SEALs. It had been bounced back and forth sixteen times between the action officer and the director, Brigadier General James Palmer, who finally put his stamp of approval on a letter that was not all that different from the initial draft. Though Delmont was confident that his letter was not going to surpass that mark, he had little doubt that it would once more find its way back to his desk, scarred by red marks annotating corrections and changes made by Palmer that did nothing to alter its content. This practice had nothing to do with any issues Palmer had with the letter's style, grammar, or content. It was simply his way of putting off dealing with an issue that he was not quite ready to address.

Ordinarily Delmont didn't mind this sort of busywork. Having spent more than eighteen years chugging along his chosen career track, he understood that every senior officer had his own peculiar idiosyncrasies that subordinates had little choice but to live with. Palmer was no different. Demanding and uncompromising, the general was the sort of man one didn't try to put something over on. Those who did were never afforded a second opportunity to repeat that mistake. For officers that Palmer deemed worthy to serve him, the general went to great pains to ensure that their time on the Department of the Army staff was educational and professionally rewarding. So long as he kept his mouth shut, did what was expected of him, and played Palmer's brand of hardball, Delmont knew that he would depart from the Puzzle Palace on the Potomac, as the Pentagon was known, with an outstanding evaluation and his choice of assignments.

Still, those distant rewards were of little consolation to him at the moment. Unable to concentrate on the task at hand, Delmont leaned back in his seat and glanced at the row of clocks arrayed along one wall of the outer office that he shared with half a dozen other action officers. Because American forces operated all over the world with various contingents in one time zone supporting others in different time zones, all directives and operational orders issued by the Department of Defense used Zulu time, or Greenwich mean time. To assist the action officers who generated those directives and orders, each clock displayed the current time in a different part of the world. He looked at the one labeled Charlie, which meant it was the third time zone east of Greenwich.

It was almost twenty hundred hours in Syria. RT Kilo would be on the move by now, he thought. While he was sitting in an office that was a stone's throw away from the nation's capital, wordsmithing a letter that was of little consequence, soldiers who had earned the right to wear the same black-and-yellow shoulder patch of the army's Special Forces that adorned the sleeve of his uniform were making their way across the Syrian desert. Closing his eyes, Delmont could easily picture what the commander of RT

Kilo was seeing at that moment. He even imagined he could taste the fine sand that tended to hang suspended like a mist in the blacked-out interior of the team leader's humvee as it bounced across the uneven desert.

Delmont knew all there was to know about Recon Team Kilo. In a locked safe, which only he and three other officers had the combination to, were files on every aspect of Operation Razorback, a black operation whose aim was to locate sites where special weapons that had once belonged to Iraq were being stored.

The mission that was about to kick off half a world away was typical of those assigned to the recon teams that represented Razorback's cutting edge. The intelligence summary that had initiated this night's mission identified the approximate location of a Syria surface-to-air missile launcher protecting a facility that was believed to be a chemical warfare lab that had once been part of Saddam Hussein's mighty arsenal. Had the analysts at Langley been sure of this there would have been no need to send RT Kilo to ferret out the lab's location. Aircraft alone would have been able to do the job. But the lab, if it were truly there, was tucked away in a small village made up of a few hundred families and protected by a small garrison and an ADA battery. Had that battery not let fly with a pair of missiles at an American drone en route to check out another site, no one would have even associated this collection of hovels with anything of military value.

The practice of tucking important military facilities in out-of-the-way locations was something the Syrians had adopted from their Iraqi cousins. Not only did the tight-knit nature of a small community make it all but impossible for Israeli agents to slip in unnoticed, it served to force both America and Israel to spread its intelligence-gathering assets out over a larger area. Adding to the problems faced by the American intelligence analysis and targeting officers was the quaint custom of placing high-value targets right next to sites that were normally immune from attack, such as schools, hospitals, and mosques. That the same international law that placed a taboo on hitting such structures also prohibited a warring party from placing military facilities in or near protected locations was freely ignored by a government that did not have to labor under the same high level of public opinion and moral sanctions that the Americans were obliged to.

It was this state of affairs that had led to the creation of Operation Razorback and the recon teams such as RT Kilo. Without an effective network of dissidents within Syria, the United States and Great Britain had to use its own people to do the things that intelligence platforms in outer space, or aircraft zipping by at six hundred miles an hour at an altitude of fifteen thousand feet could not do. Operation Razorback was a dangerous job, one that nearly everyone in Washington, D.C., wished they did not have to do, but the alternative, doing nothing, was even worse.

Though he had not been in on the initial planning of Razorback and had no input concerning day-to-day taskings of the recon teams that made up the ground component of Razorback, Delmont was responsible for monitoring their activities and providing daily briefings to his superiors and selected senior officers. Most of his peers and the other military and civilian staff within the Directorate of Special Operations knew nothing about Razorback. So it was impossible for them to appreciate the anger that would suddenly well up in him whenever the recon team currently deployed in Syria was in the midst of an active tasking while he was chained to a desk ten thousand miles away.

When Delmont felt this frustration and anger building he sought escape by putting himself in the place of the current team commander. With the same thoroughness that he had once used himself when he had been a spry young captain commanding an A team, Delmont would consider the requirements of the mission he had briefed that day in the close, quiet confines of General Palmer's office. Putting himself in the team commander's place, Delmont would plan every aspect of that day's missions. In doing so he skipped no steps. Everything from preparing the team to how he would execute the mission was considered. In this way, no matter where he was during the day or what he was doing, the labors of the recon teams were never far from Delmont's mind.

"Hey, Bobby, you gonna go out and run or join the rest of us forlorn galley slaves for lunch?"

With the suddenness of a thunderclap the voice of Lieutenant Colonel Thad Calvert broke the trance Delmont had drifted into. Turning, Delmont looked up at Calvert, who had managed to wander into his cubicle without his noticing.

Seeing that there was an open document displayed on the monitor of Delmont's computer, Calvert grunted. "Must be something mighty important there, bucko."

Embarrassed at being caught in the midst of a daydream, Delmont waved dismissively. "Oh, that. No, not really. Just busywork."

Glancing at the edited version of the document Delmont was working on and recognizing the markings, Calvert laughed. "I see that General Palmer is once more trying to prove that the pen is mightier than the sword, capable of laying low the best of the best."

Though he normally enjoyed his friend's dry humor, Delmont found it difficult to muster up a weak smile in response.

"So GI, which is it going to be?" Calvert continued. "Enjoy a fine gourmet meal at the cafeteria or pound your poor body into the ground?"

Knowing that he would be unable pick up his imaginary mission where he had left off now that he had been interrupted, yet in no mood to socialize, Delmont shook his head. "I think I'll run today."

"Okay. Your call. See ya later."

When Calvert was gone Delmont hit the save key before closing the letter that refused to go away. When he was unable to mentally play out a mission that was in progress, losing himself in a long and strenuous session of physical activity was the next best thing. Neither form of escapism did much to allay his feelings of uselessness and guilt that he harbored at times like this. He knew it was foolish and counterproductive to feel that way. The majority of his duties were necessary even if they paled in significance compared to those being executed by the soldiers of Recon Team Kilo. That he happened to be on the DA staff when America's war on terrorism was in full swing was little more than bad luck. Only keeping his mouth shut and soldiering on to the best of his abilities in his current assignment ensured that he would once more be assigned to a posting where he would be free to sally forth into battle and ply his stock-in-trade. Until that day arrived, all he could do was cope and hope.

Reaching under his desk, Delmont pulled out his gym bag and made for the door, stopping to let the secretary know where he was going and when he would be back. The Department of Defense civilian employee nodded without taking her eyes off the letter she was working on.

CHAPTER THREE

Syria
20:35 LOCAL (16:35 ZULU)

Having served in southwest Asia as a junior officer during the First Gulf War Lieutenant Colonel Delmont's fertile imagination was capable of conjuring up sensations and images that were surprisingly close to those the commanding officer of RT Kilo was experiencing. The same could not be said of Burman's leadership. The methodology he followed while preparing his command for a foray, his planning, the manner in which he organized his command, and the way he actually led his men in the course of an operation bore no resemblance to the meticulous techniques Delmont thought of as necessary and universal. Burman was like so many young officers in the field. He saw little need to slavishly adhere to a set process time and time again. In his opinion his men were professionals, experienced soldiers who allowed him to dispense with those elements of the army's standard troop-leading procedures that he deemed unnecessary and a waste of time.

The routine the drivers of Kilo's humvees had settled into was an example of why Burman was able to get away with issuing truncated orders. They knew their place in the order of march, the speed their tiny column should maintain during their movement to their assigned objective, and the necessity of maintaining a distance of one to two hundred meters between vehicles. Since none of these particulars had changed since they had crossed into Syria, Burman no longer mentioned them when he was issuing his operations order. He believed that to have done so time and time again would have been seen as an insult to Kilo's highly trained and well-seasoned professionals. The most the young Special

Forces officer said concerning these particulars was a short, crisp, "You all know the drill." This allowed him to move right to the operational matters that were particular to that night's mission.

"The drill," as run by Kilo, bore no resemblance to what a Hollywood version would look like. RT Kilo did not charge off into the trackless wastelands wily-nilly at high speed. That would have been dangerous and quite foolish since the real desert held many a pitfall and irregularity just waiting to snarl the unwary and stupid. The most hazardous obstacles to cross-country navigation were the wadis, dry streambeds cut into the desert floor by the runoff from infrequent but violent rains. Wadis came in all shapes and sizes. Some were little more than shallow drainage ditches. Others could be quite massive, barriers that required long detours and careful navigation. Though it is never dry, the Grand Canyon in the American southwestern desert is an extreme example of a wadi.

At times the actual texture of the desert itself creates difficulties. In some areas the surface is as hard as concrete and flat as a pancake, while the sand in other locales is as soft as that which you would use in a child's sandbox and as bottomless as the ocean. In the first few weeks of Kilo's deployment, it was not at all unusual for the driver of Kilo's lead vehicle to find his vehicle suddenly slowing down even as he subconsciously applied more and more foot to the accelerator in an effort to maintain a steady speed. If neither he nor the senior man riding up front in the passenger seat catch on quick enough, they soon find themselves grinding to a dead stop as the chassis of their humvee burrowes itself into the soft dirt, leaving its oversized wheels spinning about furiously in a vain effort to find traction in loose sand. On one occasion the lead vehicle had dug itself in so deep that it took the combined efforts of the other three humvees hooked up to each other end to end to extract the hapless vehicle. By drawing on the collective wisdom of past desert warriors and experiences like these, Burman developed the standard operating procedures that had become second nature to his drivers.

The prescribed twenty miles per hour at which RT Kilo

moved provided the drivers with greater response time when suddenly confronted by an unexpected obstacle. That pace also minimized the dust cloud generated by vehicular movement through the desert. While not completely eliminating the problem, this reduction in the team's signature diminished the possibility that an alert Syrian civilian would spot them on a clear, moonlit night. And even if he did, the steady, unhurried pace would convince the observer that the small convoy he was seeing was his own military. If the observer were a Syrian soldier, he would label Kilo's dust as nothing more than herders tending to their chores. Either way, unless the lead vehicle actually ran over a Syrian, odds were that Kilo would be ignored.

To keep their profile as low as possible, all of Kilo's moves were conducted at night and in total blackout. Even the blackout markers known as cat's eyes, designed to assist drivers in maintaining proper spacing, had been covered up, leaving no light outside of the vehicle visible to the unaided eye. Unfortunately, relying solely on night vision goggles could be a nerve-wracking experience for the drivers. While on the move they had to spend the entire night perched on the edge of their seats, hanging on to their steering wheels with white knuckles as they peered straight ahead into the darkness in an effort to catch an occasional glimpse of the vehicle in front of them, praying all the while that the humvee they were following hadn't come to a stop and was now stationary and hidden by its own dust. By dawn, the drivers would be exhausted by the stress this engendered.

In many ways the dark confines of the team's humvees was as stressful for the passengers, crowded together for hours on end with little to do until they reached their objective. While Captain Burman expected the senior man in each vehicle to keep tabs on their exact location and the others onboard to stay focused on what they were about to do and maintain their vigilance in the event that something unexpected happened, the men of Kilo had been doing these sorts of missions for so long that sustained concentration was difficult. If the train-up time that preceded their deployment overseas and the four weeks' acclimation and re-hearsals they went through before crossing over into Syria were added to the six weeks they had spent deployed forward in that country, the members of Kilo had been together for nearly four months. Even while still in the States, they had spent more of their waking hours with each other than with their own families. This sort of closeness created a cohesion that was almost unprece-dented in the modern American army. It also had the potential of working against them. Having exhausted their collective reservoir of jokes, stories, and tales early on, the members of Kilo had noth-ing new or interesting to discuss. By the end of their third week in Syria their conversations had become as barren as their trackless surroundings.

When a conversation did bubble up it seldom lasted long. This was due to a serious dearth of meaningful issues worth dis-cussing. Kilo had to maintain strict noise discipline during the day while hunkered down. Men who were not standing guard were sleeping. This sort of cycle limited the amount of news they received from the outside world. What they did hear came to them via the two personally owned short-wave radios that Bur-man had permitted SFC Kannen and Sergeant O'Hara to bring along. When someone was listening in for news, they usually tuned to the BBC World Service, broadcasts that contained a great deal that was of little interest to Americans, such as cricket scores between the Indian and New Zealand national teams.

In the tradition of American soldiers throughout the ages, a few members of Kilo used humor to fill idle hours. SFC Kannen was especially good at this. One night, after listening to Specialist Four Salvador Mendez's daylong rant about being unable to keep up with American sports, Kannen chuckled. "Look at it this way. When we get home, we'll be like Rip van Winkle. Only instead of waking up and finding that many years have passed, we'll discover that we were lucky enough to miss an entire political season."

A native of New York City, Mendez responded with a bit of his own humor. "That's what I am afraid of. I can see it all now.

I'll get back home and find out that the folks from upstate elected a senator who's from Kansas to make up for that carpetbagger from Arkansas."

The sort of wit and attempts to engage conversations that were not mission related tended to reflect the character of the senior officer or NCO who rode up front in the passenger seat of each humvee. By default they established the rules and tone everyone followed in their respective vehicle. This was particularly true in Kilo Six, the lead humvee, where Erik Burman literally led from the front in all matters. With Burman were Specialist Four John Laporta who drove and maintained the Hummer, Sergeant E-5 O'Hara, the team's comms specialist, and Sergeant Yousaf Hashmi, an American born to Syrian immigrants.

The conflicts in personalities and vast divergence of backgrounds that existed within Kilo tended to make long conversations difficult. This was especially true with Sergeant Hashmi. While he had never lived in Syria, Hashmi was the primary translator for the team. All of the recon teams had at least one member who was intimately familiar with the customs and culture of the nation whose sovereignty they were violating.

That Hashmi's knowledge was gained through his parents and therefore secondhand did not matter to the army. Hashmi had been aggressively recruited for just this sort of operation. Unfortunately, the qualifications that made Hashmi such an important member of the team also served to isolate him from the others in many ways. Though born and raised an American, his cultural heritage and Muslim religion were foreign to most of his fellow countrymen. No matter how hard he tried, no matter what he did, he remained very much apart from what his father referred to as real Americans whenever he was angered by the subtle prejudice that the Arab-American community lived with day in and day out.

Like Hashmi, Specialist Four John Laporta was born in the United States of foreign parentage. His Mexican mother had entered the country alone and illegally while still pregnant with him. Laporta had been raised south of Kansas City, where his stepfather, an illegal Mexican alien, worked as a stable boy at a riding club while his mother earned extra income by doing housework for the owner. Like so many of his countrymen, Laporta lived with the fear that his parents would one day be caught by an INS sweep and sent back to a country that was as foreign to him as Syria was to Hashmi. To ensure that his children would never be tormented by the same uncertainty and fear, the Mexican-American had enlisted in the army the day he graduated from high school. Only when he had an honorable discharge from the United States Army in hand and sufficient funds safely tucked away to cover the cost of advanced technical training would John Laporta feel safe enough to quietly melt into the middle class of hardworking people who populate the nation's heartland and start a family of his own, an all-American family.

Of the three enlisted men who traveled in Kilo Six only the team's comms chief, Sergeant Dennis O'Hara, came close to having anything in common with Burman. The gregarious NCO was what he liked to call "a real American," someone who could claim Irish, German, Polish, and Italian heritage. He often bragged that he could walk into most neighborhoods in Milwaukee and feel right at home. In the beginning Burman had found O'Hara's outgoing personality a welcome break from Hashmi's aloofness and Laporta's guarded nature. But O'Hara's habit of rambling on and on even when he had nothing of value to say became more and more irritating over time, very much like the fine grains of sand that tormented them all. Burman, who enjoyed an equal measure of intelligent conversations and quiet periods of meditating and thinking, quickly found ways of cutting off O'Hara that he assumed were harmless. Unfortunately, O'Hara always took great offense.

Everything about Burman, from his background and personality to his worldview, tended to separate him from his men. This, not to mention the fact that he was their commanding officer, went far in stifling chatter in Kilo Six. With a single word he could

send any Kilo member into harm's way. The plans he conjured
and the orders he issued governed every action and waking hour
of the thirteen men entrusted to him. An error on his part, a failure to properly address every possible contingency, or a lapse in
judgment could result in the failure of their mission and the death
of all of them. No one person in the entire army's chain of command, not even the president himself, had the same impact on
American combat troops as a captain leading troops on the field
of battle.

The four occupants of Kilo Two, the humvee next in the line
of march, did not suffer the same tension that those around Burman did. The senior man was Sergeant First Class Allen Kannen,
making those assigned to Kilo Two the only group that was all
enlisted. This alone did much to make the atmosphere more con-
ducive to a free exchange of views and thoughts. Though he was
RT Kilo's senior NCO, responsible for the good order and discipline among the team's enlisted soldiers, Kannen was able to lead
Kilo Two with a light hand because of the quality and professionalism of the others who rode along with him in Kilo Two.
The only topic of conversation that was out of bounds was criti-
cism of their unit's officers. Though they might make fun of Burman and Aveno on occasion by referring to Burman as Captain
Ahab, Kannen would not tolerate any disrespect. Whenever
someone in Kilo Two came close to doing so the senior NCO
would cut him off by reminding them that until they were in
charge, the only response the enlisted men would give when their
commanding officer issued an order was a crisp salute and a gusty
"Airborne."

None of the men who traveled with Kannen had any problem
with this. They had more than enough material to work with, jab-
bing fun at each other or exchanging puns when the mood struck
them. Salvador Mendez, who drove Kilo Two, was the only man
who enjoyed driving through the desert, though the experience
would have no value when he returned to New York City. "No
one will ever believe me when I tell them that I was able to drive

for hours on end without ever hitting a red light or having to lean on the horn."

Specialist Four David Davis, a young black man born and raised in rural Mississippi, and called Dee Dee by officers and enlisted alike, was never sure when to believe the stories Mendez liked to tell about his experiences in "the city." Davis had joined the army for many of the same reasons Laporta had. "I'll go back to Mississippi after I get out so I can take advantage of the cheap tuition given to in-state students at Ole Miss while living at home. But I'll be damned if I'm going to stay in that state after I graduate. Having the family close is okay. And the folks down there are friendly. But it's just too damned hot for my liking."

Whenever Davis complained about the heat, someone in Kilo Two would point out that if he was trying to escape warm climates, he had definitely made a bad career move when he enlisted in the army. Usually it was the team's weapons specialist, Sergeant Samuel Harris, who pointed this out. Like Mendez, Harris was a native of New York State. Unlike the Puerto Rican–American, Harris was from Watertown in New York, near the Canadian border. Mendez enjoyed poking fun at his fellow New Yorker, referring to him as a hillbilly without hills or an almost-Canadian. Harris took all this in stride and managed to serve up his own retorts. "I've been to New York City once or twice," he'd reply whenever Mendez would go off on a rant about how backward the people were in the region of the state where Harris came from. "The only part I was able to enjoy was the sign that reads Welcome to New Jersey." Though most of the banter in Kilo Two was rather silly, it served to pass the time and lighten the mood.

The same could not be said of the pair who made up the air force liaison team in Kilo One. While they were cordial to each other in a sergeant–lieutenant sort of way, during these protracted marches through the desert, there was little opportunity for idle banter. Nighttime was prime time for air strikes, and patrols in the no-fly zone were looking for unusual activities on the ground.

With the HF radios turned to the frequency of the E-3A AWACs on station, First Lieutenant Joseph Ciszak kept track of who was airborne, where the various aircraft were in relationship to RT Kilo, what sort of ordnance those aircraft were carrying, and who would be best able to come to their assistance if Kilo blundered its way into trouble. When Ciszak and his NCO did exchange words, it was usually in response to something heard over one of the many radios that were crammed into the rear of the humvee. After doing this work for so long, Ciszak and his driver, Airman First Class Jay Jones, were as familiar with the personalities of the AWACs' crews and pilots of the strike aircraft as they were with the other members of Kilo. What comic relief they did enjoy was derived from banter the strike pilots tossed back and forth in an effort to break their own boredom.

Bringing up the rear of the small column was Ken Aveno and Kilo Three. The silence that permeated this vehicle was due primarily to the dust that they had to eat because of their assigned position in the line of march. The only time they escaped this curse was when there was a strong wind blowing in from the side. But even then the chatter between Aveno and his fellow travelers was limited. Seated next to the executive officer of Kilo was Specialist Four Insram Amer who served as Aveno's driver and the backup translator. Amer was a Palestinian who had lived in Jordan before coming to the United States to attend college. Lacking the funds necessary to continue his pursuit of a doctorate and having no desire to return to a nation that would never be a home to his people, Amer opted to join the United States Army. Since one of Kilo's escape-and-evasion routes took them through Jordan, Amer was viewed as a valuable asset by those who had selected the personnel for Kilo.

Equally valuable to the team was Sergeant Glenn Funk, their medical specialist. Like all army medics Funk took great pride in looking after his companions. In time, if he did not reenlist, Funk planned on returning to Texas where he hoped to find a position as an EMT in the Dallas/Fort Worth area. Until then he devoted himself to learning all he could about emergency medicine by practicing his craft whenever possible.

The fourth man who made up Kilo Three's complement was Staff Sergeant Angel Ramirez. He served as Kilo's second-ranking NCO and its demolitions expert. Like Kannen, Ramirez was a career soldier, a man who had no intention of ever going back to the state he had once called home. While the two senior NCOs joked about having found a home in the army, it was painfully true for the thirty-one-year-old Ramirez. Many of the Chicano youths he had hung out with while growing up in Los Angeles were either dead or serving hard time in one of the state's prisons. The Latino NCO knew that had he not enlisted when he did, he'd be with them, in prison or planted six feet under. That his chosen career routinely put him in harm's way was of little concern. As he saw it, at least in the army his life had meaning and value. None of his former friends who were still alive could make that claim.

Behind Kilo Three, there was nothing. Ahead, the other three Hummers. And somewhere out there in the darkness that hid them all was a site they had been assigned to locate, and designate for an air strike if it turned out to be worth the risk. That people could very well die because of their actions that night didn't matter. Someone of higher rank, someone whom none of them would ever meet, had already made that decision. Nor would the members of RT Kilo actually be responsible for the dead. They were only the messengers of death, a collection of men from across the United States, brought together by their profession and a cabal of faceless staff officers.

CHAPTER FOUR

Syria
20:35 LOCAL (16:35 ZULU)

Seated upon the hood of Kilo Two with his back braced against the windshield and feet tucked up so that he could rest his elbows on his knees, Allen Kannen peered through his night-vision goggles. Slowly he scanned the horizon from left to right. He tried hard to ignore the pair of humvees that kept cropping up in his field of vision as they moved forward, but he was concerned because they were far too exposed, moving too fast, and waiting too long before dismounting. Though both Kilo Six and Kilo Three were commanded by officers who had done this sort of thing countless times before, Kannen was beginning to wonder if they were getting careless.

Behind him Sam Harris stood with his upper torso sticking up through the ring mount fitted to the hard shell of Kilo Two. Leaning forward, the team's weapons expert grasped the traverse and elevation knobs of the TOW missile launcher while keeping his right eye glued to the tracker. Like Kannen, Harris was searching for trouble. Just what sort of trouble they were looking for was as unknown as the form it would take, if in fact there was any danger out there. With a more powerful sight, Harris had the advantage of being able to stop when he came across something suspicious. With the flip of a lever on the TOW's tracker he was able to change the sight's magnification, allowing him to carefully inspect the object that concerned him. Though the sound of this action was minute, it was loud enough to put Kannen on edge every time he heard it. When he did not hear Harris switch back to the lower setting within a second or two, the senior NCO would call out in hushed tones. "What ya got?"

Though Harris knew Kannen was anxiously awaiting a response, he would say nothing until he was sure of what he was seeing. In most cases the weapons expert would heave a sigh of relief and relay a belated "It was nothing" before flipping the lever back and picking up his search where he had left off.

The other members of Kilo Two were not idle. Mendez remained behind the steering wheel with the night-vision goggles he had used during the long trek to this spot hanging down around his neck. Peering through those devices for hours on end could be very painful, feeling as though someone with long skinny fingers was reaching behind the eyeballs in an effort to pull them out. Even without the goggles on, Mendez was still watching and listening. Strange as it may seem, the basic-issue unaided M-1A1 eyeballs were still just as valuable a search engine at night as were the most sophisticated night-vision goggles in the army's inventory. Any sort of night-vision devices or binoculars tend to narrow the focus of the observer and eliminate peripheral vision. Often it was what a soldier perceived rather than heard or saw that first cued him to a danger he was not looking for.

Davis was also on his guard. Unlike the others, he was dismounted. Leaning against the rear of Kilo Two with his weapon cradled in his arms, Davis kept watch over the team's rear 180-degree arc, alternating between using his night-vision goggles and scanning the empty horizon without them. This was a lonely vigil, as demanding in its own way as were the efforts of Kannen and Harris. That Davis was not anticipating anything popping up in his sector made his task all the more tiring.

The only thing that broke up the otherwise barren landscape that Davis was assigned to cover was Kilo One, the ALO's, or air liaison officer's, humvee. While Burman in Kilo Six and Aveno with Kilo Three went forward in search of that night's target, First Lieutenant Joe Ciszak and Jones remained with Kannen and the crew of Kilo Two. When either Burman or his XO found what they were searching for, they would notify Ciszak via the team's internal radio net. The air force officer would contact the AWACs, using his radios, and pass on targeting information. Once his authority to attack was confirmed, the mission officer would hand off the action to the strike aircraft that had been specifically sortied for this task. If they were unavailable for whatever reason, aircraft that had been running routine patrols were tagged to fill in.

When all was ready and the colonel aboard the AWACs had all the data concerning the time on target and angle of attack calculated, he would send this information back to Ciszak, who would, in turn, inform whichever Special Forces officer was observing the target. The army officers never knew the identity of the aircraft that would be coming, or the type of ordnance that would be falling from the sky. All they needed from Ciszak was what the minimum safe distance was, and when he needed to switch on his laser designator and "paint" the target for the incoming laser-guided bomb. This was the American way of war—fought at a distance, relying on technology to synchronize the assets of several services, and delivering overwhelming firepower on a target with an accuracy that would have been unimaginable in past wars. For the Americans, these strikes were swift, unexpected, and damned near antiseptic. Staff officers back in Washington, D.C., charged with briefing civilians on these sorts of activities liked to refer to them as "surgical."

To the Syrian soldiers and Iraqi expatriates located at ground zero there was nothing surgical about the bombings. If they were lucky the only thing they would experience was being shredded by razor-sharp fragments from the 750-pound bomb's detonation—countless white-hot shards of metal filling the air and slicing through exposed flesh in a most efficient and completely random fashion.

Those who survived this shower of fragments suffered other, often more heinous deaths as fragments from the bomb sliced through fuel tanks or the thin casings of shells and other munitions within the targeted area. The resulting fireball and the flow of burning fuel liberated by the rupturing of their containers seared and scorched exposed flesh, setting clothing and hair ablaze and sending the stricken souls off in a wild flight that only served to fan the flames they were trying to escape.

Even those who were fortunate enough to escape being butchered where they stood or burned alive were not safe. The force of the blast radiated out in a wave that had the power to turn internal organs into jelly, toss people through the air like rag dolls, or pound them into the ground as though struck down by a Nordic god's invisible hammer. Those who had the wits and ability to crawl far enough to escape the spreading pool of burning fuel or the effects of secondary explosions that inevitably followed a successful attack suffered broken eardrums, shattered bones, and crippling concussions.

The soldiers assigned to RT Kilo never saw any of this. At most they witnessed the initial explosion and its attendant fireball. On rare occasions one of them caught a glimpse of a corpse being thrown through the air. But that was all. Once the bomb had struck home there was no time for the men who had guided it to its mark to celebrate their achievement or measure the bomb's effects. They had to swiftly turn from finding and designating to escaping and evading, for another tenet of the American way of war is to do unto others without giving them the opportunity to do it to you.

Like his predecessors, Captain Erik Burman never questioned the political wisdom of what he and his men were doing. That was not in his job description. He was an American soldier, a commissioned officer sworn to uphold the Constitution of the United States and follow all orders from his duly appointed superiors. If those orders placed him and the soldiers entrusted to his care in harm's way, so be it. Regardless of their personal motivation, everyone in RT Kilo had volunteered for some form of service at least twice—when they joined the armed forces and later again when they had chosen to become members of the army's Special Forces. Only the two men belonging to the air liaison team were part of RT Kilo against their better judgment. Joe Ciszak was fond of reminding everyone who cared to listen that he had joined the air force to thunder along at mach one plus, not sneak about in the night like a Bedouin raider. This attitude, shared by Airman Jones, tended to isolate them from the rest of the team.

What the air liaison officer thought was the last thing Ken Aveno was concerned about. At the moment his entire focus was on finding a spot that offered anything that came close to offering cover and concealment behind which he could halt his vehicle. In this he was having no luck. Nothing resembling a textbook hull-down defensive position seemed to exist in this region. When this was the case, both he and Burman in Kilo Six had to settle on creeping forward as far as they dared from different directions before simply stopping in the flat open country just outside the village they were approaching. Such compromises of acceptable doctrine were both hazardous to the max and completely un-avoidable.

Sometimes RT Kilo got lucky, and the object of their search was discovered on the periphery of a village or installation hidden in the lee of a building. On the nights that the officers found their mark exposed in this manner they were able to stand off and designate the target right from their vehicle. This did not prove to be the case tonight. As they drew closer to the darkened village where they hoped to find a chemical warfare lab the usually unflappable Ramirez assigned to Kilo Three began to wonder just how far they would go before Aveno ordered him to stop. Ramirez's position during these cautious advances was up top, training the 40-mm grenade launcher on the village ahead. From there he had an unobstructed panoramic view of the village as well as its environs. With his right index finger never more than an inch away from the trigger, Ramirez watched and waited for trouble he prayed would not suddenly pop up from out of the shadows. When they did stop, he would remain with Kilo Three to provide cover as the XO continued on foot into the village with his driver, Amer.

Inside the humvee, Ken Aveno was also becoming nervous as he squirmed in his seat and leaned forward until the brim of his cap touched the windshield. He was pushing his luck. They were already far too close and still he saw no sign of anything even remotely resembling a safe place where Kilo Three could hunker down. Though he didn't like doing so, the Special Forces officer decided he had to order his driver to stop. "Things aren't looking any better between here and there," Aveno said to Amer before ordering the halt. He drew in a deep breath. "We'll have to leave her here and hoof it the rest of the way."

The Palestinian-American said nothing. He dreaded what lay ahead. The stress and anxiety lingering just below his conscious thoughts was already twisting his stomach into knots. Both would grow by leaps and bounds from this point on as they adbandoned what little protection Kilo Three offered from hostile fire. Once out of the vehicle and on the ground, Amer would have no protection at all, with only the darkness as a shield.

Amer brought his humvee to a stop and climbed out. Sergeant Funk wasted no time sliding in behind the steering wheel. Like all the members of RT Kilo the medic was cross-trained in other duties. Funk could fill in for Amer as driver as well as operate all of the team's communications equipment except some of the more specialized air force stuff that was crammed into Kilo One. The fact was he had done just about everything else he had been trained to do except be a medic, something for which everyone in the team, including Funk himself, was quite thankful.

It always took several minutes for Aveno to collect his gear and steel himself for the coming ordeal. Besides taking his MP-5 from the bracket where he kept the weapon while on the move, the XO had to remove the laser designator from its carrying case and inspect it as best he could in the dark to ensure that it was functional. He also needed to check the small radio he carried, placing the earpiece in his right ear and adjusting the volume. During these preparations Ken Aveno reflected on how things had changed during their unending deployment in Syria. He recalled how excited he had been in the beginning. Like a child fumbling with gifts on Christmas morning, he had been all thumbs as he tried to do everything at once. Now such enthusiasm was only a memory, lost weeks ago in the monotony and strain of their daily routine and the harsh environment in which they lived. He tried hard to justify in his own mind that the time it now took him to prepare was necessary lest he overlook something. But he knew that was not the real reason. He was putting off going forward, delaying for as long as possible advancing into the heart of a hostile village in the faint hope that Captain Burman discovered their target first, thus sparing him the necessity of doing so himself.

That he harbored such feelings and thoughts shamed him. He was a professional, a West Pointer. Officers weren't supposed to think or feel like that. Yet, as their extended deployment had dragged on he found himself questioning his own fitness to be an officer, wondering if he needed to reexamine his priorities. Perhaps it was time to find a new career. His slow departure from the relative safety of Kilo Three only reinforced his self-doubt about his commitment to his current line of work.

When he had reached the end of his mental checklist and there was nothing more to keep him from leaving, Aveno turned to Amer. "Ready?" His throat parched by his own growing fear, Amer simply nodded.

Aveno turned his back on Kilo Three and slowly stepped off, advancing toward the village on foot. Amer took up his post five meters to the left and a little behind the XO. Whatever fears or apprehensions the two felt were hidden by the same darkness they relied upon to conceal their presence.

Even though Dee Dee Davis, protecting the rear area of Kilo Two, was facing in the direction of the Syrian recon vehicle, he was not the first one to become aware of its presence when it broke cover in the darkness, and began to advance on Davis and Kilo Two, and the air force team in Kilo One.

From his perch on Kilo Three Sergeant Harris heard the whine of the ancient Russian-built four-wheeled BRDM armored reconnaissance car but was unable to figure out which direction the noise was coming from. Assuming it was somewhere in or near the village, and knowing Aveno and Amer were out there, the weapons expert frantically began to sweep the area while calling out a warning to the others. *"We got company!"*

This announcement sent a shock through Kannen seated on the hood of Kilo Two. "Where? What is it?"

"I don't know, but it sounds like an armored car. A BRDM or something." After making another sweep of the village and the horizon on both sides, Harris quickly added, "I don't see it. Does anyone else?"

Kannen was still straining his eyes in an effort to catch sight of the menace when he felt a hand grab his right boot. Looking down he saw Davis standing next to the rear of the humvee.

"Back there!" Davis screeched. *"Back there!"*

Jumping to his feet Kannen stood on the hood and turned, looking out over the roof of Kilo Two. Even without his night-vision goggles he could make out the form of a BRDM barreling down on their position. That the Syrian recon vehicle could also see them was confirmed a second later when its 20-mm cannon cut loose.

CHAPTER FIVE

The eruption of gunfire in the distance found Erik Burman and Sergeant Yousaf Hashmi on foot and not far from the center of the village. Instinctively the Special Forces officer threw himself on the ground and rolled up against a building, which was, at the moment, the only thing that afforded him anything resembling hard cover. Once he came to a stop against the wall he brought his weapon up to the ready, flipped its safety off, and began to frantically scan the area around him for danger. Even in the midst of making himself as small a target as possible, it was clear to Burman that the fire was not directed at them or anywhere near. Still, he responded as if it were. Hashmi didn't wait to be told what to do either. As professional as anyone else assigned to Kilo, the New York–born Syrian followed suit, twisting himself about as soon as he was on the ground, to check their rear and make sure they were not surprised from that quarter.

Having tended to his first order of business, that of providing for his personal security, Burman now needed to find out what was going on. Fumbling until his left hand found the hand mike of the small radio that linked him to the other members of his command, Burman depressed the push to talk button. "Kilo, Kilo, this is Kilo Six. Sitrep, over."

While waiting for the scattered elements of his team to report their situation, Burman continued to look around in order to assess his own. Already he could hear the sound of the village coming to life. On the other side of the wall he was pressed up against he could hear feet hit the floor and begin to scurry about, accompanied by a flurry of excited voices. Deep down in the pit of his stomach, Burman felt a growing fear begin to well up, a fear that if left unchecked would turn into panic. He had to contain it, to keep it in check if they were to have any hope of surviving the next few minutes. Both he and Hashmi couldn't stay where they were for very long. That much was obvious. Soon, someone would come tearing around the corner and trip over them. It didn't matter whether they were civilian or military. Everyone in this village, with the exception of Hashmi, was a hostile, a person who would just as soon see him dead. They had to move. The sooner they did, the better their chances of getting away.

Only the failure to get any sort of response to his call for a situation report and a fresh burst of gunfire in the distance kept Burman in place. For all he knew there could be Syrian soldiers lying in ambush, waiting for them to make a run back to their humvee. As dangerous as it was to stay where he was, it was even more hazardous to jump up and charge off into the dark totally ignorant of what was going on out there. Crushing the push to talk button on the small hand mike, Burman frantically repeated his call to his subordinates. "Kilo, Kilo, this is Kilo Six. Sitrep, over. I say again, give me your sitrep, *Now!*"

While someone with each of Kilo's scattered detachments heard Burman's call, all were busy responding to the same threat that had sent Burman to ground, whether they could see it or not.

The members of the air liaison team in Kilo One were the last to catch on to the acute danger that faced them, or, more correctly, was rushing up at them from behind. As was his habit, Airman Jones had turned down the volume of the tactical radio net that linked all of Kilo's humvees so that Lieutenant Ciszak could better monitor those nets upon which the AWACs and strike aircraft were operating. It wasn't until Jones noticed the frenzied activities of Kannen, Harris, and other members of Kilo Two's crew, punctuated by bright orange flashes streaking through the night sky, that the airman turned to Ciszak. "LT, we've got a problem."

Jones's statement took several seconds to cut through Ciszak's mental haze. Confused, the air force officer was about to ask Jones what he was talking about when the sharp pow-pow-pow of the BRDM's 20-mm cannon provided the answer. Startled, Ciszak looked over to where Kilo Two sat. In a scene that reminded him of an old silent movie, the flash of the BRDM's cannon lit up the night, illuminating the army humvee and its crew. Ciszak watched as Harris frantically swung the TOW missile launcher around to face the threat barreling down on them. Two other men, whom Ciszak couldn't identify, had thrown themselves on the ground and opened up with their individual weapons. That they were having no effect was obvious as the unseen intruder continued to hammer away with a slow, steady pow—pow—pow.

"Lieutenant, shouldn't you be calling for support?"

Ciszak turned to face Jones, who repeated his plea almost as an order. "*Sir*, you need to inform Rainbow we're in trouble."

Rainbow was the call sign for the AWACs. The code word for "team in trouble, send immediate air strike" was Cherokee. Unfortunately, Ciszak found he wasn't able to recall that particular code word. The ones he used day in and day out were on the tip of his tongue. Those that he had no need for during the course of normal operations such as Cherokee had been stored away somewhere in his memory and quietly forgotten. Completely rattled by what was going on outside, Ciszak didn't think to ask Jones if he remembered what the call for assistance was. Instead the harried officer flicked on his small penlight and looked down at the sheet where all the code words, call signs, and frequencies for that evening were listed.

Already shaken by the surprise enemy attack, it took Jones a moment to catch on to what his officer was doing. When he did he yelled at Ciszak. "*Cherokee*, for Christ sakes! The word is Cherokee."

Embarrassment added to his befuddlement as Ciszak fumbled with his hand mike while he attempted to make the call. Unable to hold back any longer, Jones snatched the mike, mashed down the push to talk button, and screamed repeatedly into it, "Cherokee, Cherokee, Cherokee."

Two hundred fifty miles away the word "Cherokee" had the same startling effect on the crew of the E-3A AWACs that the fire from the BRDM had had on Ciszak and Jones. Caught totally off guard the AWACs controller asked to confirm their requests for assistance.

The controller's call for confirmation was heard by a number of other aircraft throughout the region as well as the operations center responsible for monitoring the day-to-day activities of Razorback in Turkey. But neither Ciszak nor Jones heard or responded to the call. By then events on the ground had spiraled out of control and overwhelmed the crew of Kilo One.

The BRDM that had initiated the frantic call for assistance was not alone. At a minimum recon vehicles traveled in pairs, allowing one to go forward and search while the other hung back and quietly watched, just as Sergeant Kannen and the crew of Kilo Two had been doing.

The sudden appearance of Kilo One and Kilo Two was as much a surprise to the Syrian lieutenant commanding the pair of BRDMs as his unit's appearance was to the members of RT Kilo. The Syrians had been returning to the village after having finished a routine mounted patrol when the gunner of the lead BRDM called out that he thought he saw something on the horizon. Startled by the sight of combat vehicles where there should not have been any, the Syrians automatically reverted to established battle drill. While his lieutenant radioed his observations to his superior, the commander of the lead BRDM continued to press on in order to investigate. With his duty of reporting his discovery fulfilled, the commander of the Syrian recon team ordered his driver to come to a halt as he prepared to support his lead vehicle. That BRDM continued to roll on, opening fire on the target nearest to it, which happened to be Kilo One. The presence of a second enemy vehicle in the area, Kilo Two, didn't become apparent to either BRDM until after the Americans manning it sprang to life and prepared to return fire.

Because the recon vehicle was parked, the gunner seated next to the Syrian officer took his time laying his sight on his intended mark with care, unlike the other BRDM, which was in motion and spewing its fire about like a drunk trying to urinate in a jar.

That they were a target was not readily apparent to Ciszak or Holton. Their vehicle's hard exterior shell as well as the supplies, equipment, and radios that Jones was using to call for help shielded them from the initial burst of 20-mm cannon fire. Only when they felt their humvee begin to rock and shake did they realize they were not only being shot at but were being hit

Jones tossed the radio hand mike to his lieutenant. "Keep trying to get them. Send them our location." As Ciszak groped in the dark interior for the hand mike that had hit him, Jones faced forward, grabbed the steering wheel with one hand, and reached for the ignition with the other. Getting out of the line of fire, if even for a moment, seemed to be a vastly superior option to simply standing fast and being chewed to pieces.

The wild spray of fire from the lead BRDM was screaming over the top of Kilo Two as Sergeant Harris brought the TOW missile launcher to bear on the advancing Syrian vehicle. Those rounds were not wasted as they managed to find a totally unexpected mark that neither Syrian BRDM had yet spotted. The shower of small explosions impacting around Kilo Three were both spectacular and unnerving to Sergeant Ramirez, who had been topside manning the 40-mm grenade launcher, and to Funk, seated at the steering wheel. The attention of both men had been riveted on the village ahead. The unexpected hail of fire directed at them from somewhere in their rear was a shock. Twisting about, Ramirez caught sight of the BRDM for the first time. When he saw the bright orange tracers of incoming rounds looming larger and larger, he naturally assumed that Kilo Three was their intended target. Dropping down into the humveev Ramirez screamed, *"Get the fuck out of here, NOW!"* as loudly as he could to Funk, who was still frantically looking backward trying to figure out what was going on.

Without the slightest hesitation the team medic started the engine, engaged the gears, cut the wheel to the left, and stomped his foot on the accelerator until it bottomed out on the floorboard. Moving through a cloud of dust thrown by Kilo Three's wheels, Ramirez and Funk chose flight over fight, totally unaware that the 20-mm rounds had been meant for Kilo Two and not them.

Though Sergeant Kannen knew his rifle fire was having no effect and the 20-mm shells weren't even coming close to hitting Kilo Two, he continued to blaze away at the Syrian recon vehicle barreling down on them. To have lain there on the ground, doing nothing as the Syrian gunner made the necessary corrections to his aim, was simply not in Kannen's nature. Only when he'd emptied the weapon's magazine and was reaching for a fresh one did he take the time to look up at Harris and yell out to his weapons expert. "What the hell is taking you so long?"

Harris ignored Kannen. With his right eye shoved against the TOW's sight he took one more second to refine his aim before bracing himself and unleashing the wire-guided antitank missile, momentarily blinding Kannen with the ignition of the missile's rocket motor. Harris stayed focused on the oncoming BRDM. Inside the Hummer Davis was already in the process of trying to unstrap a reload for the TOW launcher while Mendez squirmed in the driver's seat, waiting for someone to give the order to take off. None of them were paying any attention to Kilo One when it suddenly disappeared in a ball of flames.

Hearing one massive explosion in the distance, followed shortly thereafter by another explosion of equal force, Erik Burman realized the battle had intensified significantly, thus magnifying the risk he ran if he and Hashmi remained where they were much longer. Still, he once more delayed taking any action, waiting and listening a few moments longer until he was sure he and Hashmi were in no immediate danger. Only when he was absolutely sure that it was safe to do so did Burman rise and cautiously begin to make his way along the wall that had provided a modicum of protection and concealment. Without having to be told, Hashmi followed crouched low in an effort to make himself as small a target as possible.

They had not gone very far when a burst of small-arms fire from around the corner caused them to flatten on the ground once more and bring their weapons up to the ready. After it became apparent that the AK gunfire had not been directed at them, Burman said to Hashmi. "What are they firing at?"

Hashmi's response was short and to the point. "Not us."

Taking a second or two, Burman listened. When he was confident that Hashmi was right he pushed himself up off the ground and continued to snake his way through the back alleys of the village, hugging walls and staying as low as he could. They had not gone far before a second burst of small-arms fire broke out from somewhere behind them. This time Hashmi did not hesitate as he called out as loud as he dared, "It's not us. Keep going, sir. Keep going."

Both Dennis O'Hara and John Laporta had heard the opening burst of fire on the far side the village. Both men had heard their commanding officer's desperate plea for situation reports. When they heard no response from their compatriots or anything more from Burman, the two special fours prepared themselves for the worst. Wrapping his hands around the spade grips of the M-2 machine gun he was manning, O'Hara called out to his companion. "Well, amigo, it looks like we're finally going to get a chance to kick some ass and take some names."

Laporta clutched his steering wheel as he peered into the darkness in the hope that he would catch sight of Kilo Six's other occupants headed back their way. "I don't know if I'm ready for this, Dennis."

O'Hara said nothing for a moment as he slowly traversed his weapon back and forth, taking his time to scan the dark outline of the village up ahead in a vain effort to understand what was going on out there. "Ready or not, we're in it."

"Maybe we should go forward a bit, get closer so the captain and Yousaf can find us easier."

O'Hara shook his head even though his companion couldn't see him. "The CO knows where we are. If he wants us to move, he'll tell us. Best we stay here where we can cover them when they reach the edge of the village and make a break for it."

"And if they don't?"

"Have a little faith, Johnny," O'Hara replied without hesitation. "Don't worry about that. "They'll make it. You can bet on that."

The destruction of the first BRDM by Sergeant Harris brought no respite to the men of Kilo Two. Even before the stricken Syrian recon vehicle had rolled to a dead stop, Sergeant First Class Kannen was up off the ground and running to where he had seen a body land after being forcibly ejected from the blazing Kilo One, the air liaison team's humvee. As he ran the only thing that kept running through his mind was the hope that his efforts weren't in vain.

As he approached Kilo One Kannen saw the driver's door on the left side of the humvee fly open. A sheet of flames leaped from the open door, followed by the most horrific spectacle imaginable, a living person totally engulfed by fire struggling to climb out. Stopping in midstride, Kannen watched in horror as the human torch struggled to free itself from the inferno that had once been a tactical vehicle. Once on the ground the stricken figure stood upright with legs apart and arms held out at its side, twisting this way and that as if in a forlorn effort to escape the flames that covered it from head to toe.

There was nothing Kannen could do. The man before him was dying, dying in unimaginable agony. As he watched, the grotesque figure managed to take a step, one last faltering step away from its own funeral pyre before toppling over in a heap of burning flesh and rags.

It had never occurred to anyone in RT Kilo that having cans of diesel inside was a bad idea. No one had ever given much thought to the risk they were running by carrying spare cans of fuel inside their vehicles. They all merrily believed that because diesel had very low volatility and the Hummers had thick metal walls that were difficult to pierce, carrying fuel in the cargo bay posed no threat to the passengers. This supposition, based on the assumption that most of their foes would have only small arms, was never challenged even as Burman was arming one of the humvees to fend off tanks. No one took into account what an exploding 20-mm high explosive round would do to fuel cans wedged in between cases of spare ammunition. This object lesson, like all important lessons learned in battle, comes at an awful price, one that was often paid over and over again.

The report of another 20-mm cannon not far from where he was standing jarred Kannen from his trance. Turning away from the burning humvee, he saw a second BRDM emerge from the darkness that lay outside the flickering light of flames. Without having to see it, Kannen realized that it was another Syrian recon vehicle, the one that had destroyed Kilo One and was now preparing to take out Kilo Two as well. Jolted back to the reality of the here and now, Kannen took off as fast as he could to recover the body that had been thrown clear of Kilo One.

Syria
20:48 LOCAL (16:48 ZULU)

On the other side of the village Ken Aveno and Insram Amer emerged from the cover of the last building and into the open. In the distance Aveno caught glimpses of the exchange of fire between the Syrian recon detachment and Kilo Two, taking in the entire situation on the fly. In an instant he appreciated that this would be their only opportunity for escape, while confusion reigned and before the Syrians in the village had an opportunity to come to a full state of alert. So the two men abandoned all caution and broke into a dead run as they made for the spot where they had left Kilo Three.

As he ran to where his humvee waited, Aveno kept glancing over to Kilo Two and the pair of BRDMs that were fighting it out. The act of running as well as the sudden flash of an explosion made it difficult for him to sort out what he was seeing. Only after they had covered better than half the distance to the spot where they had dismounted was he able to assess the situation before him with any accuracy.

In the foreground stood Kilo Two, silhouetted by the flames that engulfed a freshly killed BRDM. Ignoring the stricken Syrian vehicle as fire consumed its crew and cooked off stored ammunition, Aveno looked at its sole victim, Kilo One.

Suddenly it struck him. They had lost one of their humvees, perhaps the most valuable of the four, for Kilo One was the only one that could communicate with the AWACs. As he looked at the blazing remains of Kilo One, Aveno wondered if Ciszak and Jones had managed to call for an immediate air strike to cover the team's withdrawal before their vehicle was destroyed. He wondered if either of them had been wounded or killed.

The executive officer of Kilo was not being cold or unfeeling by the order in which he assessed the situation before him. He was a professional soldier and an officer, a person who had trained his mind and body for these sorts of situations. More often than most officers would admit to outsiders, success in battle often depended on an officer's ability to subordinate his personal feelings and concerns for the welfare of the men, and instead focus on accomplishing his assigned mission. The status of equipment, the availability and disposition of weapons, and the ability of those weapons to inflict the maximum damage upon their foe were what won battles. The soldiers under his command were the currency with which victory was purchased. It was cold. Inhuman. Perhaps it was even morally repugnant. But it was war, and war, as Sherman had pointed out, was hell.

From where he was Aveno had no way of knowing how many Syrian vehicles were out there. What he was able to make out was the form of a man atop Kilo Two struggling to fit a large cylinder into the rear of the TOW launcher. It had to be Harris, Aveno thought. The team's weapons expert was in the process of reloading, meaning that there was another BRDM out there. Either that or Harris was expecting more.

Only when he took the time to look around again did Aveno belatedly realized that his own Hummer, Kilo Three, which had been parked just beyond Kilo Two, was no longer there. Stunned, Aveno called out to Amer. "Where the hell is Kilo Three?"

Before he could answer a stream of green tracers emerged out of the darkness ahead and struck Kilo Two, causing Aveno to wonder what was really going on. Why wasn't Kilo Two moving while Harris reloaded? Why were they standing there giving the bastards an easy target? Then, belatedly remembering that he was linked to the other members of Kilo by radio, he added another, even more telling question to his litany of concerns. "Why the hell isn't anyone reporting?"

At the moment the questions Aveno was posing to himself were less for information than they were expressions of his frustration at finding himself in a position from which he could neither exercise command nor control. Caught up in his own struggle for survival coupled with a futile effort to sort the situation that was playing out before him, it never dawned on Ken Aveno that he had not heard his commanding officer's voice for some time.

A fresh spate of small-arms fire followed by a chorus of frenzied cries that sounded like orders brought Erik Burman's movement through the village to another abrupt halt. Throwing himself against the wall he had been moving along, he slowly slid to the ground. Hashmi, who was watching their rear while brushing up against the same wall with his shoulder as he backed up didn't see Burman stop. Before he realized what he was doing, his boot came down onto Burman's ankle.

The sound of cracking bone indicated the seriousness of the damage. Yet despite the wave of pain, Burman somehow maintained silence as he jerked his injured leg from under Hashmi's foot. Already off balance, Hashmi fell to the ground, hitting it hard and unwittingly crying out in pain. Between his wild gyrations to keep from falling and the sudden impact, his rifle flew out of his hands. Like his exclamation there was nothing Hashmi could do to muffle the noise that his weapon made as it clattered across the loose rocks and stones that littered the narrow alley they had been moving through. Adding to his embarrassment at losing his weapon and injuring his commanding officer was a fear that his clumsiness had inadvertently betrayed their presence.

Burman was struggling with his own problems at that moment. Once the initial surprise, shock, and pain associated with his broken ankle had passed, he rolled onto his back. The Kilo commander's struggle to suppress screams of pain and anger caused his face to turn beet red and his throat to bulge and quiver. Taking as much time as he dared, Burman sat up and slowly bent over until he could reach his foot. In the darkness of the narrow ally he could see that the toes of the foot Hashmi had stepped on were pointed up just like the other foot. That was a good sign. But when he tried to move his left leg the searing pain that coursed through his body blinded him to the sudden light that was cast upon them when a boy opened the shutters of a window above the pair of Americans.

Hashmi looked up right into the eyes of the small Syrian boy who had opened the window, curious to discover what had caused such a racket. The two looked at each other for the briefest of moments before the terrified boy turned and fled into the interior of the house screaming as he went.

"Jesus!" Burman yelled, feeling the pain intensify. Hearing the boy's panicked shouts hadn't helped. "We're fucked for sure. Give me a hand."

Without giving his weapon another thought Hashmi scrambled to his feet and reached over to help his commanding officer stand. Burman flung his weapon over his shoulder onto his back and out of the way. As he fought off the waves of pain that swept over him, with Hashmi doing most of the lifting, Burman managed to get up and stand on his good leg before draping his left arm securely over Hashmi's shoulder. For the first time in his military career Burman came to the realizion that his six-foot-three, two-hundred-ten-pound frame could be a serious liability. While Hashmi was as tough as every other member of the team and almost as strong, Burman wondered if the five-foot-six Syrian-American was up to the task. When they were both set he gave Hashmi a quick nod and curt order. "Let's go."

Slowly the pair took their first tentative step together. Burman closed his eyes and concentrated on keeping weight off his broken ankle while choking down a sudden bout of nausea brought on by the pain. Struggling to support his burden, Hashmi took it easy at first. Only when Burman ordered him to pick up the pace did he lengthen his gait.

All hope of a quick and stealthy exit from the small village was now gone. Linked together the two staggered on, remaining in the shadows as best they could and halting only when the thumping of boots and sound of voices grew too close to ignore. Despite the clumsiness of their arrangement, Hashmi was able to get the hang of supporting Burman while negotiating their way through the back alleys.

Focused on each next step, Hashmi was shocked when he suddenly looked up and found that they had cleared the last building of the village and reached the open desert beyond. When he came to an abrupt halt, Burman opened his eyes.

In an instant he understood what had happened, though he didn't quite know what to do about it. In their effort to get out of the village as quickly as possible Burman had not given any consideration to how to best cross the open ground that lay between the edge of the village and where Kilo Six sat waiting. Only now did it dawn upon him that it might be a good idea to radio Kilo Six and have Laporta make a quick run in to pick them up. But just as quickly as this thought came to him he rejected it. He wasn't sure precisely where they were. That and the fact that the sound of an approaching humvee would be impossible to mask made doing so a risk he was unwilling to take. The Syrian soldiers in the village behind them would be drawn to the sound of a foreign vehicle coming toward them like moths to a candle.

"Captain, we must keep moving."

Burman could see the sweat running down Hashmi's face. He drew himself up and nodded. "Yes, let's get the hell out of here."

Tightening his grip on Burman, Hashmi headed into the open desert beyond.

. . .

Throughout their high-speed flight in Kilo Three neither Staff Sergeant Ramirez nor Sergeant Funk thought to turn the volume up on the radio that was set to monitor the team's internal net, thus missing Ken Aveno's repeated calls to them. Like bandits fleeing the scene of a crime, they sped off into the night until Ramirez was sure that they were well out of danger and finally ordered Funk to let up on the gas and slow down. Only then were the two men able to hear the voice of their XO above the roaring engine of Kilo Three.

Realizing what he had done, Ramirez grabbed the hand mike and mashed the talk button. "Kilo Three Alpha, this is Three Bravo, over."

From the vacant spot in the desert where he and Amer had expected to find Kilo Three, Ken Aveno was having a difficult time trying to decide whether he should be furious with Ramirez and Funk for disappearing or thankful that he had finally managed to establish contact with them. In the end he opted to maintain as calm and professional a tone as his circumstances permitted. "Three Bravo, what is your current location and status?"

It took Ramirez but a minute to check the coordinates displayed on the GPS and look them up on a map that he'd managed to fish out of a pile of notes and papers that had been scattered about everywhere during their precipitous retreat. "This is Three Bravo. We are about three-quarters of the way to the rally point. We're headed back your way, over." Upon hearing this Funk started doing what Ramirez had reported they'd already done.

By the time he heard the last part of Ramirez's message Aveno had already done some time-distance calculations and had come to a decision. "Negative, Three Bravo. We'll catch a ride with Kilo Two. Keep heading to the rally point and secure it, over."

Within the dark confines of Kilo Three, Staff Sergeant Angel

Ramirez's first thought was relief and joy, relief over the fact that they would not have to turn around and go back into the maelstrom they had so narrowly escaped. Only after he glanced over at Funk to see if his driver had noticed what Ramirez was feeling did that sudden and unexpected elation over being spared turn to guilt.

Firmly gripping the humvee's steering wheel and focusing on his driving Funk kept his emotions in check, his eyes straight ahead, and his thoughts to himself as he drove Kilo Three away from where his teammates continued their struggle for survival.

Ashamed of himself, Ramirez slowly turned away from Funk.

From his perch atop Kilo Six O'Hara caught sight of movement some fifty meters to the right of his position. With a single easy motion he swung the heavy .50-caliber machine gun to bear. When he was set, he pulled his night-vision goggles down over his eyes and adjusted them so he could see properly. What he saw were Syrian soldiers deployed in skirmish line, advancing through the desert as if they were looking for something, or someone.

"John!" he whispered while keeping his eyes on the Syrians and his hands on the smooth grips of the machine gun. "We've got company."

John Laporta didn't need to ask O'Hara where the threat was coming from. He could tell by the direction the .50-caliber was pointed. Catching sight of the dark figures drawing nearer, Laporta carefully groped around in the dark interior until he felt the stock of his weapon and laid it in his lap. Leaning back he cocked his head, looked up into the ring mount where O'Hara stood, and whispered, "They're not acting as if they've seen us yet."

From his vantage point O'Hara could see that the Syrian soldiers were veering away from them. Slowly scanning the horizon to the left, right, and rear while keeping the machine gun aimed at the Syrians, he searched for any sign of more of them. When he was satisfied that the dozen or so enemy soldiers off to the left were the only ones in the immediate vicinity, O'Hara lowered himself into the humvee to speak to Laporta. "See if you can contact the captain." Then, recalling that there had been firing in the village and they had not heard from Burman, O'Hara added, "If you can't raise him, try the XO."

After ordering Ramirez and Funk to keep going toward the rally point, and turning toward Kilo Two, Aveno heard Laporta's efforts to contact Burman. When Laporta's third attempt to contact Burman failed Aveno realized that something had happened to their commander. Either he was down or he was in a position that prevented him from exercising command and control either in person or via radio. Regardless of what lay behind Burman's failure to respond, it now became crystal clear to Aveno that he had no choice but to take command of the team and do everything possible to save what he could.

At the moment the prospects of achieving this modest goal appeared to be good. Kilo Three was already out of harm's way. Kilo Six was threatened but had not been spotted by the Syrians. And Kilo Two seemed to be holding its own against an enemy force of unknown size, but one that Aveno assumed to be manageable since Kannen was still there, fighting it out rather than turning to flee. After ordering Kilo Six to stand fast for as long as he could do so in the hope that Burman and Hashmi might yet show up, Aveno turned his full attention to getting Kilo Two out of harm's way and to a spot where it could pick up Amer and him. Once that was accomplished, he would then have the ability to either make a quick sweep around the village in one final effort to find Burman or break contact completely and withdraw both Kilo Two and Kilo Six to the rally point that would soon be secured by Kilo Three.

· · ·

While O'Hara was filling Aveno in on Kilo Six's situation and the executive officer was assessing the situation and determining what to do next, Burman and Hashmi were hugging the ground and remaining absolutely still as a group of Syrian soldiers slowly made their way toward where the pair lay hidden only by the cover of darkness.

By now the sharp pain emanating from Burman's swollen ankle straining against his tightly laced boot, had settled down to a dull throb. Still, the injury was clouding his judgment at a time when his thoughts needed to be clear and rational.

Fighting through his pain and growing fear, Burman struggled to assess his plight. Hashmi had lost his weapon back in the village, leaving him disarmed and unable to defend himself if it came to a fight. In order to secure his own MP-5, which was lying uselessly in the small of his back, Burman would have had to push himself up off the ground, reach around, and grope about, a series of actions that would surely betray his position to the Syrians who were now no more than ten meters away. Only his 9-mm pistol was within reach, snug and secure in a holster strapped to Burman's uninjured right leg, which was tucked beneath him. Yet even this weapon could not be accessed without him having to move his entire body. Burman feared though that any effort to roll over and retrieve it would cause too much noise. Besides, after counting his foes and doing the math, the Special Forces captain came to the unmistakable conclusion that aggressive action on his part was tantamount to suicide. Given the odds he faced, Burman concluded that his only salvation lay in trusting his luck and the darkness.

A few feet away Hashmi felt the terror gnawing at him as he lay watching the line of Syrian soldiers draw closer. As bad as things would go for his captain if they were taken alive, the Syrian-American knew that he would become the object of a particular brand of ire from his captors that they reserved for those who betrayed their people, their homeland, and their faith. For Hashmi, the stories of cruelties and torture inflicted on those who defied the Syrian leadership were not rumors or news stories. They were family legacies. Those of his uncles who had not seized the opportunity to flee Syria like his father and mother had suffered martyrdom in the most heinous manner imaginable. Hashmi knew that if he were captured, he'd be denounced as a traitor by a country that was not his. He'd considered that possibility when he volunteered for this assignment, and accepted it as part of his service. He knew that the rights and protections international law afforded to other members of Kilo would be denied to him. But Hashmi was an American soldier, a member of the Special Forces who understood his duties and obligations as an American. He knew that being born in a land dedicated to freedom and liberty often required great sacrifices.

Closing his eyes, Hashmi whispered to himself the oft-repeated prayer he had heard his father recite in moments of distress and despair, "Allah, my life is in your hands."

C H A P T E R
SEVEN

Ken Aveno's initial estimate of the situation was beginning to look less and less promising as the minutes ticked away and no one assigned to Kilo Two responded to his repeated calls on the team's internal radio net. That left him still afoot in the middle of the desert at night with little to do but keep from getting killed by the random bursts of small-arms fire coming from the village or the 20-mm rounds that flew past Kilo Two as Kilo Two continued to engage a Syrian armored vehicle he still could not see. His own vehicle, Kilo Three, was miles away by now and getting farther away by the second. Kilo One had been destroyed taking an unknown number of men with it. Kilo Six was, from his perspective, out of the picture. There was nothing he could do to assist O'Hara and Laporta who were still sitting on the other side of the village. And so long as there was a chance that Burman might still show up, Kilo Six had to remain where it was.

Seeing no good alternative, Aveno started off toward Kilo Two. Just as anxious to reach Kilo Two, Amer quickly followed, picking up his stride until he was soon pulling ahead of his lieutenant. They hadn't gone very far before Aveno found himself again questioning his decisions. This time it concerned his orders to Kilo Three to continue on to the rally point. With its 40-mm grenade launcher, that vehicle might well be the very thing they needed to lay down a hail of suppressive fire and permit Kilo Two to break contact. Slowing his pace he looked out over the desert in the direction that Ramirez, Funk, and Kilo Three had gone, wondering if it might not be a good idea to recall them.

It took Amer several seconds to notice that Aveno was no longer with him. When he did he stopped and turned to see what was wrong. Upon seeing the executive officer peering off into the distance Amer wondered if he had missed something. "What is it?"

The new commander of RT Kilo didn't respond. His mind was now on the fight that was still going on between Kilo Two and the Syrian vehicle he couldn't see, weighing the merits of recalling Kilo Three. His deliberations were interrupted by the sudden flash of a TOW missile being launched. For the briefest of moments it lit up the entire area around Kilo Two, burning an indelible image of the drama being played out there into Aveno's memory.

He could see Sergeant Harris standing in Kilo Two's open hatch hunched over the TOW launcher, struggling to guide the just-launched missile into the distant target. The flaming wreckage that had been Kilo One continued to blaze fiercely. Between the two humvees he saw a figure moving away from Kilo One with a motionless body draped across its shoulders. Whether it was Sergeant Kannen or someone else was hard to say. He was simply too far away to be sure. Aveno understood the motivation behind this valiant effort to save a fellow soldier. It was almost a tradition in the American military to do everything one could to bring everyone back, the right thing to do in most circumstances. But he also appreciated that by undertaking such a noble rescue attempt the man who had sallied forth to save a member of Kilo One's crew was endangering the other three men assigned to Kilo Two by keeping his humvee in the line of fire longer than necessary.

Of course there was nothing Aveno could do about any of that now. Besides, the would-be hero was already on his way back to Kilo Two. Just to be sure that Sergeant Kannen didn't tarry any longer than he needed to, Aveno decided to try to reach Kilo Two once more and order it to withdraw as expeditiously as possible. "Kilo Two, this is Kilo Three Alpha. Break contact and head straight back toward the village to pick me and Three Delta up, over."

Depending on one's proximity to enemy fire, time in combat either races by at alarming speed or crawls along at an agonizingly slow pace. Though it only took a few seconds for Mendez in Kilo Two to find the hand mike of their radio, Aveno's isolation from the scene of battle made that wait unnerving. Within the dark confines of Kilo Two, the bellowing voice of Sergeant Harris yelling to Davis to pass him up another TOW missile trumped the urgency of Aveno's call. Added to this was the distant report of the Syrian 20-mm cannon, and explosions of near misses accentuated the pungent scent of fear, with the sharp smell left in the wake of a freshly launched missile. As Davis scrambled to secure another missile for Harris, the impression in Kilo Two was that Mendez had responded with lightning speed to Aveno's orders. "This is Two Charlie. Two Alpha is almost here with Kilo One Alpha. We are continuing to engage a BRDM."

"Kilo Two, disengage immediately. I say again disengage and head toward the village to recover us, over."

The last part of Aveno's message left Mendez confused. None of Kilo Two's crew knew that Kilo Three was gone, leaving the XO and Amer in the lurch. They hadn't even taken note of the spate of hostile fire that had erupted in the distant Syrian village. So the XO's orders to turn their back on a Syrian BRDM they were about to destroy and head back toward the village to pick him up made absolutely no sense to Mendez. In an effort to make sure he understood, he asked Aveno to repeat his message.

Already alarmed at the situation, Aveno lost his temper. "This is Kilo Three Alpha. I say again, get the hell out of there now and head directly for the village to pick up Three Delta and me."

Though Mendez still did not quite understand what was going on, he recognized the tenor of Aveno's bark. Without hesitation he responded with a quick, "Wilco," before turning to relay the order on to Harris.

In the midst of his own crisis, Sergeant Harris yelled back down through the open hatch that the XO would just have to wait until Kannen returned from Kilo One. "Doesn't that asshole realize we've got one man out there and a Syrian BRDM trying to kill us?"

Unsure what to do Mendez glanced at the humvee to check on Kannen's progress, then back up at Harris, who was struggling to maintain his focus on the Syrian vehicle while waiting for Davis to pass a third TOW missile up to him.

Sensing that there was little more he could do to speed Kilo Two along, Aveno turned his attention to Kilo Six and his missing commanding officer. "Kilo Six Alpha, Kilo Six Alpha, this is Kilo Three Alpha, over." After waiting for what seemed to be an eternity, Aveno radioed again. "Kilo Six Charlie, what is your situation, over?"

With the Syrian foot patrol little more than a stone's throw from their position, Specialist Four O'Hara paused before he whispered his response into the hand mike. "This is Kilo Six Charlie. Ten to twelve enemy infantry less than thirty meters at my nine o'clock. They haven't located us yet, over."

"This is Kilo Three Alpha. Have you been able to contact or locate Six Alpha, over?"

"Negative. We've had no contact with Six Alpha or Six Bravo since they left this location, over."

Frustrated by his impotence, Ken Aveno decided the time had come to take decisive action and save what he could of RT Kilo's surviving members. "Kilo Six, this is Three. Break contact and move to the rally point immediately, over."

Having paid no attention to all the details of the operation when Burman had briefed them, O'Hara didn't think this was the right time to ask Aveno where the rally point was. There would be plenty of time to do that once they were out of danger. So his reply was brief and whispered. "This is Six Charlie, roger, out."

From the driver's seat John Laporta looked through the

opening in the humvee's roof to where O'Hara was standing. "Denny, how're we going to get clear of those assholes? As soon as I start cranking the engine they'll be all over us. And what about Captain Burman and Hashmi?"

Tightening his hands on the machine gun's grips, O'Hara drew in a deep breath. "I don't know about the CO and Hashmi. For all we know they could be dead. Besides, you heard the XO. He's ordered us to beat feet and that's exactly what we're going to do as soon as I open fire. Now, when I cut loose, crank this sucker up and move out."

"What direction?"

O'Hara snapped, "Go. Just go." Then, after a brief pause he added, "Anywhere that's far from here."

The sudden chatter of machine-gun fire and the pained screams of wounded men was joined by the excited barking of orders issued by startled Syrians who were but a few meters away from Burman and Hashmi. At first neither party knew where the heavy machine-gun fire was being directed, causing some of the Syrians near Burman to throw themselves facedown in the sand as if they had been shot. Others dropped to one knee and watched a stream of tracers rip through the darkness like so many shooting stars. Captain Burman and Hashmi didn't move.

The distinctive rattle of the M-2 left no doubt in Burman's mind that O'Hara and Kilo Six were in trouble. The need to find out what had caused him to open fire became too much. As carefully and cautiously as he could, Burman raised his head and looked out in the general direction of Kilo Six. Hashmi did not move, maintaining his prone position as he listened to the hurried footsteps of the Syrian soldiers grow closer by the second.

Just as Burman's picked his head up off the ground he heard the distinctive whoosh of an illumination round as it streaked skyward. Burman had only seconds to flatten out again before the flare popped overhead and lit up the entire area. The burning illumination round reminded Burman of the fiery pain in his broken ankle. He knew his injury made escape all but impossible. But if he hadn't moved, both he and Hashmi would surely be dead. Perhaps, he thought, at least one of them might make it. Perhaps if he stood his ground and took the Syrians under fire, Hashmi could make a break for it.

The brilliant light of the illumination round and the proximity of the Syrian soldiers didn't give Burman any time to think things out. Slowly, as slowly as he dared, he began to reach over his shoulder in an effort to secure his MP-5.

Whether it was the Syrian soldiers glimpsing Burman's cautious movement or the unexpected presence of an enemy vehicle firing wildly at another patrol nearby, an excited alarm was sounded from within the ranks of the Syrians, who were but a few meters from the two Americans. When Hashmi heard the cries, he turned to Burman. *"They've seen us!"*

No longer having any need for caution, Burman rose up unto his knees as he slew his MP-5 about. "Get out of here, Yousaf."

Not understanding that his commanding officer had already resolved to stand and fight so that he could escape, Hashmi did exactly what Burman did not want him to, the Syrian-American got to his feet and started to pull Burman to his. "Come on, come on."

Caught off guard, Burman turned to Hashmi in an effort to order him to leave him and to run. But he never was afforded the opportunity to issue his last command. In the midst of Hashmi's efforts to get his commanding officer up a Syrian soldier reached them. With a great arching swing, the Syrian brought the butt of his AK around and smashed it against the unprotected head of Erik Burman, sending the Special Forces officer sprawling.

The end of Kilo Two was quick and bloody. Having successfully evaded one antitank missile through a combination of luck and timely maneuvers, the commander of the only surviving Syrian BRDM knew he had to take decisive action. Since the extreme reach of the TOW missile and the flat, open nature of the terrain made withdrawing tantamount to suicide, he saw that he had but one choice left. In order to survive, he had to rush the American humvee.

Sergeant Sam Harris was reaching down for a third TOW missile when he heard a change in the pitch of the BRDM's engine as its driver threw it into gear and lurched forward. Raising his head through the open hatch, Harris watched the BRDM close with them at an alarming rate, firing as it did so. In an instant Harris realized he wouldn't have time to get off another round before the Syrian recon vehicle was inside the minimum arming range of the TOW missile. *"Everyone out!* Grab your weapons and all the AT-4s you can and bail out, *NOW!"*

Kilo Two began to shake as the BRDM's gunner finally found the range. Mendez was the first out. Grabbing his M-16 and an AT-4 light antitank rocket, Kilo Two's driver used his elbow to push the lever down and shoulder the door open. As soon as his foot hit the ground, Mendez fell forward in a controlled manner as if executing a parachute landing. Once prone, he began to roll away from the humvee, taking care to protect his rifle and the rocket launcher.

Davis was kneeling on the right rear seat facing the back of the humvee in the midst of digging through personal gear and equipment, searching for another TOW missile when he heard Harris's order. Though he was vaguely aware of the humvee's rocking motion, Davis was caught off guard by Harris's command. "What? Now?"

Having abandoned the TOW launcher and slipped down into the humvee, Harris reiterated his order. *"Get out, NOW!"*

Davis threw open the door next to him, dove through the opening headfirst and was on the ground and crawling away as fast as his hands and knees could propel him before it dawned on him that he had forgotten to grab any weapon on the way out. Angry at himself for being so stupid, Davis stood up and prepared to dash back to recover his rifle.

As soon as Davis left, Harris reached over the back of the passenger's seat to grab his MP-5, just as Kilo Two's thin armor shell gave way to the hammering of 20-mm high-explosive rounds. The interior of the humvee was suddenly alive with bright flashes of detonating small-caliber cannon shells and a shower of sparks thrown off as fragments tore through the interior, ricocheted off equipment, and ripped into Sergeant Harris's exposed haunches.

Allen Kannen had almost reached the cover of Kilo Two with the charred body of First Lieutenant Ciszak in his arms when he saw Davis dive out the rear passenger door. At first Kannen had thought that Davis was coming out to assist him. Only when Kannen saw 20-mm rounds striking the exposed rear of his humvee did he appreciate that as noble as his effort to save the stricken Kilo One members might have been, his decision to leave Kilo Two and force them to remain in place until he returned had exposed the recon vehicle and his fellow crew members to deadly fire. It was a decision that made his rescue mission a costly error.

Within the humvee, just as some shards of white-hot metal fragments from exploding 20-mm rounds peppered the exposed thighs and back of Sergeant Harris, others were tearing through the casing and warhead of the TOW missile that Davis had uncovered before he bailed out. These fragments ignited the propellant of that missile that was designed to carry it 3,700 meters. This lethal combination of hot fragments and volatile rocket fuel instantly engulfed the interior of the humvee. Even before the sheets of flame leaping out the open doors and hatch in the roof reached their peak, the warhead of the TOW missile detonated, killing Harris with merciful speed.

Outside Kannen watched as the humvee hard shell was torn from the chassis while a chain reaction of explosions erupted, caused by the detonation of another TOW missile and a pair of smaller rocket launchers that had been tucked off to one side of the cargo compartment. The successive shock waves generated by the initial blast and subsequent detonations knocked him off his feet and hammered Davis into the ground. Mendez, already down, felt the pressure push his body deeper into the sand. Those who could see Kilo Two watched with sadness and fear as a vehicle that had served them as home and transport for six weeks became a giant fragmentation bomb.

Ken Aveno watched in stunned silence as the meaning of what his eyes beheld and his ears heard sank in. His CO and Sergeant Hashmi were missing and perhaps dead. Kilo One and Kilo Two had been destroyed and all or some of their crews killed. While Kilo Three was safe, it was long gone and could do little to help him at this moment. Nor could Kilo Six, as Aveno listened to the echo of that vehicle's machine gun hammering away as it tried to make good its escape.

Dumbfounded and forlorn, Aveno felt despair overwhelm him. His command had lasted two minutes, perhaps three.

Lost in his grief and guilt Aveno did not hear Amer's warning about a squad of Syrian soldiers emerging from the village and moving quickly toward them. Despondent and forlorn, all Aveno could do was to stare at Kilo Two as detonation after detonation shook the stricken humvee. Without a word, without a whimper, first Lieutenant Ken Aveno slowly squatted down onto the ground and crossed his legs. Ignoring Amer's efforts to persuade him to get up and flee, the acting commanding officer of RT Kilo settled down to await whatever fate the cruel god of war held for him.

CHAPTER EIGHT

The Pentagon had no need for a tocsin to alert assigned personnel that there was a crisis. The hurried pace and grim expressions worn by those considered to be the Pentagon's key players as they moved through the miles and miles and miles of endless loops and corridors was warning enough. The purposeful gait of staffers quickened as they dashed from one impromptu meeting or briefing to the next. Even if certain people did not have an active role in the crisis du jour, the heightened alertness was transferred across the entire spectrum, from top to bottom and agency to agency in a manner similar to that of an excited electron transferring some of its own energy to other electrons as it pinged madly about.

Lieutenant Colonel Robert Delmont picked up on the telltale signs as he emerged from the locker room and headed back to his office, maneuvering his way through the unusually heavy flow of traffic coursing through the hall. At first he wasn't all that concerned. If the crisis had involved something he was responsible for he was confident that someone would have dispatched an NCO or a junior officer to find him.

This illusion disappeared the moment he stepped through the door of the Army's special operations section. In an instant his attitude changed and his pucker factor multiplied by a factor of ten. The tension in the air was palpable. Those staff officers who were not on phones listening intently or jabbering away were staring at their computer screens, twirling track balls or madly pounding away at their keyboards. Delmont reached his cubicle, pulled the chair out, and flung his gym bag under the desk. Peering over the divider at his office mate in the next cubicle, Delmont asked, "What's going down?"

Totally absorbed in studying a situation map displayed on his monitor, Lieutenant Colonel Thad Calvert was startled by Delmont's question. "Where in the hell have you been? The general has been screeching your name for the past half hour."

"I told Dorothy I was going out to run. Didn't she tell anyone?"

Calvert grunted. "Like everyone else, Dorothy hasn't had a chance to catch her breath since the doodoo hit the fan."

"Well, I'm here now. What's going on?"

"The general told me that as soon as you graced us with your presence, you were to grab everything you had on some operation code-named Razorback and get your sorry little ass down to the Sec Def's briefing room ASAP."

When Delmont heard the word "Razorback," he realized that RT Kilo had either uncovered the mother lode or had stumbled into a dung heap. Either way, Delmont now knew that it was "his" operation that in some way had caused the current crisis. Taking only enough time to scarf up the important Razorback files, Delmont made haste for the wing of the Pentagon where the Secretary of Defense held court.

Once the guard at the door had checked his access roster and cleared him for entry, Delmont braced himself for what awaited him when he entered the briefing room where the Sec Def's crisis action team was meeting. Compared to this, exiting out of an aircraft at forty thousand feet is a piece of cake, he thought as he entered the room. His entrance caused a pause as all eyes turned to see if the newcomer was of any importance or the bearer of fresh news from the field. Embarrassed at creating such a stir, Delmont nodded at the Secretary of Defense as a means of apologizing before he looked at his superior, Brigadier General James Palmer. With a searing glance and a slight tilt of his head, Palmer directed Delmont to an empty seat directly behind him.

The Air Force colonel who had been in the middle of his briefing picked up from where he'd paused during Delmont's entry. "We have been able to confirm that the person who initiated the request was Airman First Class Jay Jones."

At the mention of this incident Major General Worton of the Air Force turned toward the Secretary of Defense. "I would like to reiterate, Mr. Secretary, that the call monitored by the AWACs crew was not a specific request. Airman Jones initiated the call by repeating 'Cherokee,' which is a code word used to request immediate air-ground support but failed to respond to the controller's call for confirmation. Nor did Jones or anyone else follow up with any details about the nature of the emergency. We don't know why Airman Jones had to make the call when the correct procedure calls for the air liaison officer, Lieutenant Ciszak, to make the request. The only logical explaination my people can offer is that Lieutenant Ciszak, was unable to make the call himself due to enemy action, forcing Airman Jones to initiate it himself. Efforts to ascertain the nature of the emergency or reestablish contact with the air liaison party with Recon Team Kilo failed."

Sporting a grim expression, the senior rep from the Army War Room leaned forward and added his own postscript. "Efforts by group headquarters in Turkey to contact anyone within RT Kilo have also had negative results. The last transmission they received from the team commander came in just after two thousand hours local stating that they were preparing to initiate this evening's operations."

Across the table, Ted Writt, a high-ranking CIA officer in his early forties wearing a three-piece suit leaned forward. "We had a bird coming up on station at that time. An immediate request from the Air Force allowed us to focus on the area in question. Our spot analysis of the site shows three burning vehicles. As soon as we have hard copies of that imagery Langley will send it here."

The Secretary of Defense nodded before turning to the briefing officer, who responded by continuing. "As General Worton indicated, Mr. Secretary, we received only the code word before losing contact with RT Kilo. The senior controller aboard the AWACs immediately dispatched a flight of two F-15s that were on station waiting to strike the target if the commanding officer of RT Kilo was able to determine if it was, in fact, the chemical warfare lab we've been looking for. A second flight consisting of two Navy F-18s from the *Truman* carrying a mix of cluster bombs and seven hundred and fifty-pound general-purpose bombs were diverted from a routine patrol over northeastern Iraq. On reaching the area in which Kilo was operating, both flights identified the afore-mentioned derelicts as well as numerous dismounted personnel scattered east and west of the built-up area. As already mentioned, neither the senior controller aboard the AWACs or operations personnel in Turkey were able to reestablish comms with Kilo. Since the pilots were unable to tell who was who on the ground, they were unable to intervene. After staying over the area as long as their fuel permitted, the crews of the F-15s and F-18s departed without being able to render any assistance."

When the briefing officer had finished, the Chief of Staff of the Army looked at General Worton even though his question was directed at the briefer. "How high were those aircraft when they were making those observations?"

The Air Force Chief of Staff straightened up as he took up the challenge being hurled at Worton and his briefing officer. "You know very well that the minimum operational altitude is fifteen thousand feet."

The Army Chief's response irritated every Air Force officer in the room. "So, in your usual fashion your people responded to my people's call for assistance by zipping in at five hundred miles an hour and buzzing about for a couple of minutes at fifteen thousand feet before fluttering away without doing a dammed thing."

The Air Force Chief snorted angrily. "Two of those men belong to me."

"And twelve are mine!" the Army Chief countered.

At the head of the table a hand slapped the smooth surface, causing all eyes turned to the Sec Def. "I hope I do not need to remind anyone in this room," he stated calmly but firmly, "that every one of those people, on the ground and in the air, are my responsibility. When I go to the pressroom tonight it's my head the American media will be calling for. So, if you *gentlemen* don't mind, let us proceed with this briefing so I can at least create the illusion that I know what I'm talking about when I have to face the members of the fourth estate."

The Sec Def turned back to the briefing officer. "Unless you have anything of relevance to add, Colonel, you are dismissed." The Air Force colonel left the briefing room as quickly as decorum permitted. For the better part of a minute the Sec Def scanned the solemn people lining both sides of the long conference table before speaking. "Can anyone tell me what went wrong? How is it that this mission went south after all previous operations were managed without a hitch? Anyone?"

The silence that followed was oppressive, especially for those wearing Army green. The Chairman of the Joint Chiefs of Staff looked at the Army Chief of Staff, who looked at the Army Deputy Chief of Staff for Plans and Operations, who in turn looked at Brigadier General James Palmer, head of the Army's Directorate of Special Operations. Realizing this nonverbal passing of the buck stopped with him, Palmer spoke. "Although we cannot be sure what transpired on the ground, Mr. Secretary, Lieutenant Colonel Delmont, the special project officer charged with overseeing Razorback, can provide us with his assessment." Palmer turned to Delmont. "Colonel?"

With all the grace of a man upon whom a ten-ton weight had

just fallen, Delmont stood up and walked to the spot where the Air Force briefing officer had stood, collecting and organizing his thoughts as he did so. After a pause during which he cleared his throat, he launched into his impromptu briefing. "For some time now the Syrians have been employing a form of ambush designed to deal with our airborne incursions into their air space. Popularly known as SAMbushes, this tactic involves the concealment of surface-to-air missile batteries near locations that are technically immune from attack due to their proximity to sensitive nonmilitary targets such as schools, mosques, and civilian medical facilities. To draw our aircraft into these well-laid ambushes the Syrians set up dummy facilities such as chemical warfare labs that they knew our national intelligence assets were looking for. One of the primary reasons the recon teams such as RT Kilo were organized and deployed under the operational plan known as Razorback was to make up for our lack of human intelligence sources on the ground. We needed to ferret out which facilities were real and which were decoys."

Delmont paused in order to give the Secretary of Defense the opportunity to ask questions and respond to any challenges. When he saw that neither were forthcoming, he continued with a bit more confidence.

"Razorback has been largely successful. RT Kilo, the eleventh Special Forces recon team to be dispatched, was searching for an approximately located and previously unidentified Syrian battery that was deployed in an area where there were no known targets of value. The conclusion that the CIA and DIA reached was that the battery was protecting a chemical warfare lab that had once been part of the Iraqi program. While we cannot yet be sure what went wrong, we can make some assumptions as to why today's mission did not go off as planned. Either the security detachment assigned to protect the missile battery and/or lab from ground attack detected RT Kilo as they were approaching the site or RT Kilo drove into a successfully executed ambush intentionally laid for them. After we obtain and analyze the information being collected by the CIA and the Air Force my office should be better able to determine what actually happened."

With his improvised presentation succeeding, Delmont went on to describe RT Kilo's basic operational procedures even though he couldn't be sure if Kilo was still adhering to them. General Palmer, deciding that Delmont's discussion of tactics contributed nothing to what the Secretary of Defense needed to know so as to manage the crisis, let Delmont know that he needed to wrap up as quickly and gracefully as possible by employing his usual nonverbal cues.

Glad to be off the hook, Delmont swiftly finished a point he had been belaboring. Then, rather than concluding with a comment that closed all discussion on this aspect of the issue, he made the mistake of asking, "Are there any questions?"

The Commandant of the Marine Corps brought up something that had been bothering him about Razorback for months. "Colonel, what role do you think fatigue played in this incident?"

To the Secretary of Defense and most people seated about the table, the question sounded simple and practical. But a few, including Palmer and Delmont understood its significance. The Marine general who posed the question had never been in favor of Razorback from its inception. That he was using this forum to continue this debate angered Palmer and everyone who had pushed it. In the twinkling of an eye Delmont realized that his asking for questions been a mistake on a grand scale.

Even before Operation Razorback had actually begun there were those who knew that it could not be properly supported. Manpower shortages and overcommitment of Army Special Ops units around the world were already creating problems. The dearth of available units and personnel could only be made up by extending the duration of each recon team's in-country time to six weeks or more, and not the two weeks originally envisioned. After the first couple of long rotations demonstrated that this was simply too much for the recon teams, the Army had informally asked the Marine Corps if it'd be willing to help by contributing some marine force recon teams or fleet antiterrorists security teams, better known as FASTs. The addition of marine teams to the rotation would allow all of Razorback's army recon units to maintain a more practical schedule even though their deployment time would still be greater than two weeks. In his response to the Marine Commandant Delmont's Marine counterpart thought that Operation Razorback was basically a sound plan dealing with an important mission. Unfortunately, he continued, the Marines had the same problem as the Army did in terms of manpower. Their special operations forces were already overcommitted. Adding some of the Marines' teams to Operation Razorback would help the Army, but only worsen the problem the Corps was already having to deal with elsewhere. And even if Marine special ops teams had been available, the Marine special operations plans officer stated that the extended missions in Syria by both Army and Marine units would be detrimental to their operational efficiency, a state of affairs that could lead to a decline in both the effectiveness of the units and their ability to carry out their assigned missions.

"Protracted exposure to the stress of an operation of this nature, coupled with the corrosive effects of the desert environment in which the teams operate will result in a deterioration of the mental and physical health of individuals assigned to these recon teams. If these teams are not rotated before this occurs, a situation that has become routine in Syria, this deterioration will continue to a point where the ability of a team's personnel to function properly or execute their assigned tasks will be significantly compromised, increasing the risk they face to a level that is unacceptable." Between this conclusion and the fact of special ops team scarcity, the Commandant of the Marine Corps had declined to commit any of his forces to Razorback.

The reason the Commandant was posing his question at this time was clear to Delmont and Palmer. Eventually it would be learned that Palmer had authorized the routine extension of each recon teams' tours of duty in Syria. This revelation would raise the same concern that the Marine special ops officer had described in his report to the Commandant after studying the Razorback operation. By reminding Palmer of this in front of the Secretary of Defense the Commandant was putting the Army on notice that if they dared try to blame the Corps for any Razorback-related problems, he would respond by publicizing the warning that he had conveyed to the Army several months ago.

Aware that Delmont was uncertain about how to deal with the live grenade that had been tossed in his lap, Palmer answered the question himself. "As Mr. Writt of the CIA and others have pointed out, we have no way of knowing for sure what happened on the ground. Mr. Secretary, until we have more information and have an opportunity to confirm and verify it, I don't think there's any value in continuing speculation about what happened today. The media, I'm sure, will do enough of that on their own."

Sensing that General Palmer wasn't ready to reveal sensitive information the Army already had and needing time to prepare a report that would protect the Army's operations and interests, the Army Chief of Staff backed up Palmer's conclusion. "I agree with General Palmer's point. Until we know for sure what went down out there we should concentrate on collecting information and intelligence. Speculation on what might have happened is a waste of time."

The Secretary of Defense sighed. He now saw that he would have to deal effectively with a potentially explosive issue with nothing more than incomplete information. Turning to the Pentagon spokesman, the Sec Def instructed him to draft a short statement based upon what they did know for sure and have it ready for his review in fifteen minutes so he'd have something to release to the press that would keep them at bay for a few more hours. The Secretary of Defense concluded the meeting by saying he needed to call the President and fill him in. Thanking them for their input, he stood up and left a conference room full of senior officers who commanded the most powerful military force on the face of the earth but were, at the moment, completely powerless to do anything to help the surviving members of RT Kilo.

Fort Bragg, North Carolina
14:20 LOCAL (18:20 ZULU)

Diana Burman thought nothing of the strange new sound that roused her from her nap. The slow, rhythmic *kerr-plunk, kerr-plunk, kerr-plunk,* didn't cause her to immediately spring forth from the recliner she had nestled in and seek out the source of the noise. As with so many other problems that plagued the three-bedroom government quarters Diana would ignore the sound until the post preventive maintenance folks finally got around to coming by or her husband returned from overseas. With her pregnancy fast approaching its ninth month, Diana could barely keep up with her headstrong two-year-old, let alone a house that should have been condemned years ago. If it weren't for his after-noon naps which allowed her to do the same, she was sure she'd have completely lost it by now.

It wasn't until the steady splashing of water stopped that her suspicions were piqued enough to cause her to pay attention. When she heard the pitter-patter of sock-clad feet as they emerged from the hall bathroom and scurried down the bare tile floor to one of the back bedrooms she realized that her midday break was over. Still not fully awake, she waited and listened as the same little feet made the return trip up the short hallway to the bathroom. When the slow, rhythmic *kerr-plunk, kerr-plunk, kerr-plunk* resumed she knew her son was into something she wasn't going to like.

"Alex?" The splashing sound ceased but the young boy didn't answer. Again she called out. "Alex? Are you in the bathroom?"

A small boy appeared around the corner that led from the living room and into the hall. Wide-eyed and pensive, Alex Burman said nothing as he stood there sans training pants, nervously twirling a little plastic Fisher-Price figure in his tiny fingers.

"*Alex!*"

Flashing a smile that could be endearing or a prelude to mischief, the young boy disappeared around the corner. Diana knew that she had no hope of matching her son's speed. She therefore resorted to a mother's standard threat. "Alex Scott Burman! Don't you dare!"

One final *kerr-plunk* issued forth from the bathroom before she heard Alex beat a hasty retreat to the illusionary safety of his bedroom.

Like a beached whale trying to make its way back to the sea, Diana squirmed and wiggled in an effort to return the recliner to its upright position. It took her several tries before she managed to plant her feet firmly on the floor. All of this commotion was not appreciated by the tiny life she carried. Angered at being awakened, a miniature limb stomped on its nearest neighbor, Diana's bladder, forcing out a spurt of urine. Rubbing her distended stomach and trying to calm her next son, Diana spoke to her unborn child as she often did these days. "Keep that up and I swear I'll ship you off to your father."

Whether it was Diana's words or her soothing touch, the unborn child calmed down, allowing her to finish rising up out of the recliner. Waddling to the entrance of the hall, Diana decided to investigate the scene of the crime before confronting Alex and deciding the appropriate punishment for Alex's latest adventure. She didn't like playing the heavy with her young son, but in Erik's absence she had to do what was necessary.

When she reached the bathroom, Diana could see that her suspicions had been correct. There on the floor before Alex's tiny potty chair was the discarded diaper that she had put on him before laying him down for his nap. As she sniffed the air the pungent odor of urine caused her nose to wrinkle. At least Alex had made it to the bathroom and spared her the chore of changing the bed sheets.

That little courtesy on his part did nothing to mitigate the unpleasantness that fishing out whatever Alex had deposited in the toilet would evoke. To assist in his transition from diapers to training pants as well as making it easier for her to clean out her son's tiny potty, the small nonmechanical commode was located right next to the fully functional adult version. Unfortunately the proximity of the smooth, gleaming white throne to his small plastic pot created a compelling air of mystery. The convenience of this standing body of water was a temptation he was unable to resist, resulting in a proclivity for depositing inorganic odds and ends in the toilet. Despite her efforts to curb this behavior, Diana was forced to post a sign on the toilet tank reminding guests to look inside the toilet before they used it.

Diana was pleasantly surprised to find that today's offerings were a floating group of tiny Fisher-Price people, merrily bobbing up and down in the potty water with fixed smiles. Sometimes one of the figures would bump against the side of the bowl, then bounce back to join the other beaming members of its clan. "Well," Diana said, as she slowly knelt, "at least you guys seem to be having fun."

She was in the process of scooping out the figures when she heard the squawking doorbell that announced someone was at the front door. Diana hoped that whoever was at the door would be patient enough to wait until she finished so she wouldn't have to get up and down from the bathroom floor twice. She had removed two more happy little people when the doorbell rang again.

Alex seized on this opportunity to ingratiate himself with his mother by helping her. In a flash he was out of his bedroom and scampering down the hall like the U.S. Cavalry coming to the rescue, shouting as he went, "I get it!"

Diana caught a glimpse of her bare-assed son as he raced for the front door. "No, Alex! Wait."

Undeterred, he repeated his battle cry. "I get it, Mama. I get it."

As she endeavored to get up, she could hear Alex struggling to turn the doorknob. Her hope that his effort would take longer than hers did was dashed when she heard the door slowly squeak open and a male voice ask, "Is your mommy home?"

Diana was emerging from the bathroom just as Alex was scampering back down the hall to inform his mother that she had visitors. The collision between his head and her belly sent Alex sprawling to the floor and caused Diana to recoil from the sudden pain as her baby twisted and recoiled within her. Fighting back tears, Diana waddled to where her son was sitting, howling as if he had been beaten to a pulp. Despite the pain and difficulty, she gathered Alex in her arms.

Having been greeted by a naked child and hearing the sudden outburst, the caller at the door hesitantly called out, "Mrs. Burman?"

A frustrated Diana, fighting back her own tears, replied as best she could, "Just a minute, please." The unseen visitor waited silently as Diana soothed Alex until his sobs had receded to a tolerable level. Putting him down and asking him to stay there until she returned, the pregnant Army wife waddled to the front door and finished opening it.

They were all there. In the forefront was Doug Flanders, a captain from the same Special Forces group to which her husband was assigned. Behind him stood another, more senior officer in dress greens. She didn't recognize him but saw from his unit crests that he was assigned to the post's staff. The silver crosses on the collar of the third man marked him as a chaplain, telling her all she needed to know.

No one knows in advance how they will respond at times like this. While every woman married to a soldier knows the drill, none are prepared for the event. The already stressed Diana Burman snapped. She just couldn't deal this, not with a two-year-old child and another in the offing. Diana yelled out a crisp, *"No!"* before slamming the door.

The grim trio stared at the closed door before them, wondering how best to carry out their painful assignment as they listened to Diana waddling away as fast as her incredible burden allowed.

New York City
14:50 LOCAL (18:50 ZULU)

Every aspect of the offices belonging to the law firm of Atkins, Steinburg, and Silverman had been engineered to convey a regal aloofness. With the exception of select clients the partners, senior associates, receptionists, secretaries, and paralegals treated everyone with a cool indifference. This was especially true when it came to the young lawyers new to the firm. Until they had been at the firm five years or more and were entrusted with managing the legal affairs of a prominent client, freshman lawyers were merely tolerated.

None of this bothered Elizabeth Stanton, an ambitious young woman who had been with the firm for less than nine months. During her time at the prestigious firm, in addition to doing her assigned work she had done all she could to hone those skills that would one day allow her to become part of the wealth and power of a city considered by many to be more than just the true mecca of capitalism, but a universe unto itself. To a true New Yorker all the cities, lands, and people that lay beyond the five boroughs of New York were little more than client states whose sole value was providing it with the raw material and cheap labor needed to keep it running.

Not being a native New Yorker was a handicap that Elizabeth Stanton needed to overcome. In a city where one in four of its residents had not even been born in the United States and diversity was publicly proclaimed as a virtue, New York's dirty little secret was that success did not automatically lead to acceptance by the city's elite. Such acceptance was very difficult to achieve. Even those with the right name, impeccable pedigree, and high-level connections often did not become part of the city's patrician class. Those who were not born to that rare breed had to successfully pass through a series of challenging gates set up to keep the blue blood of New York City pure.

Initiation into the law firm of Atkins, Steinburg, and Silverman was similarly cruel and unforgiving. On her first day at the firm, Elizabeth had been told by Mr. Steinburg himself that the firm was not anyone's best friend. The practice of corporate law was as uncompromising as it was demanding. He pointed out that mistakes with the business of major clients had consequences beyond the loss of billions or tens of billions of dollars. It meant the wholesale slaughter of a company's senior management, the destruction of carefully crafted careers, and, most important, damage to the firm's prestige. "Every minute of every day someone in this town is making or losing a fortune. That's what this city is all about. But a reputation is different. It's invaluable, almost priceless. Damage done to it is irreparable. It takes a lifetime of hard work and dedication to build one. This firm has invested decades achieving its current acclaim and recognition. A lawyer in this firm is a force to be reckoned with. If you have what it takes, you will become part of this great institution. Your rewards will be more than money. You will have earned the right to walk with giants. If on the other hand you are not up to our high standards, I suggest you save us both a great deal of bother and leave now."

Elizabeth had not left. The prospect of a six-digit annual income before her thirtieth birthday was a minor factor. The challenge and opportunity to earn the status and power that Mr. Silverman had described were what motivated her. These were the magic keys that would unlock all the right doors and open up a future that was truly boundless.

In many ways Elizabeth Stanton had been preparing for this

job her entire life. Her father was a lawyer who had made his fortune defending the interests of several tobacco companies during the great assault on that industry in the late '90s. While not winning every case, he had legendary talents and skills for negotiating pretrial deals that saved his clients while allowing the other side to create the public perception that it had achieved an overwhelming victory. When Elizabeth began practicing corporate law at the firm she had a huge head start on all the other freshman lawyers. As her father liked to brag, being a corporate lawyer was in Elizabeth's genes.

Returning from lunch with a distinguished client whose business she was courting with promising progress, she purposefully strode through the maze of narrow corridors to her small windowless cubbyhole. Along the way Elizabeth lowered her eyes and nodded when she passed a senior associate, or lifted her chin haughtily when she saw an underling. Upon reaching her desk, she immediately turned on her computer. Like most modern businesses the firm made extensive use of e-mail for a wide range of communication from routine to transfer of vital documents. E-mail meant that anyone could send a message at any time from their midtown Manhattan office, a bedroom in the Hamptons, or during lunch at the Four Seasons. Never knowing what messages would be waiting for her when she returned to her desk, she made a habit of checking her e-mails before settling down to work in case there was something that demanded a sudden reprioritization of her schedule.

An e-mail from one of the firm's senior partners leaped out at her. Except for a quick introduction after their final interview, first-year associates had no dealings with the partners. Even at social gatherings they did not speak to Messrs. Atkins, Steinburg, or Silverman unless they were spoken to first by one of them. So the message from Ira Steinburg troubled the young lawyer, especially since she was not working on any case that he was even remotely connected with.

Elizabeth clicked open the message and read the five words. "Please see me at once." The "please" did little to take the edge off the unexpected order from the partner who handled the firm's important personnel actions. This unexpected meeting had nothing to do with any of her cases. Junior associates received all instructions and assignments from the senior associate they assisted. Nor could it involve any upward or lateral moves within the firm. Such news was delivered to the person via a letter, always written in hard copy form for diplomatic and political reasons, as well as to make the news legally bulletproof.

Like many New Yorkers who believed that their careers were forever in the balance, and could be undone by their use of a single ill-chosen word, the young lawyer assumed the worst. Because he had said, "at once," and Elizabeth always confronted any problem or obstacle head-on without hesitation she took off for Mr. Steinburg's suite of offices with her usual stylish and forceful stride.

A hush fell over Mr. Steinburg's small staff as Elizabeth entered the outer office. His executive secretary looked up. "Go right in. *He's* expecting you."

Pausing at the threshold of Steinburg's office only long enough to straighten her skirt and jacket, Elizabeth entered.

Steinberg was in his late fifties. His full head of hair was tinted to just the right amount of gray for a man of his age, wisdom, and stature. His well-tanned complexion indicated that these days he spent more time conducting business on the links than in his office. Golfing and a demanding fitness regimen gave Ira Steinburg a physique that filled his tailor-made pinstriped suit in all the right places. When his eyes rose to meet Elizabeth's he threw out his chest like a peacock during mating season.

"Elizabeth, please, take a seat."

Moving to the indicated chair, Elizabeth Stanton sat down and braced herself for whatever he had in store for her.

Stepping from behind his massive desk, Ira Steinburg moved to a chair near the one where Elizabeth sat. "I was not aware that you were married."

Concealing her surprise that her secret had somehow been betrayed, Elizabeth launched into immediate damage control mode. "We were married shortly after graduation. We were both young, and perhaps a bit foolish, thinking that love would conquer all. Unfortunately, things didn't turn out the way we would have liked."

"Are you divorced?"

"No. After we married I went on to law school and he—"

"Reported to Fort Benning. Yes, I know."

Elizabeth nodded, stunned that he knew so much about a subject that she had done so much to bury like yesterday's trash. "Ken and I met in high school. We dated on and off while I was going to college and he was at the Academy. We always tried to spend the holidays together. During our senior years, we decided to get married during June Week at West Point."

"A military wedding. I imagine there is still a certain *allure* to that sort of thing even these days." Steinburg paused before continuing. "*Ms.* Stanton, I do wish you would have been a little more forthcoming, even if you and your husband were estranged. It would have saved us both a great deal of embarrassment."

Embarassment? Bewildered, Elizabeth found herself becoming fearful. Having no idea where he was going with this she was having a difficult time looking directly into Steinburg's steel gray eyes as she waited for what might come next. She knew that there was a strong antimilitary sentiment in the legal profession and in this firm in particular, but she'd never thought that being married to an officer could be grounds for dismissal. Her concealment of her marriage when filling out the firm's various application forms, however, was probably sufficient justification in itself for termination. The only saving grace she saw at the moment was that Steinburg might buy in to her defense that her marriage was strained, that she and her husband had been informally separated for good reason as implied by his use of "estranged."

"Elizabeth, this morning my office was contacted by an officer from the Department of the Army. He asked if we had an Elizabeth Aveno at this firm. My secretary replied that we did not. It was only when he called back an hour ago and asked if we would check our employment files for an Elizabeth Stanton that we realized our mistake." Elizabeth started to panic. "Why were they looking for me?"

Wishing there was an easier way to break the news, Ira Steinburg had to tell her the blunt, painful truth. "Your husband, First Lieutenant Kenneth Aveno, is missing in action."

Stunned, her mind and emotions went whirling, leaving Elizabeth momentarily speechless. It took her a moment to recover her composure. "Missing in action? What action? Where?"

It was now Ira Steinburg's turn to be shocked. Though he had correctly assessed the state of Elizabeth's relationship with her estranged spouse, the hard-nosed New York lawyer had expected Elizabeth at least to know that her husband was on assignment in Syria. That she didn't know he was in harm's way was completely unexpected. He knew that Elizabeth was tough, but her total lack of information about her husband's current mission was bound to make the unexpected news of his being MIA that much more painful.

"I suggest, Ms. Stanton," he announced with a decided chill in his voice, "that you contact the Army directly and get the answers from them." Standing up, he looked down at the young lawyer. "May I also suggest that you take the remainder of the day off and sort this out?"

Elizabeth stood, nodded, and left without saying another word to deal with a part of her life she thought she had put behind her.

Syria
05:35 LOCAL (01:35 ZULU)

Cloaked in the darkness that precedes dawn, Dennis O'Hara and John Laporta leaned against the side of their Kilo Six humvee, munching on crackers they had saved from the previous night's rations. On the ground between them lay a map both men took turns studying under the glow of their blue filtered flashlights. "I could have sworn we went a lot farther than we did," O'Hara finally stated. His words were muffled and the map was showered with a spray of wet cracker morsels as he spoke while he pointed at a spot on the map. "I think we're here, or damned near it."

Using the edge of his flashlight Laporta pointed to their original location just outside the village that had been that evening's objective and traced a circumspect route to a point well short of that indicated by O'Hara. "We were going fast, but not that fast. I don't know if you remember, but I had to make some wide detours in order to get around and through some pretty impressive wadis."

O'Hara grunted. "How could I forget? You hit one that lifted me clean out of the Hummer. If I hadn't been holding on to the spade grips of the Maw Duce you would have turned me into a hood ornament."

"What can I say? I was driving fast and in total blackout. We were on top of the wadi before I saw it. I tried to brake before we went over the edge, but it was too late."

Though still smarting from the bruises, O'Hara nodded. "I know." Then he looked back in the direction from which they had come. "Do you think anyone else made it?"

"I can't see how the Syrians could have gotten everyone. It's not possible. Even if there was more of them on the other side of the village and they had the drop on us, at least one of the other humvees had to have gotten away."

"After we had gone a few kilometers I was able to catch a glimpse of the far side of the village. I counted three vehicles burning." O'Hara paused. "In order for us to be the only survivors all three of those wrecks would have had to have been Hummers. If you ask me, RT Kilo is too good to go oh and three against the Syrians. And since one of those vehicles I saw in flames was definitely a BRDM, that means there's at least one other humvee out there."

"You're probably right. I know I heard the XO order Sergeant Ramirez and Kilo Three to make for the rally point."

"I heard that too," O'Hara added, "even before I saw the three derelicts."

"I sure hope they *all* managed to break contact, and that at least one of them was lucky enough to have a GPS with them."

O'Hara laughed as he turned his flashlight off and sat upright. "Correction there, good buddy. You hope they have a GPS with batteries that work."

Extinguishing his flashlight, Laporta struggled to his feet, looking down at O'Hara once he was up. "I told you two days ago to go to the XO and get some new batteries for the GPS."

"I did," O'Hara countered. "And as soon as I got back I promptly put them into the CO's GPS."

Laporta grunted. "And a shitload of good that does us. The batteries were for the GPS we keep with the vehicle, not the old man's."

"Well, you didn't tell me that."

Seeing this was getting them nowhere, Laporta decided to drop the subject and move on to a more pressing concern. "Now what?"

O'Hara took his time before answering. Faced with what seemed to be an overwhelming number of Syrians, the pair had sped off in the direction that offered them their best hope of breaking contact and escaping. Regrettably this took O'Hara and Laporta due north, away from the Syrian soldiers but also away from the unit's designated rally point located south of the village. By the time their adrenaline surge had subsided and Laporta had slowed down, neither man could see the village or burning vehicles, either of which would have served as a crude but effective navigational aide and landmark.

"Well," O'Hara finally concluded as he peered off in the direction from which they had just come, "I don't think we should go back. Even if we aren't being pursued, the Syrians will be wide awake and alert back there. The chances of getting around the village in broad daylight without being seen are pretty much nil." Slowly pivoting about he looked off at the unseen northern horizon. "Our orders are for us to stay off the radio and make for Jordan or the Kurdish-held area of Iraq if things go to hell. But if we stick to those orders, we'll have to go back where the whole Syrian Army is probably waiting for us to do something boneheaded like that."

Understanding what his companion was getting at, Laporta agreed. "Turkey does seem to be our best bet. It is a big country with a long border. I'd say our chances of stumbling upon it somewhere are pretty good."

"Well, be that as it may," O'Hara concluded as he glanced nervously over his shoulder. "I daresay at the moment all that matters is putting as much distance between us and those Syrians as possible."

"Amen, Brother O'Hara. Amen."

It took Staff Sergeant Angel Ramirez longer than it should have to notice the faint glow in the eastern sky announcing that the new day had finally arrived. His long vigil and the trauma of that night's cataclysmic events had plunged him into a mental stupor that was not easily shaken. For hours Kilo Three had sat hidden away in a shallow wadi at the rally point with Ramirez standing upright in the humvee's open hatch, clutching the spade grips of the 40-mm grenade launcher and peering into the distance watching and waiting for the other humvees to appear. During this lonely watch neither Ramirez nor Glenn Funk had uttered a word. The only sound that stirred the night air was the ceaseless desert wind whipping past the solitary humvee and its forsaken occupants.

Tired, sore, and forlorn, Ramirez shifted his weight from one leg to the other, groaning slightly as his stiff aching muscles protested. Down below Glenn Funk was roused by this sudden movement. He had also been teetering on the verge of losing his fight to stay awake after spending the night seated behind the steering wheel prepared to answer the radio or continue their flight at a moment's notice. Like his companion up top, it took him a moment or two to clear his head and sort out where he was. After blinking his dry eyes in an effort to generate some moisture, his blurred vision cleared enough for him to see that they were still at the rally point. After glancing about and confirming that they were still the only ones there, he looked up at Ramirez. "Anyone coming?"

Ramirez again looked out at the tracks Kilo Three had left in the sand. With every passing minute of growing daylight he could see farther along the twin ruts that led right up to their humvee. The desert wind and its fine grains of sand had been busy erasing the ruts all night, but they were still crisp enough to provide anyone interested in following them a clear and unmistakable trail. A curt no was all Ramirez could manage. Inside Kilo Three Funk thought about this as he slowly scanned the horizon through the windshield of his humvee before he asked the question that both men had been avoiding. "What do we do now?"

Ramirez knew that there was only one answer he could give if he followed the standing orders by which RT Kilo operated. "Should the mission be compromised by hostile action and subsequent events prevent the team from re-forming at the designated mission rally point, each individual element will escape and evade on their own. As the Syrians have a sophisticated electronic warfare capability and will be monitoring the entire electronic spectrum seeking to track elements attempting to escape and evade, all radio communications and the employment of emergency beacons is to be avoided unless the tactical situation dictates otherwise." By now it was obvious that he had no choice but to proceed accordingly. Yet following this simple, straightforward order did not come easily to Ramirez. To do so would mean going against a proud Special Forces tradition that dictated that no one ever turned his back on a comrade. They didn't leave anyone behind, regardless of the circumstances. This, together with a growing feeling of guilt that was beginning to manifest itself at having fled as they had done while the battle was still in progress stayed his hand.

Squirming in his seat as he watched the sun begin to break the horizon, Funk became impatient when Ramirez failed to response to his question in a timely manner. Anxious to be doing something other than sitting still, he grabbed Ramirez's pant leg and gave it a tug. "Angel! What do we do now?"

The physical contact and the abruptness of Funk's tone ended Ramirez's internal struggle. He turned his back on the trail they had left in the sand and eased himself down into the seat First Lieutenant Ken Aveno had filled less than twelve hours before. Taking only enough time to get his bearings, he pointed toward the southwest in the direction of Jordan. "Move out."

While relieved that Ramirez had finally made a decision, Funk found the consequences of that order as difficult to accept as it had been for Ramirez. Failure of any kind was hard for proud, highly trained soldiers like Angel Ramirez and Glenn Funk. It was even worse when it meant abandoning men who had become closer to them than brothers. Having to explain how they had survived and the others had not to the widows and the fatherless children of the comrades they were now turning their backs on was a burden that would grow with every mile they put between themselves and the members of RT Kilo who were back there, somewhere.

In the darkness Ken Aveno had been able to see little of the limp figure that bounced about and slid back and forth along the steel floor of the truck that seemed to hit every pothole and bump in the unpaved desert track. When dawn finally did break and the growing daylight cast some light upon the figure, what he saw made Aveno wish for a return of darkness.

When Aveno and Amer had been captured in the desert neither man had offfered resistance. The Syrian soldiers had simply bound their hands and led them back to the village where they were separated, with Amer doing his best to contain his growing fear as he was being led away. Things, it seems, had been far different for his commanding officer. It was clear that Burman had been subjected to a merciless beating.

As distasteful as it was for him to do so, Aveno stared at his commanding officer. The severity of Burman's injuries indicated that he had resisted, something that made Aveno ashamed at having allowed himself to pass into captivity without a whimper. At the time it had seemed to be the smart thing to do. To have done otherwise would have been folly. Still . . .

Pushing these thoughts from his mind, Aveno studied Burman in the growing light of a new day. His captain's hands and feet were tightly bound with wire in the same manner as his. Aveno found the binding painful, almost intolerable. But Burman showed no indication that these restraints were causing him any discomfort. Since laying eyes on him back in the village, Aveno could not recall seeing Burman move on his own or even make a sound as the Syrians dragged his limp body to the truck and tossed it in as if he were nothing more than a sack of potatoes. The only movements Aveno had observed were those caused by the motion of the truck. The fact of the matter was that Aveno could not be sure if Burman was still alive.

Aveno studied Burman's face more carefully. It was little more than a collection of black-and-blue bruises smeared with blood, and deep red abrasions. Massive swelling hid Burman's right eye. Above that was a hairline slit from which thin rivulets of blood dribbled down across his brow and onto his cheek before falling away into spreading pool on the truck's floor. If not destroyed outright, Aveno felt sure that Burman's right eye had been severely damaged. His left eye was only a little better. The socket and surrounding area were puffy and badly discolored. Every now and then Aveno caught a glimpse of white, indicating that the eyeball was probably still intact. Burman's nose was bent to one side and clogged with dark bloody plugs that oozed a thick red-dish gray fluid. His jaw was slack and canted off to one side, his mouth agape. Between Burman's split and discolored lips, swollen to twice their normal size, Aveno could see a number of broken, blood-covered teeth. Dangling limply and off to one side was Burman's tongue, lazily swaying this way and that in rhythm with the motion of the truck like the pendulum of a clock.

Aveno found himself wondering if Burman's head injuries were severe enough to cause temporary or permanent brain dam-age. At the moment there was no way of telling. It would be only when his commanding officer recovered consciousness that he would be able to ascertain if his mental facilities were impaired, and to what extent. After that, only the passage of time would clarify whether Burman would recover fully from his injuries. Even after Burman came to, Aveno doubted if he'd be able to resume command right away. That would mean he himself would have to continue as the acting CO. The surviving members of the team would have no choice but to rely on him for leadership and inspiration.

This realization caused Aveno to look out the rear of the cargo truck he was in past the four Syrian guards seated on either side of the open flap. Shrouded in dust being thrown up by his vehicle was a second Chinese-made truck. Three other members of Kilo were in that truck. As he was lying bound and gagged on the ground in the village square Aveno had watched helplessly as Kannen, Davis, and Mendez were dragged to the rear of that truck by Syrian soldiers and tossed in. Only Kannen managed to make eye contact with him. Though it was still quite dark and Kannen was twenty meters away, he managed to convey an intense anger and loathing that Aveno felt sure was meant for him and not their captors.

Closing his eyes, Aveno rested his head against the truck's canvas side. Why had Kannen glared at him like that? Aveno had only been in command for the briefest of time. He'd done all he could given his circumstances. He had tried to sort out the confusing, complex nightmare as best he could and given the only orders that made sense. While his actions hadn't been particularly heroic, he suspected that he had managed to save two of the humvees and some of the men.

So why had Kannen been angry at *him*? What did he expect? *Did he expect me to reach into my rucksack and pull out a miracle that would save them from the Syrian BRDMs?* Aveno found himself wondering. Or perform a grand sacrifice that would inspire him and the others? Perhaps, Aveno thought, that was what Burman had been doing when the Syrians had overpowered him, engaging in a valiant and noble effort by fighting them tooth and nail before they overpowered him. Had Burman's resistance motivated and inspired the pair of spec fours with Kilo Six? Had his sacrifice allowed them to escape? Or had his resistance been for naught, a futile display of bravado that had cost him dearly?

Aveno had no way of knowing this for sure. Looking at Burman again, he wondered if he would ever know. The one thing that the Special Forces officer did know was that he wasn't capable of miracles or grand sacrifices. Perhaps Kannen already knew that maybe that was why the team's senior NCO had used his brief eye contact to display a feeling of intense anger that pierced him like a shot in the heart.

Opening his eyes, Aveno looked back at the truck following his once more. After all his long years of preparation, after four years of West Point, Infantry Officers' basic training, and the long, grueling ordeal that every volunteer for the Special Forces has to endure before he has the right to wear the coveted Green Beret, he'd had but one chance to do something meaningful, to do something important. Just one chance. And somehow, he'd blown it. Now all he had left to look forward to was pain, suffering, and shame.

The arrival of a black Mercedes limousine escorted by a pair of Russian-built Gaz jeeps caused a stir in the village marketplace. The civilian inhabitants withdrew into the shadows while Syrian officers began shouting at their soldiers to straighten up and salute as the Mercedes came to an abrupt halt. The two guards who flanked Yousaf Hashmi, who had been seated against the wall, jumped to their feet and assumed a position of rigid attention.

Hashmi casually looked around the market place and saw that everyone's eyes were riveted on the limousine, not on him or Specialist Four Insram Amer. Also sensing that he was no longer being watched, Amer stopped digging in the waist-high hole he stood in. For the briefest of moments, the two American soldiers looked at each other. Both saw that the other had suffered severe beatings that had left their faces bruised and swollen. Amer seemed to be the worse for the wear, with one eye so puffy he couldn't see out of it.

Amer's turning to Hashmi was how it had always been between them. Since the first day Amer joined Burman's team, the young Muslim had looked to the older, American-born Arab for guidance and solace. This was partly due to their shared cultural customs. But mostly it was a feeling of separation from the rest of Kilo. It was more than a matter of their swarthy complexions and the manner in which they showed their devotions to their God. Even the most liberal-minded team member looked upon them as foreigners even though Hashmi was born in America and Amer had been raised in the shadow of the Statue of Liberty.

Hashmi and Amer had long ago accepted that they would have to deal with this sort of thing for the rest of their lives. It was only their hope that their children would one day be perceived as regular Americans that kept them working to achieve the American dream.

During this interlude Hashmi nodded at Amer in the same reassuring way his father had done when his children were distressed or frightened. Understanding his gesture, Amer straightened up, his face relaxing into an expression of tranquility and confidence.

Turning away, Hashmi watched the driver of the Mercedes spring from his seat and scamper around the vehicle to open the right rear door. Taking his time as befit a man of his importance, a Syrian colonel slowly emerged. Hashmi was disappointed. He'd expected at least a general. Then he silently laughed at his own foolishness. He was thinking too much like an American. "We ain't in Kansas no more, Toto," he whispered.

Hashmi's whisper caught the attention of one of his guards, who punished his impudence with a single quick swing of the butt of his Kalashnikov against the side of Hashmi's head. The action caught the attention of the newly arrived Syrian colonel, who was being briefed by the commander of the local garrison. The colonel silenced the garrison commander, and looked at Hashmi.

As Hashmi recovered from the unexpected blow, he realized that he was now the object of the colonel's attention. He studied the colonel and realized that he was not the sort of man who cared to be trifled with. He had that look that could send chills down another man's spine. With a cold smile and his gaze firmly fixed on Hashmi, the colonel started walking toward him.

Immediately the pair of guards braced themselves as if they anticipated being smacked about for their prisoner's misconduct. Hashmi concentrated on recovering from the butt stroke while resisting every effort the guards made to get him up onto his feet. Though a prisoner, Hashmi was determined to give nothing to the people who had murdered his uncles.

The Syrian colonel came to a halt before the seated American and ordered the two guards to cease their efforts and back away. The colonel took his time as he studied Hashmi. When he finally spoke, it was almost a whisper. "You have been with the Americans too long. Their arrogance has rubbed off on you."

Though he understood the colonel's Arabic and could have responded in kind, Hashmi used English tainted with a slight New York accent. "Joseph Hashmi. Sergeant. One hundred fifty-nine-forty-two-seven thousand seven hundred and seventy-six."

"Yes, of course. Name, rank, and service number." Bending slightly at the waist, the colonel patted Hashmi on the check as an affectionate father would do to a small child. "Sergeant Hashmi, you do not disappoint me."

The Syrian colonel straightened up, looked at the garrison commander and nodded. The commander marched to the hole that Amer had been digging. Instinctively Amer's guards came to attention. The garrison commander barked orders that Hashmi at first thought he'd misunderstood. One guard snatched the shovel out of Amer's hand, while the other brought his Kalashnikov up to his shoulder before lowering its muzzle until it was within inches of Amer's forehead.

Hashmi watched in stunned disbelief as both Americans realized what was about to happen. Sensing that he had but one chance to get this right, Amer snapped to a position of attention. Closing his eyes, he titled his face to the heavens above, and raising his voice in prayer. "Allah be praised." Then, opening his eyes, the son of Palestinian refugees glared at his executioner and bellowed, "God bless America!" before the Syrian guard could pull the trigger.

CHAPTER ELEVEN

With the last of their evaluations finished and an arduous training cycle at Fort Chaffee winding down, it was time for the commanding officer of the 3rd Battalion, 75th Ranger Regiment to gather his officers together and troop them off to the officers club to celebrate the conclusion of another successful exercise. Seated in the center of a long row of tables that had been shoved together in a haphazard and thoroughly unmilitary fashion, Lieutenant Colonel Harry Shaddock sipped his beer and listened intently as his command sergeant major spun the sort of tale that had gained him notoriety throughout the special ops community. This particular yarn concerned Shaddock himself. It told of an incident when he had been a strapping young second lieutenant and Command Sergeant Major John Harris had been a newly minted staff sergeant doing time in Korea. "The day before the colonel, then *Second* Lieutenant Shaddock, arrived, Gus Franklin, our platoon sergeant, told us that we were to keep our mouths shut and let the new LT do his thing so long as he wasn't threatening to hurt anyone."

From the end of the table a captain who was a bit further along the path to inebriation, groaned. "Now, there's a tall order for you."

After a round of laughter died away, Harris continued. "The colonel, then *Second* Lieutenant Shaddock, reported for duty in the late afternoon just as we were preparing for stand-to. Well, having been told at the Fort Benning School for Lost Boys that you needed to hit the ground running when you were given a platoon, the colonel, then *Second* Lieutenant Shaddock, decided that this was an excellent time to inspect his platoon. Now, as luck would have it, he arrives at my bunker just as one of my biggest foul-ups is in the midst of making a circuit test on a Claymore mine."

Seated next to Shaddock, Major Ben Casalane, the battalion's executive officer, rolled his eyes. "Oh, Lordy, I see where we're going on this one."

Again Harris paused until the laughter died away. "As I was saying, on seeing that this man was having some difficulty with his basic hand-eye coordination, our newly arrived platoon leader seized the occasion to demonstrate his proficiency in the art of war. With a voice that he must have practiced for weeks, the colonel, then *Second* Lieutenant Shaddock, walks over to the soldier, orders him to hand over the clacker and the wire running to the mine, and states, 'Here, let me show you how to make a circuit test.' The colonel, then *Second* Lieutenant Shaddock, jammed his end of the wire into the clacker, flipped off the safety, and squeezed the clacker."

Every officer and staff NCO of the Ranger battalion roared as they pictured the scene. Standing up, Harris made like he was holding the triggering mechanism of a Claymore mine. "He just stood there, eyes bigger than saucers holding the clacker at arm's length like a viper while he watched the dust and dirt kicked up by the mine he had just set off drift away like his career. Everyone in the bunker looked at each other, not knowing what to do. Everyone, that is, except the soldier, who the colonel, then *Second* Lieutenant Shaddock, had taken the clacker away from. The soldier reaches into his pocket, pulls out the circuit tester, and offers it to his new platoon leader, saying, 'You might want to use this next time, sir. I always found it helps keep that sort of thing from happening.' Well, wouldn't you know who gets blamed for this. The man who actually set the Claymore off? Noooo! Gus and me! We spent the next two days going before every sergeant major and commanding officer in our chain of command to receive the most protracted ass chewing in recorded military history."

Another NCO yelled to Harris over the chorus of laughter. "So what was the colonel doing while you were being counseled?"

"Yes, well," Harris replied with a twinkle in his eye. "While Gus and I were having our prostate glands massaged, the colonel, then *Second* Lieutenant Shaddock, was touring the entire division, inventorying every Claymore assigned to it."

Shaddock rose to his feet. "And I must say," he shouted above the roar, "it was the most comprehensive and accurate inventory of Claymores in the entire history of the Second Infantry Division."

Having defended his honor as best he could, Shaddock raised his bottle of beer. The assembled leadership of the 1st of the 75th corralled their own drinks in preparation for the toast that their commanding officer was about to make. When he had their undivided attention, Shaddock scanned the faces of the officers and NCOs who served under him. "For the past two weeks you have been put to the test, and pronounced the best." This statement unleashed a new round of hoorahs, whistling, and the pounding of hands and bottles on tabletops.

After letting his men hoot and holler, Shaddock called for quiet. "This success did not come easy. Like everything else worth having, each and every one of you paid for this battalion's achievements through hard work and dedication. For this, I thank you."

Befitting the tone of their colonel's speech, the response this time was a more sedate clapping of hands and light rapping of bottles on tabletops. "Now that you've had a moment to bask in your glory, hear an atta-boy from the old man, and enjoy the fruits of your success, it is my duty remind you that the first elements are scheduled to depart at oh-five-thirty in the morning. So finish up your drinks, listen to another one of Sergeant Major John Harris's tall stories if you must, and then get some sleep."

As was his habit, Harris refused to let his commanding officer escape without receiving the salute that he deserved. Standing up, the battalion's command sergeant major lifted his glass. "Gentlemen, I give you Colonel Harry Shaddock, the man who is the heart and soul of this battalion."

Jumping to their feet every man present hoisted his drink and roared as one, "To the colonel!"

Having shown his gratitude to the men who had made his tour of command a successful one, exchanged salutes with them, and now suffering from the effects of one too many beers, Shaddock decided it was time to excuse himself and make his way back to his quarters. The training evaluation that his battalion had been subjected to at the Army's joint training center as well as the train-up that preceded it had been grueling. While he hated to admit it, he wasn't getting any younger. The fourteen-hour days that he had been able to take in stride when he was younger were finally beginning to take their toll. For all the technology that had become the mainstay of the armed forces, the profession of arms was still a young man's game, especially for those who wore the coveted Ranger tab.

As he was preparing to leave Shaddock saw an officer standing in the doorway to the officer club's dining room, obviously on duty because he was wearing a beret with his battalion's crest and a web belt sporting a holster. It was also clear from his expression that he was here on business.

From across the table Sergeant Major Harris noticed that something was distracting his colonel. Glancing over his shoulder he caught sight of the armed officer. "I see Lieutenant Ehrlick's found us."

The battalion's duty officer seemed unsure how best to proceed, so Shaddock took the initiative and went to him. Fearing the matter might involve one of his enlisted men, Harris followed. The executive officer, Major Castalane, watched for a second before he too decided to join his commanding officer and the battalion's senior NCO.

As he approached, Shaddock called out, "What brings you here this evening, Lieutenant?"

Ehrlick's response was crisp and cryptic. "Sir, you need to make a call on a secure line. Here's the phone number."

"All right, Lieutenant."

The duty officer saluted, pivoted, and left the officers club. Turning to Harris and Castalane, Shaddock grunted. "Best have the lads cease and desist. I might need some of them very soon."

Having expected that Shaddock would not be returning that evening and wanting to begin preparing for their imminent departure, the battalion's signal platoon had descended upon the temporary headquarters Shaddock had used while training at Chaffee, and begun the process of pulling out phones, computers, and radios. So there was some surprise and not a little embarrassment when Shaddock showed up demanding to know what had become of his secure phone. After scrambling about and reinstalling the device, the overeager communications specialists disappeared while their colonel punched in the number he had been given by the duty officer.

Shaddock was still on the phone when Sergeant Major Harris and Major Castalane arrived at the partially dismantled headquarters. Seeing that the door to their colonel's private office was closed and not knowing how long he would be, the two men took seats, Harris on a folding chair and Castalane on a vacant desk. "I don't suppose," Harris said, "this has anything to do with the flap in Syria."

Castalane shook his head. "Not our turf, Sergeant Major. There isn't a man in the entire battalion that speaks Arabic. Polish, Russian, Hungarian, Rumanian, German, Norwegian, Czech, Danish, and Finnish, yes. We even have a couple of guys who can babble in Swedish. But Arabic? Not a one."

"Something personal?"

"I don't think so. It's something else, sensitive enough that the colonel has to use a secure line."

The pair were still speculating over the sudden call when the door opened and Shaddock called them in. As they entered the small office, barren of furniture except for a small, well-used desk and a couple of chairs, they were struck by Shaddock's silence. Even after he had closed the door he said nothing as the sergeant major and battalion XO watched their commanding officer walk around in a small circle with his head bowed low. Harris's eyes met Castalane's. They both felt the same unease.

Shaddock finally stopped pacing and turned toward them. "Ben, assemble the staff. Within the hour we will be receiving new orders. Sergeant Major, have the duty officer put the word out that all personnel are to be prepared to depart by oh-two-hundred hours local. While he's doing that I want you to go to each company and talk to the first sergeants. They are to submit the name of any man with a medical profile that makes him nondeployable to you by midnight along with a fully updated morning report.

Thinking there'd be additional information, Harris and Castalane stood their ground and waited in silence. Lost in thought, it was a few moments before Shaddock realized that both men were still there. "Gentlemen," he said apologetically, "I wish I could tell you more. But I cannot."

"Yes, of course sir," Harris replied.

It bothered Shaddock that he was unable to share anything with his most trusted subordinates. But he knew how Brigadier General James Palmer was. When he gave an order, he expected it to be followed precisely. Shaddock sighed. "Gentlemen, that will be all. Thank you."

Syria
09:40 LOCAL (5:40 ZULU)

After turning their backs on the team's rally point and continuing their flight, barely a word was exchanged between the two men in Kilo Three. Staff Sergeant Angel Ramirez and Sergeant Glenn Funk simply stared straight ahead at the vacant desert before them as they tried to let the roar of the Hummer's engine drown out their troubled thoughts. When one of them did speak, his comments were abrupt and brief, his tone gruff to the point of being rude and hostile.

There was more to this than the usual psychological trauma that many soldiers experience after combat or the physical exhaustion magnified by the stresses their current plight created. Both were struggling to overcome an almost paralyzing disbelief that things had gone as badly as they had and that they were probably the only survivors. After receiving Aveno's order to move to the rally point they'd heard nothing from anyone. To some extent that was to be expected, since the standing orders dictated that radio silence was to be strictly enforced if any or all of the team were forced to escape and evade to Jordan.

That particular order had been meant to protect the survivors of any disaster that might befall the team. In an age of sophisticated electronic warfare capabilities that could ferret out confidential communications regardless of safeguards, and an intrusive media that seemed to have "unnamed sources" in every nook and cranny of the Pentagon, even the most secure means of communication were less than secure. This was not much of a departure from the manner in which the recon teams normally operated.

Except for targeting information exchanged between the air force liaison teams and airborne controllers coordinating air strikes, almost all communications with the recon teams were one-way. The highly trained members of the recon teams assigned to Razorback were expected to exercise their initiative and experience in any situation that came their way, especially in a crisis. Lacking any guidance to the contrary, and as the senior surviving member of RT Kilo, Staff Sergeant Angel Ramirez saw no reason not to follow that particular order to a T.

That decision had turned out to be the easiest one he made. All of his years in service had done little to prepare him for the confusion both he and Funk had suffered during the last few hours, or might experience in the ordeal that lay ahead. None of their previous experiences offered either of them a basis from which they could draw as they struggled to deal with a blow that was as devastating and cataclysmic as the one that had consumed RT Kilo. Compounding this shock was the realization that neither of them had done a thing to help their comrades at a time when they needed them the most. Although they believed they were under attack by the Syrian BRDM that Kilo Two had engaged, their response was not simply to move out of the line of fire from the constant 20-mm rounds. They had fled. Instead of taking a second to assess the situation and respond in a well-measured and meaningful manner, both Ramirez and Funk had given in to panic and run. And even though the Team's XO eventually gave them an order to continue their retreat to the rally point, each man knew the truth of the matter They had acted as cowards and had turned their backs on their fellow team members without a second thought, without protest.

So while the pair of NCOs remained outwardly silent, their personal struggle to come to terms with their cowardliness in the face of the enemy raged on without pause. In the course of reaching this bitter conclusion, both Ramirez and Funk seized upon the same self-serving rationale to justify their actions: their cowardly flight had been the other's fault.

These and other dark thoughts were only beginning to bubble up in their exhausted minds when Funk called out over Kilo Three's steady drone without bothering to look over at Ramirez, who was driving. "We gotta stop."

Surprised by this, Ramirez pulled his foot off the accelerator and shifted it over to the brake pedal as he began a quick, nervous search for the unseen danger that he assumed triggered Funk's unexpected command. When he saw nothing ahead but barren desert, Ramirez looked over at Funk. "What's wrong?"

"Just stop the fucking humvee."

Angered by the medic's churlish response, Ramirez stomped on the brake, bringing Kilo Three to an abrupt halt. Since he was prepared for the sudden stop and had a wheel to hold onto, Ramirez maintained his balance. Funk, however, was off guard even though he'd been the one to make the demand. His own weight and momentum flung him forward and into the windshield before he bounced back against his seat.

Unable to contain an anger he did not yet understand, Ramirez threw open the door on his side, climbed out of the humvee and stalked away before Funk could recover from being tossed about. He was some ten paces away before the medic managed to catch his breath and compose himself. Rage over what Ramirez had done trumped any regret Funk might have had for snapping at him.

Payback, however, would have to wait. At the moment, there were more important matters that needed tending to. Shaking off the effects of his collision with the windsheild, Funk dismounted, walked a few meters away from the humvee, spread his feet, unbuttoned his fly, and took care of the urgent business that had initiated his sudden call for a halt. Midway through relieving himself he gazed at the distant horizon, wondering how far had they come. Neither had cared enough about their journey to use their GPS to plot their current location or check their direction of travel. Consumed by their own personal struggles, they'd navigated by simply driving straight and keeping the rising sun at their back. That approach had gotten them this far, but in truth, it was little more than a continuation of their precipitous flight. It was time, Sergeant Funk concluded as he did up the buttons on his trousers, for both of them to start behaving like professional soldiers. Whatever personal problems each had over what had happened and how the other man had behaved would have to wait. Ready or not, Staff Sergeant Ramirez, his senior NCO, would need to start thinking things through. He would have to plan their route of march to the designated crossing point and begin to think through how he was going to deal with potential problems when it came time to cross the Jordanian border. Maintaining their simpleminded flight from both the Syrians and their responsibilities was no longer an option.

Slowly, as Funk began to make his way back toward the humvee, he began to think through how he would address Ramirez and put forth his thoughts. Fuel, water, and rations would be no problem. Since Lieutenant Aveno had been responsible for overseeing logistics for the team and Kilo Three had been his personal humvee, it had become a rolling supply dump. In terms of supplies, getting to Jordan would not be a problem, provided they didn't stumble upon any Syrians along the way. Until they crossed the Jordanian border, the operation would be a straight-up military affair. Escape and evade.

Upon reaching the humvee Funk reached through the open door and fished a map out from between the radio and the passenger seat where he had shoved it during the night. Unfolding it, he held it at arm's length as he began to scan it until he found the section that he was looking for. Crossing into Jordan, in a purely geographical sense, would not be a problem because the border was only a line on the map drawn by old men gathered in Versailles in 1919 to divide the postwar world among the victors. The potential difficulties would begin after they had entered Jordan and had to deal with the Jordanian border guards, who might not be expecting them. Funk hoped that someone in Washington was already greasing the diplomatic wheels in preparation for their arrival in Jordan. But like so much of what they were doing, he realized that they could not count on it.

While it was true that he was only an E-5 medic, like the other members of RT Kilo he had been briefed on the geopolitical realities of the region in which they were operating. Jordan was a nation in a precarious position, politically and religiously. It was a country the size of Indiana, ruled by a constitutional monarch who held a pro-Western stance. Unfortunately, the Jordanian king too often found himself politically and militarily squeezed by Israel on one side, and all the surrounding Muslim countries on the other side, most of which were culturally and religiously fundamentalist, and almost unanimously anti-Western. Even the king's own population could not always be counted on to support his decisions and actions. Among Jordan's population of 4.5 million people were many of Palestinian descent who were very pro-Syrian, an outlook that was constantly being reinforced by the uncompromising anti-Zionist rhetoric that flowed unceasingly from Damascus.

The U.S. Army had made specific arrangements with the Jordanian king and his government to use a portion of his country as a staging point for American Special Forces teams and individuals who had been running recon missions in Syria for a long time. From time to time a recon team had found it necessary to seek sanctuary inside Jordan. On every occasion, Jordan had lodged an official protest, warning the United States that it would not permit its territory to be used as a base of operations. Because the region's political, military, and religious situation was continuously volatile, Funk could not be sure if these threats were simply bluster aimed at placating the Arab states or if they were real. In addition, he had no way to know if something might have happened after RT Kilo had deployed into Syria that his officers had not told them about, something that forced the Jordanian king to curtail his nation's role in Razorback. If that had happened, the rally point would not only be nonexistent but a potential danger.

Slowly Funk lowered the map and laid it on the passenger

seat. If recent circumstances had changed the agreement between the U.S. and Jordan about the nature of the rally point, it could prove to be a trap. Funk and Ramirez would find out for sure as they tried to cross the border. Heading to Jordan would provide them with no certainties, only more uncertainties, doubts, and fears. Funk felt his anxiety growing by leaps and bounds. He and Ramirez might even have to surrender to the Jordanians and trust their fate to the machinations of self-interested, CYA-obsessed, pantywaist diplomats from the State Department.

Yet as difficult and hazardous as their immediate future might turn out to be, Funk knew that the worst part of their ordeal would not come until both he and Ramirez came face-to-face with their fellow soldiers back in the States. Whatever they had endured up to that point would be nothing in comparison to what they would suffer when it came time to atone for their sins. No matter how things turned out, they would return to Fort Bragg to face their fellow Green Berets, men who would hold them responsible for everything they had done and had failed to do.

Funk already knew that he would never be able to justify what they had done. They had run. While everyone else in RT Kilo were fighting for their lives, he and Ramirez were running away. He had failed to execute his duties and responsibilities as a soldier. He had abandoned his comrades despite an unspoken bond between all servicemen that no one would be left behind. This was simply an article of faith, one understood by all. But through his actions, Funk had broken the bond that held men like him together when nothing else could. He'd reacted to combat by becoming a coward, intent on saving himself. He had failed on every level. Regardless of whether he was punished or forgiven, Funk would have to live with this agonizing, devastating truth for the rest of his life.

He was still lost in his anguish when he looked up and saw Ramirez standing in the open door on the driver's side of the Hummer staring at him. "So, genius, have you managed to figure out where we are yet?" the senior NCO asked sarcastically.

Enraged, Funk threw the map across the hump that separated the passenger's and driver's seats at Ramirez. "You're the E-6 here. *You* figure it out."

The map didn't hit Ramirez, but Funk's anger and response enflamed Ramirez, who found it all but impossible to hold back his own rage. While he'd been away from the Hummer, walking about oblivious to his surroundings, he too had been wrestling with many of the same demons of guilt, shame, uncertainty, and fear that were troubling Funk. He'd returned to Kilo Three even more tormented than when he'd left. Only a supreme exercise of self-control and discipline prevented Ramirez from leaping across the seats of the Hummer and throttling the only friend he had left in the world. What he did instead was to expand on Funk's reference to his being the higher-ranking NCO, to reinforce the military aspect of their relationship, and exert his seniority.

"Pick up that map and get a fix on our location, Sergeant."

This resort to his military rank, one that carried with it the implied obligation to follow orders, made Funk realize that this was neither the time nor place to have it out with Ramirez. They were still in Syria and very much in danger. They both had more important issues that had to be dealt with at the moment. Whatever score he needed to settle with Ramirez, as well as his own remorse over what he had done, would have to wait. Still, Funk made no effort to hide his ire as he retrieved the map. Before looking down at it, Funk glared at Ramirez. "We'll settle this in Jordan, *Staff Sergeant* Ramirez."

"Count on it."

Syria
09:40 LOCAL (5:40 ZULU)

The ability and skill required to read a map and use that knowledge to find one's way from point A to point B, known in the military as land navigation, is a perishable skill. If personnel don't practice it they lose their ability to eye the lay of the land and accurately gauge how the terrain features they are looking at relate to the squiggly brown lines on a two-dimensional sheet of paper. The introduction of the space-based global positioning system considerably diminished their need to keep these skills sharp. Initially touted as an aid to land navigation, the GPS first became a crutch, then a handicap as a new generation of American fighting men abandoned the old tested techniques of keeping track of where they were in favor of technology that was far more accurate and almost foolproof.

Of course, as the saying goes, "almost" only counts in horseshoes, hand grenades, and nukes. Certainly the current model of the GPS used by RT Kilo, the AN/PSN-11 portable lightweight GPS receiver was a godsend, especially when someone was wandering about the desert and didn't have forty years to spare before his next scheduled appointment. Equally certain is that the swift, bold strokes employed by Coalition forces during Desert Storm to hook around through the wastelands of southwestern Iraq and around the main line of defense would have been far more difficult without the GPS. No one in his right mind would dare suggest that the American Army forsake such a wonder simply because it could lead to overreliance on a system that might fail. Still, as with anything that is almost foolproof, relying so much on the GPS meant that the Army was waging a losing war against the law of averages and increasing the probability of one of Murphy's more famous laws, which states that if something can go wrong, it will do so at the most inopportune time.

For the pair of spec fours fleeing in Kilo Six the problem was not a systems failure. All the satellites that were part of the global positioning system were still up there, orbiting the earth as they merrily transmitted their unique signals. The difficulty Dennis O'Hara and John Laporta faced was that the GPS they relied upon to intercept those signals and translate them into useful map coordinates relied upon batteries, batteries that have a finite life span, batteries that take up room in vehicles already crowded with equipment and supplies. And while both Ken Aveno and Allen Kannen had made sure that there were more than enough spare batteries on hand, their calculations had been based on a operation that was supposed to last two to four weeks, not six. Like the soldiers who used them, the precious batteries that were available were used and used and used until they had nothing more to give, until they were exhausted and failed at a critical moment.

O'Hara and Laporta understood the principles of map reading. Both had proven their mastery of that craft while earning their coveted green berets. But neither man had much of a need to employ those skills thanks to the GPS. Even if they had gone out of their way to maintain their proficiency in map reading the pine-studded hills of North Carolina and the mountainous high desert of California where their unit did much of its training in preparation for their role in Razorback bore little resemblance to the trackless wasteland now surrounding them. A closer parallel to the skills required to find one's way in the desert was what generations of mariners had relied on to cross the world's oceans before the age of electronics. Unfortunately O'Hara was a native of Milwaukee and Laporta hailed from Kansas, places where nautical skills were not required.

Both men had already come to the conclusion that their chances of hitting the precise point on the Jordan border where they were supposed to cross was nil. This much had become clear when they couldn't even agree on where they were with any degree of certainty. The best they could do was to simply keep moving north toward Turkey. Any regrets they had over not paying more attention to the team's escape-and-evasion plan were forgotten. Even Burman had not taken it seriously, choosing to ignore it except when he joked that once they crossed the border between Syria and Jordan the team would stop and break out in a chorus of "Michael, Row Your Boat Ashore."

At the time everyone familiar with the folksong had chuckled. Now, however, as O'Hara and Laporta sped across the open desert toward the invisible line that separated Syria from Turkey

there was nothing to laugh about. In the hours immediately following their run-in with the Syrians outside the village and while
still pumped up from the adrenaline rush that combat brings on,
O'Hara and Laporta had celebrated their narrow escape. Only
later, after they'd checked their map and decided to just keep
driving away as fast as they could, and after their bodies finally
managed to purge the adrenaline from their bloodstream, did
exhaustion set in. Along with it came an acute realization of what
they had done and an appreciation of the consequences of their
actions. In the course of this self-examination, they both started
to experience the same feelings of guilt, shame, and psychological
shock people experience after an accident or traumatic incident.
Shock, with all its sinister side effects, finally began to set in.

Of all their feelings, the syndrome known as survivor's guilt
began to dominate. As the distance between them and the village
continued to grow throughout the night and into the following
morning, both O'Hara and Laporta began playing what-if games
in their minds. What if they had charged forward in search of their
commander and Sergeant Hashmi instead of fleeing into the
night? What if they had ignored the XO's order to break contact
and had given Burman and Hashmi a little more time to get back
to them? What if they had stood their ground and provided covering fire for their comrades? What if? Neither man betrayed his
thoughts to the other. They didn't need to. Both suspected what
the other was thinking and feeling without having to say a word.

Overwhelmed by these grim thoughts and consumed by a
growing sense of failure, O'Hara began to sink into a state of
despondency that led Laporta to believe that his friend was asleep.
Only after he had driven all night and well into morning and
stopped to check his bearings did it dawn upon Laporta that
O'Hara was behaving strangely. At first the young Kansas-born
Hispanic thought O'Hara was simply suffering from the same
exhaustion that was beginning to take a toll on him. Having
already dismounted, he reached back into the Hummer and
shook O'Hara. "Hey, Dennis. Climb out and stretch your legs."

For the longest time O'Hara did not respond. When he finally did so, all he did was turn his head and face Laporta. In an instant Laporta knew what was happening. He had seen the same blank expression on the face of other men who had just survived a traumatic experience. Concerned now, he gave O'Hara another shake. "Hey, buddy. You with me?"

Blinking, O'Hara tried to focus. The soft, almost whispered "Yeah," he finally did manage only served to heighten Laporta's concern.

Laporta stepped back from the humvee and looked around as he struggled to collect his thoughts. It was already midmorning. After driving through the night he knew that it would be impossible for him to continue without a break. Sooner or later his weariness would hit him. Neither of them could keep up their current pace. Yet there seemed to be no alternative. Despite the risks of remaining in one place, he needed to get a few hours' sleep. So did O'Hara. Laporta knew that a troubled mind that had suffered a severe psychological blow such as the one they both had experienced needed time to recover. It needed an opportunity to disconnect itself from the conscious world so it could begin mending itself. Perhaps, he thought, all O'Hara needed was some sleep, a chance to let his brain sort things out.

Yawning, Laporta wandered away from the vehicle as he continued to look around. Maybe sleep was the answer to all their problems. Maybe when they woke after some sleep things wouldn't look so bad. If nothing else at least they'd be able to operate at something closer to near normal levels. Of course the flip side was also true, he reminded himself as he looked back at the humvee where O'Hara sat. What if the situation were more serious than they thought and the Syrians pursuing them were just below the southern horizon? What if a few hours' rest didn't do the trick and O'Hara got worse? Could he, Laporta wondered, take care of O'Hara while simultaneously driving Kilo Six through enemy territory and keeping an eye open for trouble? Would he be able to keep himself alert and ready to deal with whatever lay ahead for as long as it took them to reach Turkey, if they ever did in fact make it that far?

As he pondered these questions, questions for which he had no clear answer, Laporta could feel his own exhaustion growing. Once more he surveyed their surroundings. For as far as he could see there wasn't anything remotely resembling a concealed position that would accommodate the Hummer. Besides, with O'Hara of no use in his current state, Laporta wondered if he could even take the risk of sleeping himself, leaving them both unguarded. He had little doubt that once he laid his head down nothing short of a world war would wake him.

Heading back to the humvee Laporta looked through the open door at O'Hara, who was staring straight ahead with an expression as vacant as the desert. Then he looked over at the PRC-137F special mission radio wedged neatly between the two rear seats. With that SATCOM radio, he knew he could talk to the world. That would mean violating his orders governing the team's conduct while escaping and evading. Yet he saw that he had no choice. The contingency plan that no one had paid much attention to, had been written by someone who could never have envisioned the sort of fix Laporta now found himself in. As a Green Beret, he was expected to improvise, to use his judgment and exercise initiative in combat. Though he had no idea what the consequences would be for him and O'Hara if he violated the team's standing order and used the radio now, Laporta was fairly sure he understood what would become of them if he didn't.

Too exhausted to continue analyzing all the possibilities, complications, and consequences of his actions, he opened the rear door of the humvee, climbed in, and turned on the SAT-COM radio. Reaching over to the front, he grasped O'Hara's shoulder and gave it a vigorous shake. "Hey, Dennis. Wake up and get your butt in gear. We need to crank this sucker up."

Laporta was almost yelling as he shook O'Hara again with ever-increasing vigor in an effort to cut through O'Hara's mental fog. His roughness with O'Hara was compounded by his fear of the consequences of his decision to use the SATCOM radio.

Slowly, almost hesitantly, O'Hara began to emerge from his deep stupor. Like a man waking from a deep sleep, he looked at his companion. Laporta managed to scare up his best toothy smile as he greeted his companion. "Well, amigo. We're either about to save our collective asses or buy a one-way ticket to hell. Either way, I've decided the time has come to phone home."

CHAPTER THIRTEEN

Delmont was madly banging away in the quiet of his small cubicle when the words and letters on his computer screen inexplicably began to jump about. Leaning back in his seat he blinked his tired eyes, making them so blurry he couldn't even see the characters. When his vision finally cleared he scrolled back and reread the portion of the last couple of paragraphs of his document. What he saw appalled him. None of that made a lick of sense. Obviously he'd allowed himself to become so exhausted that he could no longer think or write straight. It was time, he concluded, to avail himself of that desperately needed break he had been putting off for better than an hour and take on a fresh supply of caffeine before attempting to finish the operations plan, or OPLAN.

With all the enthusiasm of a galley slave released after hours of incessant rowing, Delmont pushed his office chair away from the desk. The stiffness in his fingers and the amount of effort that standing up required reminded the Special Forces officer of just how fast he was losing his edge. Despite his demanding physical fitness regime he was no longer able to run as far or as fast as he used to. Of course he realized that he was getting older. The graying of his dark, close-cropped hair was a daily reminder of that. While his wife was able to soften that blow by telling him the gray made him look noble and distinguished, nothing could hide the fact that time was slipping away from him. It was more than just aging muscles that didn't recover as quickly as they had when he had been a junior officer. He was finding he wasn't able to work through the night without a break the way he used to. Even his enthusiasm for a profession that had once been an all-consuming passion was beginning to wane as he caught himself wondering what life after the Army would be like. All of these little cues served as a warning to him that he was fast approaching a time when he'd no longer have the strength and stamina to return to doing what he loved most, being a soldier.

When he reached the break area where the section's personnel gathered during normal duty hours when they needed to escape from their mundane tasks, Delmont remembered that he had consumed the last cup of coffee from the community pot during his last break. The trace amount he had left in the glass decanter had long since dried out from the heat of the metal plate, leaving only charred residue behind.

His tired mind considered the alternatives, none appealing. Coffee from the vending machine could easily be mistaken for bovine urine. To get the necessary caffeine he needed he'd have to drink a couple cans of soda, a solution that would eventually result in more interruptions in his work as he made frequent runs to the restroom. Thus he decided to commence on a coffee hunt. Picking up an empty cup, he flipped the coffeemaker's switch to the off position as he should have done long ago and set out on his lonely nocturnal quest.

He knew that in some tiny obscure corner of the Pentagon's 3.7 million square feet of office space there was a coffeepot filled with fresh-brewed coffee to keep folks like him awake and alert so they could tend to their nation's security. All he needed to do was to keep looking until he found it.

Like an old southern bloodhound seeking a raccoon, Delmont sniffed the air for that telltale aroma of hot coffee as he prowled the long empty corridors. It was when he stepped into the main corridor that the idea of going to the Army War Room occurred to him. He would surely find coffee there, he told himself. And while he was begging the staff of the War Room for coffee, he could get an update on RT Kilo's current situation. He didn't think much had changed since he'd last checked in with the ops folks, but at least he would be able to report to Palmer in the morning that he had been monitoring the situation throughout the night. The general expected his people to stay updated on what was happening outside the five-sided squirrel cage in which they toiled.

To gain access to the Army War Room Delmont had to navigate numerous security checkpoints. Unlike his own workstation, this was a secured area. Practically every document and piece of paper in the room was classified, a fact that led the people who worked there to be rather casual when handling secret and top secret documents. By making the entire area secure they were relieved of the need to close every work file on their computer or lock away every scrap of paper as Delmont and his co-workers did whenever they left their desk. Lining one wall of the War Room were shelves holding dozens of volumes of contingency plans, orders, and operational plans prepared in advance and designed to deal with any conceivable emergency that the Army might suddenly face. Highly classified information, most of it routine, as well as topographical and situation maps were displayed on monitors and overhead screens throughout the ops center. Each display was neatly and clearly marked with a date/time group that indicated the time of the most recent update.

While his duty description was plans officer, Delmont was no stranger here. His responsibilities often required him to be present when plans he had drafted were being implemented as part of a training exercise or a real-world operation. So most of the people on this evening's graveyard shift were familiar with his face, if not his name. As he stood there with empty coffee cup in hand, Delmont looked at a screen displaying the current situation in Southwest Asia, of which Syria was part. As expected, he saw that there'd been little change in the status and routine of the Army units permanently assigned to the region. Everything was about the same as it had been before an as-yet-undetermined number of RT Kilo humvees had been destroyed, and team members killed, wounded, or MIA. Only the Navy and Air Force had significantly increased their activity. Delmont knew that because the Army War Room, like the Air Force and Navy ops centers monitored the status, location, and activities of all sister services as well as military units belonging to Coalition forces, host nations, and friendly powers throughout all theaters of operations and around the world. Even military personnel belonging to nations that were playing no active role in the current crisis were watching and tracking every move that the far-flung U.S. forces made. This was especially true of those nations that believed the very forces they were intently watching would one day be dispatched against them. Each of the elements being monitored was clearly identified by type, nationality, and size.

Delmont noted that the USS *Ronald Reagan* and its accompanying battle group had turned around and was making for the eastern Mediterranean again. Once past Cyprus the *Reagan* would join the *Truman*'s battle group, which had just relieved it. That would give the Joint Chiefs two carriers' worth of aircraft to play with should the Commander in Chief decide to take immediate action.

Delmont was aware of the consequences to the navy of this change in plans. The *Reagan*'s delayed departure meant a postponement of its homecoming and well-earned rest for the crews of the carrier and its escorts. The change also meant that other carrier groups scattered throughout the world would be forced to amend their deployment schedules and activities. Scheduled training exercises were being put on hold in order to preserve the operational strength of all combat elements. Replenishment ships and tankers had been dispatched to the eastern Med to service those vessels in the *Reagan*'s battle group that were running short of fuel, rations, and supplies.

All around the world falling dominos sent others tumbling over. Spare parts that had been held at homeport awaiting the *Reagan*'s return and that were needed to repair aircraft and machinery aboard the battle group's vessels had to be rushed to the region by the Air Force's Military Airlift command. With the airlift command already overextended in meeting its commitment to support America's worldwide forces, these unanticipated airlift sorties forced the cancellation of previously scheduled airlift missions. Priorities had to be reevaluated. Some missions would be scrubbed or handed off to Air National Guard units that were being called on to augment the airlift assets belonging to the Air Force's active component. Men and women who were expecting to awake in a few hours and pilot a commercial jet filled with harried businessmen from New York to Denver would instead find themselves hauling F-18 engines and cluster bombs out of Dover to forward bases and ports in the Med.

These ramifications were of little concern to Robert Delmont. Only securing fresh coffee mattered to him. He found the coffeepot tucked away in a small break area off to one side of the Army War Room, and filled with fresh brew that he knew to be stronger than that found elsewhere. Dumping a packet of artificial sweetener into his cup, Delmont shoved it under the large stainless steel pot's spout, and opened the valve.

While he waited for his cup to fill, a member of the ops center's staff came up behind him. "Oh, Lordy. Someone let the special ops planner loose."

When his cup was full, Delmont turned around. He recognized the face but not the name of the lieutenant colonel who stood before him, only that he was part of the ops staff that worked the War Room's night shift. The two had crossed paths before when Delmont had hung around the ops center and monitored an operation that one of his OPLANs had put in motion. Delmont waited until the ops officer was finished filling his own cup before replying. "Oh, you folks down here in the mushroom patch have nothing to worry about. I'm just taking a survey on the home life and mating habits of officers assigned to the graveyard shift."

The ops officer smiled. "How can you measure something that is nonexistent? By the time I get home the wife is already on the Beltway stuck in traffic and the kids have been scarfed up by the school bus. I swear someone could kidnap my family and hold them for a week before I noticed something was amiss."

"And the downside is? . . ."

"You'd be climbing the walls within a week. Not only does working the third shift violate several laws of nature, it is a breach of the provision in the Constitution that prohibits cruel and unusual punishment."

Though enjoying the conversation, Delmont was too tired to come back with a snappy response. He still had a lot of work to do and was not interested in wasting time with idle chitchat. So he nodded and lifted his cup in a salute. "I hear you."

The two lieutenant colonels headed back to the War Room, but stopped when they saw a TV monitor tuned in to one of the twenty-four-hour news channels. It showed a gaggle of reporters and their attending cameramen milling about on the front lawn of a house that the news anchor's voiceover identified as belonging to the mother of a member of RT Kilo who was listed as missing. Both officers watched in silence as a female reporter described the anguish she imagined the soldier's mother was feeling.

Delmont sighed. "How do you suppose they managed to ferret out the names of the personnel involved? To the best of my knowledge the Sec Def's prohibition against releasing any personal information about the servicemen involved is still in place."

"Oh, I suppose one of those nefarious unnamed sources leaked the names of the fourteen men," the ops officer replied in disgust. "It seems there's always someone with access who feels the American public has a right to know."

"Well, there is something to that. We are, after all, a democracy."

"What about *their* rights?" the ops officer snapped, pointing at the TV. "What about the right of the family to be left alone, to deal with the shock of being told that their son or husband or brother is missing and may be dead? What about their right to common decency? No one has the right to treat those poor people like a freak show! No one has the right to violate a mother's mourning."

Stunned by this unexpectedly emotional response, Delmont stepped back. The ops officer countered by quickly closing the distance. "I don't know why the men in RT Kilo joined the army. I have no idea what motivated them to volunteer for the Special Forces. But I can assure you, Colonel, that it was not to defend the right of some shit-for-brains reporter to invade his mother's home and shove a mike in her face so they could secure better ratings for their program. That, *Colonel*, is worse than rape."

Realizing that the ops officer's outburst was attracting the attention of officers and enlisted personnel, Delmont decided it was best to simply walk away and say nothing. As an astute student of tactics, he knew there were some battles that were best left unfought. This was especially true in any discussion that centered on military families, who were considered a sacred institution by the Army, and the media, who were, in the eyes of most military men, little more than a collection of immoral miscreants and heartless jackals.

Delmont and other astute members of the armed forces understood that at a time like this the military needed the full support of both. Figuring out how to best protect the privacy of military families while satisfying the insatiable needs of the media was not easy. As he returned to his cluttered desk he found himself thinking how lucky he was that he didn't have that problem to solve. All he had to do was figure out how to retrieve an undetermined number of Americans being held hostage at an unknown location that was being defended by a hostile force of an undetermined size. By comparison, that was a much easier task.

With his mental batteries recharged by a fresh infusion of caffeine, Delmont turned his attention to the OPLAN he had been working on. Already knowing that the last part of the document he'd written was nonsense because he'd been so tired when he had written it, he scrolled back past the paragraphs of gibberish and began reading the first complete page that made sense. His review of what he'd previously written before he started writing again served several purposes. It gave him the chance to edit and revise his own work. Often he found that some of what he'd already written didn't make sense or was not as coherent as it could be. Then there was spelling and grammar, about which General Palmer was a stickler. Though Delmont was the author, every OPLAN that left the office of the Directorate of Special Operations did so under Palmer's signature. This meant that the work of his subordinates reflected directly upon their superior to his superiors.

Another reason for the midproduction review after every major break was ensuring that the flow of the OPLAN was maintained. Whether the project was an OPLAN such as the one he was working on or something as simple as an operational summary, a break in his train of thought often resulted in a loss of coherent narrative or gaps in the unfolding logic. While there was seldom anything wrong from a technical military sense, these narrative defects were detractors, mental speed bumps. Senior officers on the Army's General Staff take in a great deal of information in a short time before moving on to the next item in the stack of papers on their desk. They didn't have time to labor over a paper whose purpose was not immediately clear, concise, and logical. While not as irritating to General Palmer as spelling errors or violations of acceptable military grammar, a flawed staff action usually resulted in its being thrown back at the offending project officer, sometimes quite literally.

Delmont was midway through his review process when the phone on his desk rang. Annoyed at having his train of thought derailed by this intrusion, he hit the save key before staring at the ringing phone. He wondered who could possibly be calling him at this hour. He knew it wasn't General Palmer calling to check on his progress. Palmer didn't do things like that. Once he had assigned a subordinate a project, he didn't want to see or hear about it until it was ready for his review. Delmont knew it wasn't his wife. While she was a caring soul, she wouldn't interrupt him when he was doing, as she put it, his "army thing."

Reluctantly, he reached over and picked up the receiver. "Army Special Ops. Lieutenant Colonel Delmont speaking, sir. This line is not secured."

The caller was the lieutenant colonel from the Army War Room he'd bumped into during his search for coffee. "I thought you'd be interested in knowing that we have established contact with those folks you're so interested in."

Delmont all but leaped out of his seat. *"You've what?"*

"We have been contacted by your friends in the East. Well, at least some of them."

Even after the coffee Delmont was still too exhausted, and now too excited, to realize that the special ops officer in the War Room was doing his best to relay classified information over an unscrambled line by cryptically passing on all the information he dared. Wanting more, Delmont fired off a series of questions. Only when he had finished and paused to hear the answers did the officer remind him that the information that was coming in was classified. "If you want the answers to those questions I suggest you come down here. I've got a half dozen folks well above our pay grade that I need to call immediately. I just thought you'd want to know before you wasted any more time working on something that will be OBE and yesterday's news before you even send it to the printer."

Before Delmont could say thanks, the officer in the War Room hung up. For a long time Delmont stared at the half-finished OPLAN on his monitor, wondering if he should complete it or first seek out the answers to his own questions as the friendly lieutenant colonel had recommended. "Damn!" It was moments like this that make or break a Pentagon staff officer. Make a good call and you're a hero, a rising star whose name is on the lips of the Army's movers and shakers. Screw it up and you'll find your promising career is in the crapper with your next assignment more than likely being that of the officer in charge of the officer's club swimming pool at Fort Wainwright, Alaska. "Damn it to hell. Couldn't they have waited until I finished this OPLAN and passed it to Palmer?"

Having made his decision to cease and desist until he found out what was going on over there on the ground, Delmont stood and grabbed his coffee mug. "I might as well get a refill while I'm there," he grumbled. "This could turn out to be a long, long night."

Damascus, Syria
12:50 LOCAL (08:50 HOURS ZULU)

The sudden onset of pain shot through Sergeant First Class Allen Kannen's body with the abruptness of an electrical surge, jarring him from the blessed state of unconsciousness into which he had slipped. Waves of insufferable agony swept over him, overwhelming his befuddled brain's ability to absorb the shock. Blindfolded and manacled there was little he could do but squirm and convulse on the floor of his cell as his high-pitched screams echoed off the barren walls.

Slowly his howls subsided, replaced by muffled sobs and punctuated by pitiful pleas to a deity he had seldom made time for in the past. "Make the pain go away," Kannen wept. "Dear God, make it stop. *Make it stop!*"

The minutes passed but the pain did not. No one heard his pleas. No Savior came forth. Not even God. Ever so slowly it became apparent that he would have to find a solution on his own. "Salvation lies within," he muttered as he finally managed to muster up the presence of mind to resist the panic that was keeping him from thinking clearly.

Bit by bit he began to reign in his fear and set aside self-pity by recalling his training. He would need to reassert his self-control and mental discipline if he were to survive this ordeal. This effort brought to mind an old memory. It was that of an image of a Special Forces instructor towering over him after he was knocked down during a mock prisoner interrogation. With his feet spread apart and hands on hips, that instructor kept yelling for all he was worth while Kannen wallowed about in the muck trying to catch his breath. "Fear is the real bastard," the instructor bellowed. "Fear and his good buddy, Panic. Give in to them and you're dead. Master them and you'll be indestructible."

"Master the fear," Kannen whispered. "Master the fear." Gathering his resolve, he managed to calm himself. Having regained his composure, he next tried to gather himself up into a kneeling position. These efforts were not nearly as successful. The pain from numerous injuries was simply too much. The physical damage inflicted by his tormentors had weakened and exhausted him, leaving him no choice but to stay where he was with the side of his bruised and bleeding face pressed against the cold concrete floor. Out of breath from his exertion, Kannen abandoned his attempts to pick himself up off the floor as he drew in deep gulps of air. Even this modest effort brought on spasms that were almost too much to bear as the contractions and expansions of his lungs aggravated several broken ribs while his flaring nostrils caused his broken nose to throb.

As he slowly began to emerge from his stupor Kannen became aware of the distinctive and pervasive taste of blood but not its source. Whether it was from the teeth that had been knocked out during his repeated beatings or the seepage draining from a nose that felt as if it were swollen to several times its normal size was impossible to say. All he could be sure of was that this bleeding was gagging him. Each time he breathed, another wad of blood-tainted mucus was drawn down his throat.

This gagging was made worse by the stench of the air, a wretched combination of stale bodily fluids, foul dust, and other substances he couldn't identify. Simply breathing was enough to take him to the verge of vomiting. This caused Kannen to wonder if he'd been moved to a new location after passing out since he couldn't recall the air around him smelling so bad before.

Then he wondered where he was. His first thoughts were that he was in Damascus, not that this really mattered. What he could remember was that within minutes of being overrun by the Syrian recon unit the beatings had begun. Only after a Syrian officer

arrived and ordered that the surviving members of RT Kilo be
bound and blindfolded did the soldiers who had captured them
cease their beatings, but only for a while. During this process
Kannen found himself facing the blazing hulk of Kilo One. That
burning wreck and the charred corpse of Airman Jones were the
last things he saw before a blindfold plunged him into a world of
unending darkness and ceaseless torment.

Almost immediately the bludgeoning recommenced. It
wasn't long before he lost track of time. He couldn't begin to
guess at the number of beatings he had been subjected to since
then, creating the impression that it was one continuous bludgeoning. The Syrians never afforded him an opportunity to recover
from one pounding before the next started. To his befuddled
mind it seemed as if their blows ceased only when he had been
loaded into a truck and brought to this place. His only salvation
came when he passed out during an interrogation session.

Kannen corrected himself. There had been no interrogations.
Since his arrival at this prison none of the Syrians who handled
him had said a word to him. They spoke to each other while
replacing with manacles the rope and wire that had been used to
bind his hands and feet when he was captured. Kannen had listened as the Syrians chattered to one another while they publicly
inspected his penis to see if he was circumcised. Yet during this
entire process no one had asked him a question, not a single one.
When it was his turn to be beaten the Syrians simply dragged him
into a room, shoved him down onto a straight-back wooden chair
and commenced whaling upon him while they screamed and
cursed at him. Perhaps this was a preliminary stage meant to
break him down? Maybe the interrogation would start when they
were confident that his will to resist had been broken.

Yet the more he thought about it, the more confused Kannen
became. Intelligence gained from a prisoner is a perishable commodity. A soldier's knowledge of the current situation, ongoing
operations, and near-future plans becomes stale after a day or two,
as do the codes and operational procedures that he was in posses-

sion of, since a soldier's superiors change them lest they are compromised by an inadvertent slip of the tongue or forcibly extracted through the use of torture. So if the Syrians were after information regarding current operations, they weren't being smart about their timing or techniques.

Unable to resolve this apparent paradox, Kannen turned his full attention to more immediate problems. First he needed to get his face off the floor before the stench caused him to throw up. If he didn't he'd run the risk of suffocating in his own vomit. Before moving a muscle, Kannen plotted this renewed effort thoroughly, doing his best to figure out how to do so while minimizing his pain. Before he launched into this renewed effort he strove to psych himself out for the ordeal by whispering over and over again, "Ignore the pain, ignore the pain."

When he felt that he was ready he swung his legs around until he was doubled over like a half-folded jackknife. Once set, he used an elbow to force his upper body up off the floor, clenching his teeth in an effort to keep from screaming out in agony least he alert his Syrian guards. Incredibly he managed to keep the pain in check and get himself up into a sitting position. This achievement so exhausted him that he barely had strength to breathe.

During this pause Kannen slowly became aware of some of the more basic human needs, such as thirst and hunger, which he had not given any thought to since his capture. Though he tried, he couldn't remember if the Syrians had given him anything to eat or drink. The only personal need he could recall was a sudden urge to urinate that had struck him not long after he had been placed in the cell for the first time. Unable to hold back but not wanting to summon his captors for fear of what they would do to him, Kannen had simply relieved himself where he lay. With a clarity of mind that he suddenly found unwelcome, he realized that when he had been facedown on the floor he had been lying in his own filth. Appalled by this revalation, he expelled what little he still had in his stomach with a single forceful heave, adding to the disgusting mess already fouling his small cell.

. . .

The thud of boots on concrete roused Specialist Four David Davis from his stupor. He found that being blindfolded had sharpened his hearing, something that was anything but a blessing as he listened to the Syrian guards come closer. The same sort of growing panic he had felt when he had been a child seeking any means to escape punishment began to well up as he began to quietly plea for deliverance. "Oh, Lord, make them go away. Please, make them go!"

But the boots didn't go away. They only grew closer with each passing second. The sound of the hard rubber soles increased until they came to an abrupt halt just outside the door of Davis's cell. His fear mounted as a guard sorted through his key chain until he found the one he was looking for, shoved it into the lock, and twisted. Next came the snap of the bolt as it was slid aside with a brisk and exaggerated motion intended to add to the prisoner's apprehensions and fear.

If that was their intent, the Syrian jailers were succeeding. Every loud sound they made was now so painfully familiar to Davis that he instinctively began to panic even before they were finished opening the door. He knew he needed to fight this fear and resist their efforts to break him. Though he was a prisoner, Davis understood that he was still an American soldier. As such he was expected to resist by whatever means available. He was prepared to do his best to keep the faith.

He also understood there was only so much suffering, pain, and psychological intimidation he could endure, that sooner or later he would give in. Anticipating this he began preparing himself for what he'd do when he finally did break. Already he had decided that when they finally did reach that point he would tell the Syrians a story, a series of stories just like he used to tell his mama whenever she caught him doing something he wasn't supposed to be doing. He could pull this off, he told himself as he listened to the hinges groan under the weight of the steel door slowly swinging open. The only thing he needed to be careful about was that once he started spinning his little stories he would need to be consistent, keeping his lies in order while making sure that he left out all the details that he knew were classified or might be harmful to other members of the team.

Davis could now smell the men who would take him to his next beating. With all the grace of a pair of stevedores manhandling a sack of grain, two of the Syrians grabbed Davis by the arms, jerked him to his feet, and began dragging him toward the door. With his hands tightly bound behind his back and his legs manacled at the ankles there was very little he could do to make the process less painful to himself. Even before he was out of the cell the injuries that had been inflicted during previous beatings were aggravated by the brutality of the way he was being dragged, causing Davis to moan.

Annoyed by this sobbing, a Syrian behind Davis brought his AK assault rifle up and smashed the butt between Davis's exposed shoulder blades. The force of the blow caught the guards who were holding Davis by surprise, causing the one on Davis's left to lose his grip. Unable to stand on his own and supported only on one side, Davis swung about and slammed into the Syrian who had been supporting him on the other side. Amid a tirade of shouts and Arabic oaths the two of them tumbled onto the floor in a heap.

Even before the Syrian who had gone down with Davis could free himself from the tangle of arms and legs his companions were all over Davis, kicking him and yelling for all they were worth. A few of their blows missed their intended mark as Davis squirmed in an effort to escape them and hit the Syrian lying on the ground instead. Already embarrassed and angered by the incident and feeling the sting of his companions' blows, as soon as the Syrian guard untangled himself from the fray and scrambled to his feet he turned on Davis and joined the pounding his companions were heaping upon Davis with a vengeance. Screaming at the top of his lungs, the enraged guard pummeled Davis's head and shoulders with clenched fists. All he could do to protect himself was to curl up into a tight ball.

To Davis the beating seemed to go on forever. It wasn't until a Syrian officer, impatiently waiting for the guards to bring the American to the interrogation room, came down into the cell-block and brought the impromptu beating to an abrupt and merciful halt.

Making no effort to hide his anger at having been kept waiting, the Syrian officer barked a quick series of orders as he admonished the guards gathered around Davis's prostrate form. One of the guards tried to justify their actions. For his trouble this bold Syrian guard drew a fresh volley of reprimands from the officer followed by a sharp slap across the face. The officer's actions only served to increase the guard's ire. When they picked Davis up again, they used every trick they knew to inflict as much additional pain on their charge as they could. Half carrying, half dragging their prisoner, who was now sobbing incoherently, the guards continued their trek to the interrogation room where Davis would be beaten in a more professional and deliberate manner.

At some point during this journey Davis became aware that his blindfold had slipped during his one-sided melee with the guards. By leaning his head back and rolling his eyes down as low as he could, the young specialist four found that he could catch fleeting glimpses of his surroundings. Nothing he saw was very impressive or unexpected. From what he could see of them the guards hauling him around the prison were wearing the olive green uniforms and black boots that all Syrian soldiers wore. Looking down at the floor Davis noted a rut worn into the tiles. This well-trodden path told Davis that he was but one of many who had endured this ordeal.

As they went the two guards detailed to drag Davis made no effort to coordinate their efforts. The resulting twists and jerks caused the manacles about his wrists, already excruciatingly tight, to dig deeper into his torn flesh. Worse than the pain, though, was the growing terror Davis felt as they drew closer to the interrogation room. He suspected that the guards' slow pace and the roundabout route were part of their torment. The longer they took, the more time he had to think about what was coming. When they reached the interrogation room the guards would plop him into a chair before leaving him to the mercies of professional thugs who would beat him for an hour or so.

Davis used the brief interlude that passed between the time when the guards relinquished control over him and the professional interrogators took over to make a cursory inspection of the room he so feared. Like the rest of the prison he had managed to see thus far, this room was as expected. There was nothing of note, only bare floors, scant furniture, and walls badly in need of patching and painting. Whenever he saw the toes of the boots worn by the Syrians in the room turn toward him, Davis froze. He suspected that if he jerked one way or another as if looking away the Syrians would begin to suspect that he could somehow see them. If they did, his blindfold would be rebound even more tightly than it had been before, depriving Davis of sight and giving them another reason to beat him.

Davis desperately needed the freedom he had to explore his new world for as long as possible, if only to give him a faint sense of control over something and maybe even a small sliver of hope. He needed all the hope that he could latch on to. The withholding of food and water and his constant beating would eventually break him. The only question Davis had was which would go first, his body or his mind. He suspected that his tormentors knew they could not push too much further lest they run the risk of losing him completely to death or madness. Once that happened he would be worthless to them in a propaganda war that he figured they were already waging. All he had to do, Davis kept telling himself, was to hold on. Hold on to hope. Hold on to his sanity. Hold on to his life. Just hold on.

Having no practical experience to rely on except for a few watered-down training exercises that addressed the fine art of torture, Davis didn't know what his limits were. All he knew was that as long as he remained conscious, they would beat him. So when the first blow fell upon his broken cheekbone, all Davis could think was, "Bring it on, motherfucker. Bring it on and put me down."

And bring it on they did. As they had in each of the previous sessions, the pair of Syrians assigned to brutalize Davis went about their labors in silence without making any effort to question him. This continued to be a source of surprise to him. Like a couple of gandy dancers driving a railroad spike, the thugs simply took turns pounding him. Time had no meaning to Davis. All he could do was to respond as best he could to the rhythm that his tormentors fell into, first from the left, then the right. A full-bodied slap to the left side of his head by a hand in a lead-lined glove was followed by a jab from behind aimed right at his right kidney. A jarring whack delivered to the side of his face was preceded by a thrust to the side of his stomach that knocked the wind out of him. Left, right. Left, right. Blow after blow slammed into his body, sending him reeling this way, then that. In short order Davis was no longer able to separate one pain from another as the beating went on. Left, right. Left, right.

At some point during this pounding Davis lost his balance, causing him to topple off the straight-back chair he had been sitting on. Already dazed by the well-disciplined pummeling, Davis couldn't brace himself for the impact with the floor. He simply fell like a withered leaf falling from a tree. Hitting the ground as he did only increased the agony, if that were possible, and almost caused him to lose consciousness. At any other time he would have welcomed a slide into mindless oblivion. But even in his mental fog, he realized that lying on the floor as he was gave him an excellent opportunity to look about the room in an effort to see what his tormentors looked like. Knowing he had little time before he was placed back on the chair, he gazed about the room as swiftly as he dared.

Besides the Syrian thugs who had been administering the beating there were two other Syrians. From the cut of their uniform and age Davis guessed that they were senior ranking officers, though their reason for watching a routine beating during which no one asked the prisoner any questions was unclear. Slowly, ever so slowly he continued to scan the room until he caught sight of his own officers tucked away in a corner of the room, gagged and bound to chairs, but without blindfolds.

Startled, he stared at them even as the Syrian thugs were wrestling him off the floor and back onto the chair. He had no way of knowing for sure if Captain Burman and Lieutenant Aveno had been there during his previous beatings, but he suspected they had been. Their presence did much to explain why the senior Syrian officers were there. It was at this moment, as the Syrians got back into the rhythm of their beatings that it all began to make sense to him. He wasn't being asked questions because the Syrians weren't interested in what he knew or had to say. He was simply being used as an incentive. The real object of these brutal sessions was to beat him in the presence of Burman and Aveno, beatings they could stop at any time if they gave in and talked. It wasn't *his* will they were trying to break, Davis concluded. It was theirs. As they sat there watching, the two Special Forces officers would know that the longer they remained silent, the more their men would suffer. As best he could tell, they hadn't talked yet, giving rise to a new round of speculation. What would break first? His body or their conscience?

As silently as ever, the pair of Syrian tormentors went about plying their trade, delivering a blow against the left side of his skull, followed quickly by a thick stick swung across his chest. Left, right. Left, right.

The senior Syrian officer, a colonel, waited until a pair of guards had dragged Davis's limp body out of the room. As soon as the door was closed he nodded to one of the sergeants who had been beating Davis. It was time to remove the gag from the American officers. The colonel strolled over to the table where the club, lead-lined glove, truncheon, steel rod, and other assorted instruments used to torment the American enlisted men were arrayed. He looked them over until he found one that was his personal favorite. Picking up a large metal hook similar to those used to lift and carry bales of hay, he took a moment to study it before looking over at Aveno. "Your men are disappointing me. I expected soldiers of your caliber to be more resilient and durable. I do not think they will last much longer."

As the Syrian spoke Ken Aveno glanced at his commanding officer. Burman's condition had not changed since he had first seen him in the truck. Were it not for Burman's coloration, poor though it was, and a stream of drool that ran from his gaping mouth, down his chin and onto his lap, it would have been easy to mistake him for dead. But he was alive, alive and like Aveno untouched while RT Kilo's surviving soldiers were beaten before their eyes. Given the severity of those injuries that he could see and Burman's continued unconsciousness, Aveno concluded that his commanding officer was suffering from permanent brain damage. And while it was true that he wasn't in a position to exercise any authority while in Syrian captivity, Aveno slowly came to appreciate that he would remain RT Kilo's acting CO throughout this ordeal.

As the hours dragged by and his men were brought before him, blindfolded and bound to be beaten to within an inch of their lives, Aveno began to envy Burman's obliviousness to the suffering occurring in front of him. As the acting CO and the only conscious team officer, he had to endure the horrors unfolding before him alone and live with the knowledge that only he had the power to decide when the beating of his men should stop.

Unable to bear the sight of the pitiful wreckage that his commanding officer had been reduced to, Aveno looked at the Syrian colonel who was still staring at him. Aveno maintained his silence, as he had thus far. He knew that whatever happened, his last duty to his men and to his nation was to keep the faith, no matter what the cost, no matter how high the price rose. And if the time came when the Syrians lost patience and turned on him the hook that the colonel before him was holding, then he'd have to suffer as they had.

Slowly the colonel walked over to Aveno and looked down at him. "So, are you ready to talk to my superiors? Or must your men continue to pay for your pride and recalcitrance?"

Exhausted by his lack of sleep, food, and water it took a real effort on Aveno's part to raise his head and face the Syrian towering over him. When the two locked eyes, Aveno glared at his tormentor with the most spiteful expression he could muster in an effort to convey all the anger and hatred that he dared not verbalize.

When it was obvious that the American officer was not yet ready to move on to the next stage, the Syrian colonel turned and barked a series of orders. As the gag was stuffed back into Aveno's mouth, the other Syrian officer walked out of the room and headed for the cellblock to fetch the next American slated for torture.

Arlington, Virginia
18:15 LOCAL (22:15 ZULU)

Only a live broadcast of the Super Bowl beat being in the Army War Room during the execution of a real world operation. All that was missing were the nachos and beer. Anyone who could find an excuse to be in there wiggled his or her way though the throng of spectators until they found a spot that offered them a view of the screens and a place where they could hear the running narrative.

Straphangers, that gaggle of attentive minions commonly found in the wake of every general officer, were fortunate. Unlike the peons who had no real reason to be there and thus had to resort to subterfuge or begging in order to gain access to the crowded operations center, aides de camp and selected special project officers favored by their generals simply followed the star bearers that they had hitched their professional wagon to. This was how Lieutenant Colonel Robert Delmont managed to gain entry to the plusher, less crowded regions of the Army War Room. His ticket came in the form of Brigadier General Palmer, the senior Army staff officer who had responsibility within the Department of the Army for Operation Razorback. It did not make any difference that Palmer had no part in planning or overseeing the efforts currently under way aimed at extracting two survivors of RT Kilo. This operation belonged to Central Command, or CENTCOM, the unified headquarters at MacDill Air Base in Florida responsible for Southwest Asia. Success or failure for this day's effort rested upon the shoulders of the commanders and staff officers assigned to that command and not the august gathering of high-speed generals and colonels assembled in the Army War Room. Their efforts would determine whether two very young and very lost specialist fours would be rescued or fall into the hands of the Syrians at the last minute.

The race between the pursuing Syrians and American search-and-rescue teams created the air of excitement that filled the War Room. Since contact with O'Hara and Laporta had been established, every asset capable of gathering information on the comings and goings of Syrian military units in that part of the world had been focused on the area through which the stranded American Green Berets were moving. What O'Hara and Laporta did not know was that a sizable Syrian force was shadowing them. Like the breadcrumbs dropped by Hansel and Gretel, the ruts left by the oversized tires of Kilo Six provided their pursuers with a trail that a blind man could follow.

Initially the intelligence community couldn't understand why the Syrians had not simply picked up their pace a bit and grabbed the pair of wandering Americans. Only after this strange bit of information was passed off to the operations side of the CENT-COM staff did one of the more switched-on staff officers there provide a plausible explanation. O'Hara and Laporta, he speculated, were bait. According to his theory the Syrians were waiting for the American military to dispatch a search-and-rescue team to extract them. When that happened, the CENTCOM staff officer explained, the Syrians would commit everything they could in an effort to foil the rescue attempt and perhaps even increase their haul of American prisoners by scarfing up some of the would-be saviors along with O'Hara and Laporta. "It won't matter how much it costs them," he stated in the detached and antiseptic manner that staff officers use when trying to describe bloody encounters that occur when soldiers on the ground meet face-to-face. "The prestige that a coup like that would garner will be worth the sacrifice. After all, everyone knows that a video showing the corpse of a dead American being dragged through the streets after a failed operation is worth its weight in gold on the proverbial Arab street."

No one had any way of knowing for sure if this was the reasoning behind the Syrians' delay in seizing the pair of Americans. Yet lacking any other credible explanation, the commander of CENTCOM decided to list it as one of the assumptions when he issued his planning guidance for the operation. In doing so, a simple search-and-rescue was turned into a full-bore military incursion, requiring the commitment of the entire panoply of air power deemed necessary to achieve air superiority and support the hefty contingent of troops assigned the task of securing the area while search-and-rescue helicopters flew in to snatch O'Hara and Laporta from the jaws of certain death. By the time this package had been assembled, briefed, and approved, one of the more cynical members of the CENTCOM staff likened the whole affair to dispatching a carrier battle group to rescue a kitten from a tree.

If there was anyone in the Army War Room at that moment who agreed with this analogy, they held their tongue. Few watching the operation on various monitors that displayed the operational graphics and current sitreps pouring in from the field would have been amused by an observation such as that. To those who made up the various staffs that populated the Pentagon, this was simply business as usual. The American military had both the power and the willingness to use it when it came to saving their own. It was what conventional wisdom dictated. It was what their code demanded. To have done otherwise would have been seen as a breach of faith.

The data tracking events unfolding in Southwest Asia continued to stream into the Army War Room from space-based platforms designed to gather intelligence and link every unit actively involved in the operation to their controlling headquarters no matter where it was in the world. Computers gathered this information, sorted it, and distributed it to predesignated nodes all around the operations center where it appeared on screens of countless monitors and overhead displays as symbols, graphics, numbers, diagrams, or simple verbiage. Much of it was of little value to the senior army officers and their subordinates gathered in the operations center. Even those snippets of information that were worthy of serious consideration at the Department of the Army level could not be acted upon at that level during the conduct of the operation. Tactical decisions such as commitment of additional forces, shifting planned strikes from primary targets to secondary targets, and even the ultimate "Go—No Go" call belonged to subordinate commanders much further down the chain of command who were looking at the exact same information Delmont and Palmer were privy to.

Not every officer gathered to watch appreciated this. Even some of the most senior generals continued to entertain the notion at this late hour that they were still in charge. While Robert Delmont understood how some of the high-speed personalities in the room needed to think this way in order to justify their presence, he knew that their notions were little more than a fantasy, a four-star wet dream. So long as none of them tried to exercise their authority, Delmont mused, no one would get hurt. No one, that is, who wasn't scheduled to get hurt.

From among the gaggle of spectators, a full colonel called out to no one in particular, "There go the Apaches!"

Setting aside his wandering thoughts, Delmont looked up at the display upon which the current situation was being projected. Blue symbols representing elements of an air cavalry troop began to close with a red symbol used to mark the location of a Syrian ground reconnaissance unit that had been following O'Hara and Laporta. Even on the big display each of these graphic representations appeared to be no different from thousands of other such symbols Delmont had seen during countless training exercises and in the classrooms of the Command and General Staff College. It almost took a conscious effort for him to appreciate the fact that the blue air cavalry symbol was more than a visual aid used by higher headquarters to track units on their maps. The blue rectangle with the diagonal slash and designation "1-9 Cav" was the digital depiction of real people operating multimillion-dollar weapons systems that were, at that very minute, roaring across the pitch-black wastelands of a country ten thousand miles away in search of their prey. They were, quite literally, the tip of a spear that had been put into motion by some of the men and women who were now rubbing elbows with Delmont.

Closing his eyes, the special ops plans officer found that he could almost see the dark, featureless desert slipping away beneath the attack helicopters of the air cav troop as if he were there with them viewing the world through their night-vision goggles and sights. Instinctively his memory conjured up the sounds of the aircraft engines, punctuated by crisp, almost encrypted chatter, as pilot and gunner exchanged information. For a moment Delmont imagined that he could even smell the sickly sweet scent of warm hydraulic fluids and taste the bitterness that a dry mouth produces when one is about to engage in mortal combat.

Syria
02:20 LOCAL (22:20 ZULU)

The confrontation that Lieutenant Colonel Robert Delmont envisioned taking place between the AH-64s of the 1st of the 9th Cav and the Syrian recon unit was not near as dramatic as he imagined. In fact, as far as the air cavalry gunners and the pilots were concerned they were almost as detached from the engagement they were involved in as were the men and women in the Army War Room. There was very little of the underlying apprehension or trepidation that one would image a soldier going into combat would experience. All the Apache crews were professionals. If they did feel anything, it was a strange, unspoken pleasure that many soldiers feel when they are finally allowed to practice their trade. The opportunity to pit one's skills against a living, thinking foe is something few people understand, matched only by the chance to fire live missiles and kill something. If any of them felt any regret over what they were doing, it was that they, the shooters, would not be able to linger and watch as their missiles ripped through the thin armor of the Syrian recon vehicles and tore them apart.

The mayhem created by the Hellfire missiles loosed by the distant Apaches did not go completely unobserved. This honor belonged to two pairs of OH-66 Arapaho scout helicopters. Those nimble aircraft, crewed by a single pilot/gunner, were the eyes of the 1st of the 9th. Ranging far in advance of the attack helicopters, the Arapahos skimmed and wove their way along, flying mere feet above the surface of the desert. In addition to the state-of-the-art night-vision devices that allowed their pilot/gunner to view the world outside his cockpit as if it were high noon, each Arapaho sported an array of sensors that monitored the airwaves for unseen threats, such as enemy surface-to-air search radars. Thus doubly cloaked by darkness and their innate ability to avoid their foe's best efforts to detect them, the Arapahos made sure that none of the Syrian recon detachment that had been following O'Hara and Laporta survived long enough to do something foolish like rush forward and attempt to seize them before the Blackhawks arrived.

Like a pack of raptors stalking unwary prey, the scout helicopters shifted until each had found a spot in which it could observe its target. One by one, they reported to their troop commander that they had their mark in sight and were ready to light it up with a laser designator.

Within the darkened confines of his own attack helicopter, the young captain charged with "neutralizing" the Syrian recon unit studied the tactical situation as displayed on his monitor while these reports came in. After each Arapaho gave an "up," indicating that he was primed and ready to play his role in the pending attack, the troop commander replied with a businesslike "Roger."

When all his scouts had checked in, he turned his attention to his Apaches. "Red Six, this is Six. Stand by to fire, out." Without waiting for a response, the troop commander switched frequencies and informed his squadron commander that his unit was set and ready to execute even though the lieutenant colonel who commanded the 1st of the 9th already knew this. Thanks to the wonders of modern electronics, information gathered by the Arapahos was relayed simultaneously to the troop commander, the squadron operations center, and other headquarters scattered about the globe that had an interest in what was happening on the ground. Satisfied that his subordinate out in the field was indeed ready, the squadron commander gave him a crisp "Roger" before turning to the Air Force colonel who was in command of this mission. "Colonel, the One Nine Cav is ready to rock 'n' roll."

Like the director at NASA's mission control, the Air Force colonel sitting in his own operations center in southeastern Turkey methodically checked with each officer who was either in command of an element playing an active role in the rescue attempt, or was supporting it from afar. Each of them responded in turn that their particular piece was set and ready. The colonel drew in a deep breath as he lifted the receiver of the direct line to his superior. "Sir, we are set," was all he said when the general officer on the other end of the line answered.

The general did not hesitate. "Execute. I say again, execute." With that, he hung up. Having gotten "the go," the colonel relayed the order. "People, we have a go. Execute now." These words shot through the airwaves like a surge of electricity, energizing all who heard them, and raising the curtain on a deadly ballet.

Having relayed to his subordinates the order to fire, the air cav troop commander turned to his own heads-down sight. He made a quick check of the status of his aircraft's weapon system before dispatching the first of his Hellfire missiles. Once it was away he announced over the air that it was inbound. Several kilometers away the Arapaho assigned to designate that missile's target lit up the lead Syrian BRDM with its laser designator.

Arlington, Virginia
18:23 LOCAL (22:23 ZULU)

"Bingo! They've got the Syrians dead-on."

Opening his eyes Delmont found that he was sweating despite the crisp filtered air of the room. He was even shaking a bit, the way one does when the heart rate increases in anticipation of imminent danger. He scanned the assembled mass of generals and straphangers to see if anyone had noticed his behavior. Fortunately all were watching the nearest display as additional graphics suddenly began to appear. Originating at the blue air cav symbol, flashing arrows crept across the monitor toward the red rectangle. The attack had begun. While F-22 fighters hovered high above providing air cover for the entire operation, the AH-64 Apache helicopters of 1st of the 9th Air Cavalry unleashed a volley of Hellfire missiles into the Syrian recon unit that had been pursuing Kilo Six. With the F-22s keeping the skies free of Syrian aircraft and the ground-hugging attack helicopters butchering every Syrian unit that was close enough to intervene, a pair of UH-60 Blackhawks belonging to the 160th made a mad dash forward to snatch up the wandering Green Berets.

Delmont hated moments such as this. He could not view the events unfolding on the ground in Syria with the same detachment that many of the duty officers seated at monitors around the room were able to. Nor could he identify with those staff officers who let out hoots and cheers whenever a symbol of a Syrian unit flashed to represent a change in that unit's diminishing strength. The highly polished low quarter shoes and the immaculate class A uniform he wore could not camouflage Robert Delmont's true nature. He was a muddy-boots soldier at heart. His view of the world was a soldier's view; mission, enemy, troops, terrain. For him there was reason to be a soldier, one purpose in life. And that was to close with and destroy the enemy by the use of fire, maneuver, and shock effect. All of this, he thought to himself as he looked around the crowded War Room, was necessary, but it was not war.

Sensing that he was on the verge of losing the calm, detached demeanor that General Palmer expected of his staff, Delmont made his way toward the door. His absence was noted only by those officers junior to him in the food chain who saw his departure as an opportunity to move into the vacated space that was closer to the large overhead projector and "the action."

Syria
02:25 LOCAL (22:25 ZULU)

While the 1st of the 9th Cavalry was carrying out its assigned duties with lethal precision, one of the strangest participants in that night's operation was also going into action. Like other aircraft filling the night sky over Syria, the techniques and tactics employed by this pair of naval strike aircraft were no different than those perfected by American ground attack aircraft during World War II and utilized ever since. Just short of its initiation point the lead aircraft's "pilot" conducted a systems check one more time before commencing its final run against a Syrian air defense radar site that planners felt could cause problems. The only difference was that the "pilot" of the Navy F-45 Pegasus making this attack was not flesh and blood. The closest the Pegasus came to having a human pilot was the programmer who had downloaded the data for that night's mission into the aircraft's master computer. Unlike cruise missiles that are designed to crash dive into its intended target, the Pegasus was programmed to drop bombs and return, just like a conventional attack aircraft. While still few in number, the Pegasus unmanned combat air vehicles, or U-CAVs, were the harbingers of things to come. No longer would young American men and women have to place their lives on the line executing D-3 missions—those that were dull, dangerous, and deadly. The future belonged to robo-pilots and the computer geeks who programmed them.

With dimensions comparable to a single-engine Cessna but designed using the latest stealth technology, the lead Pegasus did not flinch upon reaching its initiation point, or IP. There was no hesitation, no last-minute humanitarian concerns to stay the aircraft's relentless advance as it turned and began to make its run into the target. With digital precision, the lead Pegasus assumed the appropriate glide path. Effortlessly it pressed on until the targeting node of its onboard computer signaled that it was time to release a pair of cluster bombs within nanoseconds of the time a twenty-year-old technician aboard the USS *Reagan* had programmed. Once its payload was away, the Pegasus automatically took up a new heading that would take it back to the carrier from which it was launched. There it would be caught by a net stretched across the flight deck, checked over for any damage before being wheeled belowdecks and placed back in storage where it would wait in silence, without want or complaints, until a new D-3 mission was downloaded into its computer by its human handlers.

Not everything that night played out as the operational plan had envisioned. Aboard an E-3A Sentinel flying over Turkish airspace, its all-seeing radar eye tasked with monitoring Syrian air activities, detected a pair of Syrian fighters being scrambled from a military airfield east of Damascus. Though it was far from the area where the rescue was going down, a controller on the Sentinel thought it would be prudent to take the Syrian jet out. With nothing more than a shrug, the Air Force colonel in command on the E-3A agreed. "Better safe than sorry," he muttered, before returning to the computer screen he had been monitoring. With that, the officer charged with controlling those aircraft assigned to the air superiority mission, dispatched a pair of F-22s to take out the unexpected Syrian threat. With nothing more than the click of a computer mouse he signed the death warrant of two eager young pilots whose only mistake that night was in seeking an opportunity to log a few hours of flight time.

Last but by far not the least important element set in motion by the order to execute were the UH-60 Blackhawks of the Air Force's elite search-and-rescue command. Like the other elements of this far-flung drama, they had been hovering offstage waiting for the order to go. Once this was given, the pilots turned the nose of their aircraft toward the spot where the two forlorn American soldiers waited, opened up the throttle, and roared into action.

About the only people involved in the operation who had nothing to do by way of ensuring its success were the two men who were the focus of the entire operation, Dennis O'Hara and John Laporta. Outside of the fact that help was coming their way and that they were to halt wherever they happened to be at 0100 hours, the two specialist fours knew nothing. Somewhere along the chain of command that started in Washington, D.C., and wove its way through CENTCOM headquarters at MacDill and stretched across the Atlantic and Europe to Turkey, someone had determined that it would be best if the particulars of the operation be withheld from them. Since there remained the possibility that they could be captured at any moment, this precaution was deemed to be a prudent measure designed to maintain operational security and protect the members of the rescue force.

Such logic meant nothing to O'Hara and Laporta. Not since they had broken contact with the Syrians outside the village had they been as doubtful about their chances of making it out alive as they were at that moment. While neither man openly spoke of the growing concern each harbored, they were able to read each other's mood. Unwilling to give voice to their misgivings, the pair instead worked through this growing anxiety by throwing themselves into carrying out their last orders to the letter.

As instructed, Laporta and O'Hara stopped at precisely 0100 hours and set about destroying the documents that they had not already shredded by hand or burned. As they waited for their deliverance, even their commanding officer's map was torn apart and tossed into a fire Laporta had started in a shallow hole in the lee of their humvee. While Laporta was ripping various documents into pieces and feeding scraps of paper into the fire, O'Hara was busy smashing radios and other sensitive equipment in the Hummer. The only piece of comms equipment he did not turn his ball-peen hammer on was Kilo Six's PRQ-7, also known as the combat survivor evader locator system, or CSEL. While the GPS feature on this piece of survival gear was dysfunctional, the remote tracking beacon was still capable of transmitting. It would be the signal from the CSEL that would guide the Blackhawks in. "Let's just hope," Laporta ventured as O'Hara turned the device on at 0130 hours, "that's all this squawk box attracts."

Both men were in the midst of this frenzy of destruction when the first Hellfire found its mark little more than five kilometers from where they sat. The flash, followed some fifteen seconds later by the sound of the initial detonation, caused them to stop what they were doing and turn to where the Syrian recon unit was being destroyed. In quick succession antitank missiles from other Apaches in the air cav troop found their mark.

Unsure if this was a good thing or the harbinger of bad tidings Laporta reached down, without taking his eyes off the one-sided battle being waged in the distance, and picked up his rifle. "Hey, Dennis," he called out in a subdued manner. "When was the last time you heard from the search-and-rescue folks?"

Staring at the satcom set he had just finished smashing O'Hara was overcome by a growing sense of dread. "Maybe fifteen minutes ago."

Slowly, Laporta began to make his way to the driver's side of the humvee in preparation to mounting up. "Well, I guess a lot can change in fifteen minutes."

Taking note of his companion's actions, O'Hara put down his

hammer, shifted about in the littered interior of the humvee, and slipped up through the hatch in the vehicle's roof. After shuffling his feet to clear away bits and pieces of shattered equipment scattered about on the floor, he planted his feet and grasped the spade grips of the M-2 machine gun. "Well, amigo, looks like it's time for another mad dash into the desert."

Laporta didn't say a word as he slid behind Kilo Six's wheel and prepared to start the Hummer. "Just say the word, GI, and we're outta here."

With mounting concern O'Hara watched the slaughter of the Syrian recon unit. By now he was able to count six discrete fires glowing in the distance. Unsure of what was going on, O'Hara refrained from giving Laporta the order to move out.

It was at this moment, when the full attention of both men was so riveted on the distant engagement that the covey of rescue helicopters came screaming in upon their position. Startled by their sudden appearance, O'Hara did what came naturally to him. Without thinking he swung his machine gun about and prepared to engage what he initially perceived as a threat.

With his night-vision goggles on and his focus on the humvee directly in front of him the pilot of the lead helicopter was equally caught off guard by O'Hara's unexpected response. It took everything he had to keep from jerking his joystick to the right and climbing in an effort to escape before the Green Beret pointing the heavy machine gun at him had a chance to open fire.

It took but a second for O'Hara realize that the unexpected intruders were his saviors. As quickly as he had brought his weapon to bear, he depressed the barrel of the M-2 machine gun, let go of the spade grips, and began to flap his arms. Since his aircraft was carrying a detachment of ground troops tasked with providing security during the pickup, the lead pilot overflew Kilo Six and touched down fifty meters beyond, inserting his troops between the decimated Syrian unit and the men he had been dispatched to rescue. At the same time the Blackhawk assigned to snatch O'Hara and Laporta landed as close as it could to the humvee.

Sensing that time was of the essence, O'Hara and Laporta scrambled out of Kilo Six and made for the nearest Blackhawk. Both men were on the ground and running for all they were worth for the helicopter, heading straight for the crew chief of that aircraft, who squatted in its open door, yelling to them to watch their heads at the top of his lungs. Neither Green Beret bothered to give a helicopter crewman who jumped out and ran past them a second look. They had but one goal in mind and did not deviate from achieving it until they were safely inside and being strapped into their seats. Only then did O'Hara look back at Kilo Six where he saw the lone helicopter crewman stop, pull a pin from a satchel he was carrying, and toss it inside the abandoned humvee before pivoting and running back to the helicopter.

With a hop and a bound, the last crewman flung himself back into the Blackhawk. Even as this man went sprawling across the floor headfirst to where O'Hara and Laporta sat, the helicopter's crew chief was shouting over the boom mike of his helmet to the pilot. Just as the helicopter lurched off the ground, the explosives that had been chucked into Kilo Six went off, tearing that vehicle to bits.

Ignoring the churning of his stomach caused by their precipitous takeoff, Laporta turned to O'Hara and gave his companion a broad, toothy grin. Overwhelmed by the sense of relief he felt, O'Hara tugged against his seat belt as he reached out and wrapped his arms around Laporta. "We're going home, amigo! We're going *home*."

Northeastern Jordan
07:40 LOCAL (03:40 ZULU)

The end of Kilo Three's precipitous flight from the team's rally point to the Jordanian border was considerably less dramatic than that which O'Hara and Laporta had experienced, but no less hazardous. In many ways, the easy part of Staff Sergeant Angel Ramirez's and Sergeant Glenn Funk's escape was over. The problems they would now face as they crossed over from Syrian territory into that of an unsuspecting sovereign nation could prove to be far subtler and decidedly less predictable.

Crossing Jordan's frontier at the point designated in the team's OPLAN was simple. There was no boundary fence or sand berm such as the one used to separate Iraq from Saudi Arabia. One minute the patch of desert upon which they were traversing was Syrian, the next it was Jordanian. There was no hint of the line that British and French diplomats had drawn on a map in 1919 at Versailles when dividing the Middle East between them. Only sand that knew no nationality or political allegiance.

This seemingly insignificant fact was the first problem that Ramirez had to deal with. Since there was no clear demarcation between the two nations there was nothing keeping any Syrians who might still be tracking them from continuing their quest. The legality of hot pursuit, which international jurists and diplomats love to debate in an academic setting, was meaningless to the soldiers on the ground charged with defending a nation's borders or apprehending those who sought refuge on the other side of an imaginary line. Until Ramirez and Funk were physically in the protective custody of Jordanian officials, the two Americans knew they would not be safe from being snatched by determined Syrians and dragged all the way back to Damascus.

Nervously Funk glanced in the side-view mirrors trying to see past the clouds of dust their own vehicle was throwing up as they sped toward an uncertain future. Taking note of his companion's concern, Ramirez turned in his seat and stuck his head up through the open hatch in the humvee roof. After scanning the horizon behind them, he eased back down into his seat. "I guess those mines we left behind last night did the trick."

The fear of pursuit had driven the two Americans to push on to the crossing point into Jordan as quickly as they could. Stopping only when physical necessity demanded it and refueling required them to, Funk and Ramirez had pressed on nonstop. In addition to doing their damnedest to outrun any pursuers, they zigzagged this way and that in order to frustrate Syrian efforts to set up and ambush them along their projected path of retreat. Whether the Syrians were actually doing this was impossible to tell. What was clear very early on was that they were being followed. The same sort of dust plume that betrayed their high-speed flight likewise compromised every effort by the Syrians behind them to keep their presence a secret.

This led to Ramirez's decision to set out an ambush of his own using mines Burman had insisted on carrying for just such an emergency. The six old-style antivehicle mines they had could be activated by either direct pressure or by means of a tilt rod. Deciding where to place them was easy. Assuming that the lead Syrian vehicle would take the path of least resistance and follow their humvee by driving in the same ruts that Kilo Three had left behind, Ramirez buried the first mine right in the center of one of the ruts, using the pressure detonator. Discovery of this mine, either through an alert driver or activation of the mine would stop the pursuit for a few minutes as the Syrians figured out what had happened while tending to their wounded and dead. It would also cause a bit of fear in the next driver selected to take the lead. He would be less anxious to put the pedal to the metal in order to catch the Americans. He would also avoid driving in the ruts their vehicles had made, choosing instead to drive off to one side, close enough to see and follow them, but safe from any mines that might be hidden beneath the sand.

Ramirez expected this, which was why he placed the next two mines a few meters on either side of the trail his Hummer was blazing, and attached the tilt rods on them. Unlike a pressure detonator, a vehicle's wheels or tracks do not have to make contact with a mine with a tilt rod. As the name implies, there is a long thin rod attached to the mine's detonator. All a vehicle has to do to set the mine off is to brush the rod or knock it over as it drives over it.

Surprised a second time, the Syrians would now find themselves facing a serious problem, both tactically and physiologically. While they could attempt to fan out farther from the trail they were following, there was no guarantee that this would do them any good either. The next line of mines they stumbled across just might be deployed in anticipation of this sort of response. This would more likely than not, Ramirez theorized, lead them to go back to driving alongside the ruts, just not in them, taking it slow while watching for tilt rods as they went. To frustrate this tactic, he planted the last of his mines in the burrow between the ruts, using a tilt rod on the first one, than a pressure detonator on a second a hundred meters farther along. Upon discovering the first mine, the one with the tilt rod, the Syrians would assume they now understood what they needed to search for up ahead, setting them up for the shock that would result when they discovered the second by running over it without seeing the telltale rod protruding from the ground. Whether they actually hit all the mines was not really the point. The delay, caution, and fear that these infernal devices would cause among his pursuers were what Ramirez was after.

Tired and unable to set aside the loathing he felt for Ramirez that grew with every mile they put between them and the village where they had left the rest of the team, Funk ridiculed Ramirez every time they stopped to deploy a string of mines. During one such pause, Funk put his thoughts into words. "This is fucking stupid. The Syrians aren't going to be dumb enough to fall for this."

With a disdain that matched what his fellow soldier felt for him, Ramirez turned on Funk. "Listen, you. I don't give a damn what you think. All that matters is that you do what you're told to do and keep your mouth shut. Is that clear?"

Thus the hatred each bore for the other as well as that which they harbored for their own failures tore away Funk's and Ramirez's frayed nerves, threatening their very survival in a way the Syrians never could. When they had finished setting out the last of their mines, not knowing if this effort had been of any use, they drove on as fast as their Hummer could take them in a vain effort to escape from the Syrians as well as their own guilt, a guilt that gnawed away at them no matter how hard each man tried to hide it.

Upon arriving in Jordan both Ramirez and Funk managed to set aside the animosity each felt for the other and turn their full attention to other, more pressing issues. Even if they did manage to make contact with Jordanian officials willing to entertain their request for asylum, the two knew their trials and tribulations would not be over. During one of those rare occasions when the two managed to overcome the bitterness that poisoned their efforts to work together and discuss practical matters, Funk pointed out that they had no way of knowing for sure if they could trust the Jordanians. "The bastards are just as likely to turn around and either boot us back across the border or call their Syrian counterparts to come over and pick us up. Either way, we're screwed if we don't do this right."

Though he hated to admit that the medic had a point, Ramirez found that he had to agree with him. "You know what that means, don't you," he finally replied after giving the problem some thought. "It means we're going to have to hang on to our vehicle and weapons for as long as we dare while doing our damnedest to contact the American embassy in Amman or wait for the Jordanians to do it for us."

Unable to completely set aside the anger he felt toward Ramirez, Funk used this opportunity to take a swipe at him. Making no effort to hide the cynicism of his tone, he chuckled. "Yeah, right. While you're in the phone booth dialing up the embassy I'm sure the Jordanians will be more than happy to wash the windshield of our Hummer and check the oil on the grenade launcher.

Exasperated by Funk's snide remark, Ramirez snapped back without hesitation. "Well, what the fuck do you recommend, Sergeant Funk? Maybe we should skip Jordan and drive straight through the night to Israel. Or perhaps it would be better if we forget Israel and try Germany. I'm sure they'd be thrilled."

Funk said nothing during his companion's tirade. He simply continued to stare straight ahead, grasping the steering wheel and squeezing it until his knuckles turned white. Even when Ramirez was finished, Funk said nothing.

Whether it was due to his own sense of self-loathing, Ramirez had done all he could by way of avoiding confrontation with the only man who could bear witness to his actions. Yet there was only so much that he was willing to take. Coexisting with his desire to keep from squabbling with Funk was a burning need to have it out with him. Ramirez had no doubt that Funk held him fully responsible for turning their backs on their fellow teammates. And even though Ramirez knew in his heart and soul that he had been the one who had made no effort to question the order to flee without having giving a second thought to the welfare of Aveno and Amer, the Hispanic NCO found Funk's unspoken self-righteousness intolerable. Spoiling for an opportunity to vent his own pent-up anger, Ramirez glared at the medic, waiting, almost daring him, to say something in response.

Wisely Funk did not oblige him. The team medic opted to say

nothing as he continued to peer out across the barren landscape before him, holding in check all the dark thoughts and recriminations he harbored. He knew there would come a time when the two of them would have to face up to what they had done. Either separately or together they would need to atone for their sins against their comrades back there as well as their failure to uphold the traditions of their chosen branch of service. Though the word "coward" had yet to be mouthed by either man, it was always there, lurking behind their every conscious thought.

It was not much of a town. In fact it didn't even have a name on the map that Ramirez was using. The solid black squares and rectangles used to depict buildings on the map were clustered around a junction where two desert tracks joined together with a dirt road. Even the road that began where the goat trails merged failed to pass muster and rate a name or numerical designation. In the eyes of the American who had made the map, this piece of God's green and sometimes brown earth was not worth the time or ink needed to record that information.

Such trivial concerns were of no interest to Ramirez or Funk as they approached the nameless collection of Jordanian dwellings that someone in the Pentagon had stumbled upon long ago when he was looking for a place where teams seeking refuge from Syrian pursuit could turn to. Long before they reached that place Ramirez had come to the conclusion that creeping about under the cover of darkness in search of a Jordanian border post might not be a smart thing to do. Instead, he had opted to go slowly once they had crossed the border, and proceed only after the sun began to rise. Surprisingly, when they reached the small village the appearance of a strange-looking military vehicle sporting a large-caliber weapon caused less of a stir among the handful of inhabitants going about their daily routine than Ramirez had expected. Women in the traditional black head-to-toe garb drew back into the shadows or slipped through the open doors of their modest mud-brick-and-stone dwellings but otherwise ignored them. A cluster of old men sitting around a table set outside of a small shop drinking coffee interrupted a heated discussion only long enough to look up at the American humvee as it rolled down the dusty road that doubled as the village's main street. With a collective shrug, they returned to the topic they had been debating as soon as Kilo Three rumbled by.

The response was not quite as casual when Funk reached the center of the small village where all the trails met the dirt road. At the apex of this junction was a fortresslike building sporting the Jordanian flag. When it came into view, Ramirez spotted a soldier sitting in the shade of the building on a rickety wooden chair. As Kilo Three turned the corner, the Jordanian took one look at the American humvee sporting its ominous-looking 40-mm grenade launcher, jumped to his feet, and bolted inside without bothering to close the door behind him.

Ordinarily such a response would have generated any number of snide remarks as well as chuckles. But neither of the two American NCOs found this reaction a matter to laugh at. Both knew that what came out the door next would tell them whether salvation was at hand or if another flight had just begun. Unsure of what to do, Funk let up on the accelerator and began to slow. At the same time Ramirez found himself beginning to entertain second thoughts about his decision to come blowing in from the desert in broad daylight. For several unnerving seconds he found himself wondering if it might not be a good idea to stop where they were in order to maintain a safe distance from the ominous building that stood before them.

Equally unstrung by the uncertainty of the moment, Funk called for a decision. "Well, what's it going to be?"

Having shown themselves, Ramirez realized that to hold back now would be the worst thing that they could do. He saw that they had no choice but to continue as planned. Drawing in a deep breath, he nodded toward the building. "Pull up in front of the place until my door is even with that front door. But," he quickly added, "keep the engine running and in gear until I tell you otherwise."

Understanding the purpose of this last directive, Funk eased the humvee across the road, cut the wheel to the left, and came to a stop in front of the building. Having come this far, Ramirez was faced with having to decide if it would be best simply to sit in the humvee and let the Jordanians make the next move or press on with his strategy of bluster and bluff by hopping out, walking up to the open door, and sauntering in as any wayward tourist would do.

When he saw no movement inside the darkened doorway, Ramirez guessed that it was again up to him to take the next step. Although his imagination conjured up all sorts of images of a roomful of Jordanians soldiers armed to the teeth and waiting just beyond the shadows, the Hispanic NCO reached deep down inside and drew upon the last bit of courage he had. Throwing open the door of the humvee, he stepped out, then stood up and stretched as if he did this sort of thing every day. He purposely left his rifle behind. He figured if they were waiting for him in there, he'd never get a shot off, so intimidation was no longer an option. Much better, he thought, to go with his gut feeling and play up the friendly-but-hopelessly-lost-American angle.

Back inside the humvee Funk grasped the steering wheel with both hands as he watched Ramirez move toward the open door. Like Ramirez, he considered reaching for his weapon. But he also dismissed that idea as being both foolish and provocative. He figured that if things suddenly did go south, his best chance of survival would lie in putting as much distance as possible between himself and the Jordanians inside.

In a blinding flash of clarity it suddenly dawned upon the Special Forces medic that what he was planning to do now was exactly what he had done that night back in Syria. He had been behind the wheel that night. As the driver he had really been in control of the situation and could have, if he had wanted to, stayed where they were until the lieutenant and Amer had returned. But he hadn't. When the firing had started that night he had bolted, just as he was getting ready to do that very minute. He was preparing himself to turn his back on Ramirez and run yet again. In truth, *he,* and not Ramirez, had been the coward.

As he accepted this awful truth, Funk closed his eyes, let his hands drop to his side, and tilted his head back. In a hushed, almost plaintive tone he called out to his God, "What have I done?" Though no answer came, Funk quickly decided what he would do if the Jordanians did begin to fire. He would stay, fighting if he had a chance, or dying where he stood. But whatever happened, he was determined that he wasn't going to abandon Ramirez as he had the others. He would bring his shameful flight, as well as his dishonor, to an end.

Opening his eyes, the medic caught sight of Ramirez as he began to ascend the first of three steps that led into the building. Having settled upon his grim resolve, Funk now found himself egging on the Jordanians. "Come on, you fucking rag-heads," he muttered as he watched and waited. "Give us your best shot."

Arlington, Virginia
03:05 LOCAL (07:05 ZULU)

When you're a member of the armed forces it makes no difference whether you are on duty or at home. Nine times out of ten, a ringing phone between the hours of midnight and 0600 hours is the harbinger of ill tidings. That's why in most military families, it is the unofficial duty of the spouse to answer the phone before midnight and that of the military side of the household to do so in the wee hours.

With the response of a punch-drunk fighter and pretty much the same mental clarity, Robert Delmont rolled over toward the nightstand, snatched the phone from its cradle before it finished its second ring, placed it next to his ear, and croaked, "Colonel Delmont."

"Colonel, pack up your class A's, climb into businessman mufti, and get yourself down to Andrews ASAP."

Startled by hearing General Palmer's voice, Delmont instinctively bolted upright in the bed and spat out a crisp "Yes, sir."

"There'll be orders waiting for you at flight operations," Palmer went on. "The embassy in Amman will have a car waiting for you at the airport."

In the beginning Delmont had managed to keep up with what he was hearing. The mention of Amman and the embassy, however, threw him completely. Without thinking, he stuttered, "Amman? As in Jordan?"

Peeved at being interrupted, Palmer snapped back. "Do you know of another Amman, *Colonel*?"

"Well, no, sir. It's just that—"

"A couple of our favorite alumni from the University of Arkansas have managed to run afoul of the local authorities there," Palmer explained, passing on the particulars of a highly classified military operation as best he could over a phone line that was not secure. Though still not fully awake, Delmont was finally able to sort out that Palmer was using the name of the school as a means of alluding to its mascot, the razorback. "The Jordanians are fit to be tied. It seems they are worried about what their neighbors might do after that three-ringed circus we staged yesterday in their backyard. It seems they are demanding that the government in Amman hand our people over to the neighbors."

"The neighbors," as Delmont was well aware, meant Syria.

"What are the chances of that happening, sir?"

There was a pause, which was Palmer's way of saying that he wasn't sure. When he spoke, his tone betrayed a desperate, almost worried aspect to it. "The Jordanians are cooperating for the moment. They've let our military attaché in to speak with the pair, but he knows nothing about their affairs or the deal we're working on at the moment."

Delmont needed a moment to sort out this last bit out. "Affairs," he reasoned, must be the general's way of referring to

Razorback and RT Kilo's original mission. But "the deal" could mean several different things, not the least of which was the OPLAN he was working on to go after the members of RT Kilo who were being held by the Syrians.

"I want you to go straight to wherever they're holding them," Palmer continued, "and do your best to find a place where you can speak to them without any fear of being overheard. If you do manage that, grill them. Find out for sure just how many other team members are still alive and were taken."

"And if I'm not able to gain access to them?"

The sharpness in Palmer's voice came back. "You're a fucking colonel, Colonel. You figure that out to make it happen. Now get going. Your flight is waiting."

Damascus
11:20 LOCAL (07:20 ZULU)

For the first time since arriving at the prison, Ken Aveno had been beaten. Even more surprising was the fact that the Syrian guards hadn't even bothered to take him out of his cell and down to the interrogation room where his men had been brutalized before his very eyes. Instead, four guards had simply thrown open his cell door and set upon him like a pack of wild dogs, coming at him from every direction, kicking and pummeling him with their feet and clenched fists. The Special Forces officer had no clear idea how long this assault went on. The passage of time, already difficult to measure with any degree of certainty, lost all meaning during the course of this unexpected and thoroughly horrific thrashing.

Also lost during this beating was a sense of invulnerability that he'd imagined he had from such treatment. While it was wrong to do so, Aveno had come to the conclusion that as long as his men were able to endure the physical punishment that was being meted out to them, the Syrians would not touch him. He thought he had understood what the Syrians had in mind.

Now, however, it was clear that they had a better grasp of American military psychology than he had of theirs. Their sudden change in tactics, this unexpected attack upon him, confused the acting commanding officer of RT Kilo. Was this impromptu beating simply a taste of things to come? Would more beatings such as this follow? He hoped not. He prayed that this was little more than an aberration, a spur-of-the-moment decision by a group of ill-disciplined guards hell-bent on beating an American officer for the sheer pleasure of it. If that were so, Aveno expected that there would be hell to pay for doing what they did. Doing his best not to move lest he aggravate his bruised and battered body, he imagined that an unauthorized beating like the one he had just suffered through had the potential of spoiling the little game their officers were playing. It could steel his resolve to hold out, to endure the agony of seeing his own men beaten before his very eyes.

Only slowly did it begin to dawn upon Aveno that he really hadn't been exposed to the sort of agony that his men had already been subjected to. As vicious as it had been for him, the impromptu beating he had suffered had been but his first. Kannen, Mendez, and Davis had been beaten countless times, almost ceaselessly. What he had just experienced was nothing compared to what they had endured.

Yet this really didn't seem to matter. He'd been hurt. As shameful and selfish as it might be for an American officer to entertain such thoughts, Aveno found himself hoping that the Syrians would see the error of their ways and return to the old routine. If they did not, he didn't know what he'd do. In the silence of his cell, Aveno slowly came to the conclusion that he wouldn't last very long. He wasn't that strong. Psychologically he wasn't as tough as he had once been. Whatever confidence he once had enjoyed was gone, snatched away from him just like RT Kilo had been that night. He was helpless and forlorn, shorn of his ability to control his own fate. Both the Syrians and his estranged wife had seen to that. In her own way Elizabeth had laid the groundwork for what the Syrians were now doing to him.

She had managed to strip him of everything he had once loved and had believed in. Through her actions and his inability to see things as they really were, she had broken him, leaving little behind but an emotionally bankrupt shell, a shell that the Syrians were determined to crack.

Rolling over onto his back, Aveno looked up at the ceiling, wondering what he would do when that happened. Talk? Would telling them whatever they wanted save him? Was that his key to survival? Then, from somewhere in his troubled mind, an image of his wife came to the fore. It brought neither comfort nor joy. "Survive," he muttered, not caring for the first time if the Syrian guards posted outside the door of his cell heard him. "Yeah, right. Big fucking hairy deal. So I survive. For what?" It was a question that, like all the others, he had no answer for.

CHAPTER SEVENTEEN

Standing outside the bedroom door of their small one-room apartment, Karen Green listened for the longest time, hoping she'd hear Elizabeth stirring. Any sound would have been welcome. A squeak, a sob, anything that would give her an excuse to enter the room and comfort the woman she so dearly loved. But Karen heard nothing, not even the sound of Elizabeth tossing or turning on the bed. Just silence.

Frustrated, Karen turned away and made her way back into the living room where, dejected, she plopped down onto the sofa and wondered what to do next as she waited for Elizabeth to abandon her self-exile from the world.

Sitting around quietly waiting for things to happen did not come easily to Karen Green. By necessity she was a doer, a self-motivated go-getter who could be as brazen and assertive as the most seasoned male broker on Wall Street. Not only did her job demand that she cultivate such qualities, as a native of Manhattan that sort of persona came with the turf. Living her life on what she considered to be her terms, Karen made no effort to hide her ambitions to be the CEO of her brokerage firm before her fortieth birthday.

Yet she could also be quite astute when it came to dealing with people. Karen had no problems with modulating her behavior and temperament to fit the situation and the company she was in. Some of her less gifted co-workers chided her for being manipulative and conniving. Many of the female brokers in the firm would have nothing to do with her, branding her a heretic and throwback to the bad old prefeminist days. But her clients loved her, as much for the manner in which she treated them as for the advice that she gave them, sound advice that was seldom far from the mark. Besides a genetic heritage that endowed Karen with a classic figure and amble bosom, her mother had managed to instill in her the notion that good manners and a little charm are always in style. To this mantra Karen had added the corollary that they are also sound tactics when it came to closing a deal or ingratiating herself with the boss. While no one would dare deny that she had the intelligence and savvy needed to make it on Wall Street without relying on such methods, none could blame her for using them to gain an edge in a profession that was as unforgiving as a great white shark at its dinnertime.

Karen's ability to read a situation and modify her behavior to fit the situation was not restricted to her business dealings. At an early age, she had come to the conclusion that there was no such thing as an equitable partnership when it came to relationships. At best, there might be what one could term a senior partner and a junior partner, but the idea that two people could live in perfect harmony as true equals was a notion that was as insane and self-destructive as the old feminist idea that a woman could have it all. So Karen Green felt perfectly at ease letting Elizabeth Stanton play the Alpha. The domestic tranquility and harmony this arrangement brought to their modest if pricey Upper East Side apartment was worth the effort, for it provided the pair a refuge free of the pressures and demands that their chosen careers placed upon them.

There were times, however, when outside forces conspired to invade their modest sanctuary and deny them the serenity each required after slaying corporate dragons and fending off fierce competition. The events of the past few days had resurrected the twin demons that stalked Elizabeth, her failed marriage with an Army officer and her chosen lifestyle. Unleashed by the events in Syria, they exposed both women to the unwelcome glare of the media's spotlight. Overnight Elizabeth went from being just one more hungry New York lawyer out to make her mark on the world to being hounded around the clock by journalists and well-wishers alike. Even people whom she hardly spoke to at her law firm and those that she had absolutely no use for found it necessary to go out of their way to offer their regrets over her plight at having a husband who was being held captive. That the two were estranged and hadn't spoken to each other since finishing their previous year's tax return did not seem to matter to anyone.

Needless to say, this unsolicited attention made it all but impossible for Elizabeth to carry on anything resembling a normal life. Recognizing the disruption that her presence was causing, the senior partners decided that it would be best for all parties concerned if Elizabeth took a leave of absence until the crisis in Syria was resolved. Though each of her superiors went out of their way to make sure that they conveyed their sincere regret over the situation and that this absence would in no way affect her standing in the firm, Elizabeth was shrewd enough to appreciate that her stock in the company had taken a big hit. In a fit of anger reinforced by three glasses of a delightful merlot, Elizabeth bemoaned her fate to Karen. "I can't even walk out of this building without being pounced on by every reporter and nutcase in the city."

Feeling besieged on all sides, Karen found it necessary to step in and serve as a buffer between Elizabeth and the rest of the world while doing her best to comfort her when she was willing to accept that gesture. This, of course, meant that her own work suffered. Between tiptoeing about the apartment in an effort to provide her partner as wide a berth as possible while fending off the media and screening all incoming calls at the same time, Karen found little time to devote to her clients. Though she did her best to keep up with that part of her life on-line or over the phone, Elizabeth's situation proved to be too distracting, too disruptive to Karen's ability to concentrate on the daily ups and downs of a market that also became hypervolatile anytime the Middle East blew up.

Not everyone attempting to pierce the protective barrier that Karen had erected was a journalistic leech looking for an exclusive interview. Some of the most persistent and annoying efforts to contact Elizabeth and console her came from her own family. All felt it was more than their self-appointed duty to do so. They saw in this crisis an opportunity to set aside their differences and renew their ties with a member of the family who had become the proverbial black sheep for leaving her husband, whom everyone adored, for a woman. Leading the pack whose mission was to bring Elizabeth back into the fold with some degree of respectability, and without compromising her stance over Elizabeth's separation from Ken, was Elizabeth's mother. While she could ignore her sister and other members of her extended family, Elizabeth found it impossible to deny her mother the opportunity that she insisted upon availing herself of. Not even Karen, using every ploy she had at her command, could deflect Abigail Stanton.

When the phone rang, Karen did not hesitate. In a flash, she threw down the magazine she had been leafing through and snatched up the remote receiver. By now she had learned to check the number on the small caller-ID window before pressing the talk button. If she didn't recognize the number, she didn't even bother answering.

When she saw that the caller was Abigail, Karen's heart sank. That woman always managed to irritate Karen no end by speaking to her with a chilly tone that would bring a hyena to tears. The conversations between Karen and Abigail never varied. As soon as Karen had clicked the on button of the remote, Abigail's haughty tone would blare out. "Karen, is my daughter there?" even though Abigail already knew she was.

Karen did her best to hide her ire by responding with the most sickly sweet reply that she could manage. "I'm not sure,

Mrs. Stanton. Do give me a moment and I will check." This allowed Karen to place the old bitch on hold while she put aside whatever it was that she had been doing, roused herself in a most leisurely manner, and wandered about the small apartment in search of Elizabeth.

At the moment Elizabeth was lying on her bed amid crumpled sheets, curled up and clutching an oversized stuffed panda bear Karen had given her shortly after they met. The only light in the room came from the flickering images of the television that sat tucked away in a corner wall unit. The sound was muted, as it was most of the time these days. Though both would have loved to do so, neither woman could escape their small yet supporting role in the current media event. So it behooved them to keep track of what was going on outside the fragile shell that they had erected about them. Their need to keep track of the latest events did not mean that they needed to put up with the nonstop babble, which talking heads on the twenty-four-hour news shows felt obliged to generate. Thus the silent images.

When Karen entered the room she immediately went to the side of the bed and eased herself down against Elizabeth's back. With a tenderness that expressed both her love and a deep caring, Karen laid her hand upon the distressed woman's shoulder as she glanced at the screen. Being run at the moment was footage of an earlier press conference with the now-familiar image of the mother of Specialist Four David Davis. Standing behind her as he pleaded unabashedly to a distant dictator was the Reverend Lucas Brown. The Reverend Brown was a prominent leader in the African-American community and son of a noted civil rights leader who always seemed to be at the right place at the right time, especially if there was a TV news camera around. He had both hands securely planted upon the shoulders of Davis's mother as he spoke to the reporters for her. As Karen studied the screen she could not but help wonder if the Reverend Brown were hanging on to the bereaved mother in an effort to console her or if his true intent was to aim the poor woman toward the camera that promised to present the most flattering image of him as he stood there, tending to a sister of color in her time of greatest need.

Distracted by her cynicism. Karen almost forgot that Abigail was on the line waiting to speak to her precious baby girl. With a gentle nudge Karen shook Elizabeth. "Liz, your mother is on the phone."

At first Elizabeth did not answer. When she did, her response had nothing to do with what Karen had said. "How do you think she does it?'

Unsure of whether Elizabeth was talking about the Davis woman or her own mother, Karen paused before venturing forth with a question that would cover all possibilities. "How so?"

Absorbed by her own disjointed and confused thoughts Elizabeth was slow to respond. When she finally did, her voice had a low, almost wistful tone to it. "How do you suppose she manages to go out in public like that and allow herself to express her fears or most heartfelt passions? How can any woman be so forthcoming, so open about her deepest, darkest fears, without being embarrassed?"

Karen was astute enough to appreciate that Elizabeth's internal plight went deeper than a simple inability to express sentiments. Since the crisis had erupted she had refused to share any of her feelings or thoughts with anyone, not even her chosen partner. This left Karen in a strange place, unsure of how best to deal with a situation that refused to go away. It was not that Elizabeth's response to the crisis was out of line with circumstances that she faced. If anything Karen was surprised that the woman was holding up as well as she was. Instead, Karen's apprehensions concerned other, more long-term issues. The broker found that she was unable to put aside a nagging fear that her relationship was being endangered by a man she had never met, a situation over which she had no control, and a culture that tolerated her, but gave her no firm ground upon which to stand.

As troubling as this was to her, with each passing day Karen found that another issue was beginning to rear its ugly head. Though she tried to suppress thoughts that she had initially discounted as being selfish and uncalled-for, Karen was far too involved in her own career not to wonder what all of this would cost her professionally. She had no doubt that her inability to keep pace with her most pressing business affairs, coupled with her now very public relationship with Elizabeth, would come back to haunt her. Even in the cosmopolitan and very liberal landscape of New York City, people expect those charged with handling their money and business affairs to be discreet and on the conservative side. Rock stars, writers, and artists could be flamboyant. Brokers could not. Though no one had said as much, Karen was beginning to wonder if her unflinching loyalty to Elizabeth would spell disaster for her further down the road when she was out of the limelight. She had already seen what happened when her superiors and influential clients came to the conclusion that an associate had become too much of a liability due to some personal indiscretions or unwanted notoriety.

Reaching up, Elizabeth took Karen's hand and squeezed it, breaking the momentary and very troubling train of thought that Karen had been entertaining. With a shake of her head, she cleared away those thoughts. "Abigail is on the phone, Liz."

Just the mention of her mother's name was enough to send Elizabeth's already depressed spirits even lower. "Tell her I'm not here."

"Hon, you know she'll know I'm lying. You haven't left this apartment in days, and thanks to the media, she knows it."

"Then tell her I'm asleep."

"She'll insist that I wake you."

Angered as much by Karen's insistence as she was by the prospect of having to endure her mother's effort to insert herself into her life again, Elizabeth pulled away from Karen, threw her feet over the side of the bed, and sat up. "Damn her! Damn you! And damn that Boy Scout I married!"

Miffed by Elizabeth's response, Karen stood up and glared at the back of her friend. She made no effort to hide the displeasure she felt as she pivoted about on her heels and stormed out of the room, calling out over her shoulder before she slammed the door, "Your mother is waiting."

In a final yet futile fit, Elizabeth drew her arms against her sides, clenched her fists and shook them as she repeatedly muttered, "Damn it! Damn it! Damn it!" Then, after a moment's pause she managed regain her composer. Using the same measured discipline she employed when dealing with an annoying client, she collected herself as she reached for the phone on the nightstand. By the time she had it to her ear Elizabeth was able to greet her mother with a sweet if insincere "Hello, Mom. How nice of you to call."

Damascus
07:10 LOCAL (03:10 ZULU)

For the first time since being brought to this place, Ken Aveno woke up of his own accord and not to the sound of his tormentors entering the barren cell to haul him away to the room where the enlisted men of RT Kilo were still being beaten before his eyes. At first this unexpected respite from the nonstop horrors to which he had been exposed worried Aveno. Picking himself up off the floor the young officer found himself wondering if he had missed something, if somehow during his brief if fitful sleep his sorry state of affairs had somehow changed. The first thing that came to mind was that their ordeal was over. Though he had absolutely nothing to base this supposition upon, Aveno found himself becoming excited by the notion that the Syrians had given in to diplomatic pressures and in preparation for their release had ceased their relentless torture.

As often happens to prisoners who have been beaten and deprived of even the most basic human needs such as food, water, and sleep, Aveno's distraught mind was unable to linger upon this bright ray of hope for very long. In a flash, a sound from outside his cell swept away his budding optimism and yanked him back to the harsh reality of his circumstances. In place of elation, fear once more gripped him. No longer able to muster the determination needed to resist this ever-present foe, Aveno instinctively drew away from the door as he vainly sought refuge in the corner of his dank, cold cell.

That a professional soldier of his caliber could be reduced to such a state by mere sounds no longer bothered him. Colored berets, catchy mottoes, and the best training in the world made a difference, but could not change the simple fact that Ken Aveno and the other survivors of RT Kilo were flesh and blood. Once the thin veneer is worn away, there is nothing left to protect the mind and body. Even worse than the actual punishment itself was the mind's ability to dwell upon the unknown, to seize upon every unexpected action, every new sound, and turn it into a threat. At times like this, a soldier need something more than simple courage to keep going, something that Aveno no longer had.

With each passing second the noise on the other side of the door drew nearer and became more distinct, causing Aveno to strain with all his might to press himself deeper into the corner of his cell. In the midst of this futile effort to escape this unseen menace, he made no effort to fight the panic that had taken hold. Like a wounded animal, he continued to push and press himself into a corner that would not yield. The pride in his past achievements and the rank that he had once counted on to sustain him during times of crisis were gone. Just like the approaching sound on the other side of the door, Aveno could not escape the fact that he had thrown it away again and again each and every time a member of RT Kilo was tortured in his presence and his only conscious thought was to silently thank God again and again that he was not the one being beaten.

CHAPTER EIGHTEEN

While his lieutenant was giving way to his fears on the floor above him, Salvador Mendez was busy exploring a world that he was seeing for the first time. It did not matter to him that the Syrian guards took every opportunity they could to inflict as much pain upon him as they could while removing his blindfold and manacles. Even if this were but a precursor to a new and even more horrific form of punishment the brief respite from them was a cause of celebration.

Yet for every change to the good there was a downside. After days of having his hands tightly secured behind his back by manacles, Mendez found that his arms were for the moment useless. Even worse, the sudden release of pressure at his wrists unleashed a wave of pain that the numbness of his arms had somehow managed to mask while bound. Still, this sorry state of affairs did little to dampen a feeling boarding on euphoria that the New York City native felt. With arms hanging limply at his side, Mendez wandered about the small cell exploring every nook and cranny. This didn't take very long for it wasn't much of a cell. A person standing in the middle of the floor slowly turning his head could lay his eyes on every square inch of the cell in a matter of seconds. That insignificant fact did not bother Mendez. To him, his newly reacquired sight was a precious gift to be enjoyed lest he be deprived of it again.

This last thought triggered another, more ominous one. If the Syrians had removed the blindfold and handcuffs, Mendez reasoned they could easily put them back on again. This break from those constraints might be temporary. Alternating periods of total restraint interrupted by random interludes free of them might be all that it took to shatter his already fragile spirit and push him ever closer to a total breakdown. That wouldn't have very far to go, he sadly concluded. Even the trivial effort needed to shuffle about the small six-by-ten-foot cell proved exhausting. Mendez lowered his head and shook it. "Damn, boy," he muttered. "You're gonna have to get in shape if you expect to escape from this hole."

The idea of escaping, of course, was fanciful. Even if he did manage to somehow find a way out of the cell and the building that housed it, Mendez appreciated the fact that he would be adrift in a strange and hostile land. There would be no friendly faces to provide him sanctuary and no one to appeal to for aid. And then there was the desert. Mendez was hard-pressed to decide what was more threatening; an enraged populace capable of tearing him apart or the trackless wasteland that would siphon away his lifeblood in a matter of days. Stopping in midstride, he looked about once more. For better or worse, no matter what the Syrians had in mind he had no choice but to roll with the punches, both literally and figuratively.

This realization and a fresh appraisal of his cell brought a strange smile to the young Puerto Rican's bruised and bloodied face. He had joined the army to escape living among a hostile populace and in substandard housing, only to wind up here, being held by a hostile populace in a substandard cell. *Well,* he mused as he began another circuit of his cell, *I always knew God has a quirky sense of humor.*

Specialist Four Dee Dee Davis did little with his newfound freedom. He simply sat against the wall where the Syrians had left him after removing his constraints. He was still there when the sound of the bolt on the other side of the door sliding open roused him from the stupor into which he had drifted. If he'd had the strength to do so he would have crawled into a corner even though doing so would have been futile. There was no place for him to escape to, nothing to hide behind in the barren cell. Still, the urge to do something was overpowering.

With a growing sense of alarm Davis stared at the door. Was it time for his next beating? Had they decided that he had had enough freedom for one day and were coming back to put the handcuffs back on? Or were they here to visit some new form of punishment upon him? These questions and others, each equally scary and distasteful, raced through Davis's mind as the door began to swing open.

To his amazement no one entered the cell. Instead, when there was just enough room to do so a hand appeared and set a bowl down on the floor. The hand quickly pulled away just before the door slammed shut. Not knowing what to make of this Davis stayed where he was for a moment, watching and listening as the bolt on the other side was slammed home. Even when the sound of footfalls on the other side appeared to move down the corridor he did nothing. Only when he could no longer hear anyone out- side his cell did his curiosity finally get the better of him.

His full attention now turned to the bowl that had been left behind. He stared at it for several minutes as if expecting it to do something. Could it be food of some sort? Not trusting his sight he tilted his head back, turned his nose toward the unexpected gift, and tried to sniff the air. This effort yielded little in the way of useful information since his nose had been broken at least once and was now thoroughly plugged up with dried blood and mucus. Seeing no other alternative, Davis collected what little strength he had left and prepared to venture across the cell to investigate.

Doing this turned out to be both difficult and painful. Though it had been more than an hour since his arms had been unbound, they were still of little use to him. The only thing he could feel in them was pain from inflamed joints at the shoulders and elbows as well as a terrible burning sensation that radiated up his arm from hands that felt as if they were swollen to twice their natural size. And his legs were almost as unresponsive. His first effort to stand up shortly after the Syrians had removed his restrains had ended disastrously. Unwilling to make that mistake again, Davis opted to scoot along the floor on his bottom by throwing his feet out before him, planting them firmly upon the floor, and then using what strength he had in his legs to haul his buttocks up to where his feet were anchored. Each time he drew closer to the bowl and before he threw his feet out again in order to repeat this process, Davis paused to study it. Inching along in this manner, it took him several minutes to get close enough to see that there was something in it that looked like a soup or stew. The lack of steam rising from the surface of the broth didn't bother him. As a soldier he was used to cold meals. He was also very familiar with the pangs that hunger produces when too many meals had been missed. What he wasn't practiced in was moving about without full use of his legs.

When he was in the process of making his final lurching move, it occurred to Davis that his limp arms and swollen hands would be useless to him when he reached his goal. He would be unable to pick up the bowl. Startled for a moment by this sudden reevaluation, the specialist four paused and considered his dilemma. He could, he reasoned, wait where he was for a few minutes in the hope that enough strength would return to his arms to permit him to hold the bowl and eat like a normal human being. But waiting could be dangerous. What if the Syrians returned while he was doing so and took the uneaten food away? Would they pay any attention to his pleas and leave it? Perhaps they would see his plight, take mercy on him, and offer to feed him?

That was unlikely. As far as he knew the word *mercy* wasn't in their vocabulary. Somehow he would have to find a way to eat without using his hands.

As he was pondering how to go about eating, a memory popped into his mind. As clearly as if it had just happened, Davis recalled sitting at the kitchen table as a child next to his baby brother. The two were eating lunch when his brother dropped his spoon on the floor. Unable to reach over and retrieve the lost utensil, Davis watched as his brother smiled and barked like the family dog before lowering his head to the bowl on the tray before him. Making no effort to be neat or quiet, the child of three began to lap up the stew. Wondering if this made any difference in the enjoyment of the meal, Davis had laid his own spoon aside and copied his brother. Both boys were thoroughly enjoying this experiment when their mother appeared. As she so often did when they were violating one of her rules, she shrieked their full names in a high-pitched voice that only mothers can manage, bringing their animalistic feeding frenzy to an end and announcing to the world that a beating was about to begin.

For the first time in days Davis managed to smile as he thanked the Lord that his mother wasn't there to witness what he was about to do. "Mama," he said as he pulled himself to within easy reach of the bowl, "I do hope you forgive me for this, but a man's gotta do what a man's gotta do." With that he leaned forward, lowered his head as far as he could, and stuck his tongue out until it made contact with the oily broth before him.

Sergeant First Class Kannen greeted each new display of "kindness" by his captors with growing suspicion. He was quick to appreciate that these acts foreshadowed something more than a simple change in tactics. Having studied their culture and history, the American NCO knew that the Syrians would not abandon a line of attack without good reason. While there was the possibility that whatever they were trying to achieve by beating him had been accomplished by breaking another member of the team, Kannen discounted that notion. Information gleaned from a prisoner under duress is like a piece of a jigsaw puzzle. With the exception of their team commander and perhaps the XO, no one man had all the pieces. Even when they managed to crack a key individual, professional interrogation teams used bits of information gleaned from one person to extract additional information from others or to confirm the validity of data they already had. The American NCO was also placing a great deal of faith in his teammates. As vicious and unnerving as his experience had been thus far, Kannen doubted that any member of the team had broken or given the bastards anything of value. Eventually someone would break, though. Perhaps they all would. So even while he was enjoying his newfound freedom from being constrained and savoring every morsel of food offered, Kannen began to prepare himself mentally for the next torment the Syrians were waiting to spring upon him.

The Syrians didn't give him long to ponder this question. Not long after they had deposited a bowl of watery soup in his cell, they were back. Having already been caught offguard twice during their previous visits, Kannen managed to pick himself up from the floor and shuffle over to one of the walls of his cell. From there he figured he would be able to see out into the corridor once the door was open.

Fortified by the skimpy meal he had wolfed down in minutes and buoyed by the resurgence of hope that it fostered, Kannen found that he was much calmer now as he watched the door swing open. His restored vision added an entirely new dimension to an experience that he had endured many times before. First there was the sound of the bolt being slid through its housing with a single, quick motion so that the slapping of metal on metal at the end of its run sounded like the bolt of a rifle being jerked back. Next, the door groaned as it was swung open. This opening was executed with a slow and measured pace to maximize the chilling effect that emanated from the grinding of its unlubricated metal hinges. There always was a slight pause between the time the door was fully open, and the rhythmic tromping of rubber-soled boots as they hit the cold concrete floor of the cell.

The ability to watch all of this for the first time was strange. Kannen's first reaction, as soon as the door was open wide enough to permit him a good look at his captors, was amazement. They were not the massive brutes that his imagination had pictured them to be when all it had to go on was the sounds they made while they pummeled him. Instead, the pair of Syrians who entered the cell and confronted Kannen were anything but intimidating. Everything about them had an air of shabbiness, from the hint of fading in their unpressed uniforms to the dark stubble that indicated they did not bother to shave on a regular basis. Their boots, the age-old mark of how well disciplined a soldier is, betrayed a total lack of care. Even their mannerisms came as something of a shock to him. Their placid expressions and stooped frames reminded him of day laborers reluctantly shuffling off to work in the morning.

The effect of all of this on Kannen was quite unexpected. On one hand he felt disappointed that the people who had been tormenting him were not burly fiends decked out in crisp Nazi-style uniforms. Rather than being the best of the best, Kannen's first impression was that these people were nothing more than slugs, lowly miscreants who had been assigned this duty because they couldn't hack it in a line unit. This evaluation quickly led to anger. *How in God's name,* he wondered as he watched the Syrian guards file into the cell and approach him, *did I allow myself to be frightened by these bozos?*

This question was answered almost immediately when a third guard bearing the flashings of an NCO upon his rumpled uniform entered the cell, stepped up to Kannen, and began screaming. Kannen had no idea what the short sergeant was yelling about. But the soldiers belonging to his detail did. In a flash, they leaped to either side of the American. In unison each grabbed an arm, lifted Kannen off his feet, and slammed him against the wall. Unprepared for this sudden assault, Kannen's head hit the wall, scrambling his thoughts. Before he had an opportunity to sort himself out, the Syrians spun Kannen about and pinned him up against the wall. Unable to do anything to protect himself or resist, Kannen remained motionless as their NCO pulled his arms behind his back, and slapped a pair of handcuffs on Kannen's wrists.

In an instant, the pain of the manacles cutting into his raw skin shot through him. Blinded by this pain he hardly noticed that the pair holding him had spun him around yet again until they faced the door before moving though it with great alacrity and down the corridor.

All of this occurred with such stunning suddenness that Kannen found he was having difficulty keeping up. The bump on his head only added to his inability to concentrate on what was going on around him. As with a passenger on a fast-moving train, the blurred images of what lay to his left and right whizzed by. The only thought that he managed to put together was that he had misjudged his captors. Whatever they lacked by way of appearance, they more than made up for in enthusiasm and efficiency once they had been properly motivated. He also had a vague sense that he would soon have an answer to his question as to what sort of depredations they had in store for him next as they reached their destination.

The room the Syrians whisked Kannen into was both well lit and quite clean in comparison to what he had managed to see of the rest of the prison. His eyes were immediately drawn to the right where he saw a simple, straight-back chair set against a wall that looked as though it had been freshly whitewashed. A pair of floodlights stood several feet back and away from the white wall. Both were angled so that their beams fell on the chair. Without pausing, the Syrians dragged Kannen over to the chair, twisted him aroud, and shoved him down onto it with more force than was necessary.

Though still somewhat dazed, Kannen used the little time he had to look around as his escorts left the room and the interrogation team stepped forward to take over. Having only felt the tools that his interrogators had used, the American NCO was anxious to see what the damned things looked like. To his surprise, rather than spying a table cluttered with medieval torture devices, he saw a Syrian soldier fussing with a modern video camera set upon a dolly. In an instant Kannen's mind cleared as he realized what this was all about. The Syrians were going to use him to embarrass the United States employing the same techniques that the North Koreans and Vietnamese communists had pioneered decades before.

With the object of this little excursion now established, Kannen knew what he had to do. Regardless of the cost he would have to do whatever he could to demonstrate that though he was bloodied, he was not broken. An unmistakable display of defiance was what he would have to present to the camera. Even if all he could use was his expression or the look in his eyes, Kannen was hell-bent on making a statement that even the densest TV commentator back in the United States could not miss.

As if he had read the American's mind, a Syrian colonel who had been standing in the shadows behind the floodlights stepped forward until he stood before Kannen. Using the King's English, the colonel briefed Kannen on what he expected. "Sergeant First Class Allen Kannen, once all is ready you will look straight into the lens of the camera and give your name, your rank, the branch of service to which you belong, and your hometown. Nothing more. These are things which we already know so there will be no shame in presenting them to us here in this forum. I am not going to ask you to betray any military secrets or read any sort of statement. Is that clear?"

Kannen looked up at the Syrian colonel. The urge to tell him to piss off was all but overpowering. But Kannen managed to hold his tongue. He figured he had but one chance to get it right. It would be best if he saved that opportunity for a time when it would be more meaningful. Though he had little doubt that whatever he did or said would ultimately be edited out and never see the light of day, the American NCO was determined to communicate as best he could his determination to stay true to his code of conduct and his comrades.

After waiting several seconds for some sort of response but receiving none, the Syrian colonel smiled. "I am not disappointed. I rather expected this." Without breaking eye contact, the Syrian raised his right hand and snapped his fingers.

On cue a pair of guards who had been waiting in the corridor outside hauled a limp body into the room and across the floor. With a great deal of effort they maneuvered their burden until they could place it on another straight-backed chair sitting against the wall opposite Kannen. Squinting in an effort to see past the glare of the floodlights, he managed to focus on the figure in the chair. Though the blindfold covered most of the face, and the head hung down until the chin almost rested on his chest, there was no mistaking that the bloodied and beaten person seated across from him was his commanding officer, Captain Burman. It was the first time Kannen had seen Burman since they'd been loaded on separate trucks to be brought to Damascus.

Their duty done, the pair who had hauled Burman into the room left. Once they were gone a junior officer next came up to Burman. With a great deal more precision than any of his subordinates had shown, the Syrian officer drew his pistol, jerked the slide back, and released it. With a round clearly chambered, the junior officer laid the muzzle of its barrel against Burman's head.

When he was satisfied that all was set, the Syrian colonel looked back at Kannen. "I hope I do not have to explain to you what will happen if you elect not to cooperate with my simple demands and instead attempt to play the hero in front of the camera."

Soldiers die in battle. Kannen understood that cruel yet simple premise. Death was a natural and inescapable part of a profession whose basic object has always been to destroy one's enemy as quickly and as efficiently as possible. This, however, was not battle, at least not the sort of battle that he was prepared to engage in. If Burman had died during the melee back at the village it would have been tragic but acceptable to Kannen. To have Burman die as a direct result of something he did or failed to do was something else. Even if he could manage to rationalize his defiance by buying in to the premise that he, Burman, and all the Kilo members in the cellblock were more than likely dead men, Kannen knew that he could not allow himself to be the agent of a teammate's death. RT Kilo had started out as a team and had, as best he could tell, remained one through it all. He was not about to change that now by becoming the agent of his CO's murder, even if this meant compromising his personal honor. At least, he told himself as he prepared to endure the unendurable, he'd take the responsibility of being the first one to cooperate. Perhaps the people back home would understand. Perhaps they would show him the sort of mercy that his captors were incapable of.

Unable to hold back his rage but still very much in control, Kannen looked away from Burman's pathetic figure and back at the Syrian colonel. "You fucking bastard."

The colonel smiled. "I will take that as your consent to my simple request. Good." Turning, the Syrian colonel looked over to where the cameraman stood ready. With a snap of his fingers the Syrian technician rolled the device into place and prepared to start filming as the colonel stepped out of the line of sight so that Kannen would have an unobstructed view of his captain throughout the entire session.

Fort Irwin, California
04:58 LOCAL (11:58 ZULU)

On the ground the distance from the airfield at Bicycle Lake to the mock-up of the Syrian airfield in the northern portion of Fort Irwin was a little over fifteen kilometers. It was where all major live-fire training was conducted. It was also the least accessible portion of the training facility, connected to the outside world by roads that would have made a goat homesick. Since the series of training exercises being run by the Rangers would eventually culminate in full-scale live-fire rehearsals, this choice of location for the mock-up, officially designated Objective Kansas, was unpopular. After seeing it for the first time following a truck ride that entailed an overland trek approaching biblical proportions, the Rangers charged with securing Kansas rechristened it Dust Bowl International, or DBI for short.

By air the journey took no time at all. In fact, the hop from Bicycle Lake to Kansas was so quick that Air Force transports sometimes passed over Objective Kansas during takeoff. When the training to seize Kansas reached the point where the airborne portion of the operation was included, most of the time spent aloft was needed to reach altitude, come about, and form up for the drop. During these exercises, the Rangers who were crowded into the cargo bays of the C-130s had very little time to mentally gear themselves up for the jump. As exciting as that experience can be, it was only the prelude to a tactical exercise that every man in the 3rd of the 75th suspected would be part of an effort to rescue their fellow soldiers in Syria.

On this night the battalion sergeant major spent his time during the brief interlude between the time he settled into their nylon jump seats and the order to stand up studying his commanding officer. Seated across from Lieutenant Colonel Harry Shaddock, Sergeant Major John Harris was struck by the tight, almost strained expression his colonel wore. The easygoing, almost jovial demeanor that Shack normally sported just prior to a jump was totally absent. Instead of leaning forward and kibitzing with every enlisted men who could hear him above the roar of the transport's engines, the colonel was slumped down low in his seat. Lost in his own thoughts, he remained silent throughout the entire flight with his arms folded tightly against his chest over the reserve parachute that regulations required but which their chosen altitude of exit rendered useless.

Now, Harris was no fool. He was well aware of what was at stake. He understood the pressure that his commanding officer, the staff, and all the company commanders within the battalion were under. When Shaddock was not out in the field overseeing a tactical training exercise he was in the office poring over estimates generated by his staff or locked away in highly classified briefings or on the phone with any number of higher-ranking officers from every major command and agency that had or thought they had a role in Fanfare, the name given to the operation that was supposed to free the Green Berets being held in Syria. That the battalion was being rushed to prepare itself for its role in Fanfare went without saying. This sort of thing was not at all unusual for the 3rd of the 75th. It was the nature of the beast for a unit like the 3rd of the 75th. They were expected to train flat out month after month in order to maintain peak combat readiness. Then, when something like Fanfare came their way, they were required to redouble their efforts. Those who could not maintain that sort of pace either never got on to the merry-go-round in the first place or were quickly thrown off either by the staggering tempo or by an uncompromising commanding officer like Harry Shaddock.

Having served with the colonel in this assignment and several others during the course of his long military career, Harris knew that Shaddock's behavior as of late was not due to the long hours he was putting in. Like most of the men he surrounded himself with, Shaddock thrived in this sort of atmosphere. Nor had Harris been able to detect even a hint that his commanding officer had any reservations about the role his battalion would play in Fanfare. While Shaddock would like to see some changes to the manner in which his battalion was being employed, he had stated on numerous occasions to both his superiors and the men in his command that once they were given the word, the 3rd of the 75th would be ready to execute their assigned tasks.

It was this unexplained contradiction in his commanding officer's attitude that concerned Harris. In public Shaddock continued to be as unflappable and hard charging as ever. Yet at moments like this it was clear to the sergeant major that the man he had grown to admire and into whose hands he placed his life was holding something back. Since Shaddock was the commanding officer and therefore responsible for everything that his unit did or failed to do, Harris figured that the colonel would, in his own time, sort out whatever it was that was responsible for his current mood. Until then the best Harris figured he could do was to fend off all the trivial matters that often consume so much of a commanding officer's time, and when the occasion afforded itself, do what he could to lighten the mood.

With this in mind he slid his booted foot across the floor of the transport and tapped the toe of his colonel's boot. When Shaddock opened his eyes and looked over at Harris the sergeant major shouted across the narrow space between them in order to be heard over the transport's engines. "I was reading the XO's copy of the *Armed Forces Journal* last night. It contained its annual article on how the day of large-scale airborne operations is over. It seems we're an anachronism and what we're about to do is not only militarily inadvisable but potentially dangerous."

Despite the dark thoughts that were troubling him, Shaddock laughed. "Do me a favor, Sergeant Major, and don't let the S-Three see it. I think he'll faint if he hears someone even hinted that there's the chance that there's another change to his plan in the offing."

Having achieved an opening, Harris decided to take an opportunity to do a bit of prying. "Sir, Major Montoya wouldn't be happy unless he was running around threatening to slit his wrists." Then, pausing, Harris lowered his voice. "That's to be expected. What's worrying me is you."

In a manner akin to Lord Nelson's habit of turning his blind eye to read the signals from the fleet flagship, Shaddock tended to pretend not to hear statements that he had no intention of responding to. Turning his head slightly to the side, Shaddock raised one hand and cupped it over his right ear, which everyone in the battalion knew was partially deaf. Taking the hint, Harris sighed. With a wave, he indicated that his point was unimportant.

Satisfied that he had successfully fended off the sergeant major's effort to distract him, Shaddock returned to his own troubling concerns. His thoughts had nothing to do with the exercise that his unit was about to participate in. He wasn't even worried about the plan that his operations officer had ginned up. Nor was he in any doubt that his company commanders, despite a few persistent glitches, would eventually get it right. What was troubling the commanding officer of one of the nation's most highly skilled combat commands was the role his unit was to play in freeing the members of RT Kilo who were still in Syrian hands. Having made his mark in the Army by being a straight shooter regardless of the professional risk that such an attitude entailed in the modern American military, Shaddock found it all but impossible to maintain his enthusiasm for Fanfare. In the next fifteen minutes his entire unit would be deposited over Objective Kansas. Regardless of the injuries that were suffered during the drop, and there always were on operations such as this, each of his four companies had but twenty minutes to carry out their assigned tasks and prepare the simulated airfield to receive the fixed-wing transports that would be used to extract RT Kilo and the members of Delta, the men who had the honor of liberating the Green Berets.

Once this tactical exercise was completed, each and every member of the 3rd of the 75th would undergo a series of debriefings and after-action reports during which every failure and mishap would be discussed in detail. When these were concluded, Shaddock would gather in his company commanders and key staff officer for an after-action review conducted by Fort Irwin's notorious cadre. They would review and discuss every shortcoming and misstep that had occurred during the excerise, no matter how minute.

Throughout this long and sometimes painful ordeal Shaddock would be unable to reveal to his most trusted subordinates the one piece of information that mattered the most. All their training, all their efforts, all their suffering and hardships here at Irwin would be for naught. Fanfare would never take place. Instead of being the centerpiece of the military option to free RT Kilo, it was the deception plan. The colonel of Rangers had not been briefed as to whom this deception plan was aimed at. For all he knew, the objective of Fanfare was to create an illusion for the American media that the American military was actually preparing to do something. The best he could hope for was that it was a threat designed to provide the president's team of negotiators some leverage. Regardless of the targeted audience, Shaddock found his part in this stage play to be both distasteful and disheartening. Eventually his men would learn that their endeavors during the train-up for Fanfare had been for nothing. And if there is one thing that will crush a soldier's morale with unerring certainty, it is revealing to him that his efforts and sacrifices had been, from his point of view, little more than a waste of his time. While it might have been selfish, Lieutenant Colonel Harry Shaddock could not help but become angry that his last major operation as the commander of the 3rd of the 75th would be one that would leave a bad taste in everyone's mouth for years to come.

That Fanfare was not meant to be a serious operation was clear to anyone who took the time to study the manner in which the 3rd of the 75th were going about their affairs, especially if anyone bothered to look at the way the mock-up of Objective

Kansas was laid out. Every effort was made to replicate the Syrian military airfield that was Objective Kansas. Yet nothing was done to disguise this from space-based surveillance platforms belonging to nations that were less than friendly to the United States. Satellites, both friend and foe, passed over Fort Irwin on a daily basis. So was the open secret that both Russia and communist China provided the regime in Syria with intelligence that they themselves could not gather. It did not require a genius to figure out that a unit like the 3rd of the 75th, training in a desert environment on a site that suddenly appeared overnight, was getting ready for something. Not even the Syrians could ignore why Dust Bowl International had been built and what the purpose of the exercise meant.

Having no way of knowing what success foreign intelligence agencies were having at sorting all this out, and determined to do his best to play his part no matter how distasteful it was to do so, Shaddock did as he had done since his first day at the Citadel. He accepted the lay of the land and soldiered on as well as he could. With luck his soldiers would come to appreciate that this nut roll he was putting them through did, in some small way, play a part in the freeing of RT Kilo.

The short flight reminded Second Lieutenant Peter Quinn of the five jumps he had made at Fryer Field in Alabama while going through jump school between his third- and second-class year at the academy. But that was about the only similarity that he could recall between that experience and this one. At Benning he had been nothing more than one trainee sandwiched in with fellow cadets together with other novices going through their initiation. Nothing they carried on those occasions save the parachutes was real. All he had to do then was manage to screw up sufficient nerve to waddle up to the door and on command fling his five-foot-ten-inch frame out the door. Once he had succeeded in accomplishing those feats it was, quite literally, all downhill.

Now, however, the jump was merely the beginning. As the platoon leader of Third Platoon, Company A, Quinn's real test came once he was on the ground. There would be no time for him to collect himself or reflect upon the strange mixture of exhilaration and sheer terror that paratroopers experience between the time they bomb out of the transport and feel the tug of the harness and snap of suspension lines going taut. For an officer the brief interlude while under canopy during a jump tied to a tactical exercise would be the last precious moments of peace he would be able to enjoy. After that, chaos and confusion would be the order of the day.

On this particular night that time was substantially shorter than usual. Rather than going out at 1,250 feet as was customary during training jumps, they were exiting at 500 feet. At that altitude a man had but seconds to prepare himself for impact with the ground once his canopy was fully deployed. That is, provided the canopy did function as it was supposed to. If there was a failure of any type, whether it was a simple suspension line looped over the canopy or a rare, yet not-unheard-of total malfunction, the paratrooper would have next to no time to sort out the nature of the problem and take corrective action. In the short time he had been with the 3rd of the 75th Quinn had yet to see one of those. But even the most routine of training jumps under ideal conditions produced a fair number of hard landings and mishaps.

Stepping out the door and into the stunning blast of wind paratroopers liked to call "the Hawk," the twenty-two-year-old platoon leader tried hard not to think about what could go wrong. "Count, count, count," he muttered just under his breath as his body was thrown away from the aircraft by the blast of its engines. "One thousand one, one thousand two, one thousand three," he howled without having to concern himself with being heard. In midcount, before he was able to finish "one thousand five," the last of the suspension lines cleared the deployment bag and snapped tight, jerking his heavily laden body and bringing his count to an abrupt end.

For a moment Quinn found himself engulfed by the strange silence that many jumpers experience about the time that their chute finishes its deployment sequence. Normally this tranquil experience lasts until a moment or two before contact is made with the ground. But not this evening. As if on cue the rattle of small-arms fire and the rip of machine guns shattered the stillness that Quinn had fallen into.

Without bothering to inspect his canopy, the young platoon leader looked down through the gap between his feet in an effort to see if he could tell where that fire was coming from. Not seeing anything even remotely threatening directly under him, Quinn lifted his chin and slowly scanned the horizon. Off to his right, in the area where plywood sheds had been thrown up to simulate aircraft revetments he caught sight of muzzle flashes twinkling between the structures. Since that portion of Kansas belonged to Bravo Company, Quinn didn't bother to make any sort of assessment of the situation. Instead, he continued to turn his head, searching the horizon for any trouble spots closer to him.

He was just about to heave a great sigh of relief that there didn't seem to be any other hostile activity on the ground when it dawned on him that he was about to—

His feet were still spread apart when the balls of his combat boots kissed the unyielding sun-baked surface of the desert. Obeying the law of gravity to the letter, Quinn flopped over into a heap with all the grace of a sack of potatoes hitting the pavement after being tossed out of a moving truck. The impact was so hard it was almost audible. At least, that's the way Quinn imagined it as he tumbled and rolled about on the ground. Rattled by this unexpected calamity and dazed by the force of impact, he wasn't quite sure what he should do, if anything. In the end he allowed the last of his momentum to dissipate without making any effort to interference. When he finally did stop rolling about, Quinn found himself faceup and spread-eagled on the ground. With his equipment bag strapped to his front and lying upon his midsection, the breathless and very bruised second lieutenant decided that this might be a good time to pause a moment or two while he collected himself and took a complete inventory of his anatomy.

He was still lying there, stunned by the impact but very conscious of the sound of gunfire in the distance and the scurrying of fellow Rangers nearby when a dark figure suddenly appeared towering above him. "You okay, LT?"

Recognizing the voice as that of his platoon sergeant, Quinn did his best to be as nonchalant as his pathetic situation would permit. "Oh, I'm fine, Sergeant Smart. I'm just assessing the situation."

The looming figure didn't move. "Sir, you want maybe I have one of the medics come over here and help you with that assessment?"

For the first time since landing Quinn moved his head. "No, I don't think that will be necessary. How about you hustle on over to the rally point and gather up the lads. I'll be right behind you."

Going on nothing more than the clarity with which his platoon leader spoke, Sergeant First Class Keith Smart decided that there was nothing that he needed to do here. Doing his best to suppress the grin that he felt coming on, Smart nodded. "Roger that, LT." With that, he mentally changed gears as he took charge of the platoon until such time as his lieutenant felt up to the task. With a voice that needed no artificial amplification, Smart began the process of gathering in his people. "Third Platoon, rally on me, *NOW!*"

Slowly Quinn began the painful process of picking himself up off the ground, shedding his parachute, and gathering his gear. Feeling more like a refugee from an old age home than the member of an elite unit, the badly shaken leader of the Third Platoon made his way over to where his senior NCO was preparing to dispatch each of the squads to their assigned positions. When Sergeant Smart saw Quinn amble up to where he and the three squad leaders were, he rose off his knee and turned to his lieutenant. "Sir, do you have any further instructions for the platoon?"

Embarrassed by his less-than-stellar performance up to this point and in no mood to waste his time or that of his NCO's, Quinn simply made the sign of the cross and solemnly announced, "Go forth and prosper, my children."

Having expected anything but this, everyone who heard Quinn's pronouncement chuckled. Then, without further hesitation Smart barked out his final instructions to the squad leaders to get moving. "We have a schedule to meet, people. Let's see some assholes and elbows."

For the first time since they had begun running this version of the operation to seize Objective Kansas, Captain David Carter was the first company commander to report in that all of his platoons were in place and set. Perhaps, he thought as he looked about the area through his night-vision goggles, the colonel would back off some and find a new whipping boy. Carter was tired of being the object of what he thought was more than his fair share of the ass chewing that his battalion commander had suddenly become so fond of giving. That most of them were justified didn't matter to the commanding officer of Alpha Company. He was getting tired of being the recipient of them.

This annoying fact was still rattling about in his head when the beating of helicopter blades coming from the southwest caught his attention. Glancing over in that direction, he wondered what they were doing over there. According to the plan the UH-60s belonging to Task Force 160 carrying both Delta and RT Kilo were supposed to make their approach into Kansas from the east. Ignoring the small-arms fire that continued to sputter and pop over in Bravo Company's area, Carter hesitated for a moment as he tried hard to imagine why there had been such a radical change in plan. When a sudden flurry of small-arms fire erupted, it dawned upon him that perhaps Task Force 160, better known as the Night Stalkers, had also run into some unexpected trouble. Perhaps their unexpected alteration of the plan was a wrinkle in this exercise that someone had cranked in to test the flexibility and responsiveness of the leadership of 3rd of the 75th.

With this in mind and eager to do everything he could to redeem himself in the eyes of his commanding officer, Captain Carter instructed his RTO to pass on the order to Lieutenant Quinn and Third Platoon to illuminate the spot where the rescue helicopters were to touch down. Once they were on the ground Quinn's platoon had the responsibility of protecting the members of Delta and the survivors of RT Kilo until they were all safely aboard the Air Force transports. When that was accomplished Quinn's people would follow them into the aircraft.

The fact that the transports weren't on the ground yet didn't bother Cater. Like the change to Task Force 160's approach, he figured that this was just another kink that someone had thrown into that evening's rehearsal to see how his company would react. It was only when the trio of helicopters overflew the area cordoned off by Third Platoon and instead landed over where Colonel Shaddock had set up his battalion command post that Carter began to wonder if something more sinister was amiss.

The landing of the helicopters some two hundred meters away from the spot his people had marked caught both Second Lieutenant Quinn and SFC Keith Smart off guard. For a moment they watched as troops poured out of the aircraft and deployed. Finally, Quinn asked the question that both of them had on their minds. "Now, why did they go over there?"

Sensing that something was not right, Smart flipped his night-vision goggles down and hit the on switch. He didn't need much time to confirm what he already suspected. "LT, those are not UH-60s over there. And I'm pretty sure the personnel on the ground aren't from Delta."

In an instant Quinn understood the situation. Without hesitation he began to bark orders. "Sergeant Smart, alert the Second

Squad to be prepared to engage the intruders. Tell them when they do to take care to mark their targets, otherwise they'll hit the battalion command group which is just on the other side of the OPFOR's LZ. Then hustle on over to First Squad. Pull them out of line and swing around to the right of the OPFOR LZ. Once I make my report to the old man I'll take the Third and go left. Maybe we can box them in before they scatter."

With nothing more than a crisp "Wilco," Smart was gone. Anticipating his platoon leader's next command, Specialist Four William Hoyt reached over and held the hand mike of the tactical radio he had strapped to his back. "Sir, the company net."

Quinn seize the mike and mashed down the push to talk button with more force than necessary. "Red Six, Red Six, this is Red Three Six, spot report, over."

Over the receiver, Quinn heard the muted response. "This is Red Six Alpha, send it, over."

"This is Red Three Six. Three enemy helicopters with an undetermined number of troops have landed vicinity of Bull Dog Six. I say again, three enemy helicopters with an undetermined number of troops have landed vicinity of Bull Dog Six. I am redeploying to contain and engage them now."

Upon hearing Quinn's report, Captain Carter became alarmed. Reaching over several of the soldiers who had made up his small command group, Carter grabbed the hand mike out of his RTO's hands. "Three Six, Three Six, this is Red Six actual. Belay that maneuver. Those people over there are Eagle Flight with the packages." Fearing that Quinn's precipitous move might unleash confusion and lead to friendly fire, Carter continued. "You are to ignore those people over there for now and resume your assigned positions. I'll contact Bull Dog Six and sort this out with him. Acknowledge, over."

Peter Quinn knew he had heard his commanding officer correctly, just as he had no doubt in his mind that there was simply no way that the intruders running around just outside his perime-

ter belonged to Task Force 160 and Delta, code named Eagle
Flight. The problem that he faced was what to do. He could do as
his commander ordered and go against his own assessment of the
situation, one which he was positive was correct. Or he could
ignore his captain and continue to maneuver his platoon in an
effort to contain this new threat. It was one of those awful conun-
drums that military men often find themselves confronted with.
In order to follow his orders to a T he'd have to disregard the tactical reality that faced him. But to respond to the new situation
required him to either enter into a debate with his commanding
officer via radio or flat-out defy a lawful order and do what he
thought best, consequences be damned.

For Peter Quinn the choice was a real no-brainer. Tossing the
hand mike back to his RTO, he winked. "When the old man calls
back, tell him . . ."

Hoyt's toothy white smile shone like a beacon. "I know, I
know. You're indisposed."

Quinn nodded. "Yeah, something like that," he said, before
unslinging his rifle from his shoulder and taking off as fast as his
bruised little body permitted.

Lieutenant Colonel Harry Shaddock was busy listening to the Air
Force liaison officer issuing instructions to the circling transports
when a firefight erupted not more than fifty meters from where he
stood. Stunned, Shaddock spun around. When he saw that none
of the personnel in the immediate vicinity were engaged he called
out to the assistant operations officer who was charged with monitoring the battalion command net. "Overton, what's going on?"

Not having heard any sort of spot report that even remotely
hinted of trouble, Captain Clarence Overton shot back without
hesitation. "Negative knowledge, sir. Other than the resistance
Bravo continues to meet in their area, no one else had reported
any enemy activity."

Having slid up next to his commanding officer, Sergeant Major Harris grunted. "That fire is coming from Alpha's portion of Kansas."

Shaddock agreed. "That's the way it looks. And if Captain Carter is continuing to be true to form, his boys are having a shoot-out with each other."

Harris shook his head. "Well, sir, it wouldn't be the first time."

Angered by this unexpected interruption and its consequences Shaddock made no effort to check his rage. "Sergeant Major, get on the radio and get a hold of that man. I'm going over there and sort this bloody mess out."

Though he would have liked to stop his commanding officer, Harris knew better than to try. If there was one thing that he had learned during his twenty-three years in the Army it was never to stand between an enraged bull and a red cape.

With blood in his eyes and vengeance in his heart, Lieutenant Colonel Shaddock stormed past the soldiers who manned the perimeter of his small command post and out into the void better known as no-man's-land. He was looking for someone to light into, someone responsible for this free-wheeling cock-up. At the moment it didn't really matter who his target was. All he was looking for was a target upon which he could unleash his rage, both that generated by this particular incident and the deep seething anger he carried within him over the futility of this entire exercise. It was wrong for him to do so. When it was over he would regret letting his passions override his common sense. But this was battle, and even in a simulated engagement a man's visceral response trumps logic nine times out of ten.

Catching sight of a small cluster of personnel crouching in a slight depression off to one side Shaddock veered toward them. "You people!" he shouted in order to make himself heard over the sputtering gunfire that seemed to be spreading. "What in the hell do you think you're doing?"

The answer he received was delivered without hesitation as

the crouching figures leveled their weapons at Shaddock and opened fire.

Stunned, Shaddock reined himself in. *"YOU! Soldier!"* he yelled, pointing at the tallest figure in the group. "What's your name?"

From the midst of the dark figures, the one Shaddock had singled out stood up and answered in a deep baritone voice that the Ranger colonel did not recognize. "Your worst nightmare, sir. First Lieutenant Emmett J. DeWitt."

With his anger now mitigated by a growing sense of confusion, Shaddock asked again. *"Who?"*

The next reply was delivered by a collective shout from the crouching figures that were decidedly more cheerful than Shaddock wanted to hear at that moment. "We be the OPFOR, and you be dead."

Whatever self-control he had in reserve quickly came into play as he realized that as much as he needed to vent his anger, these soldiers were not an appropriate target. They were simply doing their duty. Besides, Shaddock quickly decided, he had a far better victim in mind, one who was far more deserving.

When Captain David Carter walked out of the small office used by his commanding officer while in base camp he didn't look left or right. Stone-faced he made for the door without saying a word or making eye contact with any of the staff officers gathered in the outer office. Once he was gone Shaddock called through the open door of his office. "Major Castalane, Sergeant Major."

With a sidelong glance at each other these two men stood up, gave their uniforms a quick tug, and trooped into their colonel's office with all the eagerness of condemned men. After closing the door behind him Harris made for one of the folding chairs that accounted for the majority of the furniture in the office. "So," he stated in an effort to break the frigid silence after sitting down, "I take it Captain Carter is gone." Unrepentant, Shaddock glared at his sergeant major. "As of five minutes ago we are an Army of one less."

Sensing that it would be an exercise in futility to try to dissuade his commanding officer from this course of action, Castalane turned to the subject of a replacement. "I don't think it would be a good idea to replace Carter with his XO. Lieutenant Tatum is good, but he's not ready for a command."

Shaddock nodded. "Agreed."

When his superior made no effort to follow this up Castalane continued. "The most logical choice is Overton. He's got the experience and has already commanded an infantry company. With his knowledge of Fanfare he'll be able to step into the position without much trouble."

This time the battalion commander shook his head. "You are correct. He is a natural. Unfortunately, the operations section can't afford to lose him, not now."

For the first time Harris spoke up. "I agree. Major Perry is great when it comes to putting a plan together, but he needs Overton to run the current ops side of his shop in the field."

Shaddock nodded. "Agreed."

Not waiting this time, the battalion XO moved on. "Sir, do you want I call back to Lewis and see if they have someone they can send us?"

"No. If we did that we'd be stuck with whatever they sent us. Besides, it would take too long to get him down here and bring him up to speed."

Stymied, Castalane glanced over at Harris, then back at Shaddock. "If not Overton or someone from Lewis, then who, sir?"

For the first time the commander of the 3rd of the 75th shifted about in his seat. Leaning forward, he planted his elbows on his small field desk and folded his hands under his chin. "Ben, call over to the post commander before we leave here for the after-action review and see if he'd be willing to part with one of his OPFOR officers."

Taken aback by this, Castalane and Harris again exchanged glances. "Sir," the XO asked in an effort to clarify his instructions, "do you have anyone in mind?"

Reaching into the breast pocket of his BDUs, Shaddock pulled out a small notebook and opened it. "First Lieutenant Emmett J. DeWitt."

"Who?"

Shaddock dropped the deadpan expression he had worn since the tactical exercise at Dust Bowl International had been concluded, and smiled. "You'll be meeting him in about an hour. He's the energetic young officer who threw the turd in the punch bowl this morning."

In an instant Castalane understood his commanding officer's logic. "Not bad, sir. No doubt this DeWitt knows the layout of Kansas far better than we do. And I imagine he's already got a good idea about what our plan is."

"Exactly," Shaddock stated. "He's here, he's primed, and he struck me as the sort of officer who can motivate a corpse to rise up and follow him."

As much as he agreed, Sergeant Major Harris cleared his throat. "Sir, I hate to be the one who rains on your parade, but what if DeWitt isn't a Ranger?"

Leaning back into his seat, Shaddock waved a hand about. "Oh, I'm sure you'll be able to scrounge up some patches and take care of that."

Not sure he was hearing one of the most diehard advocates of maintaining the purity and high standards of the army's Ranger program, Harris cocked his head to one side. "Sir?"

"Sergeant Major, if it is a problem, take care of it. Enough said?"

Drawing in a deep breath, Harris stood up. "Well, sir, as you well know, you don't need to hit me over the head more than three or four times before I get the message."

Coming to his feet, Shaddock raised his arms over his head and stretched. "I'm glad about that, 'cause I'm getting tired of using the dumb stick." Then, in an instant he dropped his hands, affected a more serious demeanor and looked at both Harris and Castalane. "No matter how this thing turns out I don't want anyone to say that the 3rd of the 75th wasn't able to perform its assigned tasks. We will do as we're told in the most professional manner that circumstances permit. Do I make myself clear?"

Thinking they understood what their commanding officer was saying, the battalion XO and sergeant major snapped to attention and saluted. "Roger that, sir."

Only when they were gone did Shaddock allow himself to drop the facade of enthusiasm for Fanfare that was becoming harder and harder for him to maintain.

Fort Irwin, California
11:40 LOCAL (18:40 ZULU)

The eagerness that had driven Emmett J. DeWitt since his meeting with Shaddock suddenly evaporated when he turned the corner of the base housing area and spotted his wife's car parked in front of their quarters. He had been hoping that she wouldn't be there, that she would take her lunch in the office of the base contractor that she worked for. He had wanted to get in, pack up what he would need to take with him to the cantonment area where the 3rd of the 75th was, and clean up some before he had to confront her. Now that plan was clearly shot. Seeing that he had no choice but to get this over with, DeWitt slowly pulled into the driveway. The trials that he would have to face and overcome in the next few weeks would pale in comparison to the ordeal he was about to endure.

Creeping about the house like a cat, he took great care to open each door slowly and peek around the corner before entering the next room. He was in the middle of moving from the kitchen into the combination living room and dining room when his wife emerged from the rear of the house. With a smile and cheery tone she called out to him, "I didn't hear you come in!"

Startled, DeWitt all but jumped as a child does when caught by his mother engaged in something he should not be doing. "Hi, hon. I didn't know you were home."

Knowing better than that, Angela DeWitt walked up to her husband, placed one hand on his arm and stood on her tiptoes so that she could plant a kiss on his cheek. When he made no effort to turn toward her or bend his head down so it would be easier for her to reach her objective, Angela realized that he had come home bearing bad news. Lowering herself back onto the floor, she stepped back, sliding her hand down his arm till their fingers touched. Taking his hand in hers, she lifted it to her lips and planted a light kiss on it before looking up into his eyes. "Okay, King Kong, what's up?"

Normally when she called him that in private, DeWitt grinned. At the moment, however, he could not find it in himself to do so. With his free hand, he reached over, grasped the hand that was already holding his, and lifted it to his chest. "Hon, I've been given an opportunity that I just could not say no to."

These are the sort of words that strike terror into the hearts of every military wife, especially when they are uttered in the midst of an international crisis. Sensing the fear that sent a chill down her spine, DeWitt pulled her closer to him. "This morning a slot in the Ranger battalion that's been training here for the past week came open."

Heaped upon the growing sense of alarm that she could not suppress, Angela now felt a touch of nausea. "Is he dead?"

"No, hon," DeWitt quickly explained. "I don't know the whole story but in a nutshell one of the company commanders was relieved this morning." Seeing no need to do so, he made no effort to inform his wife that he had, in a rather roundabout way, precipitated that action. "Before the after-action review of today's operation the commander of the 3rd of the 75th Rangers asked Colonel Higgins for me by name to take that officer's place."

With a shove that caught Emmett DeWitt off guard, Angela drew away from him. "And of course you said yes."

Before he responded to her accusatory statement, DeWitt tried to close the distance. She frustrated this attempt by continuing her retreat. Flustered and unsure of what to say next, he squeezed her hands a bit tighter while he tried to put together the right words that would justify to her his decision to accept an offer that was for him a once-in-a-lifetime opportunity. "Baby, I'm a soldier. You know that. You knew that when we got married. It's my job."

"And being a husband to me or a father to your baby isn't your job? What about us? Don't we have a say in this? Aren't we part of this equation?"

Without having to think about it DeWitt knew that he could not answer that question in the manner that she wanted yet remain truthful. Fortunately for him he didn't need to. His silence was enough.

Realizing that she could no longer hold back her tears, but determined to deny him the opportunity to comfort her, Angela DeWitt tore her hand free from her husband's grasp, turned, and fled back into their bedroom. When he heard the door slam, DeWitt took a deep breath and shook his head. "Well," he muttered sarcastically. "That went better than I thought."

Damascus, Syria
18:30 LOCAL (14:30 ZULU)

Five times a day Sergeant Yousaf Hashmi was able to free himself from the steel-and-concrete cage that imprisoned his physical being. It did not matter that his prayer rug was a frayed, lice-infested blanket or that the eastern wall of his cell was covered with crude graffiti left behind by former occupants who had lost all hope. Such physical concerns faded from his consciousness as Hashmi humbled himself before his God as his father had taught him to do. Closing his eyes and bowing his head he uttered the simple statement, "All praise be to Allah," with a love and strange joy that only a true believer knows. Since he had been locked away in this place these words and actions had come to be more than a prelude to his ritualistic devotionals. They had become a shield that allowed the Syrian-American to protect himself from the fear his captors endeavored to instill in him and a sword with which to strike back in steadfast defiance. His daily prayers were also a reminder to him that there was more to this world than that which his eyes could see or his arms could embrace. When his time came to leave his mortal body behind, Hashmi found comfort in the fact that he would not die. His soul would go on as did the spirit of all those who placed themselves in the hands of Allah.

When the guards opened the cell door Colonel Mohammed Raseed found Hashmi in the midst of his evening prayers. For a moment the Syrian colonel was taken aback by the sight of this familiar rite. He did not quite know what to do. It had been his intent to make a grand entrance, strutting into the small room flanked by a pair of Republican Guards who served as his shield and sword. Yet even a man such as Raseed could not bring himself to interrupt a fellow Muslim while he was expressing his fidelity to Allah. With a wave of his hand the Syrian colonel dismissed his personal assistants and stepped over the threshold. As if sensing his mood, the guards took great care when they closed the door.

Transfixed by the unexpected passion of the moment, Raseed watched and listened in silence. The sight of Hashmi praying evoked a momentary sense of peace within him that his assigned duties denied him. He even found himself admiring his prisoner. Hashmi's role in the forthcoming drama would be a simple one. The Syrian-American had become little more than a pawn, one that was about to be used in a gambit he had been ordered to engineer. If the truth be known, and Raseed was a man who never allowed himself to forget the reality of his situation, he feared that his superiors were on the verge of making a major mistake. He had tried to tell them that there was a very real danger their next move could have repercussions that none of them could foresee. But Raseed was a colonel, and in this drama nothing more than a stage manager. He could do little but follow his orders even if he did not believe doing so was wise. After all, the Syrian colonel reminded himself, if things did not go as his superiors wished, he could very well be the next man seeking divine guidance within these walls.

Finished, Yousaf Hashmi paused before turning his head slowly toward Raseed. When he did, the American's expression betrayed no fear, no concern. "I thank you for permitting me to complete my prayers."

Again Raseed found himself once more thrown off guard by a simple gesture of a man whom he was supposed to be intimidating. Flustered and unable to find a response that was appropriate, the Syrian colonel was reduced to acknowledging Hashmi's gratitude with a shrug. After averting his eyes from those of his prisoner, Raseed grasped his hands behind his back, turned, and began to pace. "Up until now you have been spared the sort of treatment that the Americans have been subjected to."

Making no effort to rise up off his knees, Hashmi followed

Raseed with his eyes. "I know. The guards make it a point to pause just outside my door and beat upon my comrades for several minutes each time they are taken to their next round of torture."

This confession brought a smile to Raseed's face, for it meant that not only were his orders being carried out to a T but the tactic was having an effect upon Hashmi. Reaching the rear wall of the cell, Raseed pivoted about and continued his pacing. "I suspect that you have been wondering why they have been interrogated while you have not."

Hashmi's bland expression did not change as he continued to watch Raseed. "I suspect that you are here to explain that to me."

Stung by this response as well as Hashmi's demeanor, Raseed ceased his pacing and turned to confront the American. Yet even now the Syrian colonel found himself off balance as he looked down at Hashmi. Why, the colonel wondered, was he still on his knees? *Is he trying to show to me that he is a more dedicated follower of our faith than I? Is he trying to convey the idea that we are both equal in the eyes of Allah? Or is he simply assuming a position of submission in an effort to hide his defiance?* In truth Raseed was not interested in the answer, for it did not make any difference. Still, this seemingly harmless act annoyed Raseed. It disturbed him and kept him from concentrating on the task at hand. Having dismissed his henchmen and accepted a one-on-one confrontation, Raseed was at a loss as to how to handle this situation.

Stymied, the colonel turned his back on Hashmi and resumed his pacing. This caused a flicker of a smile to flit across Hashmi's face, an expression that he quickly checked.

"You are to be tried as a traitor," Raseed announced.

"I do not understand how that is possible," Hashmi replied, betraying neither surprise nor concern. "I have been loyal to my faith, to my comrades, and to my nation."

Stopping in place, Raseed spun about and faced his prisoner. "That is where you are wrong, and I shall prove it. You are a Syrian citizen, one who has raised his hand against his own people. By doing so you have gone against the teachings of the Koran."

Again Hashmi was able to maintain his stoic demeanor as he responded. "I have betrayed no one. I am a Virginian by birth and a professional soldier pledged to defend my native country, its laws, and its people. Even the prophet Mohammed could find no fault in what I have done."

Hashmi's line of reasoning angered Raseed. It was not what he saying, which Raseed realized was all true. Rather it was the manner in which the American was stating his case. Despite the kneeling position that he continued to maintain, the man showed no sign of fear, no indication that he was concerned about what lay ahead. His answers were delivered as if he were engaged in a theoretical debate. It had been a mistake, Raseed suddenly came to appreciate, to have spared him from the beatings that had been heaped upon his companions.

Then, in an instant, the colonel hit upon the course he would need to steer in the next few days. Triumphantly Raseed marched over and confronted Hashmi. With folded arms and a smile on his face he leaned over and stared into the American's eyes. "You may be prepared to accept your fate and all that it entails, but I do not think that your companions are. Nor do I believe that you have the stomach to watch as the scum you have chosen to call friends are beaten every time you choose to defy me."

For the first time Raseed could see a hint of concern creep into Hashmi's expression. Satisfied that he had finally achieved a degree of moral ascendancy over his prisoner, the colonel stood upright and grasped his hands behind his back while maintaining eye contact with Hashmi. "Tomorrow morning you will be brought before a military tribunal. It will judge you and your actions. During the course of the proceedings you will be expected to demonstrate to our people the respect and reverence that our law and the tribunal demand. Each time you fail to do so, each and every one of your companions will suffer. Do you understand?"

This time Hashmi made no effort to hide the anger and contempt he felt as he glared at the towering figure before him.

Coming to his feet, the American sergeant gathered himself up and looked into Raseed's eyes before he replied. Though his muted response was pretty much what Raseed expected, he knew that he had not even come close to breaking the American's spirit. Well, he thought as he forced a smile and turned to leave. It did not matter what the American thought. Cameras seldom captured the truth. They reflected an image, an image that could be easily manipulated and twisted.

Amman, Jordan
18:05 LOCAL (15:05 ZULU)

The orders that Lieutenant Colonel Robert Delmont had found waiting for him at Andrews Air Force Base proved to be of no help to him in delineating his duties and responsibilities. When he finally was able to arrange a private meeting with the two sergeants who had managed to make their way across the Jordanian frontier, he was on his own.

As he feared, this meeting did not happen overnight. To appease its neighbors and those members of its citizenry who were decidedly anti-American, the Jordanian government needed to make a show of publicly expressing its outrage over the incident. It took time to properly organize and stage anti-American rallies for the benefit of TV cameras. Statements condemning the violation of their nation's sovereign boundaries by armed combatants needed to be drafted and released by both the king and prime minister. Selected members of the government's inner circle had to be permitted ample opportunity to express their dismay over the affair. All of this had to be carefully orchestrated and played out before arrangements for the transfer of Staff Sergeant Ramirez and Sergeant Funk from a Jordanian military facility to the American embassy could be quietly negotiated and carried out. When Robert Delmont arrived in Amman these maneuvers were still under way, leaving the special ops staff officer little choice but to patiently wait while the diplomats of the two nations observed the dictates of protocol and performed their ritualistic dance.

This sort of enforced idleness is unnerving to a man whose routine consisted of twelve-hour workdays. To be out of the loop just as Fanfare was beginning to take shape only served to accentuate his angst. Were it not for the fact that this unwelcome interlude left him free to lose himself in the latest Tom Clancy novel, Delmont was convinced he would have gone totally mad.

When he was finally afforded an opportunity to sit down with the Kilo Three NCOs in a secure area alone, Delmont discovered that his frustrations were only the beginning. During the course of these meetings Delmont was able to confirm that any information Ramirez and Funk had concerning the status or whereabouts of their teammates who had been taken prisoner was of no use to him. Not even their knowledge of the terrain or the Syrian military was of value to the operation that he had been working on. And to make matters worse, when all was said and done, Delmont wasn't even able to ascertain with any degree of certainty what had actually taken place that night. All in all he walked away with exactly what he had expected—zilch.

As discouraging as this was, putting together a summary of his findings and conclusions proved to be equally disheartening. Using a vacant workstation in the secure area of the military liaison's office at the embassy, Robert Delmont quickly discovered that there was no way that he could piece together a full accounting of the affair without its reflecting adversely upon his own superior and a fellow special forces officer. Repeatedly both NCOs made statements that alluded to a deterioration of morale within RT Kilo and an appreciable decline in vigilance by every member of the team as they were told time after time that they would have to remain on station. Sergeant Funk was particularly bitter when this subject came up. When Delmont had pointed out that they were expected to follow orders, he snapped. "Yes, sir, we're soldiers. But there's only so much crap even the best of us can tolerate, especially when no one else back home gives two shits about what we're doing. Can you tell me," Funk asked rhetorically, "what exactly our sacrifice achieved? Can you, sir? Can anyone?"

Accusations such as this one rattled Delmont. Even as Funk was speaking Delmont found himself recalling each and every time he had walked into General Palmer's office bearing the file on Razorback along with staff recommendations that he himself had drafted. How easy it had been for him to assess RT Kilo's state of readiness and ability to continue until RT Lima could be deployed to take its place. Anything was possible when one was sitting at a desk in Arlington, Virginia, safely tucked away within the Pentagon. There is no sand in the food served in the cafeterias there. Columns of armed soldiers are not lying in ambush in the parking lot. With few exceptions every one of the thousands of military or civilian employees assigned there are free to turn their back on their labors when their shift is over and retire to their place of residence where they are free to enjoy the company of family, friends, or a few hours of calm, peaceful solitude. Even a hardcore field soldier such as Delmont found that it was easy to set aside his muddy-boots mentality and adapt to the Pentagon's prevailing psychology and mind-set. As much as he wanted to think that he had somehow managed to avoid slipping into that pit, the results of his debriefings were proving otherwise. He may not have been there. And he definitely had no control over how each of the men belonging to RT Kilo dealt with the situation that night. But in so many ways, he was responsible.

Inevitably, this train of thought came to shade how Delmont now viewed the entire incident. Unable to escape the fact that he had been a factor in creating the conditions that resulted in the demise of RT Kilo, the special ops plans officer found himself at a loss. In putting together his report, did he purge his prose of any verbiage that could lay culpability for the disaster upon someone's doorstep? Or did he draft a document that passed judgment on the whole sorry affair using what he knew as well as the information he had managed to glean from the two NCOs and the results of O'Hara's and Laporta's debriefings?

Needing time to figure out how to deal with his troubled thoughts as well as formulating an approach for his report that was factual without being controversial, Delmont left the embassy early. He reasoned that a good meal and a solid night's sleep would improve his ability to approach the subject in a more analytical and objective manner. If nothing else, the interlude would allow him an opportunity to clear away some of the mental fog generated by a lethal combination of jetlag and self-condemnation.

Unfortunately, like the solution that he sought, Robert Delmont was unable to set aside his problems. They followed him back to the hotel like an unwanted stray dog. There was simply too much going on, too many issues to be addressed, and too much that he needed to sort out. All during his meal he found himself thinking about the hardships the two NCOs had endured every time their redeployment was postponed. Even after he turned off the light next to his bed Delmont discovered that his brain refused to disengage itself from dwelling upon the challenges he had yet to deal with. In desperation, he threw back the sheets, got up, dressed himself, and made his way to the hotel's bar. While he doubted that he would find a solution to any of the issues he had to deal with there, knocking back a beer or two wouldn't hurt.

One element that confused Delmont was the attitudes of the two NCOs. During his debriefings of them he had become so obsessed with his own role in this crisis that it took him longer than it should have to pick up on the contempt each man held for his erstwhile companion. Only when he began to pay attention to their tone and choice of words, especially when referring to each other, was Delmont able to discern the hostility each expressed when the other NCO was mentioned. Mixed in with this animosity were scattered hints of self-loathing that both men continually alluded to when discussing their actions that night.

While not exactly material to his mission, his personal involve-
ment in the operation shaded everything the two NCOs told
him, depriving Delmont of the objectivity that would have
helped him to paint a more complete and factual picture of that
night and its aftermath.

Sitting at the quiet little bar, Lieutenant Colonel Robert Delmont did his best to focus his entire attention on nothing but the
beer sitting before him. Even in this modest endeavor the Fates
conspired against him. The officer had not given any thought to
which seat he took when he had entered the bar. As chance would
have it he found himself facing a television that was tucked away
in one corner of the bar. The drone of elevator music that filled
the room drowned out most of the sound but did nothing to mitigate the flickering images that caught Delmont's eye every now
and then. Like a moth drawn to a light, he found himself glancing
over at the boob tube more often than he intended.

During the first half hour or so the program the barkeep
watched between tending to customers appeared to be the Jordanian version of MTV. The beat of the local music that accompanied the relatively tame performance mixed with the soft jazz that
played throughout the lounge in deference to the Western businessmen who filled it. No doubt, Delmont mused as he watched a
comely young woman covered from head to toe in layers of silky
veils twirl about, a single showing of Madonna's latest music
video would earn the station manager an old-fashioned stoning.

The American colonel was well into his second beer, an Irish
brew that he favored, which somehow didn't quite taste the same
here as it did back in Virginia, when the bartender walked over to
the TV and changed the channel. In place of the female dancers
adorned in traditional dress, a news reader who seemed to be far
too Western for these parts appeared on the screen. In the traditions of the BBC he dutifully read the latest news in a crisp monotone. Delmont was about to turn away and survey his fellow
Occidentals who had migrated into the lounge from the dining

room when the image of a member of RT Kilo flashed on the screen. Though he had come down to this place to escape thinking about that issue, Delmont was too much of a professional to turn his back.

For several seconds the news reader rattled on about something in Arabic while the mug shot of Sergeant Yousaf Hashmi was displayed. At first Delmont thought nothing of this. It was quite natural for Arabs to be drawn to the only surviving member of RT Kilo who was a fellow Muslim. That conclusion quickly evaporated, however, when a recent press photo of the Reverend Lucas Brown popped onto the screen next to that of Hashmi.

This apparition struck Delmont as being both incongruous and worrisome, especially since the previously attentive bartender suddenly turned his attention away from what he had been doing and instead focused on what the news reader was saying. In the twinkling of an eye, the dreamy and warm state of mind into which Delmont had slipped evaporated. Shifting about in his seat, the American colonel cleared his throat and lightly tapped his half-empty glass on the bar in an effort to get the barkeep's attention. That the news item being announced had captured the full interest of the man was obvious by the manner with which he backed away from the screen without taking his eyes off it. Only when he was nearing Delmont did he bother to face him. Even then the American could tell that he was keeping one ear cocked as he tried to do two things at once.

"What's he saying?" Delmont asked when he was sure that the Jordanian was paying attention to him.

Without skipping a beat, the barkeep turned to face the screen while he answered. "The Syrian Ministry of Information has announced that the Syrian who was taken with the Americans is going to be tried by a military tribunal for treason."

Whether it was the offhanded, almost matter-of-fact manner with which the bartender spoke or the news itself, Delmont found himself stunned by this revelation. "Sergeant Hashmi is an American citizen!"

For the first time the bartender turned and seriously regarded the patron he was addressing. After giving Delmont's statement a moment of thought, the Jordanian replied in the same disinterested tone. "According to law in Damascus, at least the way they are practicing it there these days, he is still a Syrian."

Sensing that his point was lost on the bartender and eager to sort out what possible connection there could be between a Syrian-American soldier and a prominent civil rights leader, Delmont pressed on. "So what's the reverend got to do with all this?"

Missing Delmont's sarcastic tone, the bartender listened to the television for a moment before answering. "It would seem that he will be going to Damascus tomorrow to meet with Syrian officials as well as the American prisoners."

Somewhere in the back of Delmont's mind this possibility had already begun to generate a coherent thought, one that the special plans officer dreaded. Even so, when the Jordanian confirmed his suspicion Delmont found that his frustration over being so far from the action as well as the beer he had consumed kept him from checking himself. With more force than he had intended, he lifted his glass before slamming it on the bar. "Great. That's all we need."

Throughout the lounge the collection of businessmen who had gathered with their fellow travelers as well as some of the local talent stopped for a moment and turned their attention to Delmont. Ignoring their stares and glares, he stood up, pulled some money out of his pocket, and threw it onto the bar before storming out of the room, mumbling as he went. In his wake an English electronics salesman quipped, "Americans!" With that, everyone returned to whatever business proposition they had been making.

CHAPTER TWENTY-ONE

Fort Bragg, North Carolina
15:55 LOCAL (19:55 ZULU)

The media blitz unleashed by the Syrian government concerning its decision to put Sergeant Yousaf Hashmi on trial coupled with the stilted interviews of the other American prisoners had its desired effect upon the ceremonies staged to greet O'Hara and Laporta. Rather than celebrating an American success, the homecoming served to remind those who turned out to welcome home the two NCOs that the crisis was far from over.

In itself, this new propaganda campaign would have been difficult for the American military community to deal with. Unfortunately for the families of those still in captivity, the ever-voracious American press snapped up every scrap the Syrians dangled before them. Reinvigorated, legions of reporters fanned out across the American landscape as they redoubled their focus on the families, relatives, and friends of the members of RT Kilo featured in the Syrian propaganda clips. As devastating as this was to the loved ones, the effect upon efforts to resolve the crisis was nothing less than crippling. Overnight open negotiations on neutral ground and back-channel communiqués between the two nations ceased. Also lost by this unexpected change in the international landscape were several initiatives sponsored by third parties.

Even when it became clear that this unwanted attention was having adverse effects on serious efforts, the stampede to project, analyze, and predict what the national leadership would do next did not subside in the least. And when the networks ran out of talking heads, the topic merely shifted to an on-air debate by the journalists on how their compatriots were covering the story.

Throughout this media melee one topic that no one on-camera ever seemed to tire of was the search for someone whom they could hold responsible for the sudden collapse of serious negotiations. Anxious to lay the blame for this on everyone else's doorstep except their own, TV journalists and newspaper editors stood as one in proclaiming that this reversal of diplomatic fortunes was due to the manner in which the military had gone about retrieving O'Hara and Laporta. In one paper of record, the front page sported a banner headline that read "Misguided Military Misadventure Misfires."

At Fort Bragg silver-tongued commentators who mistook shouting matches between political foes for meaningful discussion of issues and considered a thirty-second film clip to be an in-depth report struggled to outdo their competition when it came to describing the somber, bittersweet occasion of the homecoming. "Even the weather has turned its back on the people assembled here to greet the returning heroes," one wag noted when commenting on the cold gray clouds that filled the sky. And in an effort to keep from offending any of their viewers who preferred redwood trees to more conventional deities, several of the networks cut to commercials when the post chaplain stepped forward to lead the gathering in prayer.

If anyone standing in the hangar was aware of these shenanigans being played out on the nation's airwaves they did not let on. Unlike the esteemed members of the fourth estate who honestly believed that they actually spoke for the American people, the leadership of the nation's armed forces kept their eye on the ball and their priorities straight. They congratulated those who had participated in the effort to snatch O'Hara and Laporta away from the Syrians, did their best to console the families of those still being held, and maintained their calm when accosted by journalists eager to cap that day's report with a crisp, candid sound bite. At no time did any of the generals, colonels, and senior NCOs allow themselves to forget what their true goal was. While shaking the hand of Specialist Four O'Hara and Specialist Four

Laporta, each and every man who had a role in planning the next operation saw their return as nothing more than a down payment.

To that end the commanding general of CENTCOM arranged a private briefing for all the family members of RT Kilo. Before launching into well-rehearsed briefings put together by his staff for the wives, children, and parents of the men still being held or missing, the general addressed the gathering in an effort to set the tone. "While our purpose here today is to welcome home two soldiers, let no one forget those who cannot be here with us today. Our goal continues to be to bring all of our people home as quickly and as safely as possible." Had the general been totally honest with the gathering he would have added, "without doing any further damage to our already tarnished reputation." Such candor, however, was not advisable even when dealing with those who understood and felt the true cost of maintaining their nation's place in the world.

Ever mindful of the need to protect the family members of its soldiers, entry into these briefings was restricted to immediate family only. Enforcement of this policy was handled by polite yet unyielding personnel from Fort Bragg's office of public affairs and the post's protocol officer. Only those who could prove that they were related by blood or marriage to one of the men still being held by the Syrians were granted full access to all the briefings. Everyone else, including in-laws and one woman who claimed to be the fiancée of Lieutenant Joseph Ciszak, had to wait in a vacant office that had been hastily converted into a temporary lounge. Among this assortment of second-tier relatives, lovers, and friends was Karen Green. When asked by Fort Bragg's protocol officer what her relationship was to Elizabeth, Karen had been as truthful as she dared. "I'm here to lend her my moral support." If she had been totally honest, she would have told the protocol officer that she had come to spare Elizabeth the agony of going there with her mother, a woman who was determined to do all she could to comfort her poor baby.

For Karen, Fort Bragg represented a sinister side of America that she and her friends delighted in disparaging and denigrating over five-dollar cups of cappuccino. Everything about the place and its people alarmed her, from the presence of gun-toting soldiers in uniform to the high fences and barbed wire that surrounded restricted areas. Never having taken the time to understand the role of the military in keeping democracies free, Karen found that she had nothing better to draw upon to regulate her experience than the popular imagery of Nazi concentration camps that the entertainment industry was so fond of perpetuating. This particular comparison had become so ingrained in her psyche that she found herself looking for MPs with snarling German shepherds to appear shouting "*Achtung!*" as they moved about the edge of the crowd. By the time Elizabeth had to part from her side in order to attend the family-only briefings, Karen had managed to work herself into such a state that it was becoming a question of whether she was providing moral support to Elizabeth or vice versa.

In the waiting area where everyone who was nonfamily gathered, Karen found herself alone and feeling quite vulnerable. If ever there were a time when she needed a cigarette to calm her nerves, this was it. Unable to escape, she did her best to be as inconspicuous as possible by tucking herself away in a corner of the room.

With nothing better to do while she waited for Elizabeth to appear, Karen tried to forget about her paranoia by studying the comings and goings of the others who filled the anteroom. Having shared Elizabeth's ordeal since the beginning, more than a few of the faces around her were familiar. Off near the door that led into the auditorium where the briefings were taking place Karen spotted the woman who was engaged to the air force officer. Sitting patiently against the wall with her feet drawn up under her chair and hands folded in her lap, the woman looked perfectly composed as she waited for her fiancée's sister to emerge from the briefing. *I wonder,* Karen found herself wondering as she looked at the woman's calm demeanor, *if the military has special programs designed to prepare the families for times like this?*

As the savvy New Yorker was pondering this question one of three chaplains who were circulating throughout the room came up to Ciszak's fiancée. Like everyone she and Elizabeth had come into contact with since arriving at Fort Bragg, the chaplains were doing their best to calm the fears of those who found themselves on the fringe of the crisis. Never having reconciled her lifestyle with the faith of her parents, Karen distrusted rabbis almost as much as she did anyone wearing a uniform. When one of the chaplains threatened to make his way over to where she stood, Karen began to look for someplace to escape to.

Just before she made her move a woman her own age whom Karen didn't recognize approached her. At first glance the stranger appeared to be a professional of some type, a lawyer perhaps, or maybe a businesswoman. Even the easy confident manner with which she carried herself reminded Karen of the sort of person that she enjoyed being around. When she was but a few feet away, the woman gave Karen one of those knowing smiles. Without hesitation she leaned forward and whispered as if they were old friends, "I could tell by the way you were watching that chaplain that you were desperate for a savior of a different sort."

Without thinking, Karen returned the smile, reached out, and took the proffered hand of the stranger. "You don't know how right you are. How did you guess?"

While still lightly grasping Karen's right hand with her own, the woman waved her left hand about. "Oh, having been around these GI Joe types before, I had a hunch you were new to this sort of thing."

Pleased to see that this woman wasn't wearing a wedding band, Karen felt whatever anxieties she had about her surroundings slip away now that she had found someone with whom to share her plight. Reaching up, Karen placed her left hand on the woman's upper arm in order to steady herself as she leaned over to whisper in her ear. "If I have any say in the matter, this will be my first and last foray into the cave of the Bear Clan."

The woman's laughter, her light feminine scent, and the feel of a soft warm hand had an almost intoxicating effect on the nervous woman. Easing back she introduced herself. "I am Karen Green. I'm here with a friend of mine, Elizabeth Stanton."

With measured ease, the stranger gave Karen's right hand a friendly squeeze. "Hi, Karen. I'm Ann."

Karen returned the gesture by placing her left hand upon their clasped hands. For several long seconds the two women stood there in silence, neither making any effort to let go. Finally Karen managed to clear her throat and speak. "I don't know about you, but I feel like a chicken on Colonel Sanders's plantation. Let's find someplace that's less crowded and a little less green, army protocol be damned."

Laughing, Ann nodded. "I know what you mean. Since this sort of military briefing and the questions that inevitably follow tend to take forever, I doubt anyone will miss us."

Thrilled that she had found someone who shared her feelings and was willing to go along with her, Karen didn't bother to ask how it was that Ann knew about briefings like the one going on. Even if she had, the woman who called herself Ann would not have told her. She had no intention of letting on that she was a journalist for a national tabloid who had been following Elizabeth for days in the hope of finding a fresh new angle that no one else had yet uncovered.

Damascus, Syria
00:25 LOCAL (20:25 ZULU)

Concerned that the Syrian government could no longer guarantee them unfettered access to the American Air Force officer, the Chinese colonel who served as the unofficial military liaison between the government in Damascus and the People's Republic insisted that First Lieutenant Ciszak be turned over to them immediately. This led to some bitter infighting between senior Syrian officials. On one side there were some who had no desire to part with any of their captives. To those responsible for generating propaganda and anti-American sentiment on the fabled Arab street as well as abroad, each and every American was a priceless gift from God whose value increased with each passing day. Like an exhibit in a private museum, profit could be reaped simply by displaying the American servicemen, especially one who was been wounded as Ciszak had been when Kilo One had blown up. Already the Syrians had recorded hours of film showing their doctors and nurses tenderly caring for Ciszak's numerous burns. Time and time again the Syrian minister of information tried to point out that they had nothing to gain by giving in to the Chinese demands and everything to lose. "By releasing our footage showing how we are caring for the wounded American we will put to the lie the rumors the Americans are spreading about the manner in which we are treating their soldiers," the minister insisted. "We have much to gain by keeping him and selectively granting access to those sympathetic to our goals or prominent figures whom we can exploit. In time I am sure we can use the wounded Air Force officer to extract concessions from the Americans they might not otherwise have granted."

The military leadership however had an entirely different perspective on the issues concerning Ciszak and the others. They saw the remaining Americans as little more than poker chips to be played when the time was right. Already they had made their influence felt in the matter concerning a trial and public execution for a Syrian traitor who had been captured. "So long as the Americans believe that time is on their side they will hesitate to take direct action to resolve the crisis. On the other hand if they feel that they have no choice but to act and act quickly, we may be able to stampede their political leaders to taking action before their military is fully prepared. By bringing on battle sooner rather than later we increase the likelihood that their attempt to rescue the others will miscarry, a disaster that will enhance our national prestige and humble the arrogant Americans." Despite the fact that those who were against trading away their captives continued to point out that battles were notorious for yielding unintended results, the hard-line military faction won.

It was in this manner that the life of First Lieutenant Joseph Ciszak was reduced to that of a commodity. In exchange for state-of-the-art-missile guidance systems for surface-to-air missiles the Syrians so desperately needed to counter American air power, the People's Liberation Army gained an intelligence asset that could be exploited in secret and at their leisure. Having done this sort of thing during the Korean War and Vietnam, the Communist Chinese understood that the knowledge Ciszak possessed concerning techniques and technologies used to coordinate air strikes was perishable. The sooner they had him in an environment that they controlled, the more valuable the information he yielded would be when it came time to hone their own tactics and countermeasures.

The transfer took place at a military airfield just outside of Damascus. Had anyone been aware of it, they would have found it ironic that the very building and room where Syrians turned the stretcher-borne American Air Force officer over to the Chinese was the same one that Robert Delmont's plan had set aside to be the operations center of the 3rd Battalion, 75th Rangers while they were on the ground executing Operation Fanfare.

Arlington, Virginia
07:15 LOCAL (11:15 ZULU)

There seemed to be no end to the surprises that awaited Delmont upon his return to the United States. The first could only be described as an absolute bolt out of the blue. With his mind still trying to adjust to the shift in time zones and cluttered with a number of unresolved issues, Delmont had not bothered to look at the newspaper he picked up in the cafeteria along with his morning coffee. It wasn't until he was standing in line waiting to pay when he caught sight of a photo of First Lieutenant Ken Aveno sandwiched in between photos of two women. Above them the headline proclaimed "Wife Dumps Army Officer for Lesbian Lover."

Normally the special operations plans officer was able to control his response even when handed orders that were by any measure farcical and outrageous. This revelation, however, struck Delmont with all of his normal safeties off and guards down. Without thinking, he let out a groan. "Jesus fucking Christ!"

A Marine colonel waiting in line behind him glanced over his shoulder at the headline Delmont was staring at. The Marine chuckled. "I second that."

Embarrassed, Delmont turned to apologize. "I'm sorry, sir. It's just that . . ."

The Marine smiled. "No need to. I'm just glad my wife wasn't in the room this morning when I heard that tidbit on the radio."

"Well," Delmont mused as he shuffled down along the counter as the line advanced to the cashier, "I hope that young Lieutenant Aveno doesn't get wind of this, just in case he wasn't aware of his wife's choice."

The Marine sneered. "Oh, please. Be real, Colonel. Do you for one minute think that those bastards in Damascus are going to shield Aveno from this? By this evening I imagine that they'll have clippings from every English-language newspaper they can lay their hands on plastered all over his cell." Then after taking a moment to think about what he had just said, and composing himself, the Marine added with a whimsical glimmer in his eyes, "I know that's what I would do."

The others waiting in line who overheard this conversation were not shocked by the Marine's statement. They were professional soldiers, most of whom still managed to remember that their primary duty was to kill people and break things. Statements such as the one just uttered by the colonel were nothing more than the articulation of an obvious course of action chosen to deal with a given situation. Though the language was a bit more colorful than most people in the Pentagon used as they went about their duties, the thought was nonetheless just as cold and analytical as any other man and woman in that line would put forth during the course of the day. They were the shield bearers for their nation, men and women hand picked to plan the unthinkable and do those things that their fellow citizens could not bring themselves to do.

The next jarring bit of news that Delmont stumbled upon that morning did not rear up and slap him in the face in the same manner as the newspaper headline had. Instead it slowly seeped into his consciousness as he went about trying to catch up to where he had left off. Under ordinary circumstances this was no easy task in a place like the Pentagon. In the midst of an ongoing crisis it was nigh impossible, particularly since no one who came into contact with him seemed to take into account the fact that he had not been in the office for several days. Inevitably his co-workers found their way into Delmont's cubicle or stopped him as he was scurrying about and started a conversation with him as if he had just returned from the men's room rather than the Jordanian capital. Being a bit too proud for his own good, the special ops plans officer seldom asked whomever he was conversing with to stop, back up, and explain just what it was that he or she was talking about. Though it was a foolish thing to do, the alternative was worse. In a peacetime military that operated on a philosophy of zero defects, a career officer could not be seen as being behind the power curve. So Robert Delmont listened attentively and nodded when it seemed appropriate as his brain did its best to catch up to the subject at hand and the time zone he was now in.

It was late morning Eastern time and early evening Delmont time when General Palmer called him in to discuss Fanfare. Having just put the finishing touches on the draft trip report that he had e-mailed to his computer in the Pentagon, Delmont felt confident that he was ready to deal with anything his superior threw at him. In fact, he was looking forward to the challenge. Trooping into Palmer's officer, he waited until the general finished a conversation he was having on the phone before taking a seat. Actually, conversation was probably not a good word to use since

Palmer was doing all the listening and the person on the other end seemed to be doing all the talking. Without having to be told, Delmont guessed that there were a minimum of three stars on the other end of the line passing on the diktat of the day. By way of confirming this, Palmer ended the call by drawing a deep breath before mumbling "Yes, sir, I understand, sir."

Slowly he replaced the receiver on the secure line and stared at it for several seconds. Then, with his hands folded on his desk before him, Palmer looked over at Delmont. "Drop everything you're doing other than Fanfare over on Calvert's desk. Tell him that until further notice he's to cover for you. If he starts squawking, tell him to see me."

Though puzzled by this order, Delmont found himself smiling. The last part of Palmer's order, the bit about telling Calvert to see him if he had a problem, was the general's way of saying, "Shut the fuck up and suck it up."

"When you're finished with that," Palmer continued, "bring me everything you have on Fanfare."

"To include computer disks, sir?"

"Everything. Once you've accomplished that, tell the sergeant major to have the automation people wipe your hard drive clean and reinitialize it."

Up to now Delmont hadn't given any of his instructions a second thought. Everything suggested that he was being cut loose from his more mundane duties so that he could deal exclusively with a new, very high priority project. All of that pleased the ambitious plans officer. But when he heard that his computer's memory was going to be purged, alarms started to sound in his head. Dumping a staff officer's working files and records like that was akin to stripping a soldier of his rank and clipping off his buttons in preparation to drumming him out of the service. Unable to hold back any longer, Delmont found himself having to ask the obvious. "Can you tell me, sir, why we are taking these steps? Has Fanfare been blown?"

For a moment Palmer looked at his subordinate as if he were

angered by the man's obtuseness. Then, recalling the fact that Delmont had been out of the loop for several days, he relented. Easing back into his chair he stared into Delmont's eyes with an intensity that unnerved the special ops plans officer. "In your absence the political landscape has been rearranged. It seems that advisors to the Commander in Chief have concluded that the administration does not have the time to allow diplomacy to resolve the situation in Damascus. Rather than allowing the Syrians to control the pace and intensity of this crisis by killing off our people one at a time, something which they now appear to be intent on doing, the president has determined that the time has come to bring this affair to a quick and decisive conclusion, regardless of the cost or the final outcome. By doing so he intends to send the Syrians and anyone else thinking of thumbing their noses at us a message, a very strong message."

When Palmer hesitated to continue, Delmont again sought clarification. "I am not sure, sir, if I fully understand."

The anger that welled up in Palmer was generated as much by the fact that he was being stampeded into a course of action that he considered to be unwise and was opposed to as by the fact that he was having to spell it out to one of his subordinates. Standing up, Palmer leaned over his desk, resting upon his knuckles in order to support himself. "Colonel, be so kind as to pull your fifth point of contact out of your third point of contact and *think!* Fanfare is no longer a deception plan. It is *the* plan of operation. In fact, it is our only plan of operation. And you, Colonel, are going to be responsible for making sure that it works. Is that clear?"

Rattled, the best Delmont could manage was a quick, "Yes, sir. Clear."

After taking a moment to regain his composure, Palmer straightened up. "Once you've taken care of things here, your first stop will be at the office of the project manager for the Land Warrior at Fort Belvoir. Lieutenant Colonel Neil Kaplan, the project manager for Land Warrior, is expecting you. He will fill you in on the role his office will play in this. From there you will proceed to Fort Irwin, where you will serve as a liaison between Department of the Army and the 3rd Battalion, 75th Ranger."

Though he hated to do so, Delmont found that he could not avoid asking another question. "How much time do we have before we are expected to jump off?"

Bothered by the answer he was about to give, Palmer hesitated. When he did his response was rather ambiguous. "That is not for us to decide. Our task is simply to make sure that if the Commander in Chief does decide to pull the trigger, the Rangers are ready to go. I am confident you fully understand your mandate."

"Yes, sir, I believe I do."

Never having given an order of this nature before, Palmer didn't feel comfortable leaving things standing where they were. Moving out from behind his desk, he stepped forward until he was standing before Delmont. With his face set in an expression that betrayed his personal concerns, Palmer slowly repeated the final instructions that the Chairman of the Joint Chiefs of Staff had just passed onto him. "This is for your ears and your ears only. Our people will not be left to fester in Syria for 444 days. Nor will we stand idly by while the bodies of American soldiers are dragged through the streets of Damascus one by one. You will bring them home, dead or alive. Clear?"

Coming to attention, Delmont nodded. "Yes, sir. Clear as a bell."

Damascus, Syria
10:05 LOCAL (06:05 ZULU)

Nothing was left to chance. The military tribunal was to be a well-staged affair that had one predetermined conclusion fashioned to serve several well-defined purposes. For the majority of the Syrian people the public trial of Sergeant Yousaf Hashmi and his subsequent execution would placate those who demanded biblical retribution for all the suffering the Americans had inflicted upon them. It did not matter that the death of one American was little more than a token when compared to the number of Syrians who had been killed by air strikes that periodically disrupted their lives. Blood was blood. The shedding of Hashmi's blood would also serve as a warning to fellow Arabs who might be entertaining the idea of lifting their hand against their fellow Muslims while in the service of America or her allies.

The true yet less obvious purpose of this exercise was to provoke a reaction from the United States. Despite the fact that it was the Syrian government that held the prisoners, they set the pace of events or regulated the intensity of the emergency on their own. These factors were controlled by the media covering the story. So long as the editors of selected newspapers and producers of news programs said that it was a crisis, it was a crisis, one that no politician in the United States could afford to ignore. Only when a story had slipped below the fold of the newspaper and American voters lost interest in it were politicians from both sides of the political spectrum free to step down from their flag-draped soapboxes and get back to the serious business of vilifying their political foes and not the Syrians. Experience tended to support the view that when this happened, the American military became dangerous. Once they were out from under the glare of the media's spotlights and were no longer the topic of discussion on twenty-four-hour news channels, the armed forces were safe to duck into the tall grass and stalk their prey until ready to strike. More than one international terrorist or national leader who thought he had gotten away with twisting the tiger's tail was awoken from a sound sleep by the sound of a precision-guided bomb stamped Made in the U.S.A. smashing through a window of his bedroom. Unlike their fellow Americans, professional soldiers understand that patience is more than a virtue, it's a military necessity.

In the face of the sophisticated and far-reaching military might of the United States, nations like Syria have found themselves forced to practice warfare by other means, sometimes known as asymmetrical warfare. Ordinarily this means terrorism or guerrilla warfare carried out using conventional weaponry, suicide bombers, or even weapons of mass destruction. An important adjunct to these activities is information warfare, a subset of the second-oldest profession that can include anything from the disruption of critical computer systems to the use of propaganda. Within this realm of warfare the media has become an unwitting conduit. By manipulating the flow of information, a well-disciplined foe can strike at a nation's ability to control the course of events as well as the will of its populace.

Over the years the ease with which the American public could be turned against its own government through the manipulation of the press had not been lost to nations opposed to the United States. The American phase of the war in Vietnam has been something of a primer for those seeking to learn how to wage effective information warfare. The leadership of North Vietnam did not have to send a single soldier across the Pacific Ocean in order to derail the Johnson administration or bring the United States to the brink of insurrection. College professors, ambitious politicians, Hollywood glitterati, and rising media stars created an army of insurgents for Uncle Ho drawn from the ranks of privileged youth of his foe, an army that won the war for him in the streets and voting booths of the United States. The debacle in Somalia in 1993 was an even more stunning victory of imagery over reality. While it was costly to the units involved and tragic to the individual American families who lost their loved ones in that engagement, the fight in the streets of Mogadishu in October 1993 succeeded in bringing the warlords to their knees. Unfortunately for the people of the region, the video clips viewed by the American Commander in Chief convinced him that the conflict there was both unwinnable and politically unsound. The precipitous withdrawal of American forces from Somalia left that nation in a state of chaos from which it has yet to recover. These lessons and countless others have not been lost on those who cannot match the United States on an open field of battle. Rather than a bane to dictators and mass murderers, the TV news crew has become the weapon of choice when those dictators, terrorists, and mass murderers wish to target the American public.

With this in mind the officers charged with preparing the military tribunal approached it not as an exercise in international jurisprudence but rather as a stage play. Since the verdict and punishment had already been decided upon, the real issues became how to present the facts that supported the tribunal's conclusions in the most dramatic manner possible. To achieve this, everything had to be just so.

The room selected for this melodrama was selected with an eye toward the Western public. It had to fit the august and somber character that they have come to associate with judicial proceedings. At the head of the room would be the panel of three judges. Though they were all officers belonging to the Republican Guard, the criteria used in selecting the men who would hand down the verdict of guilt was their appearance. Instead of lean and muscular military types sporting intimidating expressions, each of the three judges selected could have doubled as a wise, elderly mullah who had spent his days studying the word of God and not the art of war. This was done for the benefit of those Muslims who would view the proceedings in Syria and every Arabic-speaking community throughout the world. They also had to be able to maintain expressions that clearly demonstrated that they were being deliberative and reflective as they weighed the facts of the case.

Before them would be the accused, Sergeant Yousaf Hashmi. Seated in a straight-back chair the American would face his judges with nothing to hide behind. On either side of Hashmi were two guards. Unlike the panel of judges, these sentinels were picked for their size and military bearing. Standing at rapt attention while clutching their AK-74 Kalashnikovs tightly against their chests, they represented the brave and vigilant Army that stood ready to protect Syria from traitors and foreign intruders alike.

To Hashmi's left rear sat the Syrian officer assigned to plead his case. In the same way they'd chosen all the other actors, those responsible for orchestrating this event had taken great pains to find just the right person to serve as a spokesperson for the accused. Wearing an ill-fitting uniform that hung from his skinny frame as if it were draped upon a coat rack, the bespectacled defense attorney's discomfort with his role was reflected by his posture, or more correctly lack thereof, as well as the exaggerated deference with which he addressed everyone in the room. He knew what was expected of him. Even if he had a grasp of international and military law, the counsel for defense lacked the mettle necessary to withstand the whirlwind the prosecution was prepared to unleash.

The man chosen to stand up for the people of Syria was a cross between the trio of judges seated at the front of the room, the pair of guards posted on either side of Hashmi, and a Hollywood star. Tall and well built, the middle-aged Syrian officer was the epitome of what a good Arab father should look like. The hint of gray hair testified to the wisdom that only maturity can bring. An occasional twinkle in his clear piercing eyes hinted of kindness and love that had the ability to soften the firm resoluteness that his strong angular jaw established. When he spoke his tone commanded the attention of those who heard it without his needing to be shrill or harsh. Even his posture and the manner with which he carried himself marked him as a man who was confident and in control.

To support these key players a handpicked audience of "average" Syrian citizens had been assembled. They would serve as the Greek chorus, wailing their laments as each crime against their fellow citizens and their nation was described and shouting well-rehearsed adoration whenever the prosecution scored a point. Most were women wearing traditional Arabic dress, and old men. Here and there children were mixed in with the crowd to represent those orphaned by American aggression. Also scattered about in the audience were a fair number of Syrian secret police. Dressed in mufti, they were tasked with maintaining discipline among the rabble throughout the proceedings. While none of them announced that this was what they were there for, no one in the audience needed to be told. Just as they understood their purpose, they instinctively knew what would become of them and their loved ones if they failed to measure up to expectations.

On one side of the room sat a steel cage. Behind its iron bars was a row of four chairs set one meter apart from each other. These chairs were for Hashmi's fellow Americans. The Syrians brought the remaining members of RT Kilo into the room in reverse order of rank, filling the chairs from left to right. The first to be led into the cage was Specialist Four Salvador Mendez. Though haggard and clearly suffering from the beatings that had been heaped upon him, he carried himself with as much moxie and swagger as his situation and the guards would permit. He wanted all who saw him to see that he was bloodied but unbowed. Next came Specialist Four David Davis. Dee Dee tried to follow his companion's example but found that he could no longer muster the strength to do so. Every ounce of courage and grit had been pounded out of him. To his right was Sergeant First Class Allen Kannen. Whatever Kannen thought, whatever he felt, he kept to himself. He was being driven by a desire to give the Syrians nothing. To this end he made every effort to keep his emotions and expressions in check no matter what happened, trusting that those who saw the video back home would understand his silent defiance.

Over the course of their captivity all the members of RT Kilo had been kept in isolation. Unable to gauge how the others were being treated and were holding up, each man had been left to deal with his pain, suffering, and fear on his own as well as he could. So it was not surprising that each man felt a moment of joy and hope when he saw his companions. Not only did it prove that he had not been alone, it permitted each of them to judge just how bad he himself must have looked since none had been afforded an opportunity to inspect themselves in a mirror.

Guards cut from the same mold as the pair who stood behind Hashmi served as escorts to Kannen, Davis, and Mendez. They prevented the Americans from speaking to each other and limited their freedom to look around. Once the Americans were seated in the cage, each of the three guards posted himself behind one of the American prisoners. The three enlisted men were in place when Ken Aveno was brought into the courtroom. As the others had been, Aveno was led to the cage where his seat awaited him. Unlike the others, the executive officer of RT Kilo made no effort at all to put up a brave and noble front. Whereas Kannen, Davis, and Mendez had stood erect and marched forward with as much pride as their injuries and leg irons permitted, Ken Aveno shuffled forward stoop-shouldered with a faltering pace. With his head bowed low, he made no effort to look left or right, even as he was paraded before his fellow Americans. Staring down at the floor, his face betrayed a pained, almost shocked expression.

Whatever strength the trio of enlisted men had managed to garner when they laid eyes on each other was sapped in an instant by the pathetic image that their lieutenant presented. Like the rest

of the spectacle being played out in this room, this was exactly
what the Syrians had planned. They suspected that the three
American enlisted men would look to Aveno as a source of
strength and for cues on how to carry themselves during the proceedings that were about to take place. To prevent this from
occurring without resorting to the beatings that might not work
and would leave telltale signs, the Syrians chose to break the
American officer's spirit by delivering a crippling blow to him just
prior to the commencement of the tribunal. In an anteroom just
outside the courtroom, Aveno was escorted to a table. Upon it
were clippings from English-language newspapers covering the
story of the strange love triangle involving Aveno's estranged wife
and Karen Green. The Syrians had no need to embellish anything
that American and British journalists said. Every conceivable and
juicy little tidbit, no matter how perverse and twisted, was articu-
lated in the pieces before Aveno.

No amount of torture, no other psychological trick, could
have had the same crushing impact that the revelation of this
story had on Aveno. He had fallen in love with Elizabeth at college. It had been a maddening all-consuming sort of passion that
romantic novelists only dream about. He had ignored her coolness at his insistence that they marry. He even managed to disregard the stories that his friends passed on to him of what they had
heard about Elizabeth's preferences. Only when his first commanding officer found it necessary to call Aveno into his office to
inform him that Elizabeth had approached another officer's wife
with an indecent proposal did Aveno find he had no choice but to
face reality. Yet even then the young officer was unable to cast
aside his feelings. When it came time for them to part, Aveno and
Elizabeth opted to begin by going their separate ways, rather than
immediately commencing divorce proceedings. Eventually Aveno
knew he would have to do what was necessary. Eventually he
would have to take some sort of action to end the farce that his
marriage had turned into. But at the time of his separation from
Elizabeth he could not find the courage necessary to act. Con-

fused and stunned by what was happening, he had done nothing while the love of his life walked away and left him alone to deal with his failure.

This was where things had stood when RT Kilo met its demise. Now, as Ken Aveno glanced from news story to news story he came to realize that whatever hope he had of pursuing a military career was over. No officer, no matter how good or brave or technically and tactically proficient he was, could survive with something like this following him around from assignment to assignment. For the first time since he had been taken prisoner, Ken Aveno began to see that death had become more than an option.

Lost in his own private crisis, Aveno did not take note that the other two officers who had been taken prisoner were not present. All of the enlisted men, however, picked up upon this glaring omission. Though none of them were able to communicate with the other, in time each man came to the same conclusion. As near as they could figure, both Captain Burman and the Air Force officer were being kept back as hostages in an effort to ensure the NCOs' good behavior in public should the guards behind them not suffice. Just what the Syrians would do to Burman and Ciszak was less clear. Having undergone days of unimaginable torture themselves, however, Kannen, Mendez, and Davis all had an excellent frame of reference as to what could happen if they did something that displeased their captors.

Surprisingly this effect had not been part of the equation that the Syrians had so carefully worked out. The truth of the matter was that Joseph Ciszak was already gone, bartered to the People's Liberation Army for badly needed military hardware. In Burman's case, he was safely tucked away in a military hospital where life-support systems were keeping him alive. Just what they would do with Burman had not been determined. Since they had already released the names of the American soldiers killed in action at the time of their capture, it had been decided that it would not look good to announce that one had died while in their custody. So they kept him alive, figuring that even a damaged poker chip had some value in the game they were playing.

The tribunal began with the entrance of the three Syrian judges. With great ceremony they trooped to the front of the room where they took their seats under the watchful eye of a flag-draped portrait of their national leader. With a somber tone the senior officer and chief judge called the proceedings to order before reading the charges against Sergeant Yousaf Hashmi aloud. "Yousaf Hashmi, you are being accused of treason against the people and the government of Syria. You have knowingly assisted foreign invaders to violate our national sovereignty for the purpose of waging a cruel, unjust, and inhuman war against its people. As a result of your actions, untold numbers of your fellow citizens have died or suffered."

Suspecting that he was already condemned to die and unwilling to play his part in the manner that the Syrians wished, Hashmi interrupted the reading of the charges against him. "I am an American, born and raised in the United States of America. I am not a Syrian."

Before the American could finish his denouncement of the charges, the president of the tribunal slammed his fist upon the desk and barked, "*Silence!* You will be silent until you are called upon to answer."

Having ventured this far, Hashmi was determined to press on, regardless of the cost. Controlling the fear that gripped his entire body, he repeated his statement. "I am a citizen of the United States of America and a sergeant in the United States Army. I am guilty of no crimes against Syria or its people."

As the chorus of spectators drowned out his words with jeers and hoots, one of the guards behind Hashmi took a step forward and slapped the American NCO's head with the back of his hand. At the front of the room the president of the tribunal continued to pound the table and demand Hashmi be still. Having made his point and shown that he would not go quietly to his predetermined doom, Hashmi complied, for the moment.

When silence was restored the president of the tribunal nodded to the prosecutor. Taking his time, the Syrian selected to be the hero of this production stood up and approached Hashmi. When he was standing before Hashmi, the prosecutor folded his arms and looked down at the American NCO. "What is the nationality of your parents?"

Hashmi looked into the Syrian's eyes before answering. He knew where all of this was going. He knew what was going to happen. He was going to die. That was a given, which nothing he said or did here would change. The only choice he had was how the world would see him and what they would hear him say. In the heavy silence of the room, Hashmi glanced at his fellow soldiers. When he saw that his lieutenant was making no effort to look up at him, Hashmi's gaze fell upon Kannen. The NCO guessed what Hashmi was asking him with his eyes. Though he knew that it would be hard on him and the others, Kannen closed his eyes and gave a slight yet noticeable nod.

Having received Kannen's sanction, Hashmi looked up at the Syrian before him. With a steady voice that betrayed no hint of wavering, he spoke as loud as he could without shouting. "I am an American soldier, charged with the duty of defending my fellow Americans against all enemies, foreign and domestic."

It was not the words that angered the Syrian prosecutor. It wasn't even the tone of Hashmi's voice. Rather it was the glint in the American's eye, and the hint of a smile that threw the Syrian into a fit of rage. Tossing aside the decorum by which he was supposed to be abiding the Syrian raised his hand as far as he could and delivered a stunning open-handed blow that sent the American before him sprawling onto the floor. Taken aback by this breach in protocol and unexpected deviation from the script before him, the president of the tribunal stared at his chief prosecutor, then at a figure standing behind a bank of cameras at the rear of the room. With a single motion of his hand, the producer of this stage play brought the opening session to an abrupt close. For the moment he had enough footage with which to proceed. They no longer needed the Americans. Through careful editing, a body-double shot from behind, and a dubbed voice delivered by a Syrian soldier who was even able to mimic Hashmi's accent, the Syrian Ministry of Information would be able to complete the tribunal without having to worry about any further interference from the accused. Their goal would be met and on schedule. By the next day a story that had been fading from the public's radar would once more be dictating the agendas of decision makers in the United States and around the world.

CHAPTER TWENTY-THREE

Fort Irwin, California
07:00 LOCAL (14:00 ZULU)

Seated on the hood of his humvee with his feet resting on the I-beam front bumper, Lieutenant Colonel Harry Shaddock watched the Air Force transport as it taxied its way over to where the hangars were. Standing to either side were his sergeant major, John Harris and his XO, Ben Castalane. When the roar of the aircraft's engines had subsided somewhat, Shaddock grunted. "Am I the only one who feels like a Trojan soldier watching a horse being hauled through the gates of his city?"

With a chuckle Castalane looked up at his commanding officer. "What's the matter, sir? Don't trust our good buddies from Puzzle Palace?"

Shaddock looked at his XO. "You know, when I was doing my time at Fort Benning a Russian officer who was visiting us presented a briefing on the war plans the former Soviet Union had drawn up for waging war against the United States. When he listed the primary targets the Strategic Rocket Force would take out in their first strike, all of us noticed that the Pentagon was not included. Well," Shaddock continued as he waved his hand about, "being the spring butt that I am, I took the bait. In a flash I threw my hand up. When the Russian stopped and called on me I pointed this out, asking him why the Pentagon had been left out. With a straight face and without missing a beat the Russian looked at me, and replied, 'Well, after careful analysis of your nation's command-and-control structure, it was determined that destroying the Pentagon would only serve to enhance the combat capability of your armed forces.'"

Amidst the chorus of laughter, Sergeant Major Harris lifted the lapel of his uniform. "Ah, sir, could you repeat that? I don't think my hidden mike got everything you said."

Shaddock threw his hands up. "Sergeant Major, I'm only relating to you a true 'story."

Castalane chuckled. "That's right, Sergeant Major, with the emphasis on '*story.*'"

The laughter faded as the transport rolled to a stop. Not being privy to what exactly was going on behind the scenes, Harris looked up at his commanding officer. "I take it from your demeanor, Colonel, this is a new wrinkle."

Shaddock didn't respond as he sat there wondering what the sudden appearance of this aircraft, its passengers, and the cargo it carried would mean to his battalion. Those suspicions he did harbor could not be shared with his subordinates. In an eyes-only message that had been hand delivered to him the night before by a courier who had been flown in, Shaddock was made aware of how much the situation in Syria was in flux. The message was as short as it was encrypted. "Original goals of Fanfare no longer applicable. Fanfare is now the primary response. Personnel with revised orders as well as additional equipment required for execution of revised Fanfare will be arriving your location by air 1400 hours Zulu."

When his colonel didn't respond to his comment Harris let the matter drop. He had no doubt in his military mind that he would find out what all of this was about soon enough.

After easing himself down, Shaddock reached behind with his right hand and pounded on the hood, shouting to his driver who tended to drift off to sleep whenever the engine wasn't running. "Jackson, crank it up!" Turning to his XO and sergeant major, the commander of the 3rd of the 75th Rangers pointed to the transport. "What do you say we go over there and see what the pros from Dover have for us."

.   .   .

By the time the crew chief of the transport had the ramp down, Robert Delmont was up, out of his seat, and ready to go. Leaving the project manager for the Land Warrior system and his training NCOs to deal with the load of equipment, Delmont trooped down the ramp and into the bright desert dawn. Pausing as soon as his feet were on the ground, he glanced at his watch, then up at the sun. It was still early morning and already he was perspiring. By noon his brown-and-tan desert BDUs would be soaked with sweat.

He hadn't been on the ground for more than a few moments when a covey of three humvees roared up to the transport and came to a screeching halt, throwing up a cloud of dust that drifted into the open cargo bay. Despite the fact that the people who emerged from the humvees outranked him, the transport's crew chief gave Lieutenant Colonel Shaddock, Major Castalane, and Sergeant Major Harris a look that could kill.

Ignoring the Air Force sergeant, Shaddock marched up to Delmont. "Are you in charge here?"

Somewhat taken aback by Shaddock's brusque manner, the special ops plans officer raised his right hand in preparation to receive Shaddock's in greeting. "I am Lieutenant Colonel Robert Delmont from the Office of the Deputy Chief of Staff of the Army for Special Operations."

"I'm Shaddock," the Ranger officer snapped without making any effort whatsoever to take Delmont's proffered hand. "You're supposed to have orders for me."

For a moment Delmont stared at the commander of the 3rd of the 75th with his hand held out between them. When he finally realized how things stood, the plans officer withdrew his hand behind his back, where he clasped it with his other hand. Rocking back on his heels, he took a moment to size up both the man before him and the situation. *Well,* Delmont thought as they eyed each other like a pair of pit bulls in the ring, *if this is the way you want to play it, then by God that's the way it will go down.* "Is there a secure area where we can go, Colonel, and discuss those orders?"

With a smile that reflected not a whit of warmth, Shaddock reached out with his right hand, took Delmont by the forearm, and raised his left hand in the direction of the open desert. "Please, *Colonel*. Step into my office."

Making no effort to mask the scathing expression that clouded his face, Delmont fell in behind Shaddock as the two stormed off in silence. When Shaddock was sure that he was out of earshot of everyone gathered about the rear of the transport he stopped and pivoted. "Before we get started here," he stated, making no effort to hide his anger and frustration, "are you someone who knows what's going on or are you simply another messenger boy who doesn't know his ass from a hole in the ground?"

Having had a few seconds to collect himself in the wake of Shaddock's less-than-cordial greeting, Delmont folded his arms across his chest and leaned over to look down at the toes of his boots for a second. When he was ready he glanced up at Shaddock. "I suppose I could say that I understand how you feel, that I am well aware of the goat rope we have been putting you through these past few weeks without allowing you the freedom to level with your men. Well, I'm not going to bullshit you. I'm not going to because you're a professional soldier and an officer who's been in the Army long enough to know how things work."

"You have no need to remind me of that, mister."

"Then climb down off your high horse, Colonel, and start acting like it!"

Having been called on his less-than-exemplary behavior by a fellow officer, Shaddock felt a sudden pang of regret. Though he was still angry over the way he was being kept in the dark about what was going on at echelons above him, Shaddock knew that he had been wrong to carry on the way he had. Tucking his hands up under his arms, Shaddock pulled away a few steps. Looking down at the ground, he kicked some dirt about with the toe of his boot as he regrouped. "Okay, Colonel. What are my new orders?"

While the Ranger's demeanor was still far from being friendly, at least he had ratcheted down his tone to something resembling civility.

Delmont answered accordingly. "When Fanfare was originally planned it was meant to be nothing more than a deception plan, a not-so-veiled threat that would serve as a warning to the Syrians."

Without looking up from the circles he was drawing in the sand with the toe of his boot, Shaddock nodded. "Yes, that part I understood. We were to be the sword of Damocles hanging above the negotiating table."

"Something like that, yes," Delmont affirmed. "From the beginning, the administration took the position that this crisis would be resolved through diplomacy."

Glancing up from his sand art for a moment, Shaddock looked beyond Delmont and out into the open desert. "Let me guess. Someone forgot to fax the president's talking points to the Syrians."

Sharing the Ranger's contempt for the manner with which the crisis had been handled up to this point, Delmont agreed as he also gazed out into the vast, barren distance. "Yeah, something like that." Then, looking back at Shaddock, he picked up where he had left off. "The Commander in Chief has finally come to realize that something must be done to bring this crisis to an end."

It took Shaddock several seconds to realize that Delmont's pause was deliberate, very deliberate. When he looked back into the eyes of the special ops plans officer, the commanding officer of the 3rd of the 75th Rangers understood what this unexpected silence implied. Whatever bitterness he still harbored left him. "We are actually going to be sent in?" he finally managed to ask.

"There's nothing we can do to save Sergeant Hashmi," Delmont explained. "And as well as our sources can determine, both Burman and Ciszak are beyond our reach."

Shaddock didn't need to ask what the Department of the Army staff officer meant by "beyond our reach." He was enough of a pragmatist to understand.

"Even the others," Delmont went on as he began to shuffle his own feet as he started in delve into a subject that he found difficult to verbalize, "may be a lost cause."

"Yet we are still going to try," Shaddock stated glumly. "That is why you are here, isn't it?"

Delmont decided that it was time to drop his evasive manner and get to the point. Stomping his feet as if he were shaking something off his boots, the special ops officer looked into Shaddock's eyes. "Fanfare has been modified. Instead of using Delta and Task Force 160, your battalion is responsible for the entire operation, from beginning to end. Delta and Task Force 160 will now become the deception while this battalion deploys from here directly into combat."

While he had been expecting something radical, it took Shaddock a moment to do the math. "We are going to fly halfway around the world nonstop, make a combat jump, and storm a military prison in downtown Damascus."

Delmont nodded. "Yes, something like that. Which," he added as he jerked his thumb up over his shoulder and toward the transport, "is why we brought along an entire company's worth of the new Land Warrior system the folks at Belvoir have been working on. It should give us enough of an edge over any resistance we encounter to pull this thing off."

"We?" Shaddock asked incredulously.

"For better or worse, Colonel, I'm here to stay."

Try as they might, the training NCOs who had accompanied Lieutenant Colonel Neil Kaplan, could not keep the soldiers of Company A, 3rd of the 75th Rangers from tearing into the boxes and crates they had been issued. The refrain, "Take it easy on the gear" could be heard echoing around the maintenance bay that had been converted into an ad hoc issue point and classroom. Even the fact that their beloved company commander had been summarily relieved in the field and replaced by a total stranger was forgotten as the Rangers of Alpha Company inspected the high-tech gear that they would soon have a chance to play with.

In the middle of the organized bedlam, First Lieutenant Emmett DeWitt stood next to the officer responsible for issuing the Land Warrior systems to DeWitt's company and training them in its use. "You realize," Kaplan muttered, "we do not have the time needed to fully qualify your men on this system. At best they will be able to use but a fraction of its full capability."

As he watched his men go about defying the dictates of Kaplan's NCOs, and continue to rip into boxes like hyperactive kids on Christmas morn, DeWitt grinned. "Colonel, those are Rangers you're talking about. Every now and then they've been known to surprise folks with what they can do."

Making no effort to hide the deadly earnest tone of his voice, Kaplan looked over at the new commander of Alpha. "For our sake and the sake of those poor bastards in Damascus, let's hope you're right."

Taking the hint, DeWitt nodded. "Yes, sir. You do have a point."

Not wishing to linger on that grim thought any longer than necessary, Kaplan cleared his throat. "If you follow me, Lieutenant, I will introduce you to the latest version of the new and improved Land Warrior. While it pales when compared to what the folks in Hollywood can dream up, it is the system that will revolutionize ground warfare."

"Colonel, I'm the last person in the world you need to convince. I'm a believer."

With a sly smile, Kaplan cocked his head. "Good. Now, let's get down to making you a practitioner."

Weaving their way through the clutter of soldiers, instructors, empty boxes, packing material, and high-tech gear, Kaplan led DeWitt to a table off to one side of the room where DeWitt's executive officer and platoon leaders were gathered. On the table one of Kaplan's NCOs had laid out complete sets of the Land Warrior for each of them. "This is Master Sergeant Benoit, the

NCOIC of the Land Warrior mobile training team. He has set aside a complete set for yourself and each of your officers," he announced as they stood before the mass of cables, electronic black boxes, weapons, sights, vests, and helmets. "I thought it would be beneficial if we gave you and your officers a leg up on the system while the rest of your command and my people complete the process of unpacking, sorting, and issuing the equipment."

With a nod DeWitt acknowledged Kaplan's forethought and courtesy.

"While the equipment before you is basically no different than any of the other sets your company will be receiving, these computers have several additional programs, which analysts in my office have concluded a company commander and his platoon leaders might need in combat."

"Excuse me, Colonel, I don't mean to be rude or to interrupt, but are you saying what I think you are saying? As in, Gee, we haven't tried this yet?"

For the briefest of moments the self-assured confidence that Neil Kaplan had presented up to this point wavered. But only for a moment. "Well, yes and no."

Far from placating his concern, DeWitt cocked his head and folded his arms. "Colonel, if you don't mind me asking, exactly how much is yes and how much is no?"

Kaplan's expression made it quite clear that he did mind. Still, he took the time to answer DeWitt's inquiry. "The prototype of this version is the outgrowth of years of testing and evaluation. This particular model was subjected to numerous tests under every imaginable environmental and combat condition with a great deal of emphasis on desert warfare. What we have here," he stated as he laid his left hand on a stack of equipment sitting on the table, "is part of the initial low-rate engineering-protection run, or LREP, that had been slated for full-scale evaluation later this year at Fort Hood."

After studying the equipment for a moment DeWitt turned and looked at his officers. To a man they were as unfamiliar to him as they were with Kaplan's high-tech gear, so he could not read their expressions and determine what, if anything, they were thinking. Of course, he concluded, it didn't make a rat's ass what they thought. Nor did it matter if he had reservations over the reliability of the equipment before him. They were all soldiers. They had their marching orders and that, as they say, is that.

Forcing a smile, DeWitt clapped his two hands together and rubbed them as he looked over at Kaplan. "Well, that's good enough for me, Colonel. Let's get started."

20:10 LOCAL (03:10 ZULU)

Using the same well-rehearsed presentation that he used every time he was charged with presenting an initial orientation on the Land Warrior, Master Sergeant Benoit added a healthy dose of theory as he picked up each item and explained its purpose. "This version of the Land Warrior is designed to be incorporated into the MOLLE battle vest and the Interceptor body armor. The personal area network, or PAN, consists of independent communications modules which are arranged so as to distribute their weight evenly without hindering the flexibility or agility of the soldier."

Unable to keep his peace, the most outspoken platoon leader of third Platoon, Second Lieutenant Peter Quinn chuckled. "Gee, that's really nice of them."

In a flash DeWitt turned and gave Quinn one of those piercing looks that needed no translation. Sheepishly, Quinn bowed his head. "Sorry."

Having taken care of his unruly officer, DeWitt nodded to Master Sergeant Benoit. "You may proceed."

"If you would, sir," Benoit stated as he handed DeWitt the body armor and battle vest that had been set aside for him. Once he had finished adjusting the straps so that they were comfortably snug, the training NCO continued by picking up the first box on the table. "The heart, or more correctly, the brain of the system is this computer," Benoit stated as he handed it to DeWitt to inspect. "It is powered by a pair of rechargeable batteries that provide forty-eight hours of continuous use under normal conditions."

"Define 'normal' if you would, Sergeant," DeWitt insisted.

"Normal takes into account a day/night cycle," Benoit explained as he took the computer from DeWitt and slid it into the pocket on the combat vest designed for it. "It assumes the periods of rest that a soldier requires, using historical models when measuring the duration of combat in any given forty-eight-hour period. Quite naturally if the man is chatting over the wireless local area network, or WLAN, nonstop, has his thermal sight powered up and on around the clock and is tapping the GPS update button every ten seconds the batteries won't last that long."

DeWitt grunted but said nothing as Benoit continued. "There are a number of modules built into the computer itself. These include a GPS receiver, a pedometer capable of measuring the pace of the user, and a digital compass. In addition to the NAV, or navigational module, this system not only maintains your current position but also transmits this data to the situational awareness, or SA, module on other Land Warrior systems."

"So I can keep track of where each individual soldier in my company is," DeWitt stated as Benoit finished securing the computer module.

Understanding where DeWitt was going, Kaplan responded to DeWitt's question. "For some time now the problem has been not providing commanders or soldiers with information. This became painfully obvious to all the services during the First Gulf War in 1991. Information management, or packaging data into usable products is the key to success in warfare on the digital battlefield. While you could try to keep track of every single man in your command, Lieutenant, you'd quickly become overwhelmed with this chore and find yourself unable to do anything else.

Hence the special programs keyed to specific users. On your system, for example, the default settings for locations of your command are platoons, battalion combat support elements, and friendly units to your left and right. Your platoon leaders will see their squads when they access their situational awareness program and, in turn, their squad leaders will see only the members of their own squad as well as their platoon leader and any friendly troops within a prescribed radius. Of course, if you want to zero in on a particular squad or call one of your platoon leaders to meet him face-to-face, you have capability of tracking that squad or platoon leader and finding them right off."

DeWitt nodded. "Sounds like a winner to me. Next?"

"Knowing where your people are is only the beginning," Benoit continued after he finished locking in a new cable into the computer module. "The secure, non-line-of-sight wireless local area network, or WLAN, has two voiceover IP push-to-talk buttons which allow you to contact anyone operating on the net. It will negate the need for a separate squad radio system."

Lieutenant Quinn raised his right index finger in order to catch Benoit's attention. Since Benoit was involved in hooking up DeWitt's Land Warrior system, Kaplan took the question. "Yes, Lieutenant. You have a question?"

"Does this local area network negate the need for our current tactical radios?"

Without pausing, Benoit responded to Quinn's question as he made a minor adjustment on the next component he would be dealing with. "Not at this time. The current family of SINCGARS tactical radios have a greater range, frequency hopping, and secure voice capability. They will remain the backbone of our tactical command-and-control system for the foreseeable future."

"Not all units you may find yourself operating with will have the Land Warrior," Kaplan stated. "It will be some time before combat support and combat service support personnel have a system like this tailored to their specific requirements. And even then, given the attitude of many of our allies toward force modernization and the military, it is an open question as to whether other nations will field a system similar to Land Warrior."

From somewhere in the crowd, one of the platoon leaders sneered. "Three cheers for our allies."

Ignoring the interruption Benoit took up the helmet he had secured from DeWitt in advance and held it before him. "Up until now we have been dealing with command-and-control and land navigation. Now we start looking at the business end of the system, the weapons sights and laser designators."

This brought a smile to DeWitt's face. "Now, that's what I'm talkin' about. Bring it on, Sergeant."

Once Dewitt had his helmet on and had secured the chin strap, Benoit reached up and flipped a small oval disk down. "This, sir, is your lightweight thermal weapons sight, or LWTWS."

Reaching up, Dewitt gingerly touched the edges of the thin disk between his index finger and thumb. "This seems rather small."

"Until we come up with a system capable of replicating data as images that the soldier can recognize without a second thought," Kaplan pointed out, "the soldier must still be free to use his own eyes. In future versions the soldier will have a completely enclosed helmet not unlike those used by virtual reality systems."

When his colonel was finished, Benoit continued. "You're going to need to adjust this over one of your eyes, sir, to where you can easily see whatever is displayed on it. The adjustments are done like this, and this."

After watching as best he could what the training NCO was doing, DeWitt fiddled with the weapons sight hanging from his helmet until he was satisfied with where it was. "Okay. What now?"

A subtle shift in Master Sergeant Benoit's voice hinted that this was the portion of his orientation that he enjoyed. "The weapon's subsystem incorporates two sights, the lightweight thermal weapons sight and the ultralight color video sight attached to the weapon. Images generated by both of those are viewed by the soldier on the monocular display attached to his helmet."

Just as eager as his NCO, Kaplan could not help but jump in when he could to point out key points. "One of the most difficult aspects we have had with digitizing the battlefield at the individual combat soldier level has been the presentation of information in a manner that is immediately recognizable and useful. For example, humans are visually oriented. We respond to things we see based upon their shape, color, posture, and activity. A soldier on the battlefield does not have time to read a message being beamed across his field of vision stating 'Enemy, three o'clock.' The cognitive process required to translate that message or symbols into a coherent thought upon which he can then base his response takes time, time which an infantryman cannot afford. For a system to be worthwhile it has to enhance a soldier's awareness and reduce his response time to threats, not impede it. Therefore all of our efforts have been geared to delivering information and images to the soldier in a form that is natural to him and elicits a response that is more instinctive. Hence the switch to full color instead of the black-and-white imaging used in initial prototypes. In time we expect to go even further by adopting some of the technologies used by the virtual reality people. Not only will the soldier be able to see a three-dimensional world through his weapon's sight, threats will be highlighted or enhanced."

Anxious to skip the sales pitch and get down to actually seeing if the theories the colonel and his NCO were describing translated into a useful system, DeWitt nodded politely. "Yes, sir, I see, I see." Then he turned to Benoit who was in the process of making the final connections. "Now, Sergeant, how does all this neat stuff work?"

Benoit, who had been leaning over, stood up, looked DeWitt in the eye, and smiled. "Quite effectively, sir."

The quip served to lighten the mood a tad. "Okay, Sergeant," DeWitt moaned. "Target, cease fire. Now, back on your head."

For the next few minutes Benoit explained how to power up the system, switch from the thermal sight to the full-color sight and use the built-in combat identification system. "This item," he explained, "is not at all unlike the identify-friend-or-foe that the Air Force has been using for years. As squads become more dispersed thanks to the Land Warrior, the opportunity for fratricide increases. By building a combat identification system into the sight it is hoped that we can reduce friendly-fire incidents to nil."

"Hoped?" DeWitt asked. "I thought hope wasn't an option?"

Kaplan sighed. "Despite quantum leaps and bounds in technology, decisions on the battlefield at all levels will still be made by human beings."

Taking care while doing so, for fear of messing something up, DeWitt turned to his assembled platoon leaders. "Okay, you people, you heard him. Despite what you may have heard, the colonel confirms some of your speculations. I *am* human."

This brought on a ripple of nervous laughter and more than a few anxious sidelong glances. Emmett DeWitt had replaced a very popular commanding officer under very difficult circumstances. Even if he had been afforded the luxury of time, which Colonel Shaddock pointed out he did not have, DeWitt was not the sort of officer who believed that a commanding officer could be both a good buddy to his subordinates and an effective leader. Though he endeavored to be fair and just in all his dealings with the men he commanded, he always made it a point to be strict and uncompromising when it came to pursuing the profession of arms.

Both Kaplan and Benoit sensed that there was something more going on here than they knew. So they waited until their prime subject finished with his officers. When he was sure that he had made his point, DeWitt faced the training NCO once more. "Okay, where were we, Sergeant?"

Without skipping a beat Benoit picked up where he had left off. "I was just getting ready to show you how to use your sights to achieve first-shot kills at ranges of three hundred meters without exposing anything but your weapon and your sight."

Not knowing what sort of officer Kaplan was and conscious that he could not afford to compromise himself in any way in front of his platoon leaders, DeWitt chose not to make light of Benoit's choice of words. It was not that he was a prude or that he wasn't tempted to. Even after years of forced socialization and sensitivity training, the American military was still far from being gender neutral. The soldiers who were charged with the duty of doing the fighting and dying were human beings, people blessed with all their wonderful strengths and attributes as well as all their earthly shortcomings and habits. Still, until he knew how far he could go in the presence of this particular officer, DeWitt opted to fly straight and keep his colorful comments in check.

The special orientation Kaplan was holding for DeWitt and his officers was just wrapping up when Delmont and Shaddock entered the maintenance bay. From somewhere among the heaps of discarded packing materials and small clusters of soldiers and trainers, someone shouted, *"Aaaaatten-tion!"*

To a man every soul in the room ceased what he was doing and came to a position of attention. In response Shaddock acknowledged this display of military courtesy with a brisk, "As you were," that was heard throughout the bay. On cue the group of officers whom Master Sergeant Benoit had been working with arranged themselves in order of rank. With Emmett DeWitt to his left, Neil Kaplan stepped to the fore. Benoit took up a post behind and to the right of his colonel. Farther back stood the executive officer of Alpha Company with the platoon leaders trailing off to his left.

Shaddock stepped right up to Kaplan. "I hope you are receiving the full cooperation of my people, Colonel."

"They have been outstanding, Colonel Shaddock. Each of them live up to the reputation of being the best of the best."

If it pleased him to hear this the commanding officer of the 3rd of the 75th didn't show it. Rather, he looked over at DeWitt. "I expect nothing less."

Knowing this comment was intended to reinforce the initial lecture Shaddock had given him when he had assumed command of Alpha, DeWitt responded with a crisp "Airborne, sir," that bordered on being a tad too loud.

Pleased, Shaddock looked at the XO. "If you gentlemen would excuse us," he stated in a voice that left no doubt that this was an order.

Kaplan, sensing that the commander of the Ranger battalion was about to discuss something that was meant for selective ears only, glanced over his shoulder at Benoit. With a slight shifting of his eyes, he cued him in to the fact that he was also to make himself scarce. When the gathering was down to just the three lieutenant colonels and the one first lieutenant, Shaddock turned to Kaplan. "How much time are you going to need?"

Kaplan took a moment to ponder the question. He didn't need to ask for any clarification, for he knew what all of this was about and what was at stake. When he had an answer that was as definitive as he dared venture, he drew himself up and looked into Shaddock's eyes. "If we push Lieutenant DeWitt's people without physically exhausting them or overwhelming their ability to absorb what we are teaching them, they will achieve a minimum, and I emphasize the word 'minimum,' level of individual proficiency with the system within two days. Once we are there they will need an additional two, maybe three days of platoon- and company-level tactical training. I would like to have an additional two days to evaluate the company and hone their skills a bit, but—"

Shaddock cut Kaplan off. "If we have the time, fine." Looking over at DeWitt he began to issue his orders. "Coordinate your training schedule and activities directly with Colonel Kaplan using the schedule he just laid out. When it comes time for the tactical training divide the day into three parts. Tailor your predawn training to fit those tasks assigned to your company during phase one of the operation, i.e., the securing of the airfield. In the afternoon you will conduct mounted training for a new phase of the operation which you haven't been briefed on yet."

If Emmett DeWitt was taken aback by the revelation that there was a new wrinkle to Alpha's role in Fanfare he didn't let on.

"The third portion of your tactical training day will focus on clearing a building."

This time the commanding officer of Alpha could not keep himself from expressing his surprise. "What sort of building and where?"

For the first time Delmont joined the discussion. "The post commander here has graciously agreed to let your battalion 'borrow' one of his buildings."

Shaddock gave Delmont a knowing look. "I would not have used the word 'gracious' to describe the post commander's position on the matter but that's neither here nor there. Coordinate with the S-3 at least twelve hours in advance for your needs and keep him posted on your activities. You and your company have priority on everything, from training ammo to facilities. If you run into any problems with anyone see me or the XO."

For the briefest of moments, Shaddock saw a twinkle in DeWitt's eyes. "Lieutenant, I have a long memory. Don't abuse the privilege."

Realizing he had been caught contemplating how best to use his special status, DeWitt did his best to assure his colonel that he wouldn't think of doing so.

Shaddock chuckled. "Lieutenant DeWitt, you have a lot to learn about me and this battalion. One of those lessons is never try to bullshit a bullshitter. Clear?"

Grinning, DeWitt nodded. "Clear, sir."

"Good! Now, if you have no further questions for me I would advise you and Colonel Kaplan to get back to work. Time, Lieutenant, is not our friend."

Following the obligatory exchange of salutes, Shaddock and Delmont moved off to a spot from which they could watch the activities throughout the bay without having anyone overhear their conversation. "Just how much time do we have?" Shaddock asked as the pair of colonels looked on.

"Christ, I wish I could give you a definitive answer." The frustration Delmont felt was evident in his tone.

"A good guess would be nice."

Taking a moment to ponder this, Delmont weighed issues and concerns over which neither he nor any member of the uniformed services had any control. In frustration he looked up as if he were searching for the answer. "We're not driving this train anymore," he admitted. "Those people in Damascus are. We could be told to execute in as little as twenty-four hours or . . ."

When the Department of the Army special ops plans officer didn't finish his thought, Shaddock did. "Or never."

Sensing that Shaddock was still unconvinced about his battalion's new role, Delmont did his best to convey the sense of urgency that Palmer had passed on to him. "Oh, we're going. Come hell or high water we're going. It's simply a question of when."

"Well," Shaddock mused as he eyed one of his soldiers slewing a weapon about as he learned to coordinate his motions with that of his weapon while using the video sight, "at least we have a few days' grace. Not even this president would be stupid enough to send us in while the Reverend Brown is over there."

The mention of Brown's name caused Delmont to wince. "I never thought the day would come when I found myself in debt to that blowhard."

Shaddock agreed. "Yes, God does move in mysterious ways, doesn't He?"

"True, true," Delmont agreed. "All praise be to Allah."

Straightening up, Shaddock came about and looked at the DA staff officer. "It may not be original, Colonel, but I daresay this is one occasion when the old saying, 'Praise the Lord and pass the ammo' is both applicable and apropos. Now, let's leave the kids alone to finish their play."

Without fanfare the two colonels slipped out a side door and into the early evening coolness. It had already been a long day, one that would not be finished until after midnight for the soldiers of Alpha Company. Halfway around the world, where it was already the next day, others were already busy doing their best to change the equation yet again.

Damascus, Syria

10:20 LOCAL (06:20 ZULU)

The shuffle of boots, the turning of a key, and the sliding of the bolt securing the door brought Specialist Four Dee Dee Davis to his feet. As the Syrian guards on the other side pushed it open the grinding of its metal hinges sent shivers through the American. He was tired of being afraid, tired of living in dread of every sound that he heard. But there wasn't a damned thing he could do to stop it. Nothing he did seemed to make any difference. Just the sight of him seemed to provoke the anger of the guards. When they were not physically abusing him Davis was convinced that they went out of their way to mess with his mind or do things that were aimed at causing him additional anguish and grief. The torment to which he was subjected even during his daily feedings was just one example.

Instead of simply opening the small slot near the floor built into the door for that purpose and sliding the bowl of slop that passed for soup through it, the guards took advantage of the occasion to harass Davis. Three or four would enter the cell ahead of the one with the soup. While that Syrian stood in the middle of the room with the bowl precariously balanced on the tips of his fingers at the end of his outstretched arm, his companions would arrange themselves about Davis in a circle. When they were ready those in the circle would shove Davis back and forth between them trying to see how close they could push the American to the one holding the soup. Consumed by a hunger unlike anything that he had ever experienced Davis would become frenzied as he did everything he could to keep from bumping into the Syrian with the soup. Inevitably some of the bowl's content would spill, causing Davis to become more frantic and agitated. Only when the Syrians tired of this game would they finally relent and yield up to him whatever was left in the bowl.

Without taking his eyes off of the doorway, Davis slowly backed into one of the corners farthest from the door. While this maneuver offered him no protection, no real safety, it did give him a few precious seconds of time to assess the mood of the Syrian guards and brace himself for whatever mischief they had in mind.

On this occasion something very odd occurred. Instead of entering the cell one of the guards stood just beyond the threshold. Looking straight at Davis, the Syrian pointed at him. "You, come."

At first Davis didn't know what to do. As far as he could recall this was the first time that one of the guards had spoken to him in English. In the past they had shouted all their orders in Arabic, a language that Davis was all but ignorant of.

Without making any effort to enter the cell the Syrian in the doorway repeated his summons. "Come, now."

Like a beaten dog, Davis found himself unable to respond to the guard even if he had wanted to. The fear that the Syrians had instilled in him dominated his every action. Whatever it was the guards had in mind, he was in no hurry to find out or make it easier for them. So Davis opted to remain in the corner where he was as long as he could.

When it became clear to the Syrian standing in the doorway that the American wasn't going to budge, he barked an order to two of his companions before entering the cell. Already pressed against the walls as far he could, there was nothing left for Davis to do but watch him approach.

When he was but a foot away the Syrian who had been standing in the doorway stopped and stared at Davis. "You come now."

For several seconds neither Davis nor the Syrian guard before him moved. Both men were perplexed by this strange standoff. Davis found himself confused when the guards did not simply grab him and drag him away as they had done every time before. This failure served to magnify his growing sense of panic. For his part, the Syrian found himself wondering why the American was not responding to his orders. Sensing that he might have gotten his English words mixed up, the guard reached out and took Davis by the arm. "Come, now," he repeated as he gave the American a gentle tug.

The grasp upon Davis's arm was not tight. Nor did the Syrian put much effort into dislodging Davis. None of that mattered. The physical contact alone was enough to sent shivers throughout the American and sapped his ability to resist. Finally, like a quivering child being led away to some unimaginable fate, Davis allowed himself to be coaxed out of the corner and from his cell.

The calm, almost timid behavior of the guards was only the beginning. Without explanation the Syrians shepherded Davis out of his cell without stopping to shackle his hands or legs. The experience of being out of his cell while unrestrained was strange, almost frightening. Sandwiched between four Syrians Davis was totally bewildered by all of this. Not understanding the rules of this new game, he found himself trying hard not to look around for fear of violating some sort of unwritten commandment and thus incurring his captors' wrath. With measured steps gauged to match the pace being set by the Syrians, Davis was content to follow along as he was taken to a room with open showers and sinks. Once there the Syrian who had been giving him orders in broken English directed him over to a simple wooden bench against one of the walls. Upon it were arrayed an assortment of toiletries including a razor, shaving cream, soap, towels and bottles that looked as if they might be shampoo. Neatly folded on the end of the bench was a bright yellow jumpsuit. With a sweeping motion the Syrian made a show of offering the items on the bench to Davis. "Wash, change clothes."

In a flash it dawned upon Davis what was afoot. He was going home! That had to be it, he concluded as he stepped over to the bench in order to inspect the collection of toiletries. They wanted him to clean himself up so that the people from the International Red Cross were not tipped off to the appalling conditions in which he had been forced to exist. Mechanically Davis raised his hands and looked down at his wrists. That's why they hadn't placed handcuffs on him. While the wounds from earlier episodes were far from healed, the Syrians were making sure that those injuries were not reopened at this point. All of this, from the sudden change in the manner with which they treated him to this opportunity to shower and shave was an effort designed to erase every possible vestige of their savage treatment that time and a little soap would permit.

Slowly Davis let his hands fall away to his side as he looked back at the guards who stood watching his every move. For the briefest of moments his resentment over the manner with which they had treated and manipulated him ignited a sudden spark of resistance. What if he refused to clean up? What if he simply stayed the way he was, wearing the same uniform he was wearing the day he was captured, a uniform in which he had had no choice but to defecate and urinate in when he had been left bound and gagged? What could they possibly do?

Davis had no sooner posed these questions to himself than he answered them. They could make him disappear, just as they were about to do to Sergeant Hashmi. They had all the cards. They set the rules, made things happen according to their schedule, their goals. So long as he was a prisoner he had no control over anything, not even how he died. All he had left was what little pride the Syrians had not yet managed to strip away. That was not much, Davis concluded, but it was something, something that was uniquely his and his alone.

Looking back at the toiletries and bright yellow jumpsuit,

Davis realized that while he could resist, doing so would be futile and foolish. It would a symbolic gesture, which the Syrians would probably not understand, and no one back home would ever hear of. In the end the desire to survive triumphed once again. That and the fear of what might happen if he failed to play along with this new game compelled Davis to make what appeared to be the only sensible choice open to him. He consoled himself as he stripped down and prepared to shower that there would be plenty of time later to atone for giving in to these bastards. Later, when he was far away from here and out of their grasp.

The room to which Davis was taken when he had finished donning his yellow jumpsuit was unlike anything he had seen up to this point. Rich wood paneling covered the lower half of the walls. Throughout the room highly polished handcrafted furniture was tastefully set about, creating the appearance that this was some sort of lounge at an old-fashioned gentleman's club like those one sees only in movies. The floor was carpeted. While it was cheap and thin by American standards it was nonetheless spotless and well cared for. Like a stranger who has suddenly found himself transported to a distant, mystical land Davis wandered out into the center wide-eyed, gazing about as he did so.

When the door across the room from the side he had entered began to open, the same fear returned that gripped him every time he heard the bolt to his cell slid open. Without thinking he ceased his casual inspection of his new surroundings and began a frantic search for someplace to hide, a corner to which he could flee.

Davis was still in the throes of seeking some sort of sanctuary when a familiar voice called out to him. "Specialist Davis, I am the Reverend Lucas Brown."

Stunned, Davis slowly spun about and stared at the well-dressed civil rights leader as he tried hard to reconcile the apparition standing across the room from him with the reality of the hell he had just been removed from. That this man was real was without doubt. Davis had been raised by a mother who revered the Reverend Brown and his efforts to promote African-American causes.

Sensing Davis's confusion, Brown moved across the room and embraced the man. It did not matter to Brown that the stunned soldier he held did not return the embrace or cry out in glee at being in the presence of a man as great as he. So long as the camera crew following him caught the greeting and recorded the joy the reverend's expression projected, all would go well.

After maintaining the embrace long enough for the camera crew to maneuver around so that they were now behind Davis and facing Brown head-on, the reverend released his hold on the prisoner and stepped back. While keeping his right hand on Davis's arm, Brown recited a well-rehearsed message aimed at disarming any trepidation that the man before him might have about playing along with him. "Your mother sends you all of her love and wants you to know you are with her in her prayers."

This statement had its desired effect. In a flash Davis's expression changed from one of grave misgivings and wariness to one of delight at the mere mention of his mother. Caught up by the emotional response this generated, Davis reached out with his right hand and grasped the reverend's left arm. "How is she, Reverend?" he asked. "How's my mother holding up?"

Taking great care to maintain his posture, Brown smiled. This expression did not spring from the joy he felt over having an opportunity to meet the serviceman. Nor was it a sincere show of concern. Rather, its source was his satisfaction that the camera crew he had brought along with him was recording every moment of an event that promised to be politically beneficial. "Naturally your mother is very, very worried about you and your welfare, as am I. You have been with us in all our prayers every hour of every day."

Davis, having been subjected to horror heaped upon horror, was overwhelmed by the reverend's warm smile, his carefully

crafted words of concern, and the idea that he had not been forgotten. After having endured so much for so long without the
slightest hint of salvation he found himself unable to hold back
emotions that he had struggled to keep in check. Abandoning all
the pretentious pride he still harbored and with an urgency that
betrayed the desperation he felt, Davis all but lunged forward as
he seized Brown's hand between his trembling fingers and bowed
his head as if he were a sinner seeking forgiveness. "You have got
to get me out of here," Davis sobbed. "I'll die in this place if you
don't, Reverend Brown. You are my last hope. I'll just die if you
don't."

With practiced ease the Reverend Brown laid his free hand
upon Davis's bowed head as his own face assumed an appropri-
ately solemn expression. Looking up, Brown began to whisper a
prayer in a voice modulated so as to be clear when the camera's
microphone picked it up. "Lord, we beseech You to guide and
protect this wretched soul through these troubling times. We ask
that You give me the strength and the wisdom necessary to guide
Your servant away from his evil ways and free him from the sins
that he has committed against his brothers and sisters. Lord, we
implore You to open Your arms and accept this man back into
your blessed fold."

As if on cue, Davis dropped to his knees and wrapped his arms
about Brown's legs. "Forgive me," he repeated again and again as
he sobbed and wailed. In the excitement of the moment all
thoughts of his companions vanished, forgotten by a man who had
been beaten to within an inch of his life and had lost all hope. "Forgive me," Davis pleaded. Whom he was asking forgiveness from
did not matter. Neither did the price he would have to pay for this
forgiveness. "Forgive me." All that concerned this poor soul at the
moment was survival. True forgiveness and atonement could come
later when he was far from this place of pain and death, when his
body was healed and his mind was clear. "Forgive me."

The image of the yellow-clad prisoner, prostrate and weeping before the dark-suited reverend was not only powerful and heart-wrenching, it exceeded every expectation the Syrians could have hoped for. The first of the Americans had broken. It did not matter to them who had been the instrument in achieving this. All that was important to them was that Davis was vulnerable and now quite pliable. All they needed to do was provide to him the proper incentive and they would have a propaganda coup that would be worth a division.

Not every meeting between Reverend Lucas Brown and the members of RT Kilo went according to his carefully scripted program. The Syrians had expected as much. Nevertheless they had decided to afford the good reverend an opportunity to try his luck. The interview between the American civil rights leader and Sergeant First Class Kannen, laid out in the exact same manner as Davis's, never got past the initial introduction. After taking one look at Brown as he came through the door across from him Kannen pivoted and marched up to the pair of Syrian guards who were posted to either side of the door on his side of the room. "Take me back to my cell," he demanded in a voice that was loud enough to be heard by everyone in the room.

Stunned by this unexpected reaction, Brown stopped in mid-stride as the Syrians first looked at each other, then back at the American before them. Paying no attention to what Brown or his TV crew was up to Kannen repeated his demand. "Get me out of this fucking room and away from that asshole, *now!*" For this show of defiance, the American NCO was rewarded with a particularly vicious and protracted round of beatings, none of which managed to exorcise the satisfaction Kannen had derived from his response to another propaganda sham staged by the Syrians.

Specialist Four Salvador Mendez was less impressed with the appearance of the Reverend Brown than Davis had been. Though Mendez was attentive to and respectful of what the reverend was saying, the civil rights leader was never able to put him at ease. Throughout the entire meeting Mendez cast fugitive glances about the room as if he expected the reverend's camera crew or the Syrian guards to suddenly lunge at him. In the end, Brown found that he had to content himself with holding Mendez's hand while he did all of the talking.

By mutual agreement between Brown and the Syrians, a meeting with Ken Aveno was not scheduled. The Syrians didn't even mention either Burman or Ciszak and Brown didn't ask about those two officers. They also made it clear from the beginning that the pending execution of Sergeant Hashmi was a domestic issue that Brown was not to mention or inject himself into.

After meeting the three enlisted men, a deal was hammered out behind the scenes between the Reverend Brown and the Syrian foreign minister. Upon the conclusion of a press conference during which Davis read a statement prepared for him by the Syrian government, the American would be free to leave with Reverend Brown. Realizing that it would be dangerous for Davis to be allowed to read the statement beforehand and given time to think about what he was doing, Brown insisted that he be the one to handle Davis.

Meeting for a second time in the same room without benefit of guards or camera crew, the Reverend Brown informed Davis that he was on the verge of securing his freedom. "There are some in the Syrian government," Brown explained, "who would like nothing better than to see this crisis brought to an end."

Doing his best to keep his expectations in check, Davis listened intently as Brown spun his story.

"Unfortunately," Brown stated, "they are afraid that if they let even one of you go without some sort of display of contrition, then their own people will rise up and voice their righteous indignation. The people of Syria, the government insists, must be given some sort of satisfaction for the devastation and death that your actions caused them."

Slowly it dawned upon Davis what he was being asked to do. Still, that did not matter at the moment. All that was important was survival. "What do they want?"

"I know that you are a soldier," Brown expounded in a deep, empathetic tone. "As such you are bound by an oath to uphold the traditions of your service and follow its rules and regulations. Part of your obligations requires you to do everything in your power to protect your comrades and friends, a duty that even our Lord expects of you."

Looking into Brown's eyes, Davis tried to determine if the man who purported to be his savior was being completely honest and forthcoming. With Davis blinded by the promise of freedom being dangled before him, the truth never had a chance. Rather than carefully weighing each of the reverend's words Davis found himself trying to find something in them that would justify going along with whatever he was being asked to do.

"Before you were a soldier," Brown went on, "you were a man and a Christian. As such you have obligations that supersede even the most sacred and honorable oath extracted from you by your government."

Davis nodded. "I understand, Reverend."

"The Syrians have agreed to let you return home with me provided you read a statement which I have prepared for you at a press conference."

Though he suspected this sort of thing had been coming, Reverend Brown's demands struck Davis like a shot in the heart. In a flash images of Americans being held by the North Vietnamese that he had seen on the History Channel ran through his mind. His solemn pledge to uphold the Code of Conduct quickly followed. But even more disturbing than either of those thoughts was the idea that he could very well betray his comrades by doing what the reverend asked.

Sensing that he was on the verge of losing Davis and correctly guessing the reason for his sudden trepidation, Brown reached over and took his hand. "You have done all you can do for your comrades here. Staying behind and suffering alone in your cell will neither harm them nor hurt them. You have already proven your courage. You have done all that was expected of you. By coming home with me you will not be turning your back on your friends. You will be serving them. Your return will give their loved ones hope, hope that the rest will soon follow. Hope that all is not lost. No one will speak ill of you. Rather, you will be welcomed as a hero. You will be a ray of sunshine sent by God to show them that this terrible storm will soon be over." Having made his pitch, Reverend Brown leaned back and gave Davis a moment to consider the matter.

The thought of going back to his cell and enduring a fresh round of beatings carried far more weight than the message of hope that the reverend spoke of. This and this alone proved to be decisive. That he could no longer endure facing such punishment was clear to Davis. He knew what the Army expected of him. But that Army wasn't here. No one had done a damned thing to save him despite the fact that he had done all that had been expected of him and more. Now that he had an opportunity to save himself, Davis saw no dishonor in seizing it. If anything he found himself justifying his complete capitulation by reasoning that his experiences might actually prove to be of help if the Army ever did manage to get around to planning some sort of rescue attempt. So the reverend was right. His duty now was to go back with him.

Having made up his mind, Davis looked into Brown's eyes. "I will do whatever it is you think is right, Reverend."

Realizing that he had just achieved a major coup, The Reverend Brown smiled as he patted Davis's hand. "You have made the right choice, my son."

Dulles Airport, Virginia
20:45 LOCAL (00:45 ZULU)

Unable to sit calmly and pass the time as the other members of the official party somehow managed to do, Brigadier General

James Palmer paced back and forth like a caged panther at mealtime. Every time he passed his aide de camp Palmer would stop, look at that officer, and growl. "How much longer?"

Making a great show of it, the aide would lift his arm, look at his watch, and make the necessary calculations to determine how much time remained before the private jet bearing the Reverend Brown and Specialist Four Davis arrived. "Fifteen minutes, sir." Mumbling to himself, Palmer would turn and storm off as he resumed his pacing.

Seated at one end of the lounge was the Deputy Chief of Staff of the Army, a four-star general who would serve as the senior military representative at the homecoming the Reverend Brown's people had set up. When Palmer's nervous prowling brought him within a few feet of the Deputy Chief, the senior general called out to him. "For Christ's sake, Jim. Sit down. You're making me nervous."

Unfazed by this mild rebuke, Palmer stopped. "Damn it, sir! How can you sit there while the Reverend Lucas Brown is making a mockery of us? Why the Sec Def agreed to let that charlatan have his way and bring Davis straight home is beyond me."

Though he agreed with everything Palmer was saying, the Deputy Chief of Staff folded his hands in his lap and looked up at the enraged brigadier. "Both the State Department and DOD made it clear that this was Brown's show. Because he is a private citizen neither agency has any right to dictate to him how he does things. To do so now would seem as if we were trying to horn in on his success. As much as it might rankle our cockles, the dear reverend made the effort and therefore deserves his ten seconds of fame."

Palmer glared. "Oh, but if it were only ten seconds."

The Deputy Chief of Staff chuckled. "Relax. As my wife likes to say every time I get a gallstone, this too shall pass."

Finding no solace in his superior's quip, Palmer was about to take up his pacing where he had left off when a beeper being carried by the Deputy Chief of Staff's aide went off. As one, every eye in the room was drawn to him. Paying no attention to anything but his duty, the aide looked at the number displayed on the beeper. Setting it aside he pulled out his cell phone and punched in the number. "Colonel Shafter here."

When he was finished the aide clicked the off button, stood up, and looked over at his general. "Sir, that was the tower. The private jet carrying the Reverend Brown and Specialist Davis has just declared an emergency."

Blinking, the Deputy Chief of Staff came to his feet. "How far are they out?"

"Five minutes, sir. The tower has cleared all traffic and is scrambling the crash trucks."

On cue the sound of sirens coming to life broke the silence in the waiting lounge where the army delegation had gathered. "General Palmer," the Deputy Chief of Staff announced slowly, deliberately. "Get out there and find out what's going on."

Standing on the ground before the executive jet, Palmer, the pilot of the jet, and the senior rep from the Department of Transportation, stood in silence looking up at the open door. "I had just made the announcement that we were beginning our descent into Dulles," the pilot explained in hushed tones. "Everything was in order. There were no problems, not a peep from the cabin. And then, *pow*, everything went to hell."

Pausing, he bowed his head as he reached up to wipe away beads of sweat that trickled down his forehead. "According to the flight attendant," he stated in a voice that still quivered from the adrenaline that lingered in his veins, "everyone was in their seats, strapped in and ready for the landing. Before she realized what he was doing your man Davis undid his seat belt, came to his feet, and calmly walked to the door."

For a moment the trio stood there, gazing at the damaged aircraft as if they were waiting for it to provide an answer to this troubling mystery. Finally Palmer broke the silence. "And he said nothing?"

The pilot shook his head. "From what I've been told he spoke to no one the entire flight. The flight attendant said he just sat there, staring out of the window as if he were looking for something."

After a long pause, the investigator from the DOT turned to Palmer. "General, do you have any idea what could have caused the man to do something like that?"

Tugging on the hem of his uniform blouse, Palmer looked once more at the open door before turning to face the others. "Guilt. Shame. Anger. Take your pick, gentlemen."

"I can't put that in my report!"

Palmer considered the civilian bureaucrat for a moment. "Sir, I don't give a damn what you put into your report. You asked me to come here and render an opinion. I have done so. Now, if you will excuse me there are other matters far more pressing than this postmortem that demand my full attention."

Without another word Palmer began to make his way to where his aide waited with the sedan. As he walked slowly through the quiet hangar the man responsible for saving what was left of RT Kilo could not help but compare his current plight to the children's ditty that seemed so apropos to this operation. "Then there were six." And tomorrow, if the Syrians kept to their word there would be but five.

CHAPTER TWENTY-FIVE

The young officer who had led the OPFOR during that evening's exercise stood up, walked to the front of the assembled officers, and took his place. Try as hard as he might, he found that he was unable to keep himself from smirking whenever his eyes lit upon Emmett DeWitt. Knowing full well what was about to come, the best DeWitt could do at the moment was give his former compadres one of those I'll-get-you sort of looks.

As he had done a hundred times before, First Lieutenant Clarence Archer introduced himself and discussed the operations from the OPFOR's perspective. He described the role his unit had been playing during the just-concluded exercise, how he had deployed his people, and presented a concise narrative on what he saw as the engagement unfolded. It had been both a dress rehearsal and the first company-level training event DeWitt's Company had conducted with the Land Warrior. Archer's people had been playing the part of a garrison unit charged with the internal security duties of a military compound. As such the bulk of his men were lightly armed with a few crew-served weapons. To augment this force and add realism to the exercise a number of soldiers ordinariy assigned to administrative duties with the OPFOR's parent unit had been locked away in various rooms throughout the building Archer's men were protecting. DeWitt's mission was to secure these captives and withdraw from the objective with minimum casualties.

Like so many terms the American military uses, no one ever quantified exactly what the term *minimum casualties* actually translated into. If ten officers were asked to give a percentage of what they considered to be minimum casualties each of them would respond with a different answer. One thing was clear, though, even before the after-action review got under way. The simulated losses Alpha Company suffered that night would have exceeded even the most sanguine estimate. In their attempt to take down the building defended by Archer's men, DeWitt's company had lost eight dead and twenty-eight wounded, with half of the wounded winding up as prisoners.

"Just about the time it finally became clear to the command-ing officer of the assault force that none of the prisoners being held in the facility were American," Archer stated as he discussed the events, "I had finished rallying and reorganizing the survivors of my garrison at the far end of the building. When it was reported to me that the assault force was scattered in groups of three and four men searching for prisoners, I seized the opportu-nity to launch local counterattacks aimed at inflicting heavy casu-alties on the enemy. In two cases my soldiers' superior knowledge of the facility allowed them to slip a blocking force past the attackers and cut off their line of retreat prior to the commence-ment of our local counterattacks."

Since this was essentially a training exercise designed to famil-iarize Alpha Company with the capability of the Land Warrior, Lieutenant Colonel Kaplan used every opportunity he could to make important points about that system. "The Land Warrior enhances the combat ability of your soldiers," he stated, doing his best to ensure that his tone was neither demeaning nor scornful. "It doesn't make you or your people any smarter. As the OPFOR commander pointed out, their intimate knowledge of the terrain allowed them to overcome your technological superiority. While your people were reduced to groping about in a portion of the building that they had not been briefed on, the OPFOR was able to move along secondary passages and through conduits swiftly and with confidence. By the time your people who were isolated by these tactics became aware that they were in trouble, it was too late."

Though he knew better than to do so at an after-action review, DeWitt felt compelled to respond in his own defense. "Had the captives we were sent to secure been in the building anywhere close to where they were supposed to be, my company would have been long gone before the enemy had time to recover from their initial surprise and mount an effective counterattack."

It was now Lieutenant Colonel Shaddock's turn to pounce upon the hapless company commander. "I know you have heard of Son Tay," he stated in a low voice. "I intentionally had the S-3 design tonight's scenario based upon that raid. I wanted you to be faced with the same dilemma that the American commander of that operation faced when he broke into that North Vietnamese POW camp and found no POWs to liberate. The big difference between Son Tay and tonight was that the American ground force commander didn't leave any NVA guards alive."

"Sir," DeWitt responded, doing his best to maintain his calm, "my primary mission was to find the prisoners. When the team assigned to secure them failed to locate them I made the decision to dispatch additional search parties."

"And while doing so," Shaddock pointed out, "you turned your back on an enemy force that was battered but far from broken. Your decision to increase the number of teams searching for the captives was sound. Your failure to continue to maintain pressure on the enemy was not. In throwing every resource you had to achieve one part of your stated mission you set yourself up to blow another aspect of it, i.e., minimum casualties."

"So you want me to kill every one of those little suckers I can while I'm there?" DeWitt asked in frustration.

"Dead men," Shaddock stated in a tone that was as cold as the look in his eye, "can't counterattack. Besides, the bastards deserve it."

Realizing that he could not possibly win this round and

accepting the fact that he had royally screwed the pooch, DeWitt nodded. "Yes, sir. I understand."

"Good," Shaddock stated perfunctorily. "Continue."

Following their well-established format, the officers of Fort Irwin's training cadre who had been observing that night's exercise stood up, moved to the front of the small expandable van used for these after-action reviews, and discussed every aspect of that night's operation. Everything was addressed in its turn; command and control, tactics, the unit's use of intelligence, procedures employed by the unit as a whole, actions taken by individual soldiers to deal with wounded, captured enemy soldiers, and the redistribution of ammunition. For a unit commander and his staff the experience of being evaluated in this manner is pretty much the same as getting a root canal without the benefit of Novocain. This sort of inquisition is not without its benefits. Even the harshest critic of this technique is unable to discount the long-term value an unvarnished evaluation by the officers and enlisted men of the National Training Center can yield. Many veterans of the first Persian Gulf War owe their success and their very life to the lessons they learned in the crowded little vans in the Mojave Desert of California. If anything, one recurring comment after that war was that in comparison, the real thing was easy. "Not only did we have to fight the Gulf War only once," one officer stated in all seriousness after returning from the Gulf, "we didn't have to sit through one of those damned after-action reviews when it was over."

Completion of the after-action review did not close out the day's work. With much left to do, the participants belonging to the 3rd of the 75th and those helping it get ready adjourned to Shaddock's humble headquarters. Anyone entering the outer office where Shaddock's XO, sergeant major, and adjutant worked was greeted by a sign Shaddock had ordered Sergeant Major Harris to

post next to the door of his personal office. On it there was the
photo and name of every member of RT Kilo. In a box above the
photos of those who had made it out was a large blue *X*. Below
the photos was another box. In the case where a member of RT
Kilo was known to be dead, a red *X* of equal size was placed. For
those who were in Syrian hands or still missing in action, there
was nothing in either box. Shaddock had briefed his commanders
and staff when the sign had been posted that it was there to
remind each and every one of them what they were preparing for.
"Those who have earned the blue mark deserve an atta-boy, but
not from us. The men who bear the red are to be honored and
mourned. We can do nothing more for them. It is for the others
that we must bend every effort, every conscious thought. Until
they are free this battalion has but one purpose, one goal."

Upon entering the outer office that evening Shaddock was
greeted by the sight of Lieutenant Colonel Delmont standing
next to the battalion adjutant as that officer was placing a red *X*
under the photo of Sergeant Yousaf Hashmi. Shaddock watched
for a moment. "When?" was all he asked.

Delmont didn't bother to turn around as he answered. "Word
came in while you were in the after-action. I saw no need to dis-
rupt you then with this news."

Shaddock nodded in grim agreement as he continued across
the room to join the two officers before the poster. "That leaves
us how many?"

"According to DIA, five," Delmont muttered. "And if what
the CIA says is true, four."

"What do you make of that information, Delmont?"

Delmont's hesitation in answering Shaddock was caused not
by the disagreement between the two intelligence agencies but
rather by something Palmer had passed on to him earlier that evening. Glancing up, he looked at the adjutant, then Shaddock,
before walking into the latter's office without saying a word. Taking the hint, the battalion commander instructed his adjutant that

he was not to be disturbed, before following the special ops plans officer into his own office and closing the door behind him.

After the two lieutenant colonels had taken their seats, several minutes passed before either spoke. It was Delmont who broke the silence by articulating a concern that both men had but which neither had yet dared share with anyone else. "There is an opinion being expressed by some," the special ops plans officer stated hesitantly, "that we may have reached the point of diminishing returns."

Just to be sure he understood what Delmont was saying, Shaddock restating this concept in his own words. "The people back in Washington are concerned that the losses incurred in a rescue attempt can no longer be justified."

"That's about the size of it," Delmont muttered.

"What do you think?"

The special ops plans officer looked up at the man who would have to lead the ground force into Syria. He could no longer answer such a question with any degree of honesty. Somewhere along the line he had lost all sense of objectivity. He didn't know when he had crossed that line. Nor did he know what part of this whole screwed-up affair had shoved him over it. All he knew for certain was that he could no longer render anything resembling an unbiased opinion. Somewhere between the unreasonable sense of guilt he felt for sending RT Kilo on mission after mission and the prideful desire to succeed that all plans officers possess when it comes time to see one of their creations given life through to its execution, he had lost anything resembling objectivity.

Sensing that he wasn't going to get an answer to his last question, Shaddock dropped it and turned to the issue at hand. "Despite the results of tonight's training exercise, I believe that this battalion is about as ready as it's going to get." With a gesture that spoke of his frustrations as well as mental weariness Shaddock threw his hands out. "I'm not sure if we will ever be fully prepared to execute this thing. There are simply too many imponderables, too many loose ends. Perhaps the whole thing has become too complex. Instead of being a carefully crafted military operation, it's become something more akin to a crap shoot that no one seems to be willing to take. What I do know," he stated as he struggled to regain a firm, confident air, "is that within the next few days, we are going to reach our own point of diminishing returns."

"Meaning?"

"Meaning, Colonel," Shaddock explained, "that I can only keep my men holding in the starting blocks for just so long. They watch the news and listen to talk radio. They can count just as well as we can. At some point they're going to begin asking themselves if we are serious about this or if we're simply jerking them around just to make it look like the army is serious about doing something. One by one, each and every man out there, officer and enlisted alike, will find himself coming to the conclusion that we're not going. Whether they're right doesn't matter. Once enough of them decide that this has all been one big bluff, one big media scam they're going to start slacking off. The edge that we have been working so hard to put on this unit will begin to dull. Once that happens, nothing I nor anyone else says will be able to turn it around."

"What is it you expect from me?"

Having regained his poise and the fire that he used to drive himself and his men to achieve the near impossible, Shaddock leaned forward and peered into Delmont's eyes. "You're the liaison between this battalion and the decision makers in Washington. I want you to go back to whoever it is you need to see and tell them that the time has come to make a decision. We either go and go soon, or . . ."

"Or what?" Delmont demanded. "We abandon our fellow soldiers to their fate?"

"Better that," Shaddock countered, "than send more to join them."

"And if those people back in Washington give us a resounding 'Wait, out,' what then?"

Slumping back into his seat, Shaddock folded his hands in his lap and looked down at them. "I am a soldier. I follow orders. I do not believe it is proper for a subordinate commander to issue an ultimatum to his superior or tell him when it's time to shit or get off the pot. But in this case I do believe the time is drawing near when I will have no choice but to go back to my superiors and lay before them the same thing I just explained to you." After a slight pause, Shaddock glanced up at Delmont. "I do not deny that we have a responsibility to those men in Damascus. But as the commanding officer of this battalion I owe my men the same consideration. Sending these people to fight a battle they are no longer psychologically prepared to fight is worse than foolish. It's criminal."

Of the two lieutenant colonels assigned to deal with the problem, only one would be held accountable for the end result. The man who generates the plan, no matter how brilliant it may be, is seldom remembered. Whether he deserves it or not, it is the commanding officer who receives the laurels if successful, or eternal shame and damnation if not. Delmont appreciated this brutal fact of military life and found that he had no choice. "When do you want an answer?"

"Forty-eight hours," Shaddock stated without hesitation. "If I don't have a definitive H-hour by then, I will stand this battalion down."

Delmont rose to his feet, nodding in agreement as he did so. "Fair enough. You'll have your answer by then or my endorsement that Fanfare is no longer a viable option."

Arlington, Virginia
13:05 LOCAL (17:05 ZULU)

Within the military, *liaison* is defined as that contact or inter-communications that is maintained between military forces to ensure mutual understanding and unity of purpose and action. Liaison is most often conducted between combat units operating side by side, a support unit attached to a command it has been assigned to provide services to or, as with Robert Delmont, between a higher headquarters and a subordinate command. Without exception the liaison officer leaves his organization with the mandate of compelling compliance with the plans, goals, or doctrine of the parent organization that dispatched him. If the duration of this liaison mission is short-lived, executing these duties are not very difficult. If, however, the liaison officer is required to remain with the subordinate or sister unit for a protracted period, something strange happens. While the liaison officer never forgets whom he is working for on an intellectual level, living with the new unit begins to have unintended consequences. At the subconscious level the experience of sharing the physical hardships and tribulations of the host unit, dealing with its personnel twenty-four/seven, and even sharing its food creates a bond of kinship between the liaison officer and the unit. In time, rather than being an outside enforcer tasked with imposing his commander's agenda, a liaison officer can find himself becoming an advocate within his own command for the unit he was detached to.

This is not all bad, particularly when the parent headquarters is far removed from the reality in which the subordinate unit is operating. Just how great this chasm can become is startling to someone who makes the leap from one world to the next in the span of a few hours. Robert Delmont left Fort Irwin just before dawn for the commercial airport in Ontario, California. From there he flew on to D.C. Once back in Virginia he went straight to the Pentagon.

In the Mojave Desert the dominant attitude had been one of nervous anticipation. The officers and enlisted men of the 3rd of the 75th Ranger Battalion knew what they were preparing for and were doing everything possible to make sure they were ready for it. Whatever reservations their commanding officer entertained about their ability to pull that mission off were not shared with anyone other than Delmont. A good commander guards against allowing his sort of negative views to show through. Nor does he share his opinions with his subordinates on the wisdom of what they are doing, lest those opinions sow the poisonous seeds of doubt in the minds of those he must send into battle.

The stoic demeanor that Lieutenant Colonel Shaddock had adopted did not prevail in the Pentagon. Even before he reached his office Delmont was struck by the funereal pall that prevailed throughout the corridors. While smiles were rare enough in a place like the Pentagon, the total dearth of them on this day was most telling. When someone did manage to lift his gaze off the floor and make eye contact with him, the universal expression he wore was what Delmont referred to as the my-dog-died look.

If the general populace of the Pentagon came across as being despondent, then his co-workers in the Special Ops Section were downright wretched. No one greeted him as he made his way to his cubbyhole. Nor did anyone make any effort to acknowledge him or find out how things were going at Fort Irwin. Even when Delmont took the initiative, the universal response was a grunt or a simple, "Oh, hi," issued with a total dearth of enthusiasm and any interest whatsoever in engaging in conversation.

This gloom did nothing to lighten the burden that Delmont had carried upon his shoulders from the high desert of California to the banks of the Potomac. Plopping down in his seat, the special ops plans officer leaned back as far as he dared, laced his fingers behind his head, and stared at the ceiling above as he took a moment to collect his thoughts and review the situation before him for the umpteenth time.

During his tenure in the Pentagon Robert Delmont had drafted plans for many operations that had placed American soldiers in harm's way. As part of Razorback alone, he had overseen the deployment of eleven teams, and monitored their day-to-day operations for his general. Intellectually he knew that his actions were exposing men like the general to danger. He also appreciated that actions initiated in accordance with orders he had drafted resulted in the death of Syrians. In theory Fanfare should have been no different. His superior had handed him a task, he had developed a viable operational plan, and taken those actions necessary to translate concept into action.

Unfortunately, Fanfare had not turned out to be that simple or straightforward. Step by step Delmont had become more involved in this operation than any of his other creations. Through his direct contacts with the 3rd of the 75th Rangers he now could associate faces and personalities to the various units that made up the troop list for Fanfare. His assessment of whether or not the operation would succeed was no longer based solely upon sterile computer simulations and calculations of force ratios. Having seen the various companies of the 3rd of the 75th rehearse their assigned roles, Delmont's fertile imagination conjured up scenario after scenario involving numerous what-if situations that the Rangers might encounter once they were on the ground. Even now, as he sat in the rarefied air of the Pentagon he imagined that he could still taste the desert as he licked his dry lips. The feeling of fine grit thrown about by the desert wind that covers everything still clogged his pores. Where, he found himself asking as he pondered his dilemma, did he belong? Here where his duty had placed him or back there in the desert where his heart was?

As troubling as all of this was, the idea that his opinion could very well play a pivotal role in determining if Fanfare would go forward or not proved to be nothing less than terrifying. If the powers above did opt for the military solution, men belonging to the 3rd of the 75th would die. Given what the Rangers would encounter on the ground in Syria, that grim fact was a mathematical certainty. Picking up where he had left off with Shaddock, Delmont found himself weighing over and over again the wisdom of promoting an operation in which the rescuing force would sustain losses that would far exceed the number of personnel it would recover. If pure logic were used to decide the issue, the choice would be a no-brainer. Both he and his superiors would simply apply the old Russian military axiom that states that one does not reinforce failure.

While logic was a major element that would be used in determining which course of action would be followed, other imponderables that could not be measured with any sort of accuracy would have a bearing on the final decision. Within the political realm the consequences of doing nothing while a third-rate power butchered American soldiers with impunity was already having serious repercussions for a president who had made creating a strong military and waging war on terrorism something of a crusade. Day in and day out political pundits from his own party bludgeoned the president for failing to take immediate action. On the international scene, despite their calls for the American president to let diplomacy have a fair chance, responsible leaders within NATO found themselves wondering just what sort of ally the United States was. The French president was rumored to have mused that if the Americans were unwilling to come to the aid of their own in their time of greatest peril, what hope did a European have?

This very same sentiment was also being openly expressed within the armed forces. Throughout the ranks the prevailing attitude favored swift and immediate action. To most soldiers it was an article of faith that no one would be left behind, that no matter what the cost every effort would be made to bring their fellow soldiers home. And even if a full-bore military operation proved to be costly, there was the consolation that no matter how bad American casualties were, the losses and damage inflicted on the Syrians during the course of the rescue attempt would be hideously disproportionate and well deserved.

Keenly aware of all of these diverse elements, Delmont found that he had to force himself to focus on only those items for which he was responsible. On a notepad he listed in order of priority the questions that he would be expected to answer.

1. Is Fanfare still a viable option given anticipated Syrian opposition?

2. Is the 3rd of the 75th Ranger Battalion ready?
3. Is there an optimum window of opportunity, and when will it be?
4. What are the projected casualties that will be suffered by 3rd of the 75th?
5. Is it worth it?

Pausing, Delmont leaned back in his seat and studied his list. Number five, he decided, didn't belong there. Someone else many grades above his would have to make that call. Yet he could not escape the fact that the manner in which he answered the other four would have an effect on number five. A negative response to any of the other four that were within his sphere of influence would most likely be seized upon as an excuse for not going forward with Fanfare. Even a hint of hesitation on his part could be viewed as an excuse for rethinking the military option. And while it was true that others would weigh in on the subject and render their opinions before the final decision was made by the Commander in Chief himself, every nudge this way or that had an effect.

He was still sitting there staring vacantly at his list when the phone on his desk rang. Reaching out, he took up the receiver and gave the perfunctory greeting, "Lieutenant Colonel Delmont. This line is not secure."

"Well, Colonel. Are you waiting for an engraved invitation?"

General Palmer's voice jerked Delmont out of his solemn reflections and back to the here and now. "I was just going over the issues, sir."

"Cease your ruminations. Gather up whatever you need and get in here pronto. I have a meeting in twenty minutes and I need your input."

Without hesitation, Delmont stood up. "On the way, sir."

Palmer hung up before Delmont was finished. As Delmont laid the receiver back in its cradle the special ops plans officer looked back at his list. He already knew how he would answer each item on it. He even had an answer for question number five. Whether anyone further up the line shared his opinion remained to be seen.

Fort Irwin, California
19:35 LOCAL (02:35 ZULU)

The roar inside the cavernous cargo bay of the C-17 Globemaster III transport made conversation with anyone who was not seated right next to you nearly impossible. Equally futile was any attempt to navigate one's way from one humvee to another through the tangle of nylon webbing used to cross-lash the ten vehicles to the floor of the transport. This left DeWitt little to do but remain seated in the lead humvee staring at the aircraft's rear ramp. The experience was not unlike being on an old time New York City express subway. The seats were uncomfortable, the view was non-existent, the racket was barely tolerable, and the lingering stench of military equipment, diesel, aircraft hydraulic fluid, and sweaty bodies was only marginally superior to that of a subway car. Even the end of the ride had some interesting parallels. After a protracted period of boredom during which one could do little but hang on and sway with the pitching and rolling of the conveyance, exiting the Globemaster, like the subway, was a mad dash that tended to border on sheer panic.

The idea of using humvees to whisk the Rangers the nine kilometers from the airfield to the military prison where the surviving members of RT Kilo were being held became a necessity as soon as Fanfare ceased being a deception plan and became a real-world contingency operation. In the concept of operation for Fanfare as the deception plan, elements of Delta Force, flown in by Task Force 160's helicopters, had the responsibility of securing the prisoners. The third of the seventy-fifth Rangers was tasked with doing little more than seizing the airfield to which Delta, Task

Force 160, and the liberated hostages would be taken and evacuated from. When Fanfare ceased being a deception plan Delta and Task Force 160 were dropped since someone in their chain of command determined that neither of those elite units could be readied in time. So the Rangers had been handed the entire ball of wax and instructed to find a way to do it all.

At first Lieutenant Colonel Shaddock had tried going without any sort of mechanized ground transportation. "We're Rangers," he had boasted. "We can cover the distance from the airfield to the prison in no time flat." This theory was quickly shot to hell as attempt after attempt to do so in training exercises met with complete and utter failure. Even when Alpha Company encountered no opposition en route while abandoning all pretenses of a prudent and militarily sound advance, by the time DeWitt got his people to the building that had been configured to resemble the Syrian prison, his men were winded and the OPFOR was locked, cocked, and more than ready.

The next less-than-brilliant idea thrown out for consideration and trial was to seize whatever trucks were already at the airfield, load Alpha Company into them, and blitz on into Damascus. Immediately the DIA and CIA were tapped to provide an assessment of what sort of transportation was generally available and where it was most likely to be found. With this information in hand, vehicles that matched the descriptions were rounded up by the S-4 of the 3rd of the 75th Rangers and planted at appropriate locations throughout Dust Bowl International. The result of this trial was nearly farcical. Not only did DeWitt lose total control of his command within minutes of landing as search parties scattered to scrounge up their transport, but half a dozen friendly-fire incidents occurred when those who had successfully found a vehicle they could hot-wire were gunned down by personnel from other companies manning the battalion's perimeter when the newly procured transport tried to return to the company rally point.

Eventually Shaddock was driven by these dismal failures to the conclusion that they had no choice but to take their own ground transportation in with them as Delmont had originally planned. In developing their concept for this new twist, Shaddock, major Lawrence Perry, the operations officer for the battalion, and DeWitt took a page out of the history books. When the Israeli Army was confronted with a hostage situation in 1976 at Entebbe, Uganda, not at all unlike the problem the 3rd of the 75th now faced, the Israeli commandos flew in a number of gun jeeps. This expedient had allowed them to roll off the C-130 transports straight into the attack. While no one was particularly wild about adding more and more moving pieces to an already complex operation, the fact that the addition of humvees was a necessary evil could not be denied.

Of course, that did not mean that someone didn't try. Even before Delmont was finished explaining his idea of landing two transports carrying Alpha Company mounted in twenty humvees, the Air Force liaison officer had a conniption fit. With the Air Force already skittish about its role, the prospect of setting two of their valuable C-17s down even before the area had been secured horrified each and every Air Force officer who heard it. Armed with diagrams, charts, and tables of all sorts, the Air Force liaison officer and his staff took great pains to explain to Delmont and Shaddock that in order to meet the timetable they had established, the transports with the humvees would have to land on a section of the airfield that, in all likelihood, would not yet have been secured by the elements of the 3rd of the 75th that had parachuted in. "We run the risk," the Air Force officer pointed out, "of rolling right through a firefight."

Neither of the Army lieutenant colonels showed their blue-clad counterparts any sympathy. "Look at it this way," Shaddock commented dryly. "If your pilots play it right, they may be afforded an opportunity to run some of the bastards over." In the end, it took a dozen phone calls and something akin to divine intervention from the Sec Def himself to decide the issue in favor of the humvees.

Resolution of that issue was only the beginning of Delmont's and Shaddock's problems. To minimize the number of vehicles taken into Syria and maximize the number of Rangers in the mounted strike group, the two senior officers on the ground determined that the troop carrier version of the humvee was the preferred model. The 3rd of the 75th, however, had only a limited number of these available. Faced with a very real time crunch, Delmont again appealed to Olympus on the Potomac in order to secure an order to the commanding officer of Fort Irwin to hand over whatever vehicles the 3rd of the 75th required. As galling as this was to the post commander, a corollary to those instructions gave Shaddock and his maintenance people the option to reject any vehicle offered by the troop units stationed at Fort Irwin that were, in the opinion of Shaddock's people, unacceptable. Already peeved at having to put up with a unit that did whatever it wanted whenever it wanted, the post commander lost it. At one meeting he reached into his pocket, pulled his wallet out, and threw it on the floor in front of Delmont and Shaddock quickly followed by his car keys. "Here! You might as well take it all now and save us both the time and trouble of robbing me blind bit by bit."

With a calm demeanor that belied the anger he felt welling up inside, Shaddock bent down, picked up the car keys and studied them for a second. "If you don't mind, sir," he coolly asked the enraged post commander, "just what sort of car do you drive?"

What little revenge could be extracted for both the high-handed procurement of his humvees and Shaddock's comment came when it was time to sign over those vehicles selected to be handed to the 3rd of the 75th. On the express orders of the post commander every vehicle relinquished to the Rangers would have to be signed over in accordance with every military regulation

pertaining to the transfer of property from one command to the
next, using every form and procedure called for by those regulations. While this irritated everyone involved, Shaddock did his
best to keep his people in check. "I know this seems petty as
hell, especially at a time like this," he told DeWitt, who ultimately had to sign for the humvees. "But, remember, you cannot expect a zebra to change its stripes overnight. The folks here
at Irwin are not facing what we are. Even if they have a pretty
good idea what we're about it's unreasonable for us to expect
them to respond with the same sense of urgency that we do.
Even though they're wearing the same uniform they're only
human, afflicted by all the pettiness and personality quirks that
all humans labor under."

His colonel's words did little to soothe DeWitt's anger, for
the true source of the first lieutenant's ire was not the paperwork
that he was forced to deal with but the attitude his former col-
leagues were currently displaying. When he had been with the
OPFOR and part of the Fort Irwin establishment DeWitt had
viewed himself as something special, a cut above the rest. Now,
finding himself on the receiving end of what he considered little
more than an arrogant and mean-spirited hissy fit, the young officer began to have second thoughts about just how special those
belonging to the OPFOR really were.

Time did not permit DeWitt to dwell upon trivial issues such
as this. With the humvees finally in hand, the next chore was to
reconfigure them so that they were useful. Even while the paper
wars between the battalion supply officer and the Fort Irwin folks
were being waged, the ops officer of the 3rd of the 75th and
DeWitt were trying to figure out what crew-served weapons, if
any, should be affixed to the newly procured vehicles. The natural
inclination was to add some sort of weapon to each and every vehicle, whether it be an M-2 .50-caliber machine gun, an M-60D
7.62-mm machine gun, or a TOW ATGM. This was quickly seen
as impractical and unnecessary. In the end, only one out of every

two of the humvees was assigned some sort of additional fire-power. All the others would have to rely upon the weapons carried by the Rangers themselves if they ran into serious opposition going to or coming from the prison.

In tandem with this problem was the loading and securing of the vehicles within the giant transports. Adhering to peacetime regulations the Air Force demanded that the humvees be lashed down to the floor in a manner that made quick and easy egress nearly impossible. "This is an assault landing!" DeWitt kept yelling every time the loadmasters added another tie-down. "We need to get out of your bloody damned planes as quickly as we can once we're on the ground."

To this the Air Force NCOs countered that it would do no one any good if after a transatlantic flight the ramp was dropped only to reveal a jumbled heap of humvees, mangled Rangers, and twisted gear. The loadmaster on DeWitt's transport didn't budge. "My job is to get you and this airplane there in one piece, ready and able to do a job."

In the end a compromise was struck. At the takeoff and during the majority of the flight the Air Force insisted upon using the prescribed number of tie-downs on each humvee. Only when they were on final approach would all but the absolute minimum number of tie-downs be removed. And to satisfy their guests, the Air Force loadmasters promised that once they were on the ground, they would slash the nylon tie-downs rather than waste time unhooking them. "The sooner I get you people outta here," the gruff Air Force master sergeant told DeWitt as he was explaining this plan, "the sooner those people out there have something more interesting to shoot at than *my* plane."

Bit by bit, issue by issue, all of the problems with this new wrinkle in an ever-changing Fanfare were identified, addressed, and resolved. After the first rehearsal it was decided that all interior lights within the cargo bay would be extinguished twenty minutes prior to landing. Everyone within the cargo bay, to include the loadmasters, would switch to night-vision goggles.

Five minutes out the pilot would illuminate the red jump light, at which time the loadmaster would crack the rear ramp. As soon as the drivers of the humvees saw this they would crank up their vehicles. During these last tense minutes Air Force personnel located throughout the cargo bay would take up their positions. The moment they felt the C-17 hit pavement and the pilots begin applying the brakes they would begin cutting the tie-downs as the ramp was lowered the rest of the way. When the pilot of the transport judged his speed to be slow enough, he would hit the green jump light to signal that it was time for Alpha Company to exit the aircraft. In this manner DeWitt found that he could have his entire command on the ground, formed up, and clear of the airfield within minutes. While it was true that the road taken to reach this point had not been an easy one in the end, professional soldiers and airmen, common sense, and personal pride managed to overcome each and every hindrance and administrative obstacle that had been thrown their way.

To rehearse the entire sequence and ensure everyone knew the drill cold, the pair of C-17s assigned to haul Alpha Company of the 3rd of the 75th Rangers from Fort Irwin, California, to the outskirts of Damascus had to circle for close to half an hour once they were airborne. Since timing and sequence are everything in combat, taking shortcuts in training or abridging the time between actions is bad policy. DeWitt understood this and very much approved of doing everything here that his company would be expected to do over there.

DeWitt's Rangers took advantage of this interlude to do what soldiers do best when given a chance. They slept. Even before the C-17 Globemasters were airborne everyone who could manage to do so slouched down in his seat or leaned on the man next to him, taking up as comfortable a position as his circumstances would permit. With their arms tightly folded across their chest, Rangers dropped off to sleep with incredible speed. Even the platoon leaders could not help but join their men in capitalizing upon this golden opportunity to repay a sleep debt that was overdrawn. Within minutes only the sound of the aircraft's engines and a few scattered snores could be heard.

Though he would have loved to take advantage of this opportunity to follow suit, DeWitt found he was never quite able to disengage his mind long enough to relax. There were simply too many thoughts, too many concerns rummaging about in his brain housing group. Rather than seeing this interlude as a benefit DeWitt found it to be almost a waste of time. While it was necessary to this harried officer, it was a waste nonetheless. During the entire flight he nervously glanced down at his watch every thirty seconds, as he thought of half a dozen other things that he and his command would do once this exercise was over.

As soon as each rehearsal and training exercise was really over there would be the obligatory head count within each section, squad, platoon, and company to ensure all personnel and equipment were present and accounted for. Then DeWitt would meet with his own officers and senior NCOs to go over what they had just done, pointing out what he had observed and soliciting their comments. Following that he would turn his command over to his XO and head to where the Fort Irwin observers/trainers and the other officers of the battalion were gathering for the formal after-action review. When finished there, Colonel Shaddock would gather his staff and company commanders in his office to reiterate a few key points hit upon in the course of the after-action review, before turning his attention to the training schedule for the next twenty-four hours. After his commander was finished with him DeWitt would run back to his own company orderly room where he would do the same with his unit's leadership who had, in his absence, been overseeing the cleaning and repacking of all weapons and equipment. Once this was done and all questions, outstanding issues, and problems pertaining to the company, its personnel, and its mission had been addressed if time could be found to do so, DeWitt would eat, sleep, and tend to whatever personal needs he could manage to squeeze in before doing it all over again, and again, and again.

Without warning the bright overhead cargo bay lights flickered on, causing a stir among the slumbering Rangers. Amid a muted chorus of oaths and grumbled threats directed at the unseen hand that had flipped the switch, DeWitt looked about in confusion, wondering if some sort of emergency were in progress. Somewhere in the back of his mind he found himself waiting for the alarm to sound, warning everyone in the cargo bay of impending doom that the Air Force personnel were struggling to forestall.

DeWitt was still turning this way and that in an effort to figure out what exactly was going on, when he felt a hand on his shoulder. Turning, he caught sight of the senior loadmaster standing next to his humvee. Reaching up with his right hand, the Air Force NCO covered his boom mike while leaning over toward DeWitt's ear so he could be heard. "The mission has been aborted."

"Did they say why?"

The loadmaster shook his head. "Negative knowledge, sir. The pilot just said we were to return to Bicycle Lake ASAP."

"Any orders for me?"

Raising his left index finger, the loadmaster uncovered the boom mike. "Wait one. I'll check." It took a moment for him to relay DeWitt's inquiry and a few more for the pilot to check back with base operations. Finally the loadmaster turned and looked up at DeWitt. "That's a negative, sir."

Unsure what this meant DeWitt looked back at the scores of anxious faces that were now directed at him. After taking a minute to consider how best to deal with this unexpected wrinkle, DeWitt turned back to the loadmaster who had remained standing patiently next to his humvee as the giant C-17 began to make a slow bank. "When we land have your people unleash my vehicle. Leave the rest in place until I find out what's up. Clear?"

The loadmaster nodded. "Clear, sir."

With all the Land Warrior components and cables still in place and ready for use, Emmett DeWitt made his way through the battalion headquarters to Lieutenant Colonel Shaddock's office. He had half expected to walk into the middle of a command and staff meeting. Instead he took note of the staff officers who were patiently waitng outside the battalion commander's closed door. As he approached he tried to read their expressions in an effort to ascertain whether the news awaiting him was good or bad. Unable to tell this from the dispassionate stares that greeted him, DeWitt moved on and entered his colonel's office without knocking.

This sudden intrusion caused little stir among the officers gathered around Shaddock. For his part Shaddock made no effort to acknowledge his Alpha Company commander as he continued to give Robert Delmont his full attention. Without a word, and doing his best to keep from disrupting the ongoing conversation, DeWitt looked about to see who else was in the room. In addition to Major Perry, Major Castalane, and the sergeant major, he spotted the rest of his fellow company commanders seated against the wall, cooling their heels as they waited for the battalion commander to finish up with the colonel from the Pentagon and issue them new orders. Finding an empty chair, DeWitt shifted his gear and joined them.

"The biggest concern that came up during the final briefing with the Sec Def was the back-pedaling by the electronic warfare people," Delmont recounted to Shaddock. "From the start the key to this entire operation has been the Air Force's ability to shut down the Syrians' internal command-and-control system. When Fanfare was just a deception plan this was no problem. Only after it began to look as if they were going to actually execute their portion of the plan did 'serious' issues and concerns begin to crop up. As of this morning they say the best they can hope for is an eighty percent solution."

When Delmont paused, Shaddock grunted. "Eighty percent sounds good to me. We've gone forward on operations with odds that were a lot slimmer than that."

Delmont didn't like the idea of going in with the Syrians only partially defanged, but he kept his counsel.

Shaddock took note of Delmont's failure to respond. "Do you think that will be a major problem?"

Delmont shrugged. "Perhaps. It all depends on who's wired into the twenty percent of the command structure that's still operational."

"And the Joint Chiefs? Where do they stand?"

It was questions like this that caused liaison officers problems. Failure on Delmont's part to answer honestly betrayed the trust that he had painstakingly worked to build up with the 3rd of the 75th. Yet to be completely candid with Shaddock would be equally disloyal to his parent organization. In the end the special ops plans officer again opted to say nothing. Of course his silence was all Shaddock needed to hear.

After drawing in a deep breath, he turned to face his assembled company commanders, XO, operations officer, and command sergeant major. "Well, sports fans, there you have it." Looking down at his watch Shaddock waited a moment until the sweep hand reached a given point. "On my mark it will be exactly oh-three-hundred Zulu. Mark." Looking up, he gazed into the eyes of his assembled officers one by one as he spoke. "Gentlemen, you know what needs to be done. Now, unless there are any questions . . ."

Having come into this meeting after it had been under way for some time DeWitt was at a total loss as to what exactly was going on. Tossing aside any concerns about appearances or making himself look foolish, he stood up. "Sir, I believe I missed some of the meeting. If you don't mind, could you please go over a few of the key points, such as what it is we're supposed to be getting ready for?"

It suddenly dawned on Shaddock that he had been so absorbed with listening to Delmont that he had not taken note of when DeWitt had finally shown up. Having no desire to embarrass himself or the young officer because of this oversight, Shaddock took a moment to frame his answer. "Lieutenant DeWitt, unless we're waved off en route, Fanfare is a go. You and your company have eight hours to sort itself out from its training exercise, swap your training ammunition for your combat load, refuel your Hummers, recharge the batteries for your Land Warrior systems, and load out. Wheels up is eleven-hundred hours Zulu. If all goes well and no one chokes at the last minute we'll be on the ground in Damascus in exactly twenty-four hours. Any questions?"

As word made its way down the chain of command every member of the 3rd Battalion 75th Rangers threw himself into preparing for an operation that had come to dominate their lives. Weapons that were already immaculate were stripped down, cleaned, and checked for proper function once they were reassembled. Unit equipment, from satellite dishes to surgical kits, was inspected, packed, and rigged for airdrop. Individuals were issued ammunition, drew rations, and filled their canteens with fresh American water before carefully stowing each and every item they would carry into battle in a pocket, pouch, or carrier from which they could retrieve it as needed. Specialists such as radiomen had the additional requirement to report to the battalion comms section to draw their copies of the communications and electronics operating instructions that they would be using during the course of Fanfare.

At the center of all this flurry of activity were the company-grade officers and junior NCOs. Like the Rangers who made up their squads, sections, platoons, and companies, each and every sergeant, lieutenant, and captain needed to tend to his own individual weapons, equipment, and rations. But they were also responsible for ensuring that their people were ready. In an elite unit such as the Rangers where the individuals are generally more motivated and self-reliant than the average American soldier, the amount of oversight is minimal. Yet constant review is still necessary. Major Robert Rogers of French and Indian Wars fame and the great-grandfather of the modern American Rangers said it best: "Check everything, forget nothing." Each junior enlisted

member of the 3rd of the 75th understood this philosophy, and
though they would never admit it to anyone, most were glad that
there was someone watching over them, making sure that in their
excited state they did not overlook an important item or forget to
fasten a strap on their parachute harness properly. Besides, as one
wag put it, "this was the Army, where soldiers are expected to do
soldier things and officers are paid to do officer things."

After unleashing his command of highly trained and motivated soldiers, Lieutenant Colonel Harry Shaddock found that he
had precious little to do. All the orders that he needed to be
issued had been given. The plans of his company commanders
and the annexes added by his primary staff officers that supported
the battalion operations order had been reviewed by him again
and again and again to ensure that they conformed with his concept of the operation. Every aspect of the operation that could be
rehearsed had been repeated under conditions that approximated
those they expected to find in Syria. Having done all that he
could, center stage now belonged to his officers and NCOs as
they went about supervising and checking the soldiers who fell
under their direct control

During these final frenzied hours of preparation Shaddock
was reduced to the status of figurehead, the acknowledged leader
of this collection of crack troops but one who had no real need to
exercise either command or control over their current activities.
The fact was, at times like this a senior officer is a hindrance.
Shaddock understood that every time he stopped and spoke to a
soldier or asked him to hand over his weapon so that he could
inspect it he was keeping that man from doing something else
that was critical, like filling his canteen or running over to the
ration breakdown point, or checking the batteries in the company
commander's radio. They knew exactly what needed to be done.
All they needed was the freedom and the time with which to do it.

Still, as much as company commanders and squad leaders
would have liked him to, Shaddock could not simply disappear

during this crucial period. He had to be seen by his men. Even in the day of high-tech, precision-guided munitions, ground soldiers needed to be physically led into battle. All the computer chips in the world could not replace this function of the officer. Shaddock's men had grown used to seeing him in garrison and during every aspect of their training. Now as they prepared to venture into harm's way they needed to see him. Though many military men have tried over the centuries to do away with this symbolic practice, again and again combat commanders have found that there was no substitute in battle for the same sort of commanding and heroic figure that the Spartan King had immortalized at Thermopolae. Like Leonidas, Lieutenant Colonel Harry Shaddock was more than an officer in the United States Army. By virtue of his position he had become a talisman, a good luck charm that satisfied the primeval needs of the world's most sophisticated warriors. They might not understand the logic of their mission. They might not be motivated by old-fashioned patriotism. Yet there was not a soul among the soldiers of the 3rd of the 75th who did not feel a sense of loyalty to Harry Shaddock, a man who had become something between an icon and a father figure to men raised in a society in which manhood was sometimes viewed as a curse.

With no firm plan in mind Shaddock made his way from one unit assembly point to another, showing the flag while looking for something constructive to do. Like his company commanders he was responsible for overseeing the activities of his command as well as making himself available just in case some glitch cropped up at this late stage that required his personal intervention. Yet no matter how hard he searched for a situation that cried out for his attention he found no problems he needed to untangle. Nor did he come across any harried staff officer crying out for salvation. Like Diogenes wandering through the darkness in search of an honest man, Shaddock was reduced to going from one group of soldiers to another in a vain quest to find fulfillment.

In the midst of this meandering quest Shaddock came across the pair of lieutenant colonels who had attached themselves to the 3rd of the 75th during their tenure at Fort Irwin. From the looks on their faces he could tell that both Neil Kaplan and Robert Delmont desired a moment of his time. Raising his head and straightening himself up, Shaddock slipped into his battalion commander persona. "Well," he announced with far more enthusiasm than he felt, "in a few more hours we'll be ready to rock and roll."

At first neither Kaplan nor Delmont spoke as they exchanged nervous glances. Then, after taking a moment to screw up his courage, Delmont took the point. "In going over our orders assigning us to your battalion, Colonel Shaddock, both Colonel Kaplan and I have found that neither of us have been instructed as to when our responsibility to your unit is at an end."

Try as hard as he might, Shaddock found himself barely able to suppress the smirk that lit up his face. He knew what was coming and was not sure how he felt about it. Joyriding on a mission such as this was not at all uncommon. In fact, it was almost a game with rear-echelon types eager to prove something to themselves or punch their proverbial career ticket. Every professional soldier worth a damn seized upon every opportunity that came his way to go where the action was.

For the great majority of American soldiers this desire to stroll through the valley of death is not a manifestation of suicidal tendencies or a need to satisfy a sinister and savage bloodlust. Rather, the motivation that drives a professional officer to hitch on to a mission such as Fanfare even when they have no real role could be explained in one of two ways. More often than not there is an unfulfilled desire to practice all those skills that they had spent years learning and refining. To a professional soldier such as Robert Delmont, being a combat arms officer in a peacetime Army was akin to a major league ballplayer doomed to spend his entire career sitting on the bench without ever being afforded the opportunity to take the field. True, Delmont was a plans officer responsible for developing many real-world contingencies. In drafting Fanfare and providing staff oversight on behalf of his superior in Washington he had executed his assigned duties as laid out in his job description. But like most professional officers, he was a soldier first and foremost. And soldiers don't win battles by thinking about them. Nor do they derive job satisfaction from watching others go off to fight them.

A less acknowledged catalyst that compelled officers like Delmont and Kaplan to insert themselves into a situation in which they need not go was an unspoken desire to test their individual mettle. Time and time again professional soldiers reared in a peacetime army have risen through the ranks to a position of importance only to find that when they finally did face the ultimate test of battle, they came up lacking. Whether it was a dearth of the moral fiber necessary to wage war or a simple inability to subordinate personal fear, the reason did not matter. Failure by an officer to live up to expectations in combat translates into unnecessary deaths and ignoble defeat. While a good deal of blame for this shortcoming could be leveled at a system that rewards those who were most proficient at counting beans and keeping a clean motor pool rather than men who had a knack for breaking things, even the best scheme for officer selection and training could not predetermine who would buckle under the strain of combat and who would rise above the chaos to win great victories for his nation.

At the moment it didn't matter to Harry Shaddock what was driving this pair of lieutenant colonels to offer their services. As the commanding officer of a battalion about to engage in a high-risk operation, what was important was whether either or both of these people could be of use to him while on the ground in Syria. While he had no particular fondness for or loyalty to either, he at least owed them the courtesy of hearing them out. After making a show of looking at his watch, Shaddock folded his arms. "Okay, I'm game. Convince me of why either of you need to go."

Glancing at each other, both Kaplan and Delmont paused as they tried to figure out who should take the lead. In the end Kaplan deferred to Delmont. "I have not received any new orders relieving me of my duties as liaison officer to your unit. So I am assuming that they remain in force."

Shaddock knew better than to ask Delmont if he had bothered to call his superior and ask him if it was his intention for Delmont to remain with the 3rd of the 75th throughout the entire operation. After all, if their roles were reversed he sure as hell would not have made that call. "I see. And you, Colonel Kaplan?"

"Well, sir," he blurted, "while it is true that your Alpha Company has achieved a degree of proficiency with the Land Warrior, you have no one within your battalion who has the expertise to troubleshoot any problems that may crop up during the course of operations.

"If that happens," Shaddock countered, "I doubt if we would have time to sort things out."

"But if I or my NCOIC aren't around, there won't be any chance at all, will there? Besides, who will do systems and integration checks prior to dropping ramps?"

"Can't you do that now?"

Kaplan held his hands out at his side and waved them vaguely in the direction of several small groups of soldiers scurrying about as they tended to last-minute preparations. "We could try, Colonel, but at the moment it would be like herding cats. Once Alpha Company is airborne they will become the ultimate captive audience. If Sergeant Benoit and I are with them we will have thirteen hours to check the individual units, answer any last-minute questions, and sort out any problems. Besides," he added reluctantly, "this will be the first time the Land Warrior will be seeing combat on this scale. It would be useful to both the program and the Army in general if someone who is familiar with the system is there on the ground to study it under actual conditions."

"Yes," Shaddock mused, "I see your point. And once you're on the ground? What will your function be? I mean, we are going into combat."

Drawing himself up, Kaplan peered into Shaddock's eyes. "Despite what you or the Army may think, I am a soldier, no less dedicated to my profession or duty than you."

Shaddock's natural inclination was to decline the offer from his fellow officers. This was, after all, a raid. Neither he nor any of his staff would have any time once they were on the ground to deal with straphangers. Still, as he stood there looking at the pair he realized that these were no ordinary joyriders. Delmont was a trusted representative of the Joint Chiefs of Staff. His presence on the ground could be useful if things started to go south. If nothing else, he could deal with all communications directed at the 3rd of the 75th from CENTCOM or the Joint Chiefs that were not mission related.

Stepping closer, Shaddock poked the special ops plans officer in the chest with his index finger. "If you do go, mister, it will be your job to handle any and all incoming calls from anyone and everyone who is not in my immediate chain of command. Clear?"

Understanding what the battalion commander was driving at, Delmont nodded. "That's reasonable. Can do."

After nodding, Shaddock looked at Kaplan. "Colonel, I have to admit that I've not had the opportunity to study up on the Land Warrior. So I find that I am unable to tell if you're blowing smoke or on the level." He paused, looking down at the ground as he made a show of weighing the issue for a moment. When he was ready he looked up. "Rather than put this operation at risk I find that I have no choice but to add both you and your NCOIC to the troop list."

Shaddock noted how Kaplan's face lit up. "Now," the battalion commander stated, "you two need to get with my XO and let him know you're to be added to the manifest. Colonel Kaplan, you're to attach yourself to Lieutenant DeWitt's company until we're on the ground. Once there, you're to report to my TAC

CP. Colonel Delmont, you'll be with the TAC CP throughout the operation unless I have need of your services elsewhere. Any questions?"

Having achieved their aim, both Delmont and Kaplan snapped to attention and shook their heads.

"Now," Shaddock concluded, "if you don't mind, I have a battalion which I need to tend to." Of course both Delmont and Kaplan knew this was something less than truthful. Like them, the commander of the 3rd of the 75th was, for the moment, little more than a spectator as hundreds of soldiers, pumped up by the prospect of battle, prepared themselves for combat.

CHAPTER TWENTY-SEVEN

Even before the officers and men of the 3rd of the 75th Rangers departed Fort Irwin aboard giant C-17 Globemaster IIIs, the first whispers of Fanfare were beginning to sweep across the vast expanses of Syria like the stirring of the breeze before a prairie storm. Fanfare's opening gambits were not directed at Syrian troops or the facilities they manned. The targets of these long-range assaults were the systems upon which those soldiers had come to depend. Like their mark, the tip of this spearhead was not human. They weren't even machines. They were the unseen digital commandos sent streaming through the atmosphere in endless columns of zeros and ones. Their objective was to infiltrate, cripple, incapacitate, and confuse the electronic components of the fragile network that linked the Syrian air defense with its national command authority as well as the integrated communications array on which the Syrian leaders and military relied.

This was the twenty-first century version of the Trojan horse, better known as informational warfare. Launched from computers scattered around the United States, technicians unlocked back doors to automated systems all across Syria. Through those hidden portals, they unleashed worms, viruses, and other electronic predators designed to ravage programs needed to direct and coordinate the Syrian military. Each of these attacks was discrete, very narrowly targeted, and initiated in a well-orchestrated sequence so that by the time the Syrians realized what was afoot, the damage was already done.

Nothing was sacred, nothing safe. Included in this panoply of systems scheduled for disruption were nonmilitary ground- and space-based telecommunications platforms owned and operated by international conglomerates. Designed to support the global economy by linking remote areas of the world via wireless Internet connections and cell phones, these systems provided the Syrian military with an emergency backup. The same cell phones American kids carried about in their backpacks at school were standard issue to commanders of Syrian surface-to-air missile batteries. While no one doubted that there would be howls of protests from corporate CEOs and their clients when selected portions of this privately owned technological wonder suddenly went off the air, the American command authority had determined that a few hundred botched business deals and stock trades were a small price to pay for protecting its fighting men.

Fanfare's preliminary ethereal maneuvers could not play havoc forever without evoking a response from the Syrians. Eventually their command-and-control structure woke up to the fact that they were under attack. When that occurred, Syrian units began to deploy to repel the ongoing assault. To dissipate this effort and keep senior Syrian commanders ignorant of the assault's true form and the direction from which it was coming was the aim of Fanfare's deception plan. This was achieved through the use of disinformation, a more ancient form of warfare that had once been a forte of the former Soviet Union.

Disinformation is a tricky ploy that can easily backfire if not properly orchestrated. In the case of Fanfare, the primary agents of disinformation were selected members of the administration and Congress known for their propensity to leak information. In the wake of Sergeant Yousaf Hashmi's execution, these oft-quoted unnamed sources who kept the American media supplied with state secrets were fed rumors that retaliatory air strikes meant as a warning to the Syrian leadership were in the offing. Along the way these rumors of air strikes were augmented and reinforced by statements made by military analysts and prognosticators hired by twenty-four-hour news networks to fill dead air-time by rendering their views on what the administration would most likely do. Even when the more responsible journalists and editors refused to use this information, Syrian agents and people sympathetic to that nation who worked within the various news agencies passed these golden nuggets on.

Gathered by agents, this carefully seeded disinformation was lumped in with real data culled from other sources. When intelligence officers in Damascus drafted their assessment of possible and probable American military actions against their nation, the disinformation that had made its way into the mix skewed their assessments. In this way, limited air strikes rather than a full-scale rescue effort became the major concern against which the Syrian military girded itself. Rather than preparing itself to repel boarders the Syrian military dispatched its troops to key facilities where they were ordered to cast their gaze skyward and wait for an opportunity to shoot down airplanes.

Having to launch and recover aircraft from allied nations required commands supporting Fanfare from foreign soil to exercise a different and more careful blended form of deception as well as operational security. Every nation that permits American forces to operate within its borders does so under negotiated status-of-forces agreements that govern and limit American military operations and the conduct of its personnel. Without exception these status-of-forces agreements include provisions for the assignment of liaison officers from the host nation to every major American command in that nation. This makes planning and implementing U.S.-only operations such as Fanfare difficult but not impossible. To counter the threat to the security of Fanfare that foreign liaison officers posed, American counterintelligence officers waged their own disinformation campaign. The commanders and staff officers charged with preparing for Fanfare took care to ensure that those briefings that addressed Fanfare were conducted at times when the liaison officers were not around. It was not much of a stretch to claim that Fanfare's first skirmishes took place in the headquarters of Syria's pro-Western neighbors. These bloodless battles were waged between liaison officers who used every maneuver and trick in the book to sneak a peek at the documents that were sandwiched between the bright red "Secret, No Foreign Dissemination" covers, and the American counterintelligence officers charged with keeping that from happening.

The Pentagon was not immune to the need to be vigilant. In a place where handling secrets is routine, security tends to become lax. To counter this, extraordinary measures have to be taken to protect operations like Fanfare for as long as possible without alerting anyone to the notion that something out of the ordinary was amiss. This feat was accomplished by maintaining a tight control on who knew about Fanfare. Of those privy to some or all of the plan, only personnel who truly had a need to know were informed of Fanfare's actual H-hour. In being given access to this information they accepted the responsibility of doing everything within their power to keep from varying either their daily routine or that of their staff, a task that is far easier said than done.

To monitor how well the operational security plan designed to safeguard Fanfare was going at the Pentagon, a key indicator used by the counterintelligence folks there was the number of pizza deliveries made to the Puzzle Palace on the Potomac. As silly as it may sound, a seemingly mundane activity that would not cause a stir anywhere else in America is watched by both journalists and foreign agents. When the number of pizza deliveries shows a sudden spike, deductive reasoning leads those monitoring pizza deliveries to conclude that an inordinate number of Pentagon staffers are working late. During a period of crisis, this can only mean that an operation linked to that crisis is being planned or about to be initiated. Just how the counterintelligence officers go about making sure that the number of pizza deliveries is maintained at appropriate levels is a closely guarded secret that no one has yet sorted out, though it is rumored that a number of Arlington pizzeria managers are working hard to discover it.

In addition to the galley slaves manning the oars at the Pentagon, other key members in the chain of command were required to do their part to keep from tipping off the Syrians that the American military was about to pay them a visit. The Commander in Chief is no exception. To preserve the atmosphere of normalcy, the president found himself enduring a political fund-raising event that had been scheduled months in advance. Maintaining an even keel in public while hundreds of young men are about to be placed in harm's way as the result of an order that he has issued is perhaps one of the most difficult things a chief executive can be asked to do. On this night, just about the time when the president was taking his place behind a podium in preparation to deliver a political speech, Lieutenant Colonel Harry Shaddock would be standing in the door of a C-17, staring intently at a pair of warning lights waiting for the green one to illuminate. Tightly stacked up behind Shaddock would be his men, burdened by the equipment they carried and the awesome task they were about to undertake.

Syria
16:15 PACIFIC, 19:15 EASTERN, 03:15 LOCAL (23:15 ZULU)

In Washington, D.C., the president was looking out at a room of well-heeled contributors. At the Pentagon the Chief of Staff of the Army sat slumped in his seat, watching the tactical and operational displays in the Army War Room. At MacDill Air Force Base in Florida the commander of CENTCOM was alone in his office, nervously pacing back and forth like an expectant father. In Turkey, a wing commander sipped his coffee in silence as he watched the computer-generated plots track the progress of his aircraft. Over the Mediterranean the senior controller aboard an E-3A Sentinel slowly made his way along the narrow aisle of the converted Boeing jet, pausing here and there to study a display before moving on to the next. Aboard the USS *Ronald Reagan* the air group commander twisted in his chair while nervously tapping away on the armrest, an act that threatened to drive the seaman seated before him crazy. In the cockpits of strike aircraft thundering in on targets scattered throughout Syria, pilots kept their eyes glued to their sensors and instruments, praying that the next sound they heard over their headsets would not be the high-pitched tone that warned them that they had been acquired and targeted by Syrian air-defense radar. Within the transport carrying his company, First Lieutenant Emmett J. DeWitt glanced down at the photo of his wife and son one last time before slipping it back into his wallet.

If nervous anticipation was the dominant theme within the American military at the moment, panic and pandemonium were the order of the day on the ground in Syria. Throughout the Syrian countryside the men responsible for coordinating their nation's air defense were madly scrambling to assess a situation that defied their every effort to grasp while others in the military chain of command became irate when they discovered that they were unable to make a simple phone call.

This electronic onslaught did not totally paralyze the Syrian military establishment or cast its leadership into utter disarray. The Syrian military is not completely inept. It is still an organization run by a core of professionals who use the same methods the American military does to assess possible threats and prepare contingencies to deal with them. Through the employment of various alternative means of communications, including messengers dispatched on motorcycles and manual land-line systems that Alexander Graham Bell would have recognized, senior commanders began issuing orders to execute contingency plans to their far-flung subordinates. In some cases the harried dispatch rider arrived at his destination only to find that the actions he had been sent to initiate were already being implemented by officers who had correctly assessed the situation and had taken the initiative. Such occasions proved to be the exception since initiative is not a watchword within modern Syria. For the most part the bulk of the midlevel Syrian leadership restricted their actions to rousting their men out of their bunks and hounding them until they were at their assigned duty stations. Once this feat was accomplished, officers who owed their success to being cautious and operating within the accepted bounds of their military system held fast to their published orders and awaited developments. For some developments they did not have long to wait.

Informational and electronic warfare is an important element of modern war, sometimes referred to as a force multiplier. It is capable of disrupting and disorienting a foe's command-and-control system. In some cases it can even result in physical calamities. It does not, however, possess an inherent ability to kill men or physically smash things. To achieve this it is still necessary to apply copious amounts of well-directed munitions containing good old-fashioned high explosives. Over the years both the United States Air Force and Navy have raised this ancient form of warfare to a fine art. Through the employment of cruise missiles, unmanned bombers, and conventional strike aircraft these two services had the responsibility of neutralizing and suppressing those enemy units and assets that had been identified as a threat to the inbound Rangers.

Like many words in today's vocabulary, the terms *neutralize* and *suppress* have very specific meanings that sometimes conjure up an image in the mind of a layperson that does not always reflect what those words mean when used by the military. *Neutralize,* for example, is defined by the military as the act of rendering enemy personnel or materiel incapable of interfering with a particular operation. Both the word and its definition make it seem as if the actions necessary to achieve this goal can be rather innocuous. Nothing could be further from the truth. To truly neutralize an enemy unit a sufficient number of its personnel must be killed or wounded. In general terms, a unit that suffers 25 to 50 percent casualties in a short space of time is no longer able to function effectively. While some of the more humane or politically correct military types try to argue that neutralization can be achieved by destroying a foe's equipment or weapons, no one can deny that death is the ultimate form of neutralization. For a company of a hundred fifty men, this translates as thirty-seven to seventy-five dead and wounded. In a battalion with four companies, it is one hundred fifty to three hundred KIAs and WIAs. And so on, and so on, and so on.

As ambiguous as the term *neutralization* can sometimes be, *suppression* is even less exact and more difficult to quantify. One definition states that suppression is the denial of an enemy's ability to effectively move, shoot, and/or communicate. Another conception holds that suppression occurs when direct and indirect fires, electronic means, or obscurants are brought to bear upon enemy troops, weapons, or equipment for the purpose of preventing the enemy from bringing effective fire against friendly troops. However it is defined, suppressive fire does not have to actually hit and kill the enemy or smash equipment in order to be effective. It simply has to screen friendly activities or encourage the enemy to seek cover rather than fight. In reality, suppression is a means of economy. Fewer weapons and munitions are required to suppress a target than destroy it. A singe burst of machine-gun fire can send an entire platoon scurrying in search of cover. One or two bombs dropped within a military compound will cause a goodly number of soldiers to run to their bunkers rather than man their stations or weapons. Even the mere approach of aircraft can set off air raid sirens that will create a period of confusion and panic within a city that can be exploited by an attacker.

Regardless of the means used, once the method of suppression has been lifted or shifted to engage another target, the enemy is left relatively untouched and free to continue as before. This has led some commanders and trainers to unofficially advocate the notion that death is the ultimate form of suppression, a truism if ever there was one. Of course this point of view ultimately leads to the use of more assets and munitions than the original plan called for, and thus defeats the effort to economize, which the technique known as suppression was meant to provide.

Careful analysis and common sense quickly made it clear that the United States did not possess the means or have the time to kill every Syrian soldier who could potentially interfere with the efforts of the 3rd of the 75th Rangers. Therefore orders generated by subordinate headquarters supporting Fanfare included the liberal use of both terms. Besides, the stated purpose of the Rangers' mission didn't justify a wholesale slaughter. Planners like Robert Delmont had to determine which elements of the Syrian military had to be completely eliminated—a term that requires no special military definition—those targets that needed to be neutralized, and those that simply had to be suppressed during the course of the operation. It was only when one finally reaches the bottom links of the chain of command that terminology begins to become a little less important and the actual means of doing the job becomes more concrete and strangely familiar. While the means of delivery vary and the amount of force used differs from service to service, high explosives in all their modern incarnations are the principal means of eliminating, neutralizing, and suppressing.

In the end it goes back to simply dumping copious amounts of high explosives onto an enemy unit with the ultimate aim of killing its soldiers and destroying their equipment. No matter how sophisticated the means of delivery or whether the platform is manned or unmanned, upon detonation the explosives in the warhead are almost instantly transformed into heat and energy.

While it is true that heat and flame unleashed by an explosion ignites flammable material, burns exposed flesh, and can blind, it is the blast that does the serious killing. The chemically generated energy of a detonating device creates a shock wave that radiates from the point of impact in all directions. Human beings who are close enough to this can be literally torn to pieces. War stories that speak of men being blown to bits are not fabrications. They are grim fact.

Farther out, the expanding shock wave hits a human like a moving brick wall, smashing bones, pulverizing organs, and peeling away soft tissue. The effectiveness of any explosive device is defined in terms of the radius in which 50 percent of all exposed personnel are killed by this shock wave. While some people cheat this mathematical fact of life by being lucky enough to have some form of protection that shields them from the direct effects of an explosion, others find they are victims of their circumstances. When an explosion occurs within an enclosed area such as a bunker or room, the force of the blast hits the restricting walls and reflects back toward the point of origin, magnifying the effectiveness of the explosion and making kill ratios of 100 percent very achievable.

Accompanying this invisible force is overpressure. If the shock wave is analogous to the surface of a brick wall, overpressure is akin to the effect that the same brick wall would have on a person if it fell upon them. It is a crushing force, one capable of overwhelming the internal pressure of a man's eyeballs and squashing them. The air is literally squeezed out of the lungs, only to be filled by superheated air as the force of the blast wave passes on and releases its invisible grasp of the victim's chest. Other internal organs such as kidneys, liver, and heart are compressed or ripped from their internal moorings. The skull is crushed, leaving its contents to ooze out like the yoke of a smashed egg.

If the shock wave is the most deadly aspect of an explosion, the wounds created by the fragmentation of the delivery device and debris picked up and tossed around by the event are the most visually stunning. At the instant of detonation the explosive's container as well as the electronic components and propulsion system used to fly the device to the target are all torn apart and dispatched along the leading edge of the shock wave. These fragments, popularly known as shrapnel, rip, shred, gouge, and pierce any human who is not lucky enough to be under cover. Ranging from microscopic to chunks of red-hot metal the size of a man's fist, these fragments pepper the victim with all the indiscriminate randomness of a shotgun blast. If a person is close enough, death through bleeding can occur in mere minutes. Farther away, these jagged and irregular missiles embed themselves in any exposed flesh. If not removed carefully or in time, the razor-sharp edges of the fragments that have managed to burrow in or around human organs can continue to gouge new wounds or aggravate old ones every time the victim moves on his own or is shifted about by others.

The men and women of the United States Air Force and Navy who direct and deliver these agents of mayhem and death never see the true effect of their efforts. The most they are privy to are two-tone video images dispatched by sensors in the devices themselves or recorded by other aircraft that have been assigned the duty of "painting" the target with an invisible laser-aiming dot. The role of the pilots of the manned bombers and the computers guiding unmanned bombers ends when their screens are lit up by the flash of an explosion. Sometimes the manned bombers will linger in the area for a few minutes to assess the effectiveness of their attack. More often than not this bomb-damage assessment, or BDA, is done by others using space-based platforms, high-level recon flights, or by monitoring electronic and voice traffic on selected enemy command-and-control nets.

When the BDA has been complied it is reported up the chain of command, using the aforementioned terms. Thus a Syrian air defense battery that had lost half of its launchers, equipment, and personnel can be said to have been neutralized. To the men who ordered the strike and those who carried it out, a vivid description of physical carnage or exact body count is unimportant.

To some this antiseptic way of waging war is a mockery and distasteful. The more vehement antiwar crowd even goes so far as to claim that it is a convention used by policy makers in the United States to hide the truth of what its nation's military is actually doing to the enemy. While there have been times when these notions have been correct, the terrible truth is that it must be that way. Twenty-first-century America has given birth to a generation of politicians and media pundits who believe that America can actually wage war without the loss of a single taxpayer. This fantasy has forced the military into a corner that requires it to wage war at long range using technology to supplant the human whenever and wherever possible.

This is not all bad, for even the practitioners find it necessary to insulate themselves and their people from the grim, gory facts of their own handiwork. Otherwise many of the men and women who fly strike missions, push buttons to launch cruise missiles, and direct unmanned drones would never be able to do so a second time, for not all wounds suffered in a battle are physical and not all scars can be seen with the naked eye. Wars are won by force of will, by those willing to do whatever is necessary to win. Very few of our nation's sons and daughters have the psychological makeup that would allow them to go toe to toe with their foe and hack them to death for hours on end, in the same manner that was expected of ancient Sparta's youth. Even an elite soldier belonging to the 3rd of the 75th Rangers has a psychological point beyond which he cannot go and still be expected to return emotionally and mentally safe and sound. If there is one thing we have learned from Vietnam, it is that American fighting men are not automatons, machines with a "kill" setting that can be switched on and off without consequences.

As the transports bearing Harry Shaddock's Rangers lumbered on toward their objective, the men and women of the Air Force and Navy went about carrying out their assigned tasks of clearing a path for those slow-moving aircraft. The first in were unmanned bombers with short wingspans and an overall length of little more than thirty feet. Under the cloak of the electronic warfare barrage unleashed against air-defense systems and command-and-control networks these drones penetrated Syrian airspace undetected. With unerring mechanical precision they honed in on those targets that were deemed to be too risky for manned bombers. Augmenting these technological marvels were cruise missiles, the ultimate Kamikaze.

The difference between the two forms of remote-control warfare is subtle yet important. A cruise missile is a complete package

that contains a means of propulsion, a guidance system, a targeting system, and the warhead itself. Once a cruise missile is programmed and launched, it flies off to its target where the entire
package is thrown against it, rocket motor, navigational computer
and all, making it a nonrefundable commodity. The unmanned
bomber, on the other hand, is exactly like a conventional bomber
in that it is a delivery vehicle equipped with an engine, navigational aids, and a fire-control system designed to deliver a detach-
able payload. Once the payload or bombs have been expended
the aircraft returns to its home base where it is served and
rearmed with more bombs. More often than not these are good
old-fashioned general-purpose bombs or GPUs that can weigh
anywhere between 750 and 2,000 pounds. To turn a dumb GPU
into a precision-guided weapon requires the addition of fins that
allow it to glide and a guidance system designed to fly the bomb
into its designated target using a laser-designated point of impact,
radar homing, or GPS-assisted targeting. Both cruise missiles and
unmanned bombers are capable of achieving the same results of
attacking enemy targets without needing to use highly trained
American aviators. Only the unmanned bomber can do so repeatedly and far more cheaply. Whereas a cruise missile can cost as
much as $1 million a pop, a 2,000-pound Paveway GPU with all
the trimming costs no more than $50,000.

This first wave of unmanned attack aircraft and cruise missiles was directed against known air-defense acquisition radars
and surface-to-air missile batteries. This sort of mission is
referred to as SAM suppression. Destruction or neutralization of
these assets opens the way for follow-up attacks by manned
attack aircraft aimed at eliminating enemy air defenses that the
Syrian high command have held back and hidden from visual or
electronic detection. These manned SAM-suppression strikes are
flown by a unique group of aviators known as Wild Weasels.
When a sensor aboard the E-3A AWAC, an electronic warfare
aircraft, identifies a new threat the controller aboard the E-3A

charged with monitoring and orchestrating all SAM-suppression missions contacts the nearest flight of Wild Weasels and hands off the new target to them.

One of the first such missions occurred even before the last of the cruise missiles and unmanned bombers had finished their attacks. From out of nowhere an air-defense target-acquisition radar lit up and began tracking one of the cruise missiles. With a speed that defies description this event was reported to half a dozen different aircraft and operations centers scattered throughout the region. From his station aboard the E-3A, the SAM-suppression controller assigned the new target an alphanumeric designation before checking on the status and location of the Wild Weasels. The pair of aircraft he opted to dispatch to hit this new target were two F-18s from the USS *Ronald Reagan*. After contacting the commander of the F-18s by voice, the SAM-suppression controller transferred data from his station directly into the fire-control system of the F-18s via an electronic data link. Once the F-18 pilots acknowledged that they had a good copy of all the necessary target information, the SAM-suppression controller wished them luck and sent them on their way.

Anxious to achieve a kill even if it were of an unmanned cruise missile, the Syrian air-defense battery commander kept his acquisition radar on far too long. This allowed the Naval aviators assigned to silence his radar more than enough time to acquire the radiation being emitted by the acquisition radar and launch a pair of AGM-88 HARM missiles in the "range-known" mode. Sensors within the missiles themselves picked up the hostile radar, memorized its location just in case that radar was switched off during their approach, and began to make their way to it. When the HARM missiles reached the Syrian air-defense battery, their high-explosive warheads detonated, showering the entire unit with small prefragmented steel cubes that were designed to inflict maximum damage to the radar unit itself as well as other vulnerable equipment co-located with the target-acquisition radar. In the process of ripping apart the delicate electronics and mechanical devices of the battery, this rain of destruction also inflicted a fair number of casualties among the soldiers who were manning the site, causing the entire command to lose interest in the cruise missile that they had been tracking.

With Syrian air-defense units either destroyed or neutralized, the way was clear for the next wave of manned aircraft to come in. Unlike the strikes against the SAM sites, which were wide ranging, these new attacks were specifically aimed at neutralizing or suppressing those Syrian ground troops and their controlling headquarters that had the potential of interfering with the 3rd of the 75th Rangers once they were on the ground. In some cases cluster bombs were released over the motor pools of those Syrian units. By destroying their transportation the Air Force and Naval aviators took entire Syrian units out of the picture.

Not all Syrian soldiers were so fortunate. Eight companies of infantry and one reinforced tank company were located at the military airport where the 3rd of the 75th was scheduled to land, along the route of advance DeWitt's Company A would be taking, or at the prison itself. These units as well as the battalion command posts to which they reported, and the regional headquarters that controlled all military operations in the area, had to be eradicated. To simplify this task it was decided to hit them as soon as the air offensive opened, while the bulk of the personnel assigned to those units were still in their barracks. Failure to strike at that time would allow the Syrians to scatter and deploy, making the chore of inflicting casualties on them using air power alone all but impossible.

In achieving this goal, the Air Force and Naval aviators assigned to carry out these attacks were aided by the Syrians themselves. The wail of air-raid sirens and the distant rumble of bombs hitting air defense facilities made little impression on the sleeping Syrian infantrymen and tankers. They had heard all of this before and had become quite used to these nocturnal visits. Most had long ago reached the conclusion that they made poor targets. Few believed that the Americans would waste sophisticated bombs, or risk their expensive aircraft, by attacking the barracks of a lowly infantry company. Other than a grunt or groan of disgust from men roused from their sleep by the first wave of attacks, no one stirred much.

This complacency came to an abrupt end when laser-guided bombs smashed their way through the upper floors of the barracks buildings. It was only then that a handful of the startled Syrians realized just how badly they had miscalculated their odds. Unfortunately, by the time this terrifying thought was able to take hold, the two-thousand-pound GPUs used for these strikes had burrowed their way deep into the heart of the building. In all cases there was a slight pause, maybe one or two seconds after initial impact before the delayed-action fuses activated. Syrians who had been sleeping on the lower floors died quickly from the actual blast. Those who had bunks on the upper floors were killed either when their building collapsed on them or later when multiple wounds and the inability of comrades to reach them in time took their toll. Raging fires that swept through the rubble took the remainder. In this manner, a couple of dozen aircraft managed to kill or mortally wound more than a thousand Syrian soldiers within a span of five minutes. This achievement, coupled with the suppression of the Syrian air-defense system and the crippling of military command-and-control networks set the stage for the main event of the night: the assault of the 3rd of the 75th Rangers.

Syria
19:55 EASTERN, 03:55 LOCAL (23:55 ZULU)

"**S**ound off for equipment check!" Each successive command bellowed by the jumpmaster ratcheted up the tension and anticipation that permeated the transport one more notch. Already on their feet and hooked up, upon hearing this command each Ranger responded by slapping the man to his immediate front after feeling a similar tap from the one behind him, and yelling out, *"Okay!"* This action acknowledged that he had checked all of his gear, was hooked up, and ready to step off. When Harry Shaddock felt the man behind him sound off, the commanding officer of the 3rd of the 75th Rangers and first man in his stick standing next to the open door looked into the eye of the senior jumpmaster who had initiated this last check. Pointing his finger at the jumpmaster Shaddock shouted out at the top of his lungs *"All okay!"*

Having completed this last precombat check there was now nothing left for the mass of Rangers and their attending jumpmasters to do but wait until the red jump light flickered off and the green began to flash. For them everything now rested, as a devout Muslim would say, in the hands of God.

On this night God had an intermediary. This was the transport's pilot and his flight crew. In a cockpit illuminated by nothing more than the faint glow of the aircraft's instruments and computer displays the pilot of the lead aircraft carrying Shaddock, part of his staff, and most of Company C maintained the course and altitude dictated by his navigational computer. Like the rest of his crew the pilot was literally on the edge of his seat, watching, listening, waiting. He was waiting for the moment when they reached the exit point. He was waiting for the enemy air defense to come alive and light up the sky before him with antiaircraft artillery fire, known as triple A. He was waiting for a call over the radio instructing him to abort the mission. Above all he was waiting for a report from the senior jumpmaster back in the cargo hold informing him that all the Rangers were safely away and his aircraft's door was closed and secured. Only then would he be free to take command of his aircraft once more. Only then could he head back to the barn with the sense of satisfaction and clear conscience that a man feels when he has played a role in a major undertaking such as Fanfare. The success and failure of Fanfare did not rest solely upon the shoulders of Harry Shaddock and his Rangers. Were it not for the thousands of supporting players like the transport pilot and the jumpmaster who stood nose to nose with Shaddock during these last brief seconds of relative calm, Fanfare would be impossible. Like the crews of the E-3A AWACs, the pilots of the F-18s, and the men and women who readied and launched the cruise missiles, unmanned bombers, and strike aircraft, the air crews of the transports carrying the 3rd of the 75th were all part of the equation. Together with the Rangers they would determine if the survivors of RT Kilo would meet the new dawn as free men or face another day of despair.

With all the intensity of a child watching the clock on a classroom wall, the pilot kept his eye on the computer display. When the small dot following the computer-generated course he was flying finally illuminated and the tone sounded in his earphone his hand all but leaped for the switch that triggered the "go" signal. Back in the cargo bay Shaddock did not give the jumpmaster an opportunity to shout the order to go. As soon as the light on the panel next to the door changed colors the commander of the 3rd of the 75th Rangers was gone, whisked away by the jet transport's slipstream and swallowed up by the dark night sky. In his wake came an unbroken chain of a hundred Rangers, all shuffling their

feet along the aluminum floorboards of the transport and screaming *"Go! Go! Go!"* at the men before them as they pressed forward. Though the senior jumpmaster and his assistants stood
ready to literally boot any man out the door who hesitated at the
last moment, no one flinched. Within seconds the cargo bay was
empty save for the crew of the transport. After taking a moment
to catch his breath, the senior jumpmaster carefully edged over to
the open door, leaned out as far as he dared, and peered off in the
distance as the last of his former charges disappeared below. With
a wave of his hand, he murmured a heartfelt farewell that was
drowned out by the howling wind. *"Vaya con Dios, amigos."* Having done all he could to speed the Rangers along, the jumpmaster
pulled himself back in and ordered his assistants to close the door
behind him.

The blare of air-raid sirens roused Allen Kannen out of the fitful
sleep he had managed to slip into. Opening his eyes he looked
about his barren cell for a moment as he listened closely in an
effort to hear the sound of the bombs or perhaps the roar of the
attacking aircraft themselves. For the longest time he heard nothing save the mournful wailing of the sirens. As he lay there alone,
a strange and curious thought popped into his head. What if the
target of those inbound bombers were this prison? What if someone back home had finally come to the conclusion that the only
way to end this whole sordid mess was to level the prison itself
and kill them? In a twisted sort of way this idea began to make
sense to Kannen. After all, it was an accepted principle that if a
hostage could not be freed through a rescue attempt or negotiated means, the best way to end the crisis was to devalue the
hostage. And the best way to devalue them, Kannen figured as he
began to rouse himself and get up off the floor, was to kill them.
A corpse being dragged through the streets was only good for
one photo op and a single news cycle. After that, while the dead
hostage's family would always remember, the American media

would forget about what had happened in Syria and move on to the next big story, the next sensational event.

Having set this train of thought into motion Kannen found himself intrigued by the possibilities that it offered. All his suffering would be at an end. The gnawing pangs of hunger, the festering wounds that refused to heal, the constant threat of random beatings and the long hours that he had to endure alone in this cold, filthy cell would be over. Death would free him from all that and much, much more. He would no longer have to worry about the other members of RT Kilo, wondering how they were doing and when their turn to be killed off would come. He wouldn't have to endure bouts of depression during which he sobbed every time his thoughts turned to his sons, who would have to find their own way into manhood without him. Everything for him would be over. Everything would be at an end. Looking up at the ceiling of his cell as if he were trying to peer into the night sky above, Kannen began to whisper a prayer to his Lord and the pilots of the unseen aircraft that were flying around out there, waiting to deliver their payloads. "Dear God, give them the strength to do what they must do and the skill to make it sure and quick."

Kannen had become so lost in his dark thoughts that he failed at first to hear the sounds of excited voices and pounding feet in the corridor outside his cell. It was only when one of the guards stopped just outside the door of his cell and yelled down the length of the corridor at a companion that Kannen became aware of the commotion. Cocking the one good ear that he had left, he tried to determine what was going on. As he listened for the dreaded rattle of keys and the sliding of the bolt he began to notice another sound, one coming from outside the walls of the prison. Not even the layers of concrete could mask the familiar whine of jet engines that appeared to be growing louder and louder. For a moment this didn't make any sense. Air force tactics generally dictated that their strike aircraft maintain an altitude of ten thousand feet or higher in order to avoid triple A fire from the ground.

By now the American NCO was on his feet and trying to reconcile this disparity as the screech of jet engines became deafening. Instinctively, Kannen continued to look up. He was standing there in the middle of his cell peering at the ceiling when a thunderous clap and violent shudder bowled him over. As he lay flat on his back on the quivering floor choking as chips of loose concrete showered him and dust filled the room, Kannen smiled. "Thank You, Lord. Thank You."

Of all the decisions that had to be made by the people who approved Fanfare, the most difficult one involved the air attacks targeted against the prison. No one could be sure what the Syrians would do once it dawned on them that the air attacks were part of something more than simple retaliation. No one was willing to predict what the guards at the prison would do once it became clear to them that an effort to free their charges was in progress. In the wake of the execution of Sergeant Hashmi no one was willing to rule out the possibility that the guards had standing orders to shoot the surviving members of RT Kilo if that became necessary. So the question that this speculation raised was how exactly were the Syrian guards going to be kept from shooting the prisoners until DeWitt and Company A arrived?

Under the original plan of Fanfare the Deception, Delta was supposed to be dropped right onto the roof of the prison by helicopters belonging to Task Force 160. Since Fanfare *was* a deception plan, the practicality of this approach never had to be seriously weighed. Only after Fanfare became a real-world contingency plan, then an actual OP plan did Delmont and others of his ilk look seriously at this aspect of the operation. Both plans officers belonging to Delta and Task Force 160 responded with a crisp and unabashed "Bullshit! No way in hell!" when they were briefed on it.

It was in the aftermath of this universal rejection that the concept of bombing the prison was born. The idea sprang from an incident that had occurred in the first Persian Gulf War. Unbeknownst to the Coalition, the Syrians were keeping a number of POWs they had captured in Baghdad at the headquarters of the Baath Party. Since all the Iraqi national leaders were members of the Baath Party and hung their hats there, the building was a legitimate military target. Only luck kept the POWs confined there from being killed by their fellow aviators.

When it was decided to employ this high-risk strategy as part of Fanfare, the air force targeting officers and pilots who would actually make the attacks did their best to make sure that they had more than luck going for them this time. Using every intelligence source that could be tapped, a detailed layout of the prison had been created. Every known aspect of it was cranked into that layout. The areas where it was suspected that members of RT Kilo were being held were colored red and labeled No-Bomb Zone. When all parties involved were satisfied that they had done everything possible to ensure the safety of RT Kilo, they next turned their attention to those portions of the facility that would make the best targets. Areas that had been identified as barracks and mess areas were at the top of the list. Mechanical and administrative areas were next. Those that fell within those categories but were deemed to be too near the red zones were colored yellow. All others were filled in with green. It was these green spaces that the targeting officers concentrated on and it was into those areas that a steady rain of bombs would be directed.

Unlike the other air strikes being conducted in support of Fanfare, the bombing of the prison was scheduled to be a protracted assault. While no one was willing to bet the farm on it, everyone who had a part in the decision pretty much agreed that the most likely response of the Syrian prison guards would be to run to the safety of the nearest bomb shelter as soon as it became clear to them that they were ground zero. The plan called for the Air Force to maintain a steady drumbeat of bombs with an eye toward suppressing the Syrian guards or any reinforcements that might be dispatched to the prison. Only when Company A arrived would this bombing cease. To assist the Rangers in clearing a path to the cellblocks, the bomb shelters that the Syrian guards would be counting on for safety were slated for destruction through the use of special bombs designed to burrow deep into the ground before detonating. As the actual execution of the plan continued and the first wave of attack aircraft swooped in low and released their payloads, neither Kannen, who continued to lie on the floor of his cell waiting for the end nor the guards huddled in their shelters several floors below had any idea what was in store for them.

The length of time between exit and contact with the ground was but a minute, maybe not even that. But it was long enough to remind Robert Delmont just how much he hated this aspect of his chosen profession. In all his years as a Green Beret he had never found the courage to confide this sorry fact to anyone. "The only things that fall out of the sky," Delmont mumbled nervously as he closed his eyes and braced himself for the imminent impact, "are birdshit and fools." Since he was not the former, the Department of the Army special ops plans officer was left to conclude that he had to be the latter. The fact that he didn't have to be here doing this reinforced that supposition, one that was abruptly interrupted by his sudden return to terra firma.

Fortunately for the forty-plus staff officer, his responses were still keen and the patch of ground he landed on was not paved. With more grace than he gave himself credit for Delmont collapsed and rolled along the ground as if he were still at Fort Benning under the watchful eye of a black-hatted instructor belonging to the Airborne committee. Once he was stretched out on his back, he remained dead still long enough to do a quick inventory of his body parts in an effort to make sure that all were functional and undamaged. It took a spattering of small-arms fire and the eruption of grenades less than a hundred yards from him to reenergize the special plans officer.

Rolling over and rising up onto his knees Delmont gathered the suspension lines to one side of his parachute and began to haul them in in an effort to deform the canopy and keep it from reinflating while he was climbing out of the harness. He was in the middle of doing this, looking about and assessing his situation as he did, when it suddenly dawned upon him that perhaps being on this mission was not a good idea. This belated reflection was not brought on by fear. Rather, it was his realization that he had knowingly placed himself into a situation that exposed him to capture. After all, he was an officer on assignment to the plans section of the Army's General Staff, a duty that made him privy to all sorts of contingency plans and highly classified operations that were being carried out by Army personnel around the world. Razorback and RT Kilo's role in that operation were just two examples of the many things he had staff oversight for. As he finished shedding his parachute and drew his rifle out of its drop bag Delmont found himself shaking his head and mumbling "You jackass" under his breath.

A fresh outburst of gunfire jerked his full attention back to the here and now. Having sorted out his kit he dropped to one knee, and looked around, in an effort to get his bearings. Off to his right he could clearly see the hangars still lit up as if nothing were happening. To his left were the control tower and the admin building. That was where Shaddock had planned to set up his ops center once the area had been secured. Though he had exited the aircraft in the middle of a stick made up of men from Company C, Delmont had no way of knowing if the men running past him belonged to that unit. Once he was sure that it was safe to do so he stood up, swallowed his pride, and called out to a Ranger who was double-timing over to a clump of dark figures that had begun to gather. "Company C?"

Without breaking his stride the man shouted back. "This way. Follow me."

Delmont found himself chuckling as he fell in behind the

young Ranger and picked up the man's pace. "Follow me. Now where have I heard that before?"

The group he would soon find himself with all belonged to the Third Platoon of Company C. A young second lieutenant leading them counted heads as his people settled into a shallow depression in the sand that ran along one of the airfield's concrete aprons. When Delmont and the Ranger he was following were within a few meters of this rally point, the platoon leader called out to them. "Hayden, who's that with you?"

After acknowledging his lieutenant as he joined his comrades, the Ranger whom Delmont had been following looked over his shoulder at him. "Who the hell are you?"

"Lieutenant Colonel Delmont."

In unison Hayden and his platoon leader shot back *"Who?"*

"It doesn't matter, Lieutenant. Just get on with whatever you're supposed to be doing and ignore me. I'll stay out of your hair as best I can."

Delmont's words were heard by all, but did little to allay the young officer's concerns about having a high-ranking officer he didn't know suddenly show up at his rally point. Realizing what was amiss the platoon sergeant spoke up. "Sir, he's the DA colonel from the Pentagon who's been hanging out with Colonel Shaddock."

A simple "Oh, I see" was all the young officer managed before turning his full attention back to the tactical situation at hand and his platoon sergeant. "Sergeant Owens, we can't wait for the stragglers to wander in. You stay here with one man. I'm going to take the rest of those we have on hand here and move on the admin building. When you've gathered the rest of our people approach the objective from this direction if you can. We'll keep our eyes open for you."

The senior NCO nodded. "Roger that."

After taking a moment to gather his nerve and look around at the men who had managed to reach the rally point, the young platoon leader pointed to one of his squad leaders. "Okay, Sergeant Bellamey, you know what to do."

Without the slightest hesitation the squad leader who had just been tagged pushed himself up off the ground, wrapped his hands about his rifle, and took in a deep breath. "Second Squad, move out."

As one, the men who made up his squad rose, climbed out of the shallow ditch they had been gathered in and stepped out onto the concrete apron. In silence they took up positions on either side of their squad leader. When he saw that Second Squad was halfway to the admin building the platoon leader stood up. "All right, Third Platoon, let's go."

When a hasty check of the area failed to reveal any sign of Shaddock's command group, Delmont saw that he had little choice but to follow this platoon he had managed to link up with. Drawing in a deep breath, he got up and trotted onto the apron, picking up his pace in an effort to catch up with men who were far younger and considerably more agile.

It was only after they had left the ditch and were out in the open that the special ops staff officer bothered to assess his current situation. When he did he found that he didn't much care for it. The lead squad that the young platoon leader had dispatched was just about to enter the admin building they were headed for. The rest of the platoon, minus the platoon sergeant and one man who were still back in the ditch, was advancing in line with one squad on either side of their platoon leader. No one, Delmont realized, was providing them with a base of fire. The platoon sergeant, as near as he could figure, was busy rounding up strays. Not only was there no one in position ready to provide covering fire for the maneuver element, which in this case was pretty much the whole damned platoon but Delmont saw that none of the Rangers were paying much attention to what was going on to their left or right. Like their platoon leader they were all suffering from a serious case of target fixation. That, and a burning desire to get to where they were going. The farther they went the more it became painfully clear to Delmont that Shaddock's order to move quickly and be aggressive had been taken far too literally by this particular platoon.

Identifying a problem such as a faulty tactical deployment is one thing. Having the ability to do something to rectify it is an entirely different matter. In Delmont's case he was twice handicapped. First, he was not part of the platoon's normal chain of command. He didn't even belong to the battalion, a fact that made it doubtful that anyone would pay attention to his orders since in combat a superior ranking officer does not always carry the same horsepower he would under normal circumstances. And even if he did try to sort things out in midstride, the resulting confusion would only serve to prolong their exposure to enemy action. Thus Delmont opted to keep his mouth shut and go with the flow, hoping nothing would happen between here and there that would make him regret his decision.

In the Army the saying goes that hope is not an option. No sooner had Delmont concluded that it would be best if he said nothing than a trio of figures emerged out of the shadows off to his right. Instinctively the special ops plans officer turned his head and brought the muzzle of his rifle to bear upon them. A single glimpse of the floppy black berets worn by soldiers of the Syrian Army was all Delmont needed to see. Without a second thought he pulled up short and dropped to the classic kneeling position. With his right knee on the ground and his left elbow firmly planted on his left knee, Delmont took aim, brought his breathing under control, and flipped the selector switch of his rifle onto the three-round burst. When he had the lead Syrian in his sights and was ready, he let a volley fly.

This burst caught that unfortunate soul's center of mass. The first two rounds ripped into his abdomen, and the third penetrated his chest cavity sending him sprawling onto the hard concrete. With a slight twist of his torso and head Delmont brought his weapon to bear on the next mark. Again the special ops officer took aim and exhaled a bit before holding the rest of that breath and squeezing the trigger.

The rounds struck slightly higher this time, with one boring into the Syrian's right lung, the second entering and exiting his neck and the third missing completely. Like the effect on his companion, the impact of the rounds and his own forward momentum were sufficient to send him careening out of control and onto the ground.

Having been afforded sufficient time to figure out that he was in trouble, the third Syrian soldier managed to stop, turn around, and take off at a dead run in the same direction from which he and his two dead companions had come. Determined to keep him from reaching safety Delmont began to draw a bead on him but found that he was not quick enough to finish the job. From somewhere off to his left a volley of machine-gun and rifle fire directed at the Syrian erupted. Peppered by this hail of small-arms fire, the Syrian staggered and spun around before flopping onto the ground.

When he was sure that they were in no immediate danger Delmont stood up and trotted over to where a cluster of Rangers maintained their readiness to engage any new threats. When Delmont was close enough the platoon leader called out to him. "I hope you don't mind sir, but we thought we might join in on the fun."

Still keyed up by what he considered to be a narrow escape, it took every bit of self-control that Delmont could muster to keep from lashing out at the younger officer. But control himself he did. He even managed to respond in a tone that was almost civil. "Nice save, Lieutenant. Now, let's say we get this gaggle over to where we have some cover."

Unable to see the colonel's expression in the dark and unsure how to take the comments directed at him, the lieutenant turned to his men. "Okay, Third Herd, let's move out with a purpose.

Squad leaders," he quickly added, "watch your left and right as we go."

The bulk of the Third Platoon reached the admin building without further incident. Upon entering, Delmont noticed a Ranger who had been with the advance party carefully stepping over half a dozen lifeless bodies scattered about on the floor, poking each one with the muzzle of his rifle as he did so. Both the Ranger and Delmont froze in place and looked up as a burst of rifle fire followed by the pounding of feet reverberated through the ceiling. When the young Ranger who had been checking the dead Syrians was sure that this latest outburst was of no immediate concern he looked over at Delmont, then to his platoon leader. "Sir, I am proud to report Allah has six new martyrs."

Fixated on pressing forward, the young lieutenant had not taken notice of the bloody heaps that lay scattered about the open room. When he did look down at the first men killed in battle he had ever seen up close and personal, the effect upon him was quick and obvious. In an instant the color left his cheeks as his eyes grew large and round.

Sensing what was going on Delmont stepped over a body and drew himself up in front of the platoon leader. "I'll stay here and wait for your battalion commander. You'd best get upstairs and make sure the rest of the building is secure."

With the Pentagon staff officer standing before him the young officer turned his eyes away from the dead Syrian on the floor and lifted his face to Delmont. "Yes, of course."

Like his words, the platoon leader's actions were hesitant and faltering. But he managed to pull himself together and carry on.

The departure of the Third Platoon left Delmont and the Ranger who had been checking the dead Syrians alone in the main room of the admin building. Other than an occasional smattering of small-arms fire from outside and a steady tramping of boots on the floor above, the room was silent. With nothing to do until the battalion staff arrived, Delmont watched as the Ranger returned to his grim task of inspecting the dead. That all of the Syrians on the floor were stone-cold dead suddenly struck the staff officer. He had always imagined that even in the most vicious firefight a number of those who fell would be wounded. Close combat however has its own rules. It pits men who are animated and inflamed by the prospect of imminent danger and death eye to eye. Under such circumstances mercy and the granting of quarters is trumped by the drive to kill or be killed. It was only after the danger had passed that people like Delmont who had not been part of that killing frenzy can look upon such a scene with a clearer, more objective eye and think of compassion.

In the middle of this interlude a phone on the reception desk began to ring. Startled, the Ranger spun around bringing his weapon to bear as he gazed at the phone for a second, then over at Delmont. "Sir, you think should we answer that?"

Delmont made a face. "Hell, no! The fastest way to let someone in Damascus know that they're being invaded is for one of us to pick that thing up and respond with a nice cheery 'Hello' in the King's English."

Dropping his eyes, the Ranger sheepishly muttered, "I see your point," before turning his attention back to the grisly task of poking the bodies scattered about with the toe of his boot.

Having no desire to watch this any longer Delmont walked behind the reception counter and began to poke around in the documents left lying on desks and the counter as well as those stacked in the bookshelf behind the desk. Though he didn't speak or read a lick of Arabic, he thought he might find something of interest for the intel folks back home.

Like an Old-West town sheriff bursting into a saloon after a gunfight, Harry Shaddock stormed into the admin building with his staff on his heels. When he saw Robert Delmont poking through a bookcase as if he were whiling away a few spare minutes by browsing through a local library, Shaddock stopped in the middle of the room as members of his staff and battalion comms section streamed past him. Satisfied that all was in order and with nothing to do until his staff had set up his command post, Shaddock placed his hands on his hips and looked over at Delmont. "Where the hell have you been? You were supposed to rally with the headquarters section out there before heading in here."

Knowing that the Ranger battalion commander was not the least bit angry with him, Delmont shrugged. "Sorry. I guess I didn't read that part of the OPLAN."

Shaddock grinned. "A likely story."

Judging from his expression and the manner in which he was conducting himself, Delmont figured that all was going well in securing the airfield. Of course this was just the preliminaries, something both colonels knew. But it was a good start. Delmont found himself thinking as he stepped aside in order to give the people from the operations, intelligence, and comms sections room to set up, now it's time for the main event.

True to his word, the loadmaster aboard DeWitt's transport leaped out of his seat as soon as the first wheel of their C-17 thumped down on the runway. Without waiting for the aircraft to come to a complete stop he began to hack away at the last of the nylon tie-downs that secured the Hummers to the floorboards. They had practiced all of this so many times before that it was no big deal doing so in the dark interior of the transport, with all the engines of the Hummers revved up and the adrenaline glands of every person in the cargo hold madly pumping away. The only difference now was that there were no neutral observers standing around, watching every move and making notes. That, and the fact that the opposing force Company A was about to take on had real bullets.

Such trivial nuances were the furthest thing from Emmett DeWitt's mind. Seated in the lead Hummer he was leaning so far forward that the seat belt strapped about his waist seemed to be the only thing keeping him from springing up and out of his vehicle. Like every man in his command who could do so, DeWitt was staring at the partially open rear ramp of the transport waiting until it dropped away completely to reveal what lay beyond. They did not have long to wait.

With a lurch the pilot brought the massive transport to a complete halt. When the loadmaster felt this, he finished dropping the ramp. Having gauged the time that this would take during repeated rehearsals back at Fort Irwin, DeWitt had no need to wait for a signal to go. Thrusting his clenched fist forward, the young company commander let out a shout that had become something of a motto for Company A. *"Let's roll, Alpha!"*

Forward they rolled, squirting out of the C-17 as fast as they dared. In quick succession each Hummer charged down the ramp and onto the concrete runway. In an instant everything was familiar and everything strange. All of the structures DeWitt laid eyes upon were familiar, every major landmark where it was supposed to be. But now it was all so real, all so correct and clean and solid. There was none of the rickety ad hoc appearance of the mock buildings that they had trained on in California. Everything that DeWitt's eyes took in as his humvee sped across the open runway was so real that it bordered on being almost surreal.

But real it was, as real as the wind whipping across his face as his driver raced for the front gate of the airfield. With a quick shake of his head DeWitt cleared his thoughts and slipped back into his company commander mode. His Hummer had neither top nor full doors, giving him an unobstructed 360-degree view. Unhooking his seat belt DeWitt grasped the frame of the windshield, pulled himself up, and looked behind him. Through the night-vision device that was part of his Land Warrior system he could see the line of Hummers flowing from the pair of transports in a fast-moving and unbroken chain. So far so good.

Easing back into his seat, DeWitt keyed his radio transmitter. "Black Six, this is Red Six. Red is on the ground and rolling. Do we have a go, over?"

·   ·   ·

In lieu of full radio call signs it had been decided to use abbreviated call signs that would be easy to recall during fast-moving operations, thus expediting rapid and clear communications. Battalion used the pro-word *Black* followed by a number such as six, which has become over the years the universal numeric designation for a commander. The companies used the colors, red for Alpha, white for Bravo, blue for Charlie, and green for Delta.

In the admin building where the battalion operations section of the 3rd of the 75th had set up Shaddock's command post an assistant operations officer heard DeWitt's call. Snatching up the radio hand mike, he called out to Shaddock. "Sir, Red Six is on the move and asking for permission to proceed."

In an instant all conversations came to an end. Making every effort to maintain an aura of calm, Shaddock reached out and took the proffered hand mike. Clearing his throat he keyed the radio. "Red Six, this is Black Six. Wait, over."

Lowering the hand mike, he looked at his operations officer. "Well?"

The battalion S-3 nodded. "All companies have secured their assigned objectives. The road to Damascus is clear."

While taking in a deep breath, Shaddock glanced at Delmont. "Well, here we go." Lifting the hand mike to his mouth, the battalion again keyed it. "Red Six, this is Black Six. You are a go, over. I say again, you are go."

From somewhere out on the runway, just outside the open doors of the admin building DeWitt came back with a quick, crisp "Roger that. Red Six out."

With nothing left for him to do at the moment, Shaddock gave the hand mike back to the assistant ops officer, turned, and walked out of the bustling ops center. After looking around and sensing that he was simply getting in the way, Robert Delmont followed. By the time Delmont caught up with the commanding officer of the 3rd of the 75th, DeWitt's company was roaring by. When Delmont fell in on Shaddock's left, Shaddock glanced at him, then back at the Hummers. "Is this going to work?"

The question came as no surprise to the special ops plans officer who had given birth to and nurtured Fanfare. Having asked himself the same question over and over again, Delmont now found that he was unable to respond with the same forcefulness that he had been able to use so many times before when senior officers back in Washington had asked the same thing. Like DeWitt and the platoon leader he had accompanied to the admin building, Delmont found the experience of coming face-to-face with the reality unfolding all around him almost overwhelming. Almost, but not quite.

Syria
04:15 LOCAL, 20:15 EASTERN, 00:15 ZULU

There is only so much that training can do to prepare a soldier for the experience of combat. This truism quickly became apparent to Second Lieutenant Peter Quinn as he led his Third Platoon down the road from the military airfield and into the heart of the Syrian capital. The transition from open desert to city was startling. As his Hummer charged down the broad and deserted boulevards Quinn found he was unable to keep himself from glancing left and right, catching glimpses of the same sort of urban landmarks and features that were at once familiar to him and yet strange. Unremarkable was the sight of shops and restaurants lining the streets Quinn's platoon traversed. Like any city just before dawn, automobiles sat idle at the curbside, patiently awaiting their owners, who lived in the apartments that towered above them.

Yet there were more than enough cues to remind the young platoon leader that he was going into battle. Over the roar of his Hummer's engine Quinn could discern the wail of air-raid sirens that continued to blare a warning to people who had long ago fled to shelters and basements. The weight of his high-tech battle gear and the weapon lying across his lap served to keep him focused on his duties. Still, he found it all but impossible to shut out the guilty childlike exhilaration he was experiencing at being in a military vehicle bristling with guns as it flew along in total darkness at breakneck speed. The muted reports being rendered over the radio by the other platoon leaders calling in the checkpoints along their route as they crossed them added to the excitement. All of this brought the young officer to a state of heightened awareness unlike anything he had ever experienced before. It was an intoxicating feeling, an all-consuming sensation that bordered on being erotic.

If it were to succeed, the assault on the prison had to be swift and decisive. The walled complex of buildings that occupied a city block and included the prison where RT Kilo was being held would be hit from two directions in quick succession. The first in would be DeWitt's First Platoon. Their task was simple and straightforward. They were killers, men tasked with seeking out, engaging, and eliminating those Syrian soldiers who had managed to stay alive up to that point. In executing this duty the members of the First Platoon had been instructed to be bold, ruthless and conspicuous. By going in first the First Platoon would offer itself up as a matador's red cape. Though the cape is flashy and inflaming, it is the sword that is held back until the right moment that presents the real threat to the bull.

In executing their duties the First Platoon was ordered to do everything it could to restrict its activities to that portion of the prison complex where the garrison was billeted in and to reduce the chance of friendly-fire incidents. Of course there was always the possibility that the Syrians would not cooperate with the American plan. Just in case a Syrian officer did manage to correctly assess the situation and attempt to keep First Platoon in check while turning on the rest of Company A, the First Platoon had the freedom to push on beyond the garrison area in an effort to keep pressure on the enemy and off the rest of the company. If this became necessary the First Platoon would be greatly assisted in sorting out Syrians and fellow Rangers by employing the identify-friend-and-foe feature of their individual Land Warriors. Since the prisoners would be locked away in cells anyone who was up and running about had to be either a member of Company A or a Syrian. When confronted with a target in the open, if the IFF didn't squawk out the code for friend, the Rangers of the First Platoon would be free to fire. In another day and age the rules of engagement might have required both visual as well as some other sort of confirmation like a password and countersign. But the young men belonging to the First Platoon were comfortable with their electronic gadgets and computers. They had no reservations whatsoever about betting their lives and that of their fellow Rangers on the highly sophisticated system designed to enhance and magnify their abilities to carry out their grim and bloody undertaking.

While the First Platoon was in the process of hunting down their hapless prey, Quinn's Third Platoon would hit the prison from a point directly opposite of where the First Platoon was busily slaying the garrison and raising hell. The task assigned to the Third Platoon was decidedly less dramatic, but no less important. Supported by a section of combat engineers it had to first breach the outer wall that ran along a side street not much bigger than an alley. Once it had secured this point of entry as well as both ends of the street, the bulk of the platoon would press on into the prison building itself. Upon reaching that structure rather than storming the main entrance, the combat engineers would once more execute a tactical breach through the wall of the cellblock where RT Kilo was believed to be. That was as far as the Third Platoon would go, since by now it would be spread rather thin.

At that point the Second Platoon came into play. They were the chosen few, the select handful of men who would make or break Fanfare. The efforts and labors of thousands of American servicemen and women scattered around the world as well as the other platoons of Company A had one purpose and one purpose only: to support the thirty Rangers of Second Platoon. For the next fifteen minutes success or failure hung in the balance as those men swept into the cellblock and secured the surviving members of RT Kilo.

To carry out their assignment, DeWitt had divided each of Second Platoon's squads into two teams. Led by an NCO each of these teams carried all the wherewithal needed to overcome any barriers that barred their way or take out any opposition they met. Once in the cellblock area of the prison the teams would move from cell to cell, conducting a methodical search until they had secured all of the American prisoners. When a four-man team did come across a member of RT Kilo, it would hustle him out through the pair of tactical breaches defended by the Third Platoon and back into the alley where the Hummers of both Second and Third Platoons were parked. Only when all personnel from both platoons and all members of RT Kilo were accounted for or all possibilities had been exhausted would Company A break contact, withdraw, and charge back to the airfield.

Throughout this entire operation, First Lieutenant Emmett DeWitt would be with the Third Platoon's squad assigned the task of securing the cellblock breach. With him was a radioman and Lieutenant Colonel Kaplan. DeWitt's executive officer was with the First Platoon. For DeWitt this part of the operation would be the most difficult, for he was right there, literally standing in the open door where he would be able to watch the men of his Second Platoon going about their tasks. Yet there was nothing for him to do during this portion of the raid. Everyone knew what was expected of him. Each and every officer, NCO, and enlisted man had rehearsed their part over and over again until they knew it by heart and could execute the entire operation without saying a word. In theory, if all went the way it was supposed to, DeWitt could go through this entire operation uttering nothing more than an occasional "Roger" as his subordinates rendered updates on their status and progress. Of course, if there is one thing that history does teach, it is that theory is little more than an academic exercise. War is not. It is instead an affair of chance.

. . .

Just before the transport carrying the Hummer driven by PFC Bryan Ulysses Pulaski, and the rest of Quinn's First Squad, had touched down, Pulaski's squad leader had repeated DeWitt's orders. "We do everything just as we did during the last rehearsal. Don't change a damned thing." Unfortunately Staff Sergeant Henry Jones had forgotten to remind Pulaski not to slam on the brakes when he brought the Hummer to a stop, a habit he had developed at Irwin. So it should have come as no surprise to anyone that Pulaski, pumped up by the excitement of the moment, instinctively stomped down on the brakes as soon as he rounded the corner and entered the back street that ran alongside the outer prison wall. Only the fact that they were going into combat kept Jones from slapping his driver up the side of his helmet as he repeatedly did at Irwin whenever Pulaski's precipitous braking launched Jones headlong into the Hummer's windshield.

The other members of the squad who shared this vehicle weren't as forgiving. Using the butt of his rifle, PFC Johnny Washington thumped Pulaski from behind. "Asshole! You do that on purpose. I know you do that on purpose."

"Hey, Johnny! You're broadcasting over the squad net." The warning from Specialist Four George Bannon, the squad's SAW gunner did nothing to mitigate Washington's anger.

"I don't care if I'm going out over Armed Forces Network. The man's a menace."

Already on the ground and ready to go forward, Jones looked back and caught sight of the lieutenant colonel who had been foisted upon him at the last moment. Like the others who had been sandwiched into the rear of the Hummer, Neil Kaplan was doing his best to regain his balance and sort himself out while simultaneously trying to climb over the side. "Come on, people," Jones said in a low voice. "We've got a wall to breach."

He had no sooner made this statement than he felt the presence of someone next to him. "What's holding you up, Jones?"

Turning to Quinn, Jones did his best to cover the hapless deployment of his men. "We're on it, sir."

Quinn was in no mood to brook any delay. "The hell you are. The engineers are already at the wall. Now get your people over there and give them cover."

Spinning about, Jones echoed his platoon leader's command. Grabbing a handful of uniform belonging to the first man he could reach Jones tugged and shouted. "You heard him, people. *Move! Move! Move!*"

The last of Jones's squad was sliding into position to cover the engineers working at the wall when DeWitt arrived. Pausing next to Quinn and on the opposite side from where Kaplan stood, DeWitt said nothing. Instead he nervously glanced down at his watch. Though it was not meant to, this action did nothing to quell the uneasiness that Quinn felt building up within. For a moment he debated if it would not be better to move closer to the wall and join his First Squad if for no other reason than to escape the proximity of his superior. Then, as quickly as that thought had entered his mind he dismissed it. He had never done that during their rehearsals. Like DeWitt, he had held back in the lee of the Hummers until the first breach had been executed. Going forward now would only add to the confusion and pass onto his men the same sort of disquieting effect DeWitt was having on him. So he did his best to contain his mounting anxiety and put up a brave front.

The command barked by the senior engineer NCO, "Clear the site," brought an immediate response. Jones's men scattered. DeWitt, Kaplan, and Quinn crouched low behind the Hummer. And the engineers, save for their squad leader, sought cover. Even before the last of the engineers had settled in, their senior NCO bellowed, "Fire in the hole!" as he gave the friction fuse a quick jerk before scrambling to his feet and dashing off.

The detonation, while somewhat less than spectacular, was

more than effective. The roar of the blast was still echoing off the buildings and walls lining the street when Jones was up and charging headlong into the cloud of smoke and dust. "First Squad, go."

After having run this drill countless times this bit of bravado was technically unnecessary. Everyone in his squad was already on his feet and headed toward the breach by the time Jones had shouted. His men knew the order that they would assume as they passed through the freshly excavated hole in the wall. Bannon didn't need to be told that as soon as he was through it he was to rush forward fifteen yards, flop down, and take up a good firing position, ready to engage anything that moved. Pulaski would be next, as he always was moving over to the left of Bannon once through the breach. The lead-footed driver would be followed by Jones, who would shoot off to the right of the vigilant SAW gunner. Without a word, each and every member of Quinn's First Squad went through the still-smoldering hole and squirted out the other side to a predetermined position from which he would be able to cover the advance to the cellblock. Still, Jones had felt the need to sing out his order, just as he always did, for these were men, his men. In combat as in training soldiers need to hear familiar voices, whether they be giving orders, shouting warnings, or sounding off with words of encouragement. The familiar sounds tended to steel their resolve and remind them that they were not alone.

Within seconds the entire First Squad was set and all was clear, a fact Jones broadcast over the platoon net. Upon hearing this the combat engineers scrambled through the first hole they had created and rushed forward toward the cellblock where they would repeat this feat.

Both Quinn and DeWitt waited until the last of the engineers had cleared the breach at the outer wall before moving up to it. Standing on either side of the breach, the two officers peered into the open courtyard. Through the lingering smoke and dust they could see Jones's men scattered on the ground. Each man had taken up a prone firing position from which he could cover his assigned sector. Without pausing engineers rushed through this thin skirmish line, crouching low as they made their way to the point at the prison wall that they were to penetrate.

Stacked up behind both DeWitt and Quinn and crouching against the outer wall were members of Quinn's Second Squad. As soon as the prison building had been breached they would do as Jones's men had, rushing through the second breach forming a tight horseshoe perimeter once they were inside the cellblock itself. Only when they were set and all resistance within the cellblock had been quelled would DeWitt's Second Platoon, followed by DeWitt himself, go forth and commence their search for the members of RT Kilo. Quinn, with one squad in the alley watching the Hummers, one squad in the open courtyard keeping the escape corridor open, and a third inside the prison covering the search-and-rescue effort, would remain at the first breach site. From there he would be able to directly oversee the activities and control two of his squads. He would also provide DeWitt with a point of contact who could move the Hummers if the need arose. Though no one stated as much, this made Quinn little more than a highly paid horse holder and an officer with nothing to do but watch and wait.

Since he had not participated in any of the rehearsals and no one had taken the time to sit down and discuss his role in any detail with DeWitt, Neil Kaplan was pretty much left on his own when it came to determining where he should place himself during the assault, and the search and rescue. Instinctively he wanted to rush forward in the wake of DeWitt and get right up there where the real action was. As a professional officer, however, he managed to restrain this urge and hold back. Rather than getting in the way he remained behind with Quinn. From there he would be able to concentrate on monitoring the operation using the Land Warrior system he wore and had programmed especially for this. With practiced ease he scrolled through his special menus, calling up data on the status and location of each platoon in turn and then the company as a whole. To his satisfaction he found he was able to read the entire situation down to the individual soldier from where he sat balled up with his back against the outer wall. The system was working. And so too, to his satisfaction and relief, was the operation.

After a pause of a couple of minutes, the ear-shattering explosions and thunder of low-flying jet engines were replaced by the rattle of small-arms fire, the rumble of nearby explosions, and the hurried thump of boots running. Sergeant First Class Kannen, having resigned himself to the fact that the Air Force wasn't going to deliver him from this hell on earth with a quick and merciful death, suddenly found himself becoming irritated. Not only had the flyboys screwed up by not bringing this entire affair to a quick and merciful end, they had pissed off the Syrians.

Even as he went about picking himself up off the floor and turning to face the door, Kannen could hear the excited voices of guards outside in the corridor shouting back and forth to each other as they made their way past his cell. He was in for a painful round of beatings for sure, he told himself. They weren't the sort to just walk in and shoot him out of hand. No, they were simply too cruel and too callous to be quick. They would make him and whoever else from RT Kilo had survived thus far suffer for the visit the Air Force had paid them before killing them. Having resigned himself to this fate Kannen drew himself up in the center of the room faced the door, and waited. As he did so, he cleared his mind and began to make his peace with God.

He was in the midst of preparing for his final ordeal when Kannen's trained ear alerted him to inconsistencies. The first was the sound of two low-grade explosions. Instead of the shattering roar that a bomb makes, these rumbling detonations reminded the Special Forces NCO of demo charges. And the smattering of small-arms fire didn't sound right at all, either. Some of it was quite near while most seemed decidedly far off and distant, as if it were coming from other parts of the prison complex. Only after he abandoned his communion with God was Kannen able to note the difference in pitch that some of the small arms gave off. Though his surroundings distorted the sound, once he turned his full attention to the matter it became clear to him that most of the firing was not being done by AKs like those carried by the Syrian guards. Rather, the distinctive pop-pop-pop he managed to discern was that of 5.56-mm rounds being fired, ammunition common to M-16s and M-4s, American-made weapons.

Like a thunderclap it finally dawned on him what was happening. They were coming. They were finally coming for them. After all this time, after all his prayers, after all his suffering, his fellow soldiers were here to save him.

Yet as the din of battle drew nearer Kannen found that this revelation brought him no joy, no relief. Rather, he was all but paralyzed by a sudden rush of contradictory feelings and thoughts. The first response that gripped him was fear. After having survived for so long and endured so many horrors the idea that he could still be killed by his captors to keep him from being saved or even his saviors during a wild firefight in the dark took hold. Shaking his head, Kannen struggled to regain his composure even as tears began to well up in his eyes, and he found himself muttering out loud, "No. Not now."

He was still struggling to maintain his composure and brace himself for whatever came next when he heard a chorus of screams just outside his cell door. *"NO SHOOT! NO SHOOT!"*

In response to these pleas screeched by the panicked Syrians in the outside hallway, Kannen heard an American bellow out, "On your knees, motherfuckers. On your knees, and hands behind your head!"

After a moment of shuffling and scuffling in the hallway, Kannen could hear an American who had moved closer to his cell order a Syrian to start opening the cell doors. Still standing in the middle of the floor, Kannen's troubled mind now turned to what he should do. His first thought was to rush to the door and start pounding on it while shouting, *"I'm in here! I'm in here!"* But after giving it a second thought he dismissed this as being unwise since the Americans out in the corridor were keyed up and working on a hair trigger. Any sudden and unexpected noise could unleash a hail of gunfire directed at the source. So Kannen decided the best thing he could do was to stand there and wait. After having endured so much he figured he could hang on a few more seconds.

Then came the sound of something pounding on the door. A rifle butt, Kannen guessed. "*Hey!* Anyone in there?"

This was a new voice, not the same one that had spewed the profane string of orders to the hapless Syrian guards who had been in the corridor. It took Kannen a moment to clear his throat and respond. When he did, the calmness and correctness of his reply surprised him. "Sergeant First Class Allen Kannen, U.S. Army."

After a brief moment of silence, Kannen heard a chatter of voices. "All right!" and "Hey, we found one," were all he could distinguish, as the American on the other side of the door shouted to someone else and then back to Kannen. "Hang on, good buddy. We'll have you out of here in a sec."

True to his word, it took but a moment. After a brief pause, a rattle of keys, and the familiar sound of the steel bolt being snapped back the door swung open to reveal a pair of heavily armed Rangers decked out in full battle gear standing to either side of the doorway peering in through the opening. Still finding it hard to believe that his deliverance was at hand, Kannen moved slowly through the open door taking time to glance to the left and right into the faces of his saviors as he passed them. Once out of his cell, Kannen found he had to step aside in order to avoid the cluster of Syrians who had been corralled in the hallway by the Rangers. One of the Americans whom Kannen assumed to be the senior member of the group standing before him ordered his men to hustle the Syrians into the cell. "Get 'em in there and slam the door."

Like a disinterested observer, Kannen watched as the Rangers kicked and shoved the frightened guards into his now-vacated cell. When the senior Ranger noticed the expression on Kannen's face, he called to him. "We can't take the bastards back with us, so we're going to lock 'em up."

It was at that moment that the injustice of this struck Kannen. From the depths of his soul, a voice called out, "This cannot be allowed to stand."

Even as the last of the Syrians was booted into the waiting cell Kannen inspected the Rangers who stood around him. When he saw what he was looking for he walked over to him, reached up, and removed a hand grenade from the strap that secured it to the Ranger's flak vest. In silence the Rangers watched as Kannen walked to the still-open door. As he stood there the Special Forces NCO pulled the pin, let the arming spoon fly, and tossed the grenade into the room that had imprisoned him for so long.

Without having to be told, the Ranger holding the door open slammed it shut and jerked the bolt closed.

After what seemed like an eternity, the first of the search teams from Second Platoon reappeared at the outer breach with a newly liberated American in tow. No one said a word as the four Rangers and their charge made their way through the hole, into the street and over to one of the waiting Hummers.

From his post at the breach Quinn watched the entire process impassively. Somehow he imagined that he would have felt some sort of joy or elation. Yet the emotions that he experienced at that moment of triumph were nothing of the sort. If anything, he had become so desensitized by rehearsals and repeated drills that the actual event was turning out to be anticlimactic. The first cognitive thought that came to mind as he watched the men of the Second Platoon scamper away was the trite old saying, "Is this all there is?"

The young platoon leader was reflecting upon this when Staff

Sergeant Jones called over the platoon net. "Here comes Number Two."

Leaning over, Quinn peered through the breach catching sight of the second search-and-rescue team as it emerged from the prison building and began to make its way to where he waited. From the other side of the hole, Kaplan called out. "Two down, three to go."

Quinn looked up at him but said nothing. He found himself quite embarrassed by the growing sense of disappointment that he was experiencing. The event that had come to dominate his every waking hour for so long was about to come to an end without his having to do anything but drive through Damascus, stand next to a hole in the wall, and then drive back. Instead of being the shining moment of his short military career, this entire raid was turning out to be something of a disappointment. As unprofessional as this thought was, and as much as he wanted to dissociate himself from this sort of thinking, Quinn knew in his heart and soul that it was true. Success was depriving him of the sort of excitement that he had come to expect from close combat, something that he suddenly found himself craving.

The young platoon leader was struggling with this moral dilemma when an order blared over the company net that caught Quinn by surprise. "Red thirty-six, this is Red Six. Report to my location immediately with our technical advisor, over."

Confused, Quinn shook his head, and mumbled to his radioman, "Technical advisor?"

The radioman, Specialist Four Robert Hoyt, who had nothing to do at the moment thanks to the Land Warrior's integrated radio network, returned Quinn's blank stare and shrugged.

From the other side of the breach Kaplan reached across and lightly touched Quinn's sleeve. "Lieutenant, I think he means me."

Glancing up at the lieutenant colonel, Quinn blinked. "Oh, yeah. I guess so."

Positive that he was correct and not wishing to waste any time waiting for the young officer to sort all this out, Kaplan ducked through the hole in the wall and took off, shouting as he went, "Let's go, Lieutenant."

Knowing an order when he heard it, Quinn followed suit, as did his radioman.

Not having been privy to the company net, the sound and reverberation of pounding boots approaching his position from behind caught Staff Sergeant Jones off guard. Rising onto his elbows and turning, he caught sight of the trio rushing up to where he was. "What the—"

Jones's movement caused Washington and Bannon to follow suit. By the time they had managed to twist their heads about, Kaplan had reached their skirmish line and was passing through it. In quick succession Quinn, with Hoyt on his heels, made their way through the prone figures of Jones's squad. By now everyone was watching the trio as they disappeared through the second tactical breach. Only after the trio were in the prison building did Washington put to words the thought that had crossed all of their minds. "Shit. Something's gone wrong."

Though he suspected that this was the case since nothing in the plan called for Quinn to move forward like this, Jones said nothing. Until he received further orders, the mission of his squad remained the same. "Okay, folks, heads up. Open your ears and eyes, watch your sectors, and stand by for a change in mission."

DeWitt wasted no time with any longwinded explanations. "Two of the Green Berets are unaccounted for. Second Platoon has completed its sweep of all the cells in this part of the building and has been unable to find them."

This statement came as no surprise to either Kaplan or Quinn. At each and every step of planning and preparation for Fanfare this sort of situation had been addressed and debated. Some, recalling the aborted attempt to liberate POWs during the Vietnam War, referred to this as the Son Tay scenario. After considering all possibilities, it had been decided that in the event some or all of the members of RT Kilo could not be found in those places where intelligence stated they were supposed to be, the operation would be terminated and the 3rd of the 75th would immediate withdraw. Everyone knew this. No one much liked to think about actually having to execute this contingency, but they all understood the practicality of it. The worst thing they could do, Shaddock had pointed out while covering the contingency during his briefings, was to run about willy-nilly, searching for people who might be long gone.

"The XO of the Special Forces team here," DeWitt continued, motioning toward a bedraggled figure squatting next to him, "told me that their CO was severely injured when they were captured. The XO thinks Burman is alive but that he may be in the prison's clinic."

Kaplan immediately understood the problem. The Son Tay scenario assumed an all-or-nothing situation. Either everyone was where they were supposed to be or they were not. This situation presented DeWitt and the 3rd of the 75th as a whole with a real predicament. They suspected they knew where at least one of the missing men was and they believed that he was close at hand. But to explore that possibility required a radical alteration of the plan, one that would extend their time on the ground and place a fair number of Rangers at risk.

"My first thought is to go after him," DeWitt declared, "but we've got other issues that we need to consider."

Kaplan looked at Quinn, then at the battered figure that he assumed was Aveno, who was listening but not really part of the circle.

"The First Platoon is running into some vicious resistance. The XO with them seems to think the Syrians are throwing everything they have at them."

For the first time Kaplan spoke. "That doesn't make any sense. The prisoners are here. This is where I would expect the Syrians to send reinforcements."

DeWitt grunted. "Yeah, I know. Those were my exact thoughts. That's why I'm thinking there's more going on than meets the eye. Either we're being set up for one hell of a trap or we've stumbled onto something bigger than anyone who planned this thing imagined."

Quinn chimed in. "Such as?"

"Negative knowledge, Lieutenant. All I know is that we have a hard decision to make and not much time to make it."

Without hesitation Kaplan volunteered his opinion. "We have to go after Burman. To come this close and fail now would be disastrous."

Again, Quinn spoke up. "Okay, that's one. But what about the second man who's missing? Is he with the team CO?"

For the first time since this debate began, Ken Aveno spoke. "I haven't seen Lieutenant Ciszak since the night we were captured. If he's not in the hospital ward where they're keeping Burman, he's either dead or he's been taken someplace else for special handling." Having no way of knowing for sure just how Aveno knew this, none of the Fanfare team questioned his statement.

"Okay," DeWitt blurted. "here's what I've decided. The First Platoon is decisively engaged. They can hold their own but won't be able to look for Burman and Ciszak. Second Platoon is already pretty much used up, given the need to escort and cover those Green Berets we already have. So, I'm going to change roles here. What's left of the Second Platoon will cover the two breaches. Lieutenant Quinn, your two squads that are posted at the breaches will become the search-and-rescue teams that will go after Burman and Ciszak. We'll use this spot here as our jump-off point. Once we've finished the search everyone will rally point here and we'll execute our egress as briefed. Quinn, I'll go with you and your two squads. Lieutenant Hatterman will stay here with his platoon and what's left of yours. Questions?"

Kaplan looked around, then at DeWitt. "Where do you want me?"

For the first time he detected a hesitation as DeWitt spoke. "If you don't mind, Colonel, I'd like you to come with me. It seems that I can't make heads or tails of some of these navigational programs and I don't have time to sort them out at the moment."

Under ordinary circumstances this sort of confession by a combat arms officer to him would have evoked a smile. But these were not ordinary circumstances. "I am at your disposal, Lieutenant. I'll inform battalion of the situation and your decision while you sort out your company."

DeWitt nodded. "I appreciate that." Then he turned to the assembled group. "Okay, people. We have a lot to do and not much time. Let's make it happen."

Syria
04:35 LOCAL, 20:35 EASTERN (00:35 ZULU)

The silence that gripped the airport admin building was ominous as DeWitt described the situation he faced and his plan for dealing with it. Listening to this from opposite sides of the room Shaddock and Delmont exchanged glances. As the commanding officer of the 3rd of the 75th, it was up to Shaddock to approve his subordinate's actions or order him to cease and desist. Yet even he could not deny that Delmont had the power to veto any decision Shaddock made that deviated from the approved plan of action. It wasn't something that either man had discussed. It was just an acceptance of the reality of their relative positions. Shaddock was a battalion commander, an important part of the chain of command, but one that was, in the scheme of things, pretty low on the ladder. Delmont, on the other hand not only rubbed shoulders with the Army's senior decision makers, he generated and wrote the plans they used in carrying out their Commander in Chief's directives. So it was no great stretch for anyone who thought it through to appreciate that when it came time for a decision to be made, Robert Delmont's opinion would weigh heavily.

Having finished rendering his report, DeWitt asked the assistant battalion ops officer, who had been serving as the radio telephone operator on the battalion command net, for a decision from the battalion commander. Looking over to his commanding officer, the captain who had been talking to DeWitt called out. "Sir? Your response?"

In the ensuing stillness the two lieutenant colonels stared at each other. Any effort by Shaddock to figure out what Delmont was thinking by reading his expression was defeated by the poker face that a staff officer in Delmont's position quickly developed. For his part, Delmont understood what Shaddock was asking without the need to have the question spelled out. Still, he held back if for no other reason than to preserve the illusion that Shaddock was the man who would make the ultimate decision.

Finally, Shaddock began by clearing his throat. "Well, Colonel?"

Delmont made a show of shrugging as if his opinion didn't matter. "Your lads came here to do a job. It would be a pity to come all this way and not finish it."

Shaddock nodded. "I agree." Then he looked at the assistant ops officer. "Tell Lieutenant DeWitt to get on with it." He wanted to add, "and be quick," but didn't feel that he had any need to. DeWitt and every member of Company A was already well aware that the clock was ticking.

In the distance the firefight between First Platoon and the Syrian garrison ebbed and flowed. Just when it seemed as if it were subsiding a sudden outburst would revive the din to its former intensity. With each step these renewed outbursts grew more distinct, as Quinn and his two squads made their way through the long dark corridors, up several flights of stairs, and closer to the deadly standoff. In response to the heightening of the tension that gripped them, each and every member of this ad hoc rescue group redoubled his vigilance as they tightened their grasp of their weapons.

Up front, just behind the two men who were on point, DeWitt and Kaplan hugged the wall as they made their way forward. In whispered tones Kaplan called out directions. "Right at the end of this corridor. There will be double doors on either end of the corridor we'll be moving into."

DeWitt slowed down. "Any idea what those doors are made of? Are they swinging doors?"

In response to this question, Kaplan accessed the detailed schematics of the section of the building they were in. These particulars, along with numerous other items of interest, had been provided to the Army by the CIA and the Israeli Mossad and uploaded into the memories of Kaplan's and DeWitt's computers. When he found what he was looking for he read off the information. "Steel doors with small windows. The ones we'll be moving toward open out and away from us. On the other side is the dispensary."

Instinctively, DeWitt replied, "Okay, good," even though he had no clear idea if the data he had been provided was a plus or a minus.

Clicking his fingers, DeWitt caught the attention of the two men on point. Specialist Four Rodriguez Sanchez placed a hand on his partner, PFC Anthony Park. Together the two men paused. As Park watched their front, Sanchez looked back at his commanding officer. Using a standard hand-and-arm signal, DeWitt indicated the new direction that he wanted the pair of riflemen to take. With a nod, Sanchez acknowledged the order before he passed it on to Park.

From behind DeWitt, Kaplan watched in silence. On one hand he felt a keen sense of disappointment that the officer in command wasn't using the Land Warrior as he should be. DeWitt could just as easily have contacted his men on point using the radio built into the system and then, if he really wanted to be fancy, zip the visual schematic of their planned route to the pair up front. Still, he was not surprised by the young officer's actions. This sort of thing was to be expected. The entire company simply had not had enough time to become comfortable with all the features of the system. Until they were afforded the opportunity to work with it on a daily basis, soldiers like these Rangers would never be able to maximize Land Warrior's full potential. That and the appreciation that old habits died hard mitigated his frustration. In a pinch, people tended to resort to the tried and true methods that had served them so well in the past. The situation DeWitt was currently facing was the textbook description of being in a pinch.

Up front Sanchez had other, more immediate concerns. After slowly making their way forward as far as they could without exposing themselves, the pair came to a halt. Leaning his right shoulder against the wall, Sanchez poked his rifle out into the intersecting corridors, pointing its muzzle and the thermal weapon sight mounted on it in the direction of the doors Kaplan had described. This was not as easy as it sounded. Being right-handed, Sanchez held the pistol grip of his weapon with that hand, and supported it by grabbing the hand guard with his left. This placed the weapon in a natural, streamlined posture that allowed him to bring it up into a good firing position in a flash. The act of using it and the Land Warrior sight as a probe, how-ever, was awkward at best. After extending his rifle and its high-tech sight out and away from his body, Sanchez had to cross his arms so that the left hand gripping the hand guard was now opposite his right shoulder and his right hand on the pistol grip was off to the left. Not having had the time to get used to the necessary hand-eye coordination needed to maximize the thermal sight's potential when used under these circumstances, it took Sanchez a few seconds to sort out which hand he needed to move in order to obtain a clear and steady image of what lay ahead. This juggling act, conducted with the sharp echo of battle reverberat-ing through the corridor and the pressure of getting on with their duties proved to be frustrating as hell to Sanchez. "Christ! This is worse than wrestling with a snake."

Park laid his hand on Sanchez's shoulder. "Slow down, my good man. You're doin' fine."

In his excitement, Sanchez was mashing down on his transmit button, which meant that every man in the First Squad as well as DeWitt and Kaplan heard his muttered complaints. Yet no one said a word.

"Okay, got it." Once he had achieved a balance of sorts and was able to observe the double doors just ahead, Sanchez took a moment to study them, focusing on their small windows. When he saw nothing that presented an immediate threat, Sanchez pulled his weapon back and prepared to take a peek around the corner. For as good as the thermal sight was, it did have its limitation. Thermal sights function by detecting subtle differences in the amount of heat an object throws off. Sensors in the thermal sight collect these variations in radiated heat. Through the use of gee-whiz electronic wizardry, an image based upon this collected data was created and displayed in the sight's eyepiece. The problem was that anything that blocked or mitigated radiated heat has the ability to defeat this system. Glass, such as that in the door, is one such material. So it came as no surprise that it wasn't until Sanchez poked his head around the corner, and used his good old standard-issue M-1A1 eyeballs that he saw beams of light fluttering on the other side of the double doors.

After watching for a few seconds he pulled back and reported. "There's activity on the other side of the doors. Looks like people shining flashlights all around."

Back down in the corridor, DeWitt took in the report before turning to Kaplan. Even though he didn't ask, he guessed what he was thinking. "It makes sense," he stated. "If that is the dispensary then that's where the wounded Syrians would be taken and treated. With power out all over the city, the medical staff would have to rely on flashlights."

DeWitt grunted. "Great, combatant, noncombatants, and unarmed wounded all mixed together."

"Lieutenant, as far as I am concerned there's only one person in that room we need to concern ourselves with. Everyone else is roadkill."

For the first time, DeWitt took a hard look at the officer whom he had tended to dismiss over the past weeks as little more than a run-of-the-mill support weenie. Even in the dark he could see that the expression on his face was as cold and unfeeling as his words had been. He was of course right. Collateral damage had been expected.

Seeing no need to make a direct response, he turned his attention back to the situation at hand. "Okay, Third Platoon, here we go. First Squad will move round the corner and into the next room. Mark your targets, take 'em out, and don't use grenades. Our boys are in there somewhere. The first man to find them is to sing out as soon as he does. Once we have both of them out of the dispensary we'll withdraw by two. Second Squad will hold at the intersection of the corridors and cover our rear while we're in there and during our withdrawal. Acknowledge, over."

Over the radio, Lieutenant Quinn came back with a question. "Red Six, this is One Six. Where do you want me?"

"Stay with your Second Squad, One Six. I'm going forward with the First Squad."

Upon hearing this, Quinn found he could not contain his anger. "Shit! Not again?"

Hoyt, crouching next to him, looked at his platoon leader. "Excuse me, sir?"

"Nothing," he mumbled "It's nothing."

Hoyt knew better than that. As he waited next to his platoon leader, the radioman could almost sense the frustration his platoon leader was feeling at being left behind again.

Up front, Sanchez and Park led off the advance as soon as DeWitt and the balance of the First Squad closed up on them. When they reached the double doors, Park, keeping as low as he could, reached up, grasped the door handle, and slowly gave it a twist to see if it was unlocked and could be opened. When he was satisfied that this would be no problem and had done the same with the other door, Sanchez looked back at DeWitt and gave his commanding officer a nod.

Glancing back over his shoulder, DeWitt looked at Staff Sergeant Jones, who was right behind him. "Okay, here we go." Then, facing front, DeWitt pointed at Sanchez.

Twisting his head, Sanchez stared at Park and whispered, "On the count of three, two, one . . ."

In unison the two Rangers threw open the double doors and lunged forward, bringing their weapons up to the ready as they did so. By the time they had accomplished this, Jones and PFC Johnny Washington had reached the open doorway and stormed into the dispensary side by side.

For a fraction of a second there was a stunned silence as every Syrian in the dimly lit dispensary stopped whatever they had been doing and turned to gaze in horror at the oncoming Rangers. Having been taken by surprise each of them suddenly found himself faced with a simple decision that had to be made without hesitation, without thinking. Their choices were simple: flight, fight, or surrender.

Most were not given a chance to act upon their choice. Brought to a fever pitch by the presence of danger and prospect of impending combat, Jones and his companions executed their commanding officer's last order to a T. With measured ease each man selected his target, brought his weapon to bear, and fired. In the twinkling of an eye pandemonium in the close confines of the dispensary area of the prison reigned supreme. Over the chatter of rifle fire, the screams and cries of panicked men mixed in with the shrill screeches of the wounded and dying. To this was added the shouts of excited men as they pushed and shoved their comrades aside in an effort to flee, or duck for cover from the charging Rangers. Some who had not been in the main area of the dispensary inexplicably rushed out of rooms where they had been safe and into the line of fire.

Added to these sights and sounds was a riot of peculiar smells. Some of these were smells one normally associated with battle, such as the pungent odor of gunpowder, the stench of loose bowels, and the sickly sweet smell of freshly shed blood. To these were added the scents familiar to any medical facility, such as alcohol, disinfectant, and medications. Through all of this riot of sight, sound, and smell Staff Sergeant Jones, Washington, Sanchez, and Park pressed forward like the Four Horsemen of the Apocalypse, slaying all before them and adding to the carnage with each step they took. This was war at close quarters, combat at its basest, purest form, up close, impersonal, cruel, vicious, and completely uncompromising.

In their wake came the rest of the First Squad led by DeWitt with Kaplan right behind him. In pairs this follow-on party ducked into each room they came across. When they were met by a threatening figure that stood in their way the members of these search parties dispatched the hapless Syrian with the same unflinching speed as that employed by Jones and his trio. Only the thoroughness of their search equaled the ruthlessness with which they dealt with those who stood in opposition on purpose or by happenstance.

It was the lead-footed Pulaski, moving through a room with George Bannon, who found what they had come for. "Hey, he's in here!"

This announcement caused everyone on the net to pause for a second. Jones ceased his advance, and yelled to his companions. "Hold back!" At this, the two men on the outside, Sanchez and Park, pressed themselves against the walls. Both Jones and Park simply dropped to one knee.

From the room where he was DeWitt called out over the radio. "Where are they?"

"Third room on the right."

In response, everyone who had been in other rooms emerged from them, moved through the main area of the dispensary, and converged on that third room. Kaplan was first in. Without ceremony he made his way through the pair of enlisted men who guarded the bed, and inspected the motionless figure before him. Unable to get a good view of Burman in the dark, he pulled his miniature flashlight out of its holder and flicked it on. He was conducting this head-to-toe inspection when DeWitt arrived. "Well?"

Kaplan shook his head. "No blood or open wounds. And he's breathing. But he's out cold."

Without hesitation, DeWitt turned to Pulaski and Bannon, who had stepped back from the bed to make way for the two officers. "Find a stretcher or something."

In unison, the pair looked at each other, then began gazing around the room. When he saw this DeWitt bellowed as loudly as he could, *"MOVE IT, NOW!"*

The two Rangers dance about and rushed to the door. In their haste, they collided when they both tried to squeeze through the door at the same time. Under ordinary circumstances this would have been amusing. At the moment, however, it evoked only rage, a rage that DeWitt could not vent since Pulaski and Bannon quickly sorted themselves out and disappeared before he had a chance to yell. Clenching his fists, DeWitt found the strength to hold his tongue in check as he turned back to inspect the motionless form of Captain Burman.

Kaplan, who had been taking a closer look at Burman, sighed. "I don't think there's much left here."

Caught off guard by this remark, DeWitt looked at him. "Excuse me?"

Moving the beam of his flashlight along Burman's body, he stopped when its beam fell on Burman's bruised and bandaged face. At the same time he reached over, lifted one of Burman's arms and let it flop. "Either he's on strong drugs, or he's more dead than alive."

While his comments were crude, DeWitt thought he understood. "Be that as it may, Colonel, I don't see that we have any choice but to take him with us."

Confused by this comment, he looked at the company commander. "I'm sorry, but what made you think otherwise?"

Embarrassed by this misinterpretation of his comments, DeWitt was scrambling to come up with an appropriate response when the two Rangers that had gone hunting for a stretcher returned. "We found one, sir," Pulaski called out. "The Syrian soldier on it didn't seem to mind us borrowing it."

If he was trying to be funny, his effort failed miserably. At once DeWitt and Kaplan threw back the sheets that covered Burman and hoisted him onto the waiting stretcher. This sudden burden caused Pulaski to grunt.

At first, Kaplan wondered if the pair would have trouble carrying the comatose captain as well as all the equipment they were fitted out with. He was about to suggest that they shed some of their gear when DeWitt headed for the door, calling out over the net as he went, "Okay, let's find that other guy,".

Even before he was out of the room Jones responded to DeWitt's order to continue the search for First Lieutenant Joseph Ciszak. "Six, we're at the end of the dispensary and there are no more rooms that haven't been gone through."

Confused, DeWitt stopped in midstep. "Are you saying no one has seen the other prisoner?"

One by one the members of Jones's squad came back with a negative. Stymied yet again, DeWitt turned to Kaplan. "Now what?"

Remembering what Aveno had said about the Air Force officer, Kaplan did not hesitate. "There's nothing more we can do. We've already been on the ground longer than we should have. To spend more time bumbling around looking for him would be to put everyone in jeopardy. We have to go."

Knowing that the colonel was right and having no desire to dally here any longer than they needed to, DeWitt put aside whatever reservations he had about terminating the search. "Okay, Red, we're headed back to the cellblock."

At the corner where DeWitt had kicked off his assault, Quinn watched his First Squad emerge from the dispensary. First out was the stretcher party carrying Burman, led by Kaplan. They came charging down the corridor, whipped around the corner, and continued without pausing. Next out was DeWitt with three members of First Squad on his heels. When DeWitt drew up even with Quinn he waved the others on and turned to the platoon leader. "Once everyone is out of there give your First Squad a few seconds' head start, then follow with the Second Squad. Maintain contact with the First Squad while covering our egress with the Second." Without waiting for Quinn to acknowledge, DeWitt turned away and rejoined the First Squad as Staff Sergeant Jones and the trio who had spearheaded the attack came sprinting up to the corner. Only Jones bothered to slow a bit to yell out to Quinn, "I'm it. No friendlies behind me." Like DeWitt, he took off, headed back to the cellblock, leaving his platoon leader to his own devices.

It was for moments like this that the old saying, "Be careful what you wish for," was coined. The First Squad was still in the process of making its way down the corridor, when Quinn caught sight of something flying through the double doors leading out of the dispensary. With a sharp crack it hit the floor and bounced once before it began to roll toward him. It took far too long for the young platoon leader to recognize the grenade headed his way for what it was. By the time he did, he had just enough time to throw himself on the floor, landing on his side.

Kaplan took the stairs leading back down to the cellblock two at a time only to find that he had to pause at each landing in order to wait for the heavily burdened stretcher party to catch up. During these brief intervals that seemed to last forever, his attention fluctuated between what lay ahead and how Pulaski and Washington were progressing. Holding himself at the ready, he would wait until the pair of struggling Rangers were but a step or two away before turning to dash off again.

Trailing along behind the stretcher party was the balance of the First Squad. Whereas Kaplan alternated between dashing forward at full tilt and periods of dead stop, Staff Sergeant Jones found he had no choice but to advance at the same laborious pace as Pulaski and Washington. Every so often he contemplated taking advantage of a gap that was created when his two men bearing the stretcher slowed down to maneuver their way around a corner. Only the chatter of small-arms fire coming from the corridor that they had just vacated and the spat of harried reports telling of enemy troops putting pressure on their rear guard kept him from doing so. If the situation demanded that the balance of his squad go back and help extract the Second Squad, Jones knew he needed to be in a position from which he could lead that effort.

At the tail end of this file was DeWitt, who was finding that he was even more conflicted than Jones as to where he should be. His mind was that of a professional soldier and an officer. He was trained to be analytical and conditioned to be callous to the harsh realities of war, which included the need to place the men he led in harm's way. Yet his heart called upon him to go back to where his Second Squad was engaging the enemy in desperate rear-guard action and join them. He was torn between marching to the sound of the guns or staying where he could best oversee the evacuation of the prisoners his company had been sent to rescue. Either decision could be justified. Both could turn out to be wrong.

Up front, Kaplan faced no such impasse. His only concern was balancing his desire to move things along by setting as rapid a pace as possible and giving the two Rangers hauling Burman the time necessary to safely navigate the dark stairwell they were winding their way through. He was standing on the second-to-last landing they would have to pass, looking back at Pulaski when a commotion from below caught his attention.

The Land Warrior is a marvelous state-of-the-art system that combines and integrates various functions that enhance the effectiveness of the soldier. Various sights extend and improve the soldier's ability to acquire and engage targets. Networking provides leaders and commanders the ability to maneuver and control their subordinates. And the improved armor provides a higher degree of survivability. One thing that the Land Warrior does not enhance, however, is a soldier's hearing. If anything, the Land Warrior headset and the helmet design tends to degrade a soldier's ability to detect sounds. In the overall scheme of things it's a minor sacrifice since man is a visually oriented creature. But there are times when audio cues can make a difference, a big difference.

Deafened by his own arduous breathing and the clamor caused by the gyrations Pulaski and Washington were forced to go through in order to negotiate the stairwell, Kaplan did not become aware of the party of soldiers rushing up toward him until they were literally face-to-face. Turning toward a vaguely heard threat, Kaplan was greeted by an excited scream that issued from the lead Syrian. Startled by the sudden appearance of this dark apparition before him, and its unholy screech, Kaplan instinctively did what any well-trained soldier would do under these circumstances. Without thinking and without hesitation, he brought his rifle up, flipping the safety to the three-round-burst mode as he did so, shoved the muzzle into the face of the foe before him, and fired.

The sudden and totally unexpected outbreak of gunfire from the front of the column on the stairwell below caught everyone by complete surprise. All debates that both Jones and DeWitt had been struggling with as to where they should be disappeared in a flash of gunfire. Jones, who was close enough to see what was going on, did not hesitate as he leveled his weapon and forced his way past the stretcher party, who did their best to make way for him. In the tight confines of the stairwell this was all but impossible. Still, somehow Jones managed to squeeze through, while Pulaski and Washington struggled to keep from dropping the stretcher or dumping Burman over.

From his position in the rear of the column, DeWitt tried to do the same thing. His efforts to do so were frustrated by the balance of Jones's squad as they dashed forward to join their squad leader. He watched the man before him make his way forward as quickly as the congestion on the stairs permitted. To DeWitt it seemed that he was doomed to be in the wrong place at the wrong time every time something happened. Still, that did not make him impotent or unable to influence the situation that was developing below. It was in this sort of situation that the Land Warrior more than proved its worth. Mashing down on the transmit button of his radio, DeWitt called the platoon leader of his Second Platoon. Without waiting to explain the situation in detail, he ordered that officer to bring forward as many men as he could scrape together to the base of the stairwell they were in and hit the Syrians from the rear.

Up front Kaplan was trading shots with the Syrians. Ignoring the zing of bullets flying past him he pressed forward in an effort to put as much space as he could between the enemy and the pair of men behind him carrying Burman. This effort was both hampered and helped by the corpse of the man he had shot dead with his first volley, slowing his advance as he struggled to maintain his footing while stepping over it and pressing home his solitary attack at the same time. This delay, though, allowed Jones to catch up to him. Without thinking the Ranger squad leader pushed Kaplan aside, yelling, *"Comin' through!"* as he did so.

Without hesitation Kaplan pressed his back against the wall of the stairwell in order to let Jones and the squad's SAW gunner rush on by and take up the fight. Like DeWitt, even in the heat of battle, his training checked the visceral responses that had been driving him up to this point. The time had come for him to get out of the way and let the Rangers do what they did best. Besides, even though he hadn't run out of ammunition during his short-lived and mad, impetuous charge, Kaplan figured the time had come to change magazines and catch his breath.

By the time DeWitt managed to make his way to where he stood, Kaplan had managed to collect himself and swap his nearly empty magazine for a fresh one. On his way by, DeWitt slowed down, "You okay?"

Kaplan nodded. "Fine.

"If you could, Colonel, take up a position behind the stretcher and watch our rear."

DeWitt's last comment came out as an order, one Kaplan had no problem with.

"Wilco."

With that the two officers parted, Kaplan going to the rear and DeWitt doing his damnedest to get a handle on a situation that was threatening to spin out of control.

Syria
04:50 LOCAL, 20:50 EASTERN (00:50 ZULU)

In the street adjacent to the prison the Third Squad of Quinn's platoon, the Rangers of the Second Platoon who had liberated the members of RT Kilo from their cells, and the trio of Green Berets waited in silence for the order to move out. All could hear the scattered firefights raging in the prison that lay on the other side of the wall. Most of the Rangers, wired into the company, platoon, and squad nets, were able to keep tabs on what the situation was as they watched and waited.

The men whom they had come to rescue, on the other hand, were left figuratively and literally in the dark. Once out of the cellblock and through the second tactical breach Aveno, Kannen, and Mendez had been gathered in one of the Hummer transports. There they had been given a quick exam by a medic whose sole concern was obvious wounds and injuries. After that, they had been left on their own as the unexpected change in the situation forced DeWitt to mobilize every man he could to fill out the search-and-rescue party that had gone after Burman and Ciszak. This left the Rangers charged with guarding the vehicles and their three charges spread thin. The anxiety and vulnerability that these Rangers had already felt at being posted on an open street of the Syrian capital were magnified by the changing situation they were now facing. In all the excitement and sudden change in plans, no one thought of going back to where Aveno, Kannen, and Mendez sat to apprise them of what was going on. Since no one had foreseen a need to do so, it had never been planned or rehearsed.

From where he sat the only way Sergeant First Class Kannen could gauge how things were going was by studying the expressions and behavior of those Rangers near at hand. Their expressions told him that their worries were far from over. In the course of evaluating their situation, it quickly became clear to him that they would not be moving out anytime soon. Faced with this distressing reality, Kannen decided to make himself as comfortable as possible while he endured their current situation. In an effort to find some shelter from the wind that cut through his thin uniform he lowered himself off the wooden slat seat and onto the floor of the Hummer's cargo compartment. Scooting across the floorboards and over into a corner, Kannen drew his knees up to his chest and curled into a tight ball in an effort to fend off the predawn chill.

Once he had settled himself, Kannen looked at Aveno and Mendez. Neither of them had spoken a word or made a sound since they had climbed into the Hummer. Even now they both seemed to be reluctant to shift from one position to another, as if they feared that in doing so they would draw unwanted attention to themselves. Under ordinary circumstances this would have been an irrational fear, one a man like Kannen would have found worthy of scorn. But rationality was a commodity that had long been beaten out of them. During their captivity their world had been turned inside out and upside down. They had learned that anything and everything they did, including doing nothing at all, could and usually did result in a beating. It would be a while, Kannen reasoned, before any of them could regain the sort of self-confidence and assuredness that they had possessed before their capture.

As the minutes dragged by and the rattle of gunfire continued to drift over the wall of the prison in fits and starts, Kannen found himself studying his executive officer. Seated at the very rear of the Hummer First Lieutenant Ken Aveno sat hunched over with his arms drawn up tightly against his chest. His face was turned away as if he were searching for something in the distance. In a way Kannen found that this was fortunate. Had Aveno been facing him he would have been obliged to look him in the eye. For some reason he could not quite articulate he found that he had no desire to confront Aveno, not until he had been afforded the opportunity to sort out a nagging feeling that somehow that officer had failed him. How he had come to this conclusion was far too complex an issue for Kannen to deal with at this moment. But deep down inside he knew that it was one of many questions he would one day have to resolve.

What Kannen did not know was that his executive officer was trying to sort out the same issue. As all soldiers do as they train for battle, Aveno had spent a great deal of time contemplating how he would perform in various situations. Playing these mental what-if games is natural and healthy, provided one is honest with oneself. It was only now, when their terrible ordeal was about to come to an end, that Ken Aveno realized that he had neither been candid nor objective when he had assessed his personal ability to deal with such imponderables.

Only now, as this sad chapter in his life was about to conclude, did he realize how woeful his performance had been over the past few weeks. Not only had he failed to measure up to his own inflated expectations, he had failed to keep the faith with his fellow soldiers. He had not been brave and selfless. He had not been inspirational or noble. When his men had needed an example he had not found it in himself to provide it. Rather than rising to the occasion when he had been afforded the opportunity such as at the trial of Sergeant Hashmi, he had sat there like a mute, allowing himself to dwell on petty personal issues and concerns. Only now, when physical salvation was at hand did Aveno come to appreciate that his trials and tribulations would not end when they left this place. Rather, his most difficult days lay ahead. In the days and weeks that would follow his liberation he would have to recount over and over again every action he had taken, every decision he had made. Even worse, he would have to face the very men whom he was now convinced he had failed. When he did face them, Aveno wondered how he would find the courage and strength to atone for his shortcomings as an officer and a man when he had failed to do so here, when it had really mattered.

Concerns over what would happen in the next hour, let alone the next day, were the furthest things from DeWitt's mind at the moment. Throughout his foray into the prison dispensary he had quite literally lived second by second, focusing on his next move, his next step, his next order, and little more. It wasn't until they were safely back in the prison cellblock, an area that he was familiar with and where he knew friendly forces were waiting, that the young company commander finally began to feel as if he were back on track and in control again. There was of course still the need to disengage and withdraw from the prison, then make a mad dash through the streets of Damascus to the airfield. But these phases of the operation were part of the OP plan and had been rehearsed. His brief sortie into the unknown was over. As things now stood, success was within his grasp.

Behind him came Jones's squad. To a man their hearts were still pounding from their precipitous retreat from the dispensary and the vicious encounter in the confines of the stairwell. They were still animated by that encounter as they spilled out into the open space of the cellblock where the second tactical breach and point of exit was. Their sudden entrance caught the squad defending the breach off guard. Like everyone else, they were nervous as hell and teetering on a hair trigger. Startled by the First Squad's sudden and tumultuous appearance, the defenders of the breach trained their weapons on the mass of soldiers coming their way, flipping their weapons' safety to the fire position as they did so. Only the squawk of the "friend" ID over their Land Warrior earpiece and well-drilled restraint kept a bad situation from becoming a disaster.

Ignoring the danger that he had just escaped, DeWitt headed straight for the Rangers manning the breach. "Where's your lieutenant?"

A sergeant stood up and pointed out through the hole in the wall. "He's back at the first breach, sir."

Coming up to the sergeant who had replied, DeWitt whipped around and waved on Jones and the stretcher party that had been following him before turning his full attention back to the man next to him. "You're to stand fast here until Lieutenant Quinn and his rear guard have passed. Give them ten seconds before pulling out. Clear?"

The sergeant in charge of the inner breach nodded. "Roger that, sir."

By then Kaplan was in sight. When he saw DeWitt he shouted to him as he went by. "That's it for this squad. Quinn and his people are right behind me."

"Good, good."

With that, Kaplan ducked through the hole in the wall. For a moment a strange silence returned to the cellblock. Even the distant firefight that DeWitt's First Platoon had been engaged in ceased, indicating that the platoon had successfully broken contact and begun to make its way back to the airfield. This brief interlude did not last long as the hurried pounding of boots on concrete announced the approach of Quinn's rear guard.

Anxious to pull out of the prison compound as soon as he could, and have his company mounted and moving DeWitt called to the NCO next to him. "Okay, here they come. Remember, give them ten seconds and then go."

"Yes, sir. Ten seconds."

DeWitt was just about to head out into the open courtyard when he paused to take one more look back. When he did he saw something that brought him to a complete stop. Watching the figures approach he was taken aback by the sight of two men dragging a third seemingly lifeless form between them. Instead of leaving the cellblock DeWitt pivoted and all but leaped forward toward the trio. "Who's that?"

Specialist Four William Hoyt called back as he and the medic assigned to third Platoon staggered on as best they could while pulling the limp body between them using the man's flak vest. "It's Lieutenant Quinn. Grenade fragments."

As the radioman and medic rushed by DeWitt called out, "Where was he hit?"

Leaning closer to his company commander without stopping, the medic lowered his voice. "The buttocks and back of the legs. Messy but not fatal."

Despite the fact that his company's tactical situation left it quite vulnerable, DeWitt could not help thinking that the injuries suffered by Quinn would forever be a source of embarrassment to him. As he watched Quinn's faithful radioman and the medic pull their platoon leader through the breach, DeWitt shook his head. "Poor bastard."

Once he saw that the stretcher bearing Burman was secured in the Hummer, Kaplan stepped back to allow the Rangers of the First Squad to climb in while he caught his breath. They were almost done, he told himself. They were almost finished. Now all they needed to do was mount up and move out. In fifteen minutes they would be at the airfield, where the giant open maws of the cargo bays of the Air Force transports would be waiting to greet them. That was true, he suddenly corrected himself, provided the way back was still clear.

This thought caused him to pull out his handheld display and keyboard. Laying the keyboard and display on the hood of a nearby Hummer he pulled up the joint tactical and common operating environment program. In an instant a map filled the screen. One by one, as fast as the computer spit out the data, tactical symbols began to crop up on the display. Even before the program had completed spewing the information it had gathered and stored while he had been tending to other, more immediate concerns, Kaplan could see they were not quite out of the woods yet.

Battles are won by those who have superior information concerning their own tactical situation and that of the enemy. Knowing where your enemy is and what he is doing are perhaps the most important elements of warfare. This knowledge allows a commander to exploit his foe's weaknesses while avoiding his strengths. It gives him the confidence to go forth and do things that logic and common sense would otherwise veto. Arming himself with as much knowledge as possible about the enemy before battle has been a goal of every commander since the age of sharp sticks and rocks. To achieve this the Armed Forces of the United States has dedicated enormous resources. From satellites to high-tech optics, electronic eavesdropping to computer hacking, the modern American military has created a panoply of intelligence-gathering devices that would impress Buck Rogers.

Yet as important as gathering information is, it is useless unless it can be delivered to the commander in the field and the soldier on the ground in a timely manner. It is in the area of processing, packaging, and disseminating combat information where the most noted failures of combat intelligence occur. To this end one of the most useful features of the Land Warrior that the Army insisted upon including was a means of plugging the combat soldier into the massive informational web that it was developing. On the Land Warrior this feature is known as the user interface, a program that provides commanders both tactical and mission-support data in near real time. These data, gathered by platforms and agencies scattered around the world, allow the modern infantryman to literally see what is on the other side of the mountain.

After studying the tactical situation on his display, Kaplan looked up and glanced to his left and right. When he didn't see DeWitt, he keyed his radio. "Red Six, this is Black Niner Two. We need to talk."

"What's up?"

Startled by the deep booming voice behind him that had responded to his radio call, it took every bit of self-control that he could muster to keep from jumping straight up. Turning around, Kaplan pointed at the display, "The Syrians are on the move. Look here."

Moving closer, DeWitt surveyed the tactical map Kaplan had called up. He remembered Kaplan's briefing him on how this feature of the Land Warrior worked in conjunction with an all-source joint service intelligence system, but had forgotten about it in all the confusion. "Tanks, huh?"

"At least three, according to this latest intel dump. And all three are sitting on our primary egress route."

DeWitt grunted. "And the secondary route?"

With a whirl of a track ball and a couple of keystrokes Company A's secondary route popped up on the screen. After a cursory inspection of it and the adjoining streets Kaplan grunted. "At the moment it's clear. But this unit here is moving on a road that runs parallel to that route."

"Are those troops truck-mounted or in APCs?"

Kaplan shook his head. "Negative knowledge. Regardless of what they are," he quickly added, "the last thing we want while we're beating feet back to the airport is to turn the corner and run into them."

"Agreed. Any ideas?"

By way of answering, Kaplan called up another program that displayed a larger tactical image that showed all U.S. forces in the area. When he found what he was looking for he highlighted the unit and clicked on its ID. "There, an AC-130 loitering just north of the city. According to this program it has just the sort of ordnance that this situation calls for."

As Kaplan typed away on the keyboard, DeWitt continued to study the tactical display as he prepared to contact battalion. "Okay, great! I'll make the request and see if battalion can task those naval aviators to lend a hand."

Kaplan answered as he continued to pound away on the keyboard. "No need to bother with that. I've already e-mailed the AC-130 and tasked them. Since we have priority and I have access codes and a direct link to the joint targeting folks on the AWACs, our request trumps everyone else's. They'll be rolling in on target in three minutes. May I instead suggest you get your people mounted up and moving?"

DeWitt blinked, knowing full well that this short-circuiting of the traditional system and chain of command was unusual, but given the situation, a necessity. "With pleasure."

Not being privy to what was passing directly from Kaplan and the AC-130, using the Joint Tactical Operating system that was part of his Land Warrior, the announcement that an air strike was in progress stunned Lieutenant Colonel Harry Shaddock. His first response was concern over the prospect of mistaken identity and a friendly-fire incident. Even before anyone had a chance to explain, he was yelling at his ops officer. "Who the hell called that in and where?"

Equally surprised by this development, the ops officer turned to the Air Force liaison officer who had been attached to the 3rd of the 75th to coordinate these sorts of missions. "Get hold of your people and find out what they're doing."

All of this excitement came as something of a surprise to the Air Force captain who had been monitoring the close air-support net. "Excuse me, but that strike was called in by someone with Company A. It's being directed against a mech infantry column."

Both Delmont and Shaddock simultaneously converged on the map on which all of the operations graphics were displayed. "Show me where those strikes are."

Reaching in between the pair of lieutenant colonels, the Air Force officer placed his finger on the map. "Right there is the center of mass. I assume that it's a linear target that is moving along this street."

"And where exactly," Shaddock asked, "is Company A?"

The assistant ops officer who was monitoring the battalion command net called from his post. "They're currently approaching check point Three Seven, sir, moving along their alternate egress route."

When he located that point on the map, Shaddock placed his finger on it. "Jesse, that is close."

Sensing that the battalion commander's comment was a rhetorical one, neither the Air Force liaison officer or the ops officer responded. Instead, they simply stood back and watched as the man who had planned this operation and the one charged with pulling it off stared impotently at a map and waited for word from the people upon whom its success now rested.

It's called Spectre, the son of Vietnam's Puff the Magic Dragon. The converted C-130 Hercules is designed to support special operations such as Fanfare. To accomplish this task it totes a most impressive array of weaponry. This inventory includes a 105-mm howitzer, a pair of 20-mm Vulcan Gatling guns, and a Bofors 40-mm cannon. The teeth of the gunship are controlled by an equally impressive computer-driven fire-control system that allows the pilot to aim and fire any and all of the weapons with an unimaginable accuracy. When called upon, Spectre has the ability to literally chew up its target with an unerring accuracy that is both startling and inescapable.

The rumble of the AC-130 lumbering along at rooftop level followed by the sharp report of its awesome arsenal ripping into the Syrian convoy one block over from the street that he was driving down startled PFC Pulaski. Instinctively he jerked the Hummer's wheel away from the unseen pandemonium that the AC-130 was creating. More concerned about his driver's erratic behavior than what was happening on another street, Jones reached over and slapped Pulaski's helmet. "Pay attention to the road, damn it."

It took Pulaski a moment to regain control of his vehicle.

Even when he did, he found he was unable to ignore the rumble of secondary explosions and the sudden flashes of light that lit up the night sky. "Christ, I hope those guys over there know what they're doing."

Jones snapped back. "It's not them I'm worried about. It's your driving that's scaring the hell out of me."

Ignoring the banter between Pulaski and his squad leader, Kaplan monitored the air attacks as best he could, Company A's progress, and the tactical display that he was struggling to balance on his lap. Only when he saw the buildings of Damascus begin to thin out and then suddenly disappear behind them did he turn his full attention back to the keyboard. In addition to the order to cease the attacks, he added a thank-you.

When the screen flashed an acknowledgment Kaplan tucked both the display and keyboard back into their pockets on his load-bearing equipment. Finished with that, he flipped his helmet-mounted display up and out of the way. Turning around in the Hummer he took a moment to study the column of vehicles that trailed off behind the one he was in and watched the skyline of Damascus disappear in the dark.

The sky was alive with streams of tracers racing up in a vain effort to lash out at aircraft that were no longer in range. Here and there he could see flames leaping over the roofs of buildings. Every now and then an explosion erupted on one of the streets, throwing off a bright orange fireball into the sky. Slowly, almost reluctantly, he turned around and stared down at the stretcher at his feet. Even in the dark he could see the bloodstained sheet that covered the body that lay on it.

How ironic it was, he found himself thinking as he looked back at the ravaged city that was fading in the distance. For all of the precision and exactness that every participant had demon-strated that night, the one round that killed Captain Burman had been a stray shot fired during a confused and vicious firefight that no one had planned for or rehearsed. Like war itself, his death had been nothing more than an accident, a simple twist of fate. Even in an age of high-tech weaponry and instantaneous communications, war was still very much an affair of chance.

From his position, Captain James T. Stone watched the last of the transports bearing the 3rd of the 75th Rangers, thunder down the runway and leap into the night sky. After giving the now-abandoned airfield and its immediate environs a quick once-over, Stone eased himself back and away from his concealed perch. When he was back under cover, he rose and headed for the cluster of vehicles where his team was waiting for his order to move out. "Okay, folks," he called out in a low voice. "Time to go."

As one the members of RT Lima gathered about their vehicles, climbed in, and prepared to head out into the open desert where they would hide. Dawn would be breaking soon, and Stone was anxious to put as much distance between them and this spot as possible. They had executed their part in that night's operation flawlessly. Now it was time for them to disappear as completely as they could and wait for their next mission, their next opportunity to place themselves in harm's way.

EPILOGUE

The fourteen men who had been collectively known as RT Kilo had lived in the shadows. Some of them died there. Their deeds and accomplishments were not trumpeted across the land that they served. Even those who loved them and shared their lives with them would never know exactly what they did. The carefully crafted and well-chosen words on the citations and letters of condolence lavished upon bereaved widows and grieving parents spoke of courage and dedication, but made no mention of the squalid conditions or the fears that each of their husbands and sons faced as they executed their assigned duties. In the end those who remained would be left to deal with the harsh reality of their loss without ever being subjected to the horrific details.

All of this was not the result of some great government conspiracy to hide the truth. Nor was it part of a sick propaganda ploy designed to keep those who would follow RT Kilo into the shadows from losing heart. Instead, this reliance upon sentiments that appealed to the noblest aspects of service to one's country and its people was the result of an unspoken desire that each and every member of RT Kilo be remembered as a man standing tall and proud. This longing for dignity in the face of death is shared by many, military and civilian. It was a last wish that those who survived did their best to honor.

Of course it would be a lie to deny that the Army did not take advantage of the situation to do more than simply honor the men of RT Kilo and the 3rd of the 75th Rangers who were killed in action. The dedication of a monument to them was used to acknowledge the sacrifice of those hereto unheralded souls who lost their lives in other black operations that were just as much a part of America's worldwide war against terror and evil.

The event was conducted with all the pomp and ceremony that are the hallmarks of a proud and professional military. The soldiers of the Army's Old Guard maintained their poise and dignity that was very much symbolic of the manner in which Erik Burman and his tiny command had gone about their assigned duties day in, day out. The somber notes of muffled drums tapping out the half-step cadence tempered the joyous riot of red, white, and blue flags and buntings meant to stir the soul. Dignitaries and honored guests greeted one another in hushed, sober tones as they set aside petty differences and partisan concerns and prepared to honor those who sacrificed for something greater than themselves.

The monument that would be the center of attention that day was a strikingly modest affair. The four-sided block of shiny granite was said by some to be as black as the shadows that those it was meant to memorialize died in. There was no bold statement setting forth in clear and concise terms the cause that demanded such a sacrifice. Rather, there was an extract from a 1919 poem entitled "Old Valiant Hearts" written by John Stanhope Arkwright.

> *Proudly you gathered, rank on rank to war,*
> *As you heard God's message from afar;*
> *All you had hoped for, all you had, you gave*
> *To save mankind—yourself you scorned to save.*

On the left side of the monument were the names of the men and women who had lost their lives during operations conducted in Afghanistan. While they were not the focus of this day, it had been decided that this was an appropriate place to record both their achievements and the price of their devotion to their fellow countrymen. It was on the other side where the names of Erik Burman, Joseph Ciszak, Samuel Harris, Yousaf Hashmi, Jay Jones, Insram Amer, and David Davis were engraved together with those of the Rangers who died during freeing their comrades.

The inclusion of Ciszak's name had caused some heartburn among those who knew the true story of that officer's fate. The reality of international politics, however, dictated that rumors floated by the CIA that the Air Force officer was still alive had to be ignored. Even if they could be proved, few doubted if anyone in a position to do so would make his return an issue.

Seated front and center before this stark panel was Diana Burman. On one side of her sat a small boy whose age and curiosity demanded that he fidget throughout the course of the entire affair. On the other was the man who had once been her husband's Commander and Chief, the man who bore ultimate responsibility for the events that led to this occasion. Arranged about this trio were the spouses, children, and parents of the men who were no longer with them. Others had come to grieve the loss of a comrade out of a sense of duty, or simply because they were expected to be there.

Foremost among those who were there who would have preferred to have been elsewhere was Ken Aveno, the senior surviving member of RT Kilo. To either side of him were the other men who had survived. As they had on the night they left Baghdad, Allen Kannen and Salvador Mendez stood next to Aveno because they had no choice. While none of the after-action reports and inquires examining the destruction RT Kilo and its captivity found fault with Aveno's conduct, no one could convince Kannen or Mendez otherwise. Neither man could put his finger on why he felt as he did. They simply knew that somehow he had failed them.

Another cluster of officers had no qualms about their seating assignments. In fact, they were quite pleased to see each other again. It was the first opportunity Robert Delmont, Harry Shaddock, and Neil Kaplan had to congratulate each other on their promotions. Each had gone back to his previous assignments in the aftermath of Fanfare. In the hushed prelude to the ceremony, these officers took the opportunity to exchange some personal chitchat.

Of the trio only Shaddock had subsequently been reassigned, a fact that Delmont was quick to comment upon. "I hope you're managing to find some fulfillment at the Infantry School."

Shaddock responded with a chuckle that did little to hide the letdown he still felt after going from command of a Ranger battalion to being little more than just another colonel at Fort Benning. "Let me just say that you've not experienced culture shock until you've made a transition like that. My kids still call their mom to ask if it's safe to come home from college during the holidays."

Delmont did his best to maintain the decorum that their circumstances dictated. Turning to Kaplan he asked him how the Land Warrior project was going. "Well, there are days when I get the same feeling I do when talking to my cat. There's just too many hard-liners out there in the bushes who haven't heard that we've entered a new millennium that demands new methods."

Having experienced a similar response from senior officers he had to brief, Delmont nodded in agreement. "You've used the Land Warrior in battle, Captain DeWitt. Do you think it's the way to go?"

Stepping forward from the shadow of his former battalion commander, the commanding officer of Company A, 3rd of the 75th sighed. "It's no different than any other weapon, sir. When push comes to shove it's not the equipment that matters. It's the men who have to hold the line that decide the issue."

Glancing over at Delmont, Kaplan pointed at DeWitt. "See what I mean?"

"I'm afraid," Shaddock chimed in, "I have to agree with our young Ranger here. The best equipment in the world is worthless unless there are men willing to close with and destroy their nation's enemies."

"And," Delmont quickly added, "well-trained officers to lead them."

Sensing that he wasn't going to win any points here, Kaplan raised his hands in mock capitulation. "Okay, okay, gentlemen. You win. Turn in your muskets and I'll see that you get your crossbows back. Fair enough?"

Before anyone could respond the signal announcing the commencement of the dedication ceremony was given. Taking their places, the four officers who had been brought together by battle prepared to pay tribute to those who had perished in the course of that struggle. Their collective efforts would never bring about an end to war. But so long as there were soldiers, men and women who were willing and ready to place themselves in harm's way, the nation they served and the world they lived in would continue to prosper. Call it dedication, call it commitment, but whatever it is, it takes more than simple courage to stand a watch and sally forth into harm's way.